MIDNIGHT SURRENDER TO THE SPANIARD

CAROL MARINELLI

HER DIAMOND DEAL WITH THE CEO

LOUISE FULLER

MILLS & BOON

First published in Great Britain 2023
by Mills & Boon, an imprint of HarperCollins*Publishers* Ltd,
1 London Bridge Street, London, SE1 9GF

www.harpercollins.co.uk

HarperCollins*Publishers*, Macken House, 39/40 Mayor Street Upper,
Dublin 1, D01 C9W8, Ireland

Midnight Surrender to the Spaniard © 2023 Carol Marinelli

Her Diamond Deal with the CEO © 2023 Louise Fuller

ISBN: 978-0-263-30680-4

06/23

Th ... paper
... en.
Pr ... tricity

MIDNIGHT SURRENDER TO THE SPANIARD

CAROL MARINELLI

MILLS & BOON

CHAPTER ONE

'MARRIED?'

At first Anna Douglas thought her friend was joking. After all, you couldn't read facial expressions in a phone call, and Emily had only been in Spain for six weeks.

'Anna, I know it's fast, but I want one person at least to be happy for us...'

The smile on Anna's face faded as she heard the slight desperation in her friend's tone.

'His whole family are against it. Sebastián thinks I'm some sort of gold-digger...'

'What?'

'Oh, yes. While Alejandro was in the States, Sebastián fired me and terminated my accommodation at the bodega in an attempt to break us up. He practically threw me out...'

'Sebastián?'

Anna frowned, because he was one of the Romero brothers. She'd heard that name a few times in recent weeks. Emily had been working on the website of some luxurious sherry bodega, and from everything Anna had gleaned he didn't sound in the least pleasant.

'Hold on a moment. Just who are you marrying?'

'Alejandro,' Emily said, and Anna's heart sank when she realised her shy friend was actually involved with one of the Romero brothers.

They were billionaire playboys with dreadful reputations.

Anna only knew this because she'd read up on them when her friend had taken the role.

It got worse.

The wedding was to take place in two weeks' time and, yes, her friend confided, she was pregnant...

'We're only telling his parents.'

Anna, a little bolder and rather more forthright than her friend, had been about to advise her to slow things down, but when she heard about the pregnancy she closed both her lips and her eyes.

'Anna, I need your support on this.'

'You *always* have my support.'

Unequivocally.

After all, Emily was the only one in the entire village who had stood by her during the darkest of times.

It was quite a long phone call, filled with a mixture of tears and excitement from Emily as Anna did her best to remain calm and sound upbeat about this sudden May wedding!

'Please say you and Willow will be there.'

'The thing is...' Anna halted, not sure what to say to her dearest friend.

For once it wasn't about money, because Emily had told her that Alejandro was insisting on paying for their flights and accommodation. The issue was that Willow had had a string of painful ear infections and was waiting for minor surgery.

'Anna, please. You have to be there.'

It was a relief when the call ended. Anna sat on the sofa and, resting her elbows on her knees, scrunched her fists around handfuls of her long blonde hair and let out a tense breath.

Do something, Anna!

She was soon on the computer, on the very website her best friend had designed, reading about the groom, his brother, and their younger sister Carmen—who, Emily had told her, had also done her best to break up the couple.

Her eyes met those of Sebastián Romero—the eldest of the siblings and the one most opposed to the marriage. He was leaning against a wall, or a balcony, high up on a roof terrace, and smiling into the camera. Anna ignored his dark good looks and suave appearance. Instead she noticed that his smile didn't reach his black eyes...

He looked a formidable opponent indeed.

'Oh, Emily...' she groaned.

Anna made her way up the stairs and quietly pushed open the bedroom door to see her daughter asleep on top of the bed, with all her soft toys tucked up inside it.

Gently, trying not to wake her, Anna put Willow in with the toys, tucking them all in, and then sat on the edge of the bed for a moment and looked at the bottle of eardrops on the bedside table.

Of course Anna wanted to be there to support her friend, but she knew that the changes in pressure caused by flying would likely cause her daughter pain. Until she had the surgery it was out of the question for Willow to fly. Yet Emily had been there for Anna every step of the way—even if Anna hadn't quite told her everything about Willow's father...

She hadn't been able to tell anyone. She had clammed up so badly when she'd tried to tell her parents that they'd wrongly concluded that their daughter had fallen pregnant after some nameless one-night stand.

Four, almost five years later, her relationship with them was still incredibly strained. They adored Willow, though, determinedly not blaming the child for the sins of the mother...

It was to be Anna's second difficult phone call of the night: explaining to her mother that Emily had invited her and Willow to her wedding in Spain in just a fortnight...

'What about Willow's ears?' Jean Douglas immediately pointed out. 'Do you really think she should be flying?'

'No, I don't,' Anna admitted. 'That's why I'm calling you. I was wondering if you'd be able to look after her for the weekend. I'd fly out on the Friday and be back on Sunday.'

She listened to the long stretch of silence that followed. Anna's mother had the same pale green eyes as her, and though

Anna could just picture them, rolling at her daughter's audacity, she pushed her request.

'You did say that you wanted to be more involved with Willow.'

'And what if we can't look after her?' her mother said. 'It's Ascension Day, and—'

'I know that,' Anna broke in. Because of course she knew that the fortieth day of Easter—Ascension Day—would fall on that Sunday. Her father was the parish vicar, and their lives ran on church time. 'If you can't have her, then I completely understand.'

'What would you do?'

'I don't know,' Anna admitted. 'I'll speak to her GP and see if there's…' She swallowed.

It would be a two-hour flight from London to Seville, followed by a train journey to Jerez, and Willow, with her adventurous spirit, would be thrilled to go.

She asked herself the very question her mother had.

What *would* she do if her mother said she couldn't have Willow?

'If you can't take her then I won't go,' Anna said, though it tore her apart to say so. Emily had been there for her all her life—more than her blood family in recent years. Yet Willow had to come first. 'There's no one else I'd consider leaving her with.'

Even though her parents' reaction to her pregnancy had broken her own heart, she trusted them with Willow's. Willow saw her grandparents at church, and for birthdays and such, and loved them dearly. She adored spending time with them and was always pleading for a sleepover.

Her parents had so far refused.

They'd told Anna, even before she'd given birth, that they would not be used as a babysitting service.

'Very well.' She could hear her mother choking on her magnanimous words. 'We'll have Willow for the weekend.'

And even though she thanked her mother profusely, in truth she'd almost wanted her to say no.

Anna hadn't had a single night apart from Willow since she was born, and two nights felt by far too many.

CHAPTER TWO

THERE WOULD BE no train journey to Jerez.

Anna had been told that Sebastián Romero would be waiting to greet her at Seville Airport.

Apparently it was a tradition that the *padrino*—the Spanish equivalent of a best man—took care of such details on the eve of the wedding.

Anna had been warned about him, so she had read up on him some more.

It had never entered Anna's head that she might like him.

She wore a loose skirt and halter-neck top with flat sandals—a pretty non-descript outfit—and so on stepping into Arrivals she expected to have to cast her eyes around to find a guy holding up a sign with her name or...

Yet straight away her eyes locked with his.

He was tall, and wore a suit and loosened tie. He looked bored, brooding, and although she was both shocked and loath to admit it, he was beautiful.

He gave her a nod, and as she wheeled her case around and walked towards him, he gave her a sort of half-smile.

Well, a quarter of a smile.

'Sebastián...' She didn't know if she should offer her hand, nor quite how to greet this reluctant *padrino*.

'Sebastián?' he frowned. 'No.'

Realising she'd been mistaken, Anna backed away. 'Oh, gosh, sorry...'

'*Es broma...*' he said. 'Joking.'

Anna was surprised by her own smile.

'Is there a problem with your luggage?' He glanced at her small case. 'Has it not come through?'

'No, I've just got carry-on. I'm only here for two nights.'

'One of them *is* a wedding,' he said.

Anna took that as a criticism.

He must have seen her lips pinch. 'I meant that is the size of a make-up bag for most women…' He rolled his beautiful black eyes as if he knew he'd possibly offended her again. 'Let's get to the car.'

Surprisingly, she wasn't offended.

Anna was actually somewhat startled by the ease of her smile at his little joke about not being Sebastián when just moments before, as she'd exited the plane, she'd called the vicarage and spoken on the phone to an excited Willow. The conversation had left her fighting tears.

'Nanny and I are making scones!'

'How lovely.'

'Give Em a kiss for me.'

'I shall.'

'Send lots of pictures too.'

Anna had felt too far away from her daughter, and tearful that it had taken nearly five years for this to happen.

Yet Willow had sounded completely happy, and so she'd blinked away the tears. Moments later, when she'd been met by Sebastián and his dry humour, Anna had found herself smiling.

Despite the joke, it was clear he did not want to be here. She didn't take it personally, and knew it was because he was vehemently opposed to the wedding. He was scrupulously po-lite, despite his feelings about his brother's decision to marry Anna's friend.

As they left the airport, stepping out into the gorgeous May sun, Anna got her first glimpse of Emily's new world.

'Anna!' Sebastián called her back.

It was then that she realised they were *not* walking with the masses to the car park.

A low silver car was mere steps away, and Anna saw a

valet hand Sebastián his keys before stowing her carry-on bag in the boot.

'So,' Sebastián said as he manoeuvred the car out on to the main road, 'it's about an hour to Jerez. I'm to drop you at the bridal boutique and then I'll take your case to the hotel.'

'I can manage my own case.'

'You are the *dama de honor*. It is expected.'

Those last words told her everything she needed to know about his attitude towards his reluctant duty.

'How was your flight?' he enquired politely.

'Fine, thank you.'

'There was a wedding rehearsal last night...'

'I know. I couldn't get away sooner.'

Her throat went tight at the thought of Willow, so far away, and, not wanting to start crying, she hurriedly looked out of the window rather than mention her daughter.

Aside from the threat of tears, she doubted this sophisticated man would be remotely interested in her babysitting arrangements.

They drove in silence for most of the way, but as they approached Jerez he leant over, and she felt his arm brush her thigh. She was startled, but it turned out he was just opening up the glove box and taking out an envelope.

It was for her.

'That's your hotel card. It is close to the church.'

He explained the details and she tried not to blush, but found she was just so *aware* of how she had reacted to the brief contact.

'Whatever you may have heard about me, I'm not *that* bad...'

Anna frowned, and then realised he was addressing her overreaction when he'd reached over.

When it registered, she laughed. 'Sorry, I just—'

'It's okay.'

He glanced over again and gave her a smile.

Definitely a half-smile this time.

Or at least more than a quarter.

'You didn't miss much at the rehearsal,' he said, turning

his eyes back to the road. 'You are to stay with the bride and walk in with her.'

'Behind her?'

'I don't know,' he admitted. 'I wasn't taking notes.'

'You must know what usually happens at a Spanish wedding.'

'We don't usually have bridesmaids.' He shrugged. 'You'll be fine. Just make sure the bride and groom don't come in contact tomorrow until the church. You and Emily are both staying in the hotel. I am too...'

'Is that where the function's being held?' Anna asked.

'No, apart from the service, everything is taking place in the bodega.'

'Oh.'

She knew that Alejandro had a residence in the bodega, and had assumed Sebastián must too, but he said nothing to further enlighten her.

'I'll call you when we get to the church and then you'll walk the bride over...'

'Walk her over?' Anna checked. 'In brand-new shoes I've never even seen, let alone tried on?'

'You can blame your friend for that. Emily wanted a very quick wedding.' He stared pointedly ahead. 'I wonder why that is?'

His words dripped sarcasm but Anna said nothing. She knew he was testing her reaction and refused to give him one.

Instead she carried on gazing out of the window as they drove through Jerez. Emily had not overstated its beauty and Anna was enjoying the view.

Sebastián wasn't much of a tourist guide, though he did comment when they passed the esteemed equestrian school where the famous dancing horses performed.

'My sister Carmen practically lives there.'

Apart from that he left it to Anna to take in the Moorish buildings on her own. The stunning Alcázar with its ancient baths looked incredible, and there were beautiful plazas with fountains and tiny streets she would have loved to explore.

'It's a shame I'm only here for two days.'

He gave a slight mirthless laugh. 'I'm sure you'll be back to visit your friend.'

He didn't say *your newly rich friend*, but she knew she was meant to infer that.

As he pulled the car to a halt, Anna realised they were outside the bridal boutique. She decided his words merited a response.

'Oh, I shall certainly be back, Sebastián.' Her eyes met his, and now that the car had stopped he fully met her gaze. 'Emily is more than a friend. I consider her to be my sister, so I'll definitely be visiting in the future.'

Anna had been determined to remain smiling and polite throughout the proceedings, but had nevertheless felt every barb about Emily. Now that she'd realised something of what her friend was up against, she decided she would speak up.

'You're not the only one who has concerns about the suddenness of this wedding.'

He gave the slightest of sardonic smiles, clearly not believing her for a moment, so Anna let him know that she'd done her research on the man who would marry her friend.

'Your brother doesn't exactly come with the best references, and as for—'

She stopped herself then, but knew there was a flush spreading across her neck and cheeks. Because taking the groom's *brother* to task for his sexual history was not part of a bridesmaid's or a best friend's job description. Though it had gone unsaid, Anna rather guessed she'd revealed that she'd done her homework on him...

Oh, indeed, she had.

And if she'd thought Alejandro was bad... Sebastián was wicked.

It wasn't just stories of the wild parties aboard his yacht that had shocked Anna and kept her reading late into the night, but the stream of tearful women who had tried to love him.

The *endless* stream!

There was even a devastated ex-fiancée, whom he'd allegedly broken up with a couple of weeks after she'd lost their baby. All the scurrilous gossip sites managed to get the word *allegedly* in, presumably for legal reasons, and yet he'd done nothing that Anna could see to dispel the widespread rumours.

Even though she hadn't voiced any of this to Sebastián, Anna wondered if she'd gone too far.

Not that it seemed to bother him. He barely blinked—just coolly held her gaze.

Flustered suddenly, she looked down a little, but only got as far as his mouth.

It was *such* an exquisite mouth. His lips were full and the cupid's bow so defined that not even an hour with a lip liner brush could have made it better.

'Finished?' he checked, and Anna realised her eyes were still on his full mouth.

So, no, she had not finished looking. His white front teeth had met his bottom lip as he'd pronounced the *F* and then his teeth had pressed together on the *D*, and then his lips had stayed slightly parted…

She dragged her eyes back to his.

'Finished.'

She attempted a firm response but heard the tremble in her voice as she said it. She turned her head to the front window. Why had she said that? Why had she been about to allude to his reputation when it had less than nothing to do with her?

'Let's just get through tomorrow,' he suggested, although there was an edge to his voice that told her he wasn't best pleased. *'Hasta luego,'* he added.

She blinked, wondering if she'd just been insulted.

'It means *goodbye*,' he translated. 'Or rather, *until later.*'

Until later!

Sebastián did not help her with her luggage. He was through with being polite and pointedly just popped open the boot, remaining in the driver's seat.

There was fire beneath that rather icy exterior, he thought.

Reluctantly, he admired her for standing up for her friend, and for facing him as she told him what she thought of Alejandro and this sudden wedding. But then she had alluded to his own behaviour… He had thought himself numb to those accusations. After all, he knew the truth. Yet her green kitten eyes had felt like a flashlight, aimed directly at him.

For a second he had actually considered tartly suggesting that she should not believe everything she read…

No.

He would not be explaining himself and he did not care what anyone else thought, Sebastián reminded himself, watching her wheel her case towards the boutique.

This *dama de honor* also had a very beautiful back…pale and straight. He had noticed it at the airport as she'd walked ahead to the car, her slender frame accentuating the winged scapula.

Watching her walk to the boutique now, he found the pale blonde ponytail a mild irritant—but only because it concealed her graceful spine.

Perhaps she'd felt his stare, because he saw she'd stiffened briefly and halted as she arrived at the door of the boutique.

And then he further admired her, because she turned and faced him again. For a moment contempt was written on her features, but then she smiled a wide smile, turned away, and went in to greet her friend.

Unseen, Sebastián smiled too. His smile was surprisingly genuine, even though he knew Anna's was fixed in place for her friend—which let him know she was going along with this damned wedding just as reluctantly as he…

Indeed, Anna had fixed on her smile for Emily's benefit, and while she was thrilled to see her friend, she really was concerned.

'Anna!' Emily hugged her fiercely. 'I am so sorry to have inflicted Sebastián on you.'

'He was fine.'

'Please!' Emily was disbelieving. 'If I hadn't had to get my dress let out I'd have been there to greet you and to hell with tradition. Come and see it.'

Her friend was ecstatic, Anna realised. Glowing...

'And come and try yours on. If you don't like it then there are others.'

'I love it,' Anna said—and she did. It was made of heavy silk in a very deep amber colour, and possibly—probably— the most beautiful item of clothing she'd ever held, let alone tried on.

The dressmaker gestured for her to put a scarf over her head and face.

'The dress goes on over your head,' Emily said, smiling at Anna's bemused expression. 'The scarf's so you don't get any make-up on it.'

'I'm not wearing any.'

But still, she complied, and the dark silk slid over her head and down her body. As the dressmaker did the zip up Anna held her breath—and not because the dress was tight...

It was definitely the most beautiful thing she'd ever worn.

'You look stunning, Anna!' Emily beamed. 'I haven't seen you all dressed up in...'

She didn't finish.

Even Anna couldn't remember when.

Her last night out had been a Christmas function with the staff from the school where she worked as a part-time receptionist, and it had hardly been dressy.

And the time before that...

Rather than dwell on her lack of social life, Anna tried on the shoes her friend had chosen. They were neutral, but strappy and high—especially given Anna didn't usually wear heels.

'I hope I don't trip...'

In the end, it was a day of much pampering. The hotel was elegant, with uniformed doormen and bellboys, and there was even a lift man who pulled back the ancient iron gated doors of the elevator and did the same again when you reached your floor.

Her suite overlooked the beautiful Plaza de Santiago. Anna looked down at the square and to the fountain, then across to the church where the wedding was going to be held. It looked more like a cathedral, she thought.

'Are there are a lot of guests coming?'

'Hundreds.' Emily nodded. 'And half of them are Alejandro's exes—or at least it feels that way. Mariana's coming...'

'The one he was supposed to marry?'

'According to his father and brother,' Emily said. 'Apparently they wanted to merge the bodegas. I think that's why Sebastián's so angry. He only cares about the business.'

'Emily...' Anna took a breath. They were finally face to face and alone and it had to be said. 'I'm only going to say this once—'

'Please don't.'

They had been friends long enough that Emily had guessed what she was about to say.

'We're not just marrying because of the baby. Anna, I've seen how marvellously you've done on your own...'

'Hardly marvellously!'

'You've done it though—all by yourself. If Alejandro and I weren't in love then I'd go it alone. You've shown me how!'

'Okay... Well, it looks like we've got a wedding to get to tomorrow.'

After Emily's reassurances, Anna wished she could simply relax and enjoy it, but even as they sat at the elegant hotel restaurant she felt unusually flustered.

She was missing Willow, Anna told herself as they ate paella. But she'd just called her daughter, and everything at home was fine. So was it just that she felt out of place in such luxurious surroundings? Especially as she so rarely went out?

No, it wasn't that, Anna acknowledged to herself. She was by far too aware that Sebastián was staying in the same hotel.

'Why is Sebastián staying here?' Anna asked. 'I thought there were residences on their property.'

'They have places all over,' Emily said. 'It's only Alejandro who lives at the bodega. Sebastián goes there just for work, thank goodness. I'd hate to be his neighbour.'

'What about the rest of the family? Are they *all* against the wedding? You said Alejandro's father was coming round?'

'José's starting to—but only because of the baby. Carmen actively dislikes me. Incredibly, the only one who seems remotely supportive is Maria, their mother.'

'She's the famous flamenco dancer?' Anna checked. 'Why is it incredible that's she's supportive?'

'Because apparently she's the coldest fish of the lot.'

Later, as they left the restaurant, Anna found out she had been right to be on high alert—because she came face to face again with Sebastián. He was talking to the concierge, but when he caught sight of them he turned and called for them to wait.

Goodness, he was so commanding, Anna thought as he walked confidently towards him.

'Everything is organised,' he informed Emily. 'Is there anything else you need?'

'We're fine, thank you, Sebastián,' Emily replied.

And then his black eyes moved to Anna.

'Our most important role before the wedding is to ensure the bride and groom do not see each other prior to the church.'

'Yes.' She gave a tight smile. 'It's the same in England. We—'

He cut her off, clearly not willing to make idle conversation. 'I'll call you when we have arrived at the church.'

'Okay.'

'So I will need your number.'

Call Emily, she wanted to say. But of course she did not want him to see how much he rattled her. It was clear they would have to correspond on the big day, so she gave him her number and watched as he typed it in.

'Thank you,' he said, and then turned his stern attention back to Emily. 'Best wishes for tomorrow.'

He stalked off—though not in the direction of the elevators, nor the exit. Instead he walked down a long stone corridor towards a huge intricately carved arched wooden door.

'Best wishes, indeed,' Emily muttered sarcastically.

Anna found she was still watching him. She saw him take out a key and open the door, through which she glimpsed a courtyard. She had to mentally shake herself to force her attention away.

'Let's head up,' she said to the bride-to-be. 'You've got a big day tomorrow.'

So did Anna.

Her nails and make-up had been professionally done, and her hair cut, blow-dried and smoothed until it was as silky as the dress she slid on.

Now there was nothing left to do other than make the promised video call to Willow.

'Mummy!' She was so excited. 'You look lovely!'

'So do you, darling.'

Anna smiled, because Willow had dressed for the occasion and was wearing the flamenco dress that Emily had bought for her.

'I wanted to wear lipstick...' Willow's voice dropped to a whisper. 'But Nanny doesn't have *any*!'

'You look beautiful without. Now, are you ready to see how gorgeous Emily looks in her dress?'

CHAPTER THREE

'SE VE HERMOSA...' She looks beautiful...

As the bride entered the magnificent church Sebastián Romero gritted his jaw, yet he turned and looked down the aisle, ready to force a smile, willing to do his duty as his brother's *padrino* and murmur appropriate words to his brother and all the guests.

Just for today.

Of *course* the bride would be looking beautiful—who wouldn't be glowing and smiling when they'd guaranteed themselves a meal ticket for life?

He was certain Emily was pregnant—and, no, he did not believe it was possible to fall in love and decide you wanted a baby all in a matter of weeks.

He knew from bitter experience.

And Sebastián's hardened, cynical nature wasn't reserved for the bride.

He glanced over to his parents. His father, four weeks out of surgery, was determinedly standing. As for Maria—who did not deserve the title of 'mother'—for the first time in twenty-five years she was by her husband's side.

Sebastián had no doubt her return was down to the fact that José Romero was dying. The ink on his newly written will was barely dry and Sebastián was certain it would be in Maria's favour...

Hell, yes, he was jaded and bitter—unlike Alejandro, who had stars in his eyes. English stars! The woman they had hired to revamp the Romero website had revamped much more than they had intended.

He looked back to the bride, resigned to saying the right thing—only his black gaze didn't make it that far. Instead it fell on her *dama de honor*.

Anna.

Her long blonde hair was straight and worn down, held back from her face with a couple of sprigs of orange blossom.

The dress was elegant and a deep amber—almost the colour of the sherry the Romeros produced. Certainly the silk was just as fluid as it skimmed her slender body. The spaghetti straps showed her clavicles, and his eyes moved up her long neck to her face.

'*Sí, se ve hermosa,*' Sebastián finally said to his brother. *Yes, she looks beautiful.*

Sebastián had said the appropriate words to Alejandro—and with conviction.

Only he wasn't referring to the bride...

Closer now, he saw Anna's made-up eyes and mouth and noticed that her pale cheeks were rouged—or perhaps she blushed a little as she met his gaze. He nodded to her—an acknowledgement, thanking her for delivering the bride—then turned away.

He was actually a touch disconcerted by the force of his attraction towards Anna.

Although, he thought, on reflection, he appreciated the distraction on this hellish day.

The priest spoke of love eternal and again he tightened his jaw unconsciously. He took a deep breath and tried to decide if he preferred Anna with make-up or without. He might kiss that lipstick off later...

Now he was being asked for the rings...

Sebastián wished he could toss them away.

Truly.

He was tempted to fling the rings into the congregation to register his protest.

Not for a second did he believe that this was a love match.

Not for a second did he believe in love.

Even when he'd been engaged himself it had been about duty, about doing the right thing…

His mouth pressed together.

Had there been love?

Not for Ella, who had briefly been his fiancée.

For the baby?

A baby that hadn't even existed…

One was crying in the church now. Loudly. Then another baby joined in, and then another… In this sacred space their screams felt like a mockery, a pertinent reminder that it had taken a lie about a baby for him to even consider becoming a husband.

Never.

Anna's doubts were fading.

She didn't doubt her friend was in love, and the way Alejandro smiled at Emily and recited his vows told Anna it wasn't as one-sided as she'd feared.

It looked like love—not that Anna had much to go on when it came to judging.

Had she just been jealous? Or was she right to have been worried by this whirlwind romance?

Here she was, standing in a gorgeous old church, watching her best friend get married. Her eyes came to rest on Sebastián. He was looking fixedly ahead, allowing Anna a quiet moment to observe his serious beauty.

It felt odd to register attraction.

To notice how his perfectly cut suit adorned broad shoulders and to try not to wonder whether or not they would dance later.

Odd to be so fascinated by the back of his head and to notice that his hair had been trimmed since yesterday, those thick black strands growing into a V at the back of his olive-skinned neck.

Just bizarre to stand in a church in front of two hundred

or so people and for the first time in years feel her heart trip like a schoolgirl's.

Or, to blush like a naïve university student when a good-looking visiting professor smiled.

She quashed down that memory and got back to focussing on Sebastián.

No, it didn't just feel odd to be so drawn to another—it felt unfamiliar and new. Anna had never been so violently attracted to anyone.

But this was a physical reaction.

Purely physical.

Because, from everything she'd seen and heard so far, she didn't like Sebastián Romero very much at all.

Yet her lips betrayed her…because they seemed to smile or laugh at his bidding.

And her heart seemed detached from her logical mind whenever he was near and it beat more rapidly.

She watched as he was prompted to hand over the rings.

He reached into the pocket of his immaculate dark suit. Was it just her or was there a slight hesitation as he held them over the bible and then dropped them onto the pages? Anna found that her lips were attempting to betray her again, because she had to pinch an incoming smile at his truculence. He continued his vigil, staring fixedly ahead, but as the vows were exchanged and the babies started wailing again he arched his tense neck and looked up at the magnificent roof.

He was, Anna knew, hating every second of this.

Still, he was supremely polite when they went through to the vestry for the signings.

'Did I mess up the vows?' Emily asked.

She had made hers in Spanish, and Alejandro had given his in English.

'You were wonderful,' Anna said, smiling. 'Not that I speak Spanish, but it all—'

'Ladies,' Sebastián interrupted, 'the photographer wants a picture of the four of us with the priest.'

'Of course,' Emily said, and made her way over to the large table and took a seat as the photographer said something in Spanish to Anna.

She didn't understand. 'I'm sorry?' she said.

'He wants you to stand behind the bride,' Sebastián translated. 'Next to me.'

'Okay.' She took her place by his side and felt a frisson of awareness, as if the heat from her body had met the heat from his, even though they stood apart from each other.

Sebastián took her arm to guide her closer.

Don't react, she told herself. *You shouldn't even notice.*

The photographer was moving them like chess pieces, but Sebastián's light touch had her fizzing with awareness.

'Más cerca,' the photographer said, waving his hands at them.

'We are to move closer.' Sebastián translated again. 'And we are to remember to smile.'

'He didn't say all that.'

'He said one of those things,' Sebastián responded—and Anna found that she did both: she moved closer *and* she smiled.

And then it was all over and they made their way to the reception. The bodega was incredible, and every bit as beautiful as Emily had described. What they called the cellar was in fact a huge churchlike area supported by arches and filled with black barrels of the Romero sherry. There were round stained-glass windows and a stage at one end of the room. Anna knew it was also used as a restaurant, and there was a *taberna* too, which Emily whisked her off to see.

'This is where we met.'

'I've never seen anything like it,' Anna said as she stared at walls lined with photos of flamenco dancing.

Staff were passing around trays of coffee and sherry. It was the perfect opportunity for guests to catch their breath. Anna had been told the wedding would go on deep into the night.

Emily was soon called away and Anna found herself back

in the courtyard, helping herself to some food at a delicious-looking spread of tapas.

'Take it slow…'

Even before she heard his voice, Anna knew it was *him*.

'Believe me, there is more to come.'

'Oh!' She looked down at her rather full plate. 'I thought this was dinner.'

'Oh, no,' he said, taking one of her pastries. 'For now it is just food while there is talking. Later we have a sit-down dinner, and that goes on for hours.'

'Do you have your speech ready?' Anna asked.

'No speeches.'

'Pity…' Anna started, and then bit down on the remaining words, for she'd been about to say that she'd been looking forward to finding out more about him. She never flirted. *Ever*. She did not even know how. And yet she realised she had been about to with him.

'Are you okay?' he asked.

'Of course.'

'I'm aware you don't know anyone here. Just call out if you need a translator or anything.'

Anna knew he was just being polite. 'I'll be fine.'

But then he surprised her: 'Do you want a quick rundown?'

'Sorry?'

'If you're going to be people-watching?' He looked out at the other guests. 'Right…see the woman in silver with the *peineta*?'

'Yes.'

'That's Maria—our mother. With her stands my devoted father, José. See the young lady with black hair?'

'There are a lot of ladies with black hair,' Anna pointed out.

'Her dress is bronze and she's sulking and drinking champagne. That's Carmen—my sister.'

'Okay…' Anna was reluctantly touched that he would take the time to make being on her own at the wedding a little more fun.

'That one...' He'd turned his back to the crowd now and was talking directly to her. 'Don't make it obvious you're looking,' he warned. 'She has shorter black hair and her dress is...' He hesitated. 'I don't know the English for that word.' He thought for a moment. 'She looks as if she is sucking lemons...'

'In pink?'

'I know *that* word.' He shot out a laugh. 'Ugly pink.'

'That's not nice.'

'It's an actual shade,' he informed her. 'Anyway, that is Mariana!'

'Ooh!' Anna was intrigued that he had pointed out the main characters in Alejandro and Emily's whirlwind love story, but soon he was being called away.

'I have to go now.' He took another pastry from her plate. 'I'll come and get you when it's our turn to dance.'

He was so arrogant, clearing her plate when there was a full tapas bar behind him, but as it turned out she ended up being rather grateful, because the evening meal was huge.

Huge and long.

She was seated with Emily on one side of her and—with only Anna to represent Emily's family, perhaps to add balance to the table—on the other side, the very sulky Carmen.

Anna attempted conversation. 'I passed the equestrian centre yesterday.'

Carmen barely looked up.

'I hear you like horse riding?'

'I would hope so, given that it's my profession.'

Anna gave up trying to get blood from a stone, and was grateful when the meal seemed to be over. But then, just when she thought it was finished, a team of waiters filed out, carrying more plates above their shoulders.

For a brief second, and actually by accident, she caught Sebastián's eye and he smiled and mouthed, *Told you.*

Again her lips betrayed her and she smiled.

And so to the dancing...

Anna had not been looking forward to it. In fact, she'd been dreading it a little. But not any more. For now she found she was tense with anticipation.

As she watched the bride and groom dancing together, out of the corner of her eye she saw Sebastián approach. He stopped by her chair and offered his hand.

'Anna?'

'Thank you.'

She took his hand and stood, and of course then he released her, but that brief touch of his cool skin was their first real contact.

How could his hands be so cold on this hot night? She already knew he did not have a warm heart, but his fingers were like ice!

He reclaimed her hand again when they were on the dance floor and his other hand lightly held her waist. It was all very formal and polite—but the conversation, on the other hand, was not.

'It's a lovely wedding,' Anna said.

'Oh, please. Don't tell me you're a believer now?'

'They seem happy.'

'Even those babies registered their protest,' he said as they twirled and spun about the floor.

She thought of him arching his neck in the church—looking heavenwards for the strength to endure it, perhaps.

'My father lets children run up and down the aisles during the service,' she said, then added, 'He's a vicar.'

'Oh.' He thought for a moment and looked around. 'Then he would love a Spanish wedding. There's no such thing as bedtime here. Unfortunately!'

'You don't think children should be allowed at the reception?' Anna asked, and thought of Willow who, if she were here, would be dashing around and making friends, as well as a whole lot of noise. 'I think it's lovely.'

'Then welcome to Jerez,' he said dryly, and gave a small laugh. 'I am the...' His voice paused, perhaps in order to select the correct word, but his body kept moving, lithe and strong.

He never missed a beat and carried on smoothly, turning and guiding her through the steps. Then his voice came deep in her ear—deep and close. 'I am the killjoy.'

Anna said nothing, but as another couple moved a little too near she was momentarily grateful that he pulled her in close. Then it dawned on her that her face was on his chest, and she felt less relieved.

He never stopped moving—just effortlessly corrected their position and shielded them from the rather more flamboyant displays on the dance floor. Despite being on show, in front of two hundred people, she felt hidden—as if he'd taken her into an alternative world for two where they shared private thoughts and conversation.

'Maybe I am too cynical...' Now he did pause, that effortless grace momentarily suspended, as if he were deep in thought. 'I just question people's motives...'

'Not everyone has a motive, Sebastián. Some people are just...' Anna hesitated. She didn't want to call her best friend naïve on her wedding day, even if that was what she privately thought.

'Some people are...?' he queried, prompting her to go on.

But Anna had lost her train of thought.

The music had slowed and she wished the dance would end.

Not because of the discomfort.

More because of the awareness.

She was a young woman—a mother—so clearly not naïve, and yet that was exactly the word she would have chosen for herself now, if asked.

Naïve because she had never known how alive her body could feel.

Naïve because she'd thought she'd known what attraction felt like, and yet what she had felt before was pale and drab in comparison to what she was experiencing now.

'Some people...?' he said, prompting her again.

She lifted her head and looked into his black eyes for a moment before answering.

'Are too trusting,' Anna said.

'You are not?'

'Oh, no.' She shook her head. *Not any more.* 'But you're wrong about Emily.'

'I hope so.'

'They're clearly in love.'

'Please!' He gave a mocking laugh, but then conceded a touch. 'Well, if it's the love match of the century then good luck to them. *I* wouldn't want it.'

'You don't want love?' Anna frowned.

'God, no. Another damn person to worry about? No, thank you.'

She laughed—actually laughed—understanding a little what he meant. Because since Willow had been born she'd felt as if she was walking around with her heart in her mouth. Then she heard her own laughter and it sounded so carefree... a sound she had forgotten—almost foreign. Perhaps it was the sound of *Spanish* laughter!

But the moment was short-lived, for the music had ended. The dance she had both anticipated and dreaded was over, and she found herself wishing that he might not notice...that their dance would go on...

Instead, duty done, he thanked her and let her go.

It was possibly just as well, because there was stamping from those on the stage, and shouts of *'Olé!'* from the guests, and the tempo of the music picked up in response.

Anna was ill equipped for any of that.

'I must go and do my best man duty and dance with my mother...'

'Is it a tradition?' Anna asked.

'No...' He shrugged. 'But it is necessary if she is to be prevented from making this *her* night. She loves the spotlight. If I don't stop her it will become the Maria de Luca show.'

'Olé!'

'Olé!'

'Olé!'

Gosh, thought Anna, the Spanish really danced! Emily was showing off the results of her flamenco lessons as Alejandro encouraged her. Maria had started stamping her feet, clearly having fun. Even José got up—to the delight of everyone. And Sebastián could stamp his boots with the best of them.

Only the sulking Carmen remained seated.

Anna danced with a couple of other guests, but found her eyes kept drifting towards Sebastián. He had a cigar in his mouth, and although she *hated* smoking, it seemed that was what all Spanish guys did at a wedding. His hands were above his head and he was clapping and stamping and very possibly the sexiest man alive.

Oh, my!

Willow would have loved this, Anna thought, when her dance with a man who wasn't Sebastián ended. She decided now might be the right time to slip outside and call her daughter.

'Do you miss me?' Willow asked.

'Very much,' Anna said, looking at the black barrels piled high in the vast Romero bodega and the stained-glass windows above. Then she noticed a young couple kissing in the shadows, and turned her back.

She envied them, Anna realised as she ended her call with Willow after telling her to be a good girl for Nanny and Grandpa and... 'go to bed when they tell you. Sweet dreams...'

Her attention returned to the couple in the shadows. Dancing the night away and then sneaking off for a kiss...

It was romantic—all the things a perfect night should be—and something she had never properly known herself...

She didn't even like kissing, Anna reminded herself with a little shake.

Heading back to the table, she felt betwixt and between not just two worlds—her life in England and this glamorous night in Spain—but another life too...one she had been on the threshold of...

During her third year at university she'd hoped to join in more, have fun, loosen up a touch. While her friends had all considered her to be forthright and bold, when it came to intimacy, Anna hadn't been.

Anna had hidden.

She'd always dressed conservatively—the judgemental sniffs from her mother at her clothes not worth the effort of rebelling. And she'd always had the eyes of the entire congregation upon her in the village.

University had been overwhelming, and she'd focussed on studying rather than revelling in her new freedoms. Then, in her final year, she'd met someone—or rather had been flattered by the rare attention he had bestowed upon her.

But despite enjoying the attention, kissing and touching—*anything* physical—had had to be coaxed out of her. She'd kept on waiting to enjoy it, and until now she'd assumed it was guilt that had held her back, or that she just wasn't a particularly sexual person.

She took her seat at the almost empty head table, grateful not to be the only one. Carmen was still sitting everything out—though she did at least acknowledge Anna's presence.

'God, I wish this was over.' Carmen pouted and then glanced up and rolled her eyes as Sebastián came over and said something scathing in Spanish.

He took a seat beside Anna, because Carmen was at the end of the table and he had no choice but to do so. He at least had the grace to apologise before talking across Anna in Spanish.

'Carmen…' Whatever he said to his sister in rapid Spanish caused her to flash Sebastián an angry look.

'No!' she said angrily, and they argued on.

Possibly because their father had come to sit at the table they switched to English, perhaps not wanting him to understand, and Anna, who wasn't generally a nosy person—well, perhaps just a bit—felt as if her ears were on elastic as she eavesdropped unashamedly.

'Carmen, talk to your father,' Sebastián told her.

'He's making a fool of himself.'

Anna realised then that they were speaking about José,

who sat watching his wife dance, surrounded by male admirers. As Sebastián had predicted, Maria was making the night all about herself. Anna wondered if they were all being just a little harsh in their judgement, but she knew she did not know the full history.

Not that Emily and Alejandro seemed to mind... They were locked together, swaying with the music.

'Tonight is Papá's dream,' Sebastián said.

'No, he wanted Alejandro to marry Mariana.'

'Well, tonight romance wins,' Sebastián said with a wry edge. 'Carmen...' His voice was low. 'He's sick. God knows, there might never be another night like this when we're all together at a celebration.'

'Sebastián, por favor no digas eso.'

The desperation and expression in Carmen's voice meant that Anna, even with her very basic Spanish, knew what had been said: *Sebastián, please don't say that.*

And such was the rasp in Carmen's voice that José looked over. They switched rapidly back to English—or rather Sebastián did, his voice low, clipped and authoritative.

'Get up and ask your father to dance. And even if you have to glue your teeth together, smile and talk to Maria.'

No one, Anna noted, referred to her as *Mother*.

'Never!' Carmen said, with Spanish passion. 'I would rather die.'

'Very well. You can regret it when Papá dies, then,' Sebastián said, his voice low and harsh. 'Grow up, Carmen. We can all play a part for one night.'

His stern lecture worked, because Carmen flicked back her long black hair and somehow forced a smile as she got up and went over to her father, holding out her hand. 'Papá?'

Jose was clearly tired, but his face lit up at the invitation. He was more than delighted to get up and dance with his daughter.

'I apologise for speaking over you,' Sebastián said, and Anna turned her head in surprise.

'It's not a problem.'

'Watch this,' he said darkly, and she turned her eyes from his beautiful face and watched as—of course—Maria moved over to join in with José and Carmen.

'Good girl,' Sebastián said under his breath, when Carmen didn't flounce off but instead danced with both her parents.

How rich his praise was, Anna thought.

'You adore your father,' she said.

'Not always.' Sebastián shook his head. 'I love Carmen, though, and I don't want her to regret things if she ignores him tonight.'

'Is he very ill? Emily said he's just had surgery.'

'It went well.' He gave a tight shrug. 'But, as I just said to my sister, there won't be many more celebrations like this. I am never going to be married, nor have children.'

'That sounds very certain.'

'More certain than the sun rising tomorrow,' he confirmed. 'And given that Carmen just broke up with...' He screwed up his nose in distaste, no doubt referring to Carmen's ex. 'Perhaps a christening, though?' He gave her a smile that said again that he was certain of the reason for this wedding. 'Who knows?'

He really was the best man, working for peace and harmony behind the scenes, thought Anna. Emily constantly criticised him, and although Anna completely understood why—after all, he had done everything he could to break the happy couple up—there was a lot her friend didn't see.

The faultlessness of the wedding preparations...how he'd danced with his mother just to stop her spoiling Emily's night...how he'd insisted Carmen get up and at least appear to be celebrating. How he took the time to talk to a woman who was here without friends...

Anna knew it was simply out of duty, but she admired it all the same.

'Are you close to *your* family?' he asked.

Anna gave a vague nod, but it faded, and she found herself answering more honestly than she'd intended. 'I used to be...' She felt the threat of tears when she thought of how it once had been. 'Not now.'

She could have amended her words and said that Willow was now her family, and she considered Emily to be a sister of sorts, but she couldn't do that without crying and she refused to do that.

Or she could have qualified what she'd said and say that they would be close again if she would just apologise for her behaviour and repent, voice regret... But to do so would mean she'd have to declare that she regretted Willow, and she would not do that.

Damn! She was going to cry.

She reached for her glass of champagne, or a napkin, or for her bag—perhaps she'd make a dash to the ladies'—but her fingers met his hand instead.

'Dance?'

'I don't think—'

'Come on,' he said. 'We have to keep this party going.'

'You take your duties very seriously.'

'I do,' he said, as he pulled her to her feet and onto the dance floor. They swayed politely, his hand holding one of hers, the other on her waist. 'Tomorrow I will get back to telling my brother what a fool he is.'

'You'd have preferred he married Mariana?'

'Of course. A sensible marriage that would have made good business sense. None of this love nonsense.'

'So why don't you marry Mariana, if it makes such good business sense?'

'I would never tie myself to one person,' he told her. 'Also, Mariana would expect children.'

A change in the music halted their conversation. There was more clapping and stamping, and a lot more shouts of *'Olé!'* that should have sent her scuttling back to her seat, and yet it no longer mattered that she couldn't dance, because his fluid movements made up for it.

There was serious music being made, and for the first time

in her life Anna was being partnered by a man who could seriously move. He even dipped her, and then, when the music calmed again, to a slower tempo, he pulled her in close.

'See?' he said as he held her.

'See what?' Anna asked, wondering if in her daze she'd missed something he'd said.

'We move well together.'

'I think that's all you.'

'How are the heels?' he asked.

Why did he make her smile so much? 'Agony.'

'Lean on me, then,' he said, pulling her in even closer.

Her head was close to his chest now, and his hand was a little higher on her waist, and for Anna it felt as if he had located her dimmer switch and was slowly cranking it up and up. The energy that had been crackling away since she saw him at the airport was starting to spark and ignite now.

Then he lowered his head so that his deep voice was solely for her. *'"If the shoe fits, the foot is forgotten..."'*

Her mind felt misty, his words taking a moment to appear in the haze of being held by him and the low throb of his voice.

She did her best to sound unaffected and raised her head to meet his eyes. 'Did you just make that up yourself?'

'Yes,' he said, and then smiled to tell her he was fibbing. 'No, it was Zhuangzi.'

'I like that,' Anna said, hoping she could remember the quote and then resting her head on his chest. He smelt divine— of bergamot and citrus and, yes, smoke too.

Then she felt the slight stroke of his hand on her ribs.

'Do you like that?' he said, and she knew he was referring to the hand that was doing a lot more than politely resting on her waist as part of a duty dance.

She hadn't been intimate with anyone since Willow's father, and his hands had never caressed her so slowly, so lightly, so seductively. How could that slight brush of his fingers make her want to sink in, to lean in, to stretch her neck upwards and find his mouth?

'Yes,' she said—because she did like it.

This dance seemed to be an education in itself, for he was teaching her something she had not known before: that a palm on the small of her back could cause a tension so low in her stomach that it made her weak in the knees...that the fabric of a jacket could feel too warm against her cheek—so much so that she ached for the crisp white cotton of his shirt, and yet when he shifted so that her cheek rested there it still it did not suffice.

Now she wished her burning cheek was on his skin...

Anna found herself pondering the body beneath the suit, and that was most unlike her. Would he have chest hair? She couldn't imagine Sebastián being waxed, or bothering with laser treatments. He felt like more of a man than she had ever thought she might want.

'Look at me, Anna,' he said.

She had to peel herself back from his chest to do so, but, oh, he was stunning. His jaw was dusty with new growth now, and his facial symmetry was perfection.

Sebastián Romero was, quite simply, the most beautiful man she had ever seen in the flesh. And she wanted to kiss him. Desperately.

'We would move very well together.'

She frowned, unsure if she'd misread his meaning. But, no, she looked into black eyes that beckoned her into bed.

'Excuse me?' Anna said, affronted—or rather trying to be, because in his arms she didn't quite know who she was. 'I leave tomorrow.'

'That gives us tonight.'

If it had been anyone else she'd have turned on her heel and walked off, or slapped his cheek, or...

But it wasn't anyone else.

He made the inconceivable—a one-night stand—somehow seem viable.

Anna felt the pull to step into a new persona.

And she felt danger. Not the type where your hair stands

on end in fear, or your heart pounds at the prospect of imminent disaster. It was more that she felt the danger of recklessness calling to her. Because instead of walking away, she
remained in his arms.

Anna felt flustered. Indignant. Curious. Bewildered…

'We haven't even kissed,' she pointed out.

'I can remedy that now, if you like.'

'No!'

Yet still she didn't walk off. Instead, her burning face returned to his chest.

One night…

It should offend her—it *had* offended her—but now the
initial sting of indignation had gone his response played over
and over in her head as they continued to dance.

A remedy.

This night felt exactly like that. A remedy. Dancing, laughing, flirting, wanting…

Anna hadn't dated in years. There were slim pickings in the
village. Aside from her being a single mother, there was so much
gossip—as well as the fact that her father was the local vicar…

There was the internet… And yet she couldn't imagine paying a babysitter and leaving Willow to go and meet someone
she'd met online.

'Everything you do reflects on us.'

That had been the mantra repeated to her since before she
could walk—and, given she'd let her parents down so badly,
and had been so badly let down herself, Anna was now cau-
tious to the extreme.

But she was in Spain for one more night, and Willow was
safe at home…

There was a refreshing simplicity in that it could only be
one night…that it could only be *this* night…

Anna was curious too, because she didn't recognise her
own body and its response to his touch…

'Don't look now,' Sebastián said, breaking into her decadent thoughts, 'but the bride is looking worried.'

Anna jolted to attention. 'If something's wrong, I should go.'

'Shh…' He pulled her closer into him. '*We* are what is wrong,'

'Oh.'

'Emily is not a fan of mine.'

'I'd worked that out.'

'Why don't we finish this dance now?' he said in a low, deep voice. 'Then I will dance with a few others and you will do the same.'

'Okay…'

'But don't dance with them like this,' he warned.

'I don't think I could dance like this with anyone else,' came her honest response, for it felt to her as though their bodies were melded together.

'*Maldita!*' he said, as if her words had hollowed him. 'I don't want to let you go…'

It was necessary, though, and not just to put Emily off the scent. Seriously, if they did not part now then they would have to kiss, so painfully did her mouth ache for his.

'You know where my suite is,' he said as the music faded.

'I don't,' she denied.

'Anna, you saw me go in.'

She screwed her eyes closed, but the vision of that wooden door he had walked through last night was burnt into her mind.

Anna felt cold on this hot Spanish night when he let her go.

Bewildered.

Excited.

Things she had never felt before.

She walked back to the table and took a long drink of iced water, and sure enough Emily was over in a couple of moments, looking concerned.

'What's going on with you and Sebastián?'

'I was just dancing with the best man.'

'Come off it.' Emily's eyes were wide. 'Anna, do *not* fall for his slick charm. He's an utter bastard. He spits out women like olive pips.'

Though she winced inwardly, Anna kept her response light. 'He's a brilliant dancer, Emily, that's all.' She looked in Sebastián's direction and, sure enough, he was dancing with a gorgeous raven-haired woman. 'He's working the room.'

'I'd just hate you to get hurt.'

'Emily, it's your wedding. Please don't worry about me. It's going great, isn't it?'

'It is, but we're about to head off. Although I think the party will go on for ages. Don't forget—breakfast in the hotel with the family tomorrow.'

And then back to the real world.

Emily continued, 'Oh, Anna, I'm so pleased you're here.'

'As if I'd miss your wedding!'

Anna felt a stab of guilt, because had her mother refused to look after Willow then she would have missed it. Of course she would never tell Emily that. Perhaps when she had her own baby she might understand the constant push and pull of motherhood—it would have been hell to miss Emily's wedding, but Willow came first.

Willow would *always* come first.

And, because of that, she hadn't danced or been held in four years. Then she amended that thought. She hadn't *ever* danced or been held the way Sebastián had danced with her and held her...

There was cheering and clapping as the happy couple headed out through the gorgeous cellar, waving to their guests and moving into the plaza, where they were sent off with more cheering and good wishes, and then the exuberant Spaniards turned back to party on in the bodega.

Returning to the party, even though it remained lively and noisy, Anna knew immediately that Sebastián had gone...

'Would you like to dance?' a young man invited, but Anna politely declined.

She didn't want to dance with anyone else. She knew absolutely that it would never be as good as the dance she'd shared with Sebastián.

She walked out of the bodega in heels that now really hurt and tried not to notice again the stained-glass windows that reminded her of a church...

As if serving her a warning...

Anna sighed as she acknowledged it.

She would not be spending the night with Sebastián.

She stepped out into the square and walked past the stunning water fountain towards the hotel. The concierge gave her a nod, and the night porter greeted her and pulled back the heavy metal doors of the elevator that would take her up to her suite.

Tonight they reminded her of the bars of a prison.

And Sebastián had offered her one night of pure freedom...

'Perdóneme,' she said, blushing as she turned away from the lift and walked across the reception area before turning to the left towards the arched wooden door.

It was unlocked, so she opened it, then stepped into what looked like a forbidden garden. It was another courtyard, with romantic Spanish music playing and soft lights twinkling.

And waiting to greet her as she entered was Sebastián.

He had removed his shirt and tie and she discovered she had been right: he didn't wax or shave.

Goodness, he was stunning...

'Now,' he said, walking over to her and then dropping to his knees and removing her shoes, 'we can dance as we want.'

CHAPTER FOUR

THE RELIEF OF shedding her shoes was nothing compared to the relief of his naked skin on her cheek.

No, not relief…

She was shaking as his hand went to her underarm zipper and slid it down.

'Did your friend warn you about me?'

'She did.'

Her voice was unfamiliar, shaky with lust, and when his mouth found hers she almost sobbed in relief.

He parted her lips further with his tongue, deep kissing her hard, and Anna found a side to herself she had never known before. Because her hands shot to his head and then she was gripping and twisting his silky black hair as she came alive beneath the demands of his mouth.

Sebastián did not have to coax reluctant lips. He lit a flame inside Anna that had previously been unknown to her. For once she was, oh, so very willing.

'I've wanted to kiss you all night,' he said. 'Since yesterday, in fact.'

He picked her up and carried her through the courtyard. She kissed him all the way to the bed, stopping only as he put her down on the cover.

She lay breathless, her mouth swollen from their kisses and her body taut with arousal as he looked down on her.

'I'm going to undress you now,' he said, pushing the skirt

of her dress to her waist and skimming his hands along her thighs.

She sat up and raised her arms as he removed the dress, and there was not a whisper of anything other than bliss as he draped it carelessly over a nearby chair.

He unhooked her strapless bra and reverently touched one breast while he kissed her hot cheek. But just as Anna closed her eyes and lay back down, to enjoy the bliss of his touch, he removed his hand.

He focused his attention on sliding her knickers off, and Anna was surprised to find that she did not feel her usual shyness at being naked. Instead, she revelled in his dark stare and the way his breathing quickened as he looked down at her.

'Anna?'

'Yes?'

'You made the day better.'

'You did too.'

'Not just because of this,' he said as he unbuckled his belt.

'I know,' she replied.

For she knew what he meant. His presence, however temporary, had made her feel better too. She had really enjoyed their time together. All of it.

She propped herself up on her elbows so she could admire his naked body—his strong arms and his long, muscular, hairy legs. She tightened her jaw as she looked at the magnificent erection that rose from him, and any lingering shyness was forgotten as she sat up and reached over to where he stood.

His hair was like fine silk, Anna thought as she touched first the black strands on his stomach and then moved her hand down and held him, stroked him, explored him for a moment, before he stepped away from her hand.

He took a condom from the bedside table and she watched as he carefully rolled it down. She lay back, fizzing with anticipation.

'I'm going to kiss you everywhere later...' he said as he knelt on all fours on the vast bed.

'So will I you,' she whispered, in a seductive tone she'd never heard from herself before.

And then she just sank into the bliss of their naked kiss.

The need he had exposed in her continued to rise as his thighs parted hers. She was ready...so ready!

The bliss of him entering her was sublime, and as he pushed up onto his forearms he stared down and started to move deep within her.

'You feel fantastic.'

Anna could hear the little panting sobs she was making. 'I'm crying!' she said with a breathless laugh.

'Because now you can give in.'

'Yes.'

She was giving in to her body and so was he to his, because he began to thrust faster and faster, and her small sobs turned to moans of treacle-thick desire.

'Yes!' she said again, but to what she didn't know.

His breathing was ragged, in time with their movements, and then he thrust one final time—hard and fast—and stilled. His shout was the most welcome sound. It was as if her body recognised it...as if her energy raced to meet his, hurtled towards an intimate centre where she was locked with him, pulsing around him, so that they were released together.

'Dios...' he said, as if he were dizzy.

For a moment perhaps he was dizzy, because he did not want to pull out. He wanted to rock them slowly back to a second pleasure. But he was too careful for that and instead slowly withdrew.

'You okay?' he asked as they lay in the soft glow of twinkling lights and he pulled her against him.

'Very.' Anna nodded. 'Though I don't want anyone—'

'Anna,' he interrupted. 'I don't discuss my life with anyone.'

Not with *anyone*.

And yet he was aware that he had spoken rather too freely with her already.

This had been an impossible day, made better by Anna. It was rare that he dropped his guard, and he never dropped it as much as he had with the intoxicating woman in his arms. He had told her more about his family than he usually would. More about himself.

Sebastián knew he needed to halt this now.

'Anna...'

He stopped, because he didn't know what he was going to say. She didn't answer anyway, and he realised she was asleep.

He started to remove his arm, because he did not do the 'lying together afterwards' thing—he could not, would not, allow himself to do that. And yet he left his arm there, and thought he would close his eyes just for a moment...

It was a couple of hours later when he finally removed his arm, then climbed out of bed and headed to the shower, knowing he had got too close, knowing she had affected him too much...

But why?

Anna woke—but only because the real world was waking too.

She heard the buzz of her phone and saw there were several missed calls from Willow.

'Darling,' she said. 'How are you this morning?'

'We're going to church,' Willow said. 'For *two* services.'

'Ooh!' Anna smiled, remembering it well. 'Well, I'm going for breakfast and then heading to the airport. I'll be in the air and on my way back to you by the time you're leaving church.'

'Really?'

'Yes.'

They chatted about the wedding for a bit longer, and then she heard her mother calling for Willow.

'I'll be home before you know it,' Anna said, and then listened to another minute of excited chatter before Willow said she had to go. 'I love you, my darling,' Anna said.

Unfortunately it was just as Sebastián came out of the shower, and she saw a look flash across his face.

'Sebastián...' She ran a hand through her hair. 'That's not... That wasn't—'

'It's fine.' He shrugged. 'You don't have to explain. We both know it's one night...'

'No!' She didn't want to leave things like that. 'That was my daughter—Willow.'

Sebastián met her eyes then, and for reasons he couldn't fathom right now realised he'd possibly have preferred to be her illicit lover. He understood that she might have hidden the fact she had a partner, but as he looked at the rumpled bed and her body he realised that, for all they had shared over the past day or so, she hadn't once hinted that she was a mother.

He felt lied to.

'You never said.'

He thought of how he had taken care of his baby sister and younger brother when Maria went on her endless tours, and how conveniently she'd forgotten she had three children at home...

There was a cheap shot, forming in the dark corners of his mind: 'Out of sight, out of mind, is it?'

Yes, a very cheap shot, but he said it anyway.

Anna felt as if she had been turned to stone. It wasn't just the words—it was the malice with which they'd been said.

'I wasn't aware we were trading life stories.'

She awkwardly pulled on her dress and picked up her shoes, not even attempting to strap them on for her walk of shame back to her hotel room.

She seethed in silence, but turned back to him as she opened the door. 'If I were a man it wouldn't be an issue.'

He stared back at her but said nothing.

'Chauvinist p—!'

Anna halted abruptly. She'd been about to say *pig*, but she never used language like that and wasn't about to do it now.

'Thanks for a great night,' she said dryly, and walked out.

Breakfast was hell.

The Romeros and the De Lucas and all their guests attacked the food with relish. Anna merely drank strong coffee and nibbled a pastry and felt shaken inside.

Sebastián's sense of duty was clearly over, because he declared himself too hungover to drive Anna to the airport and quickly arranged for a driver to take her instead.

'Thank you, my dearest friend.' Emily hugged her goodbye. 'I wish you could stay longer.'

'I'm sure you don't.' Anna smiled. 'You've got a honeymoon to get to…and we'll get together soon.'

She kissed Alejandro on the cheek and waved to the other guests.

Sebastián didn't so much as look up.

She bristled at the feeling of having had her commitment to motherhood challenged by Sebastián—and then felt guilty as hell on the plane ride home.

Despite what her parents thought about Willow's conception, she had never had a one-night stand in her life. Willow's father had been a visiting professor during Anna's final year at university and, unused to male attention, Anna had thought for a time it might be love.

Unable to believe how immature she had been back then, Anna snorted, and the man sitting next to her jumped.

She turned and looked out of the plane window at the grey clouds forming and amended that thought: how inexperienced she had been *until last night*. Oh, all her feelings for her ex had long since been severed, but until last night he'd been her one and only lover.

When she arrived back home, and was sitting in the kitchen of the vicarage where she'd grown up, she put on a bland face and ate a rather stale scone. But inside she felt reckless and wild, unable to believe that last night she'd slept with a man she barely knew… And she felt gullible too, because she'd honestly thought they'd connected on a deeper level…that her friend was wrong in her opinion of him.

Yet it would seem that Emily had been right. His sudden contempt had made her feel abandoned and rejected, like she had with her ex. Discarded.

And the most confusing part…

The hardest part…

Her one night with Sebastián had been the most exciting night of her life.

And now she knew exactly what she'd been missing all these years.

CHAPTER FIVE

UNFORGETTABLE...

Despite their awful parting, her encounter with Sebastián was something she couldn't shake off or forget—and not just because Emily soon sent a link to the wedding photos.

Her daughter snuggled on her knee while they went through the images.

'Who's that?' Willow asked, pointing straight at the glamorous Maria, dressed in her flamenco regalia.

'That's Maria,' Anna explained. 'She's Emily's mother-in-law and a famous flamenco dancer.'

'I want to be a flamenco dancer *so* badly,' Willow sighed.

'I know!' Anna laughed, because Willow had put on the garish green flamenco dress that Emily had bought her just to look at the pictures.

'Is that Alejandro?' Willow pointed to a tall, dark and exceptionally good-looking man.

'No, that's his brother,' Anna responded casually.

She hastily clicked on to the next image, but there was no escape there—it was a picture of her and Sebastián standing next to each other in the vestry.

She had been so acutely aware of him in that moment, Anna thought. Her arm had still been recovering from the lightest touch of his fingers, and if she allowed herself to she could close her eyes and capture again the sharp, clean scent of the cologne that enhanced the essence of the man.

'What's his name?' Willow asked. 'The brother?'

'Sebastián,' Anna said, curiously relieved to say his name out loud.

His impact had been so strong, it felt almost as if it had left some kind of residue behind.

From that day forward, every night, when Willow had gone to bed, Anna resisted the urge to look at those photos. She would pick up her sewing, or the blanket she was embroidering for Emily and Alejandro's baby, but it was like knowing there were chocolate biscuits in the tin...

Sometimes she would put her sewing down and sit in her little garden on warm summer evenings, breathing in the scent of lavender, trying to escape the memories of him and hating him for that final one.

And it wasn't just the evenings when there were too many moments when he came to mind—no, he popped into her head at the most random times.

Once, busy at work, she'd slipped off a shoe under her desk, just to wiggle her toes, and that simple, unthinking motion had taken her mind straight back to him.

She'd looked up the quote from Zhuangzi.

When the shoe fits, the foot is forgotten; when the belt fits, the belly is forgotten. When the heart is right, 'for' and 'against' are forgotten. No drives, no compulsions, no needs, no attractions: Then your affairs are under control. You are a free man.

Anna felt she didn't quite get it, and yet she set it as the wallpaper on her phone.

Sex, she now knew, had been dreadful with Willow's father. But it wasn't just the soul-shaking sex with Sebastián that she yearned for, it was the smiles and the honesty—well, apart from her omission about Willow—and how it hadn't felt like bitching when they'd shared their mutual concern about the haste of the wedding.

Needless concern, it would seem, because Emily and Alejandro were besotted and eagerly awaiting the arrival of their baby—though Emily kept inviting Anna to come out and see her.

And now Willow was having her surgery, and although it was just a day case, Anna felt grateful that her mother had come too, and was there in the waiting room when she had to let go of Willow's hand as she was wheeled off after having been put under anaesthetic.

Things were getting better with her mother.

It still wasn't brilliant between them, but she knew her parents adored Willow, and now, as she sat with her mother in the hospital waiting room, Jean Douglas surprised her.

She was talking about her and father's annual trip to Scotland, to visit cousins and aunts there. Anna was only half listening, her eyes on the door, waiting to hear that Willow's surgery was done and her daughter was well.

'...if Willow might like to come? A little holiday before she starts school?'

Anna turned and looked at her mother, who repeated what she'd been saying. The invitation was clearly for Willow only. Jean didn't want her single mother daughter too much on show with the cousins, but apparently her granddaughter was acceptable.

Then her mother surprised her again. 'You could maybe go and see Emily.'

'Really?' Anna checked.

'I know you miss her, and...' Jean gave a tight shrug. 'Well, it's something to think about.'

Then a doctor in scrubs came to the door and smiled, and for a while summer and holidays were forgotten.

Her mother raised it again a couple of weeks later, and Anna realised it had been more than an idle suggestion. They *really* wanted to take Willow with them, and Willow *really* wanted to go.

Emily was thrilled when Anna called.

'Oh, my goodness. Yes!'

'Seven nights,' Anna said. 'I'd arrive on Saturday and leave on the following Sunday, if that's okay?'

'I can't wait!'

At six months pregnant, Emily clearly wanted to show off her lovely tummy and see her friend.

'Alejandro keeps asking when you'll be out to visit. He's having to travel a lot, but that's so he can take time off when the baby arrives.'

'How have things been?' Anna asked. 'With the family?'

'José seems to be doing well, although Maria's still rubbing everyone up the wrong way. She's moved back into the family home, so Carmen's incensed.'

And...? Anna wanted to ask. *What about Sebastián?*

But she didn't want to give even the slightest hint she might be remotely interested. As well as that, she wasn't entirely convinced that Emily didn't already know. So she listened as Emily asked about Willow.

'Next time bring her. Honestly, once I have the baby it will be so much fun for us all to be together.'

But then finally, near the end of their conversation, Anna got a little sliver of the information she was desperate to hear.

'Bloody Sebastián,' Emily said. 'Honestly, he's off on his yacht...barely here...'

'Things are no better between you guys?'

'To be honest, I hardly see him.'

Anna saw him every time she closed her eyes...

Life for Anna was expensive, with school starting soon for Willow, as well as new clothes for her holiday in Scotland. Add to that a flight to Spain, and things were tight.

Emily had offered to pay for the flight, but Anna didn't want things to be like that between them. She would be staying with her and Alejandro, so wouldn't have to worry about accommodation.

She had saved hard, and had an emergency fund, but would prefer not to dip into that—after all, a holiday was hardly an emergency. And by trimming all excess off her own holiday wardrobe—apart from a gorgeous red bikini and a red and white sarong that had been on sale at the supermarket—plus the help of her sewing machine, Anna had managed to keep the emergency fund intact.

Come mid-August, she sat with Willow as they both packed their cases. Anna carefully added the blanket she had so painstakingly embroidered for the baby. Usually sewing was her means to relax, but since Sebastián had arrived and then so swiftly departed from her life she'd had to fight hard just to concentrate on the basics.

'Are you going to give Emily the blanket now?' Willow asked, and Anna nodded. 'But she hasn't had the baby.'

'I'd like to give it to her myself,' Anna said, 'and I won't see her again for a while.'

She looked at her gorgeous daughter, who didn't have a jealous bone in her body and was simply happy that her mum was going on holiday too.

'We'll go to Spain together next time,' Anna promised.

Willow gave a squeal of delight. 'Can Nanny and Grandpa come?'

'Just us.' Anna smiled. 'We'll have our own little holiday and see the baby.'

A delighted Willow skipped off to find some hair ties to put in her little toiletry bag and Anna added the bikini and sarong to her case. It had looked so pretty in the shop, but in natural light the colour was more violet than red...an ugly kind of pink...

Anna laughed to herself, remembering Sebastián's opinion of Mariana's dress at the wedding. He was still a constant in her thoughts. She was nervous about the possibility of seeing Sebastián when she was in Spain, but tried to console herself that he would probably be out on his yacht and their paths would not cross at all.

It didn't feel like a consolation, though.

'What are these?' Willow asked, standing at the bedroom door holding a slim, shiny foil package of pills.

'Willow,' Anna said calmly, 'you know better than to touch someone else's medicine.'

'Medicine?' Willow frowned. 'Are you ill?'

Possibly in the head, Anna thought. Because there was no way she could justify, even to herself, her recent trip to the doctor to get the contraceptive Pill.

You hate him, she'd reminded herself.

And she hated herself every morning when she took a tiny tablet.

And yet she wanted him still.

He fascinated and confused her, and he angered her too, but most of all she couldn't get that flash out of her mind—the look that had darted across his face when he'd heard her say 'I love you, my darling' to what he'd thought was another man.

On the morning both Willow and Anna were to depart, she dropped her daughter off at the vicarage.

Anna wore the same long skirt and flat sandals she had the last time she'd flown to Spain, but with a high-necked sleeveless top and the silver earrings that Emily had bought for her birthday.

'That's a bit dressed up for flying,' her mother commented, when she saw the sleeveless top and jewellery.

Anna didn't respond, just told her that Willow already had her travel sickness band on, ready for the car.

'Mummy's got travel sickness tablets too,' Willow declared.

'You've never been travel sick,' her father said, frowning.

'Just when I fly.' Anna hid her blush by dropping to her knees to hug her daughter goodbye. 'Have fun,' she said as she held her. 'And be good for Nanny and Grandpa.'

'Do I have to be good *all* the time?' Willow pouted.

Even Jean laughed.

Willow was a light in all their lives, and Anna kissed and hugged her fiercely.

Her father, who had always been gentler than her mother, announced her imminent departure. 'Your taxi's here,' he said as he hoisted Willow onto his hip and gave Anna a kiss. 'Don't let me mix up your suitcases!' he teased as he picked up one to take it out to the car. 'Give our love to Emily and her husband.'

'I will.'

Her mother's farewell was less effusive, even though she gave her a small kiss on the cheek, she offered a parting shot as she walked down the path. 'Make good choices, Anna.'

Anna felt her back stiffen. She wanted to turn around and say something—to point out that she was twenty-six and not a teenager going off to a school disco. Instead, she took a deep breath and decided, as she always did for the sake of peace, to just let it go.

She'd made only one terrible choice that they knew of, Anna thought as she waved goodbye to them all, but especially to Willow, whom she knew would wave until she was out of sight.

And just look at the gorgeous consequence.

The other terrible choice…

Anna took out her phone and looked at the quote.

She thought of Sebastián and the wedding.

And still she did not regret it. For in their short time together he had taught her so much about how good sex with the right man could be.

Apart from the cruel parting.

Just to be safe, and so as not to appear pathetic if he inadvertently saw it, she deleted the quote from her phone.

On the flight she tried to focus on a biography she'd been saving to read but, gritty though it was, she couldn't focus. Instead she felt butterflies leaping in her stomach and chest, accompanying her all the way to Seville.

Anna walked out of Arrivals at Seville, trying to forget the last time she had done so, and trying not to recollect how she and Sebastián had locked eyes, and the little joke he'd played, telling her that she'd got the wrong man.

Looking around for her friend, she was suddenly startled. She must be imagining things…because it couldn't be him.

Him.

Sebastián.

This time he was unshaven, and his hair was longer than she remembered, and he was wearing black trousers and a pale grey rumpled linen shirt.

Maybe by some coincidence he was here to meet someone else—but, no, he put one hand up when he saw her.

Anna's first thought was that he was too suave to wave.

Her second—selfish—thought was that she wished she wasn't wearing the same skirt and sandals he'd seen her in before.

But then the nerves set in.

If he was here then something must be wrong!

Telling herself that there were a hundred reasons why Alejandro might have asked Sebastián to pick up his wife's friend, she made her way over to the man who had haunted her dreams for weeks.

'Hey,' he said as she approached.

He must have seen her frown, then appear confused, and then seen her eyes widen in sudden concern that something might be wrong with her friend, because he was quick to reassure her.

'It's okay. Everything is okay.'

He touched her bare arm, but clearly things were not okay—because if they were, given how they had parted, *he* would not be here.

'Where's Emily?' Anna asked, desperately hoping to be further reassured.

But when he paused before answering she knew that there was something amiss.

'In hospital. The baby is not behaving.'

Anna swallowed.

'She was taken into hospital earlier. You were in the air by then, and Alejandro asked if I would collect you.'

The fact that his hand was still on her arm told Anna that there was more.

'Alejandro has just called and said she's about to be flown to Marbella, as there is an intensive care neonatal unit there.'

'So they think she might have the baby? But it's too soon!' Anna's heart leapt into her throat.

'I don't know any more than that.'

He must have become aware that he was still touching her arm, because he dropped contact and stepped back just a fraction.

Anna stood, her head spinning with the news.

What should she do?

Should she fly to Marbella, or would she only be in the way?

Should she change her flight and just turn around and go home?

'She was there when I had Wi—'

Anna stopped, feeling the stinging hurt he had caused the last time she had mentioned her daughter return. She absolutely would not be discussing her daughter with this man.

'Thank you,' she said. 'For coming to the airport and telling me.'

'What do you want to do?' he asked.

'I'll work it out.'

'I don't think I'm supposed to report back and say I left you here *working it out*.'

Anna looked up, and although he looked back at her he did not quite meet her eyes. She guessed this must be the very last place he wanted to be.

'I'm driving up to Marbella,' he informed her. 'You're welcome to join me. I'm getting my yacht moved and docked there, but in the meantime I'll get my PA to sort out accommodation.'

Anna instantly shook her head, well aware that she couldn't afford any hotel that a Romero would stay at. But surely she'd be able to find somewhere cheaper once she got there, as well as change her return flight. She couldn't really deal with the logistics right now. All she could think of was that her best friend's baby was possibly about to be born too soon.

'I don't know what to do,' she admitted.

He made the decision for her.

'Come on,' he said. 'You'll drive up with me. You can change your return flight when we know more.'

His was the voice of reason, so she nodded and started to walk.

'Your case,' he reminded her, but didn't retrieve it himself. The kid gloves were clearly off.

The silver car was familiar this time. 'How far is it to Marbella?' she asked.

'A couple of hours,' he said, and then amended the time frame. 'Maybe two and a half if I have a tense passenger.'

Of course he had a tense passenger, after the way they had parted and now Emily's situation was so precarious.

They drove in silence for a considerable while, during which Anna's mind was going in every direction.

'Anna, could we discuss—?'

'No.' She cut him off, because she could not discuss that horrible morning—especially as she was sure now that were it not for this emergency she wouldn't even have seen him once on this trip.

Her phone buzzed and Anna quickly swiped to answer it. She saw it was Emily.

'Em!'

Sebastián listened to the one-sided conversation and heard her calm, upbeat voice, though he could see that her knee was bobbing up and down.

'That's good. Give the medication some time to work...'

There was a pause while she listened.

'Don't worry, I'm in the car with Sebastián...'

And another.

'It doesn't matter if I'm not allowed in to see you. Just stay calm...'

And finally, 'Love you too.'

Then the call ended and she passed on the little news she had.

'They're trying to stop the labour and they've given her

some medicine for the baby's lungs, just in case, but things seem better now than this morning.'

'Okay,' he said, and then he glanced over. 'Anna, I just want to say that I was wrong—'

'I do *not* want to talk about that morning,' she said firmly.

'What…?' He looked over again. 'You think *that's* what I want to discuss?'

'Just watch the road.'

'I was about to say that I was wrong in what I said about Emily and Alejandro. They are happy together. Even a cynic like me can see it.'

Sebastián saw her tight shrug and also her blush.

He knew he had just bluffed his way out of a necessary conversation. The truth was he *had* been about to discuss that morning, and to apologise. But then he'd heard the raw hurt in her voice and decided that the conversation might be better conducted when he was not driving.

As well as that, after all this time he still didn't know what to say. He didn't quite understand himself why he'd reacted as sharply as he had that morning.

He breathed out in frustration—but then his assistant called and told him where she had made reservations and gave him the exclusive address.

'I've booked you a beachfront room,' she told him. 'What do you want for your companion?' she asked.

'I'll sort it when we arrive,' Sebastián said, then clicked off.

As they zipped through mountainous countryside Anna was embarrassed to have assumed that their bitter parting was at the forefront of his mind, and was relieved when her phone buzzed again, to break the tense silence. But then she saw that it was Willow.

'Hello, darling!' Anna attempted to sound upbeat. 'I'm in a car,' she said, smiling deliberately and hoping it might show in her voice. 'How's Scotland?'

'Is Emily there?' Willow asked. 'Can I talk to her?'

'Not now because we're still driving, Willow,' Anna said. 'What are you up to?'

She spoke for several minutes, and reassured her daughter that she'd send some photos when she could, and then finally said goodbye.

'We're almost there,' Sebastián informed her as they came around a bend.

And there was the sparkling blue of the Mediterranean stretched out before them.

Anna didn't say anything at first, just looked at the sun-drenched view, knowing that somewhere down there was Emily, and that her friend was feeling scared.

Then the car turned and they drove parallel to the bright sea. She looked out at the yachts and expensive cars and the sheer glamour of the place.

When he'd said Marbella, she hadn't really known what to think.

But then she saw a sign for Puerto Banús and felt her chest tighten. Anna knew this place was way over her budget. She looked at the huge, luxurious residences, the ridiculously flashy cars and snow-white yachts, silently willing him to drive further on, past the golden mile.

It was not to be, though, for his car slowed and the indicator clicked.

He pulled into the beautiful gated grounds of a hotel shaded with palm trees and not a high-rise in sight.

Anna shook her head. 'I'm going to need to find somewhere a little more…' *Or rather, a lot less.*

But Sebastián was having none of it, and he told her so before she got out of the car.

'Don't be ridiculous. Nobody's expecting you to pay. We are—'

'I am *not* sharing a room with you.'

'Believe me, I wasn't offering,' he said.

Well, that told her!

'We are close to the hospital here,' Sebastián said, 'and for now that's the only concern.'

'I don't want you paying for me.'

'I'll charge it to my brother, then. Don't make an issue when there isn't one,' he said. 'But feel free to wander off in the heat and find a hostel, just to make your point.'

She moved to get out of the car, but suddenly it all caught up with her. Emily must be so scared, and the baby was at risk, and Willow would be in Scotland for a whole week... And then there was the shock of being met by *him*.

Anna did the last thing she wanted to do and leant back in the car seat and started to cry...

She saw him wave away the approaching bellboy and he remained seated beside her and did nothing, for which Anna was actually grateful. Because she knew that if he touched her arm again—or, heaven forbid, *held her*—she'd howl.

'I have no handkerchief to offer,' he finally said, as she rummaged in her bag.

Somehow he managed to force a smile, and Anna knew she had to swallow both her tears and her pride. She found a tissue to mop her tears and nodded. 'I'll stay tonight...until we know more about Emily.'

'Good.' Sebastián nodded.

He too was struggling. Tears usually didn't move him in the least, yet he sensed hers were rare, and it killed him just to sit there and do nothing. He'd heard the anger in her tone, though, and doubted any attempt to comfort her would be welcome.

As well as that, he did not do *comfort*.

'Why don't we get checked in?' Sebastián suggested. 'And then we can get the hell away from each other...'

'Yes, okay. Good idea.'

They entered a very cool air-conditioned lobby. So cool that the receptionist wore a smart blazer and full make-up and looked as if she'd stepped off the cover of a glossy magazine.

'Señor Romano.' She smiled and welcomed him. *'Bienvenido de vuelta!'*

The admin was all speedily dealt with, but something the receptionist said caused him to respond with a very blunt, *'No.'*

He explained it to Anna as they walked past a sign indicating *habitaciones contiguas*. 'She asked if we wanted adjoining villas.'

'No!' Anna repeated with the same blunt edge to her voice.

They walked beneath palm trees and he told her to order whatever she wanted to the villa, then added, 'Breakfast on the terrace is nice here, though. It's down that way.'

'Okay…'

'This is you,' he said, and handed her a folder that held a card to open the door to her villa.

'Where are you?'

'Down there.' He pointed to another path. 'I'll call you if I hear anything from the hospital.'

'Likewise.' She nodded.

'I still have your number,' he said. And then, rather reluctantly, Anna thought, added, 'I was going to text you an apology for what I said that morning.'

'Yeah, right…'

'And you were right. I *was* trying to talk about it in the car, but then I thought it better not to discuss it on a mountainous road.'

'I don't want to discuss *anything* with you—on a mountainous road or anywhere else.'

Anna flounced off, and it was such a relief to get away from his assault to her senses that it took the edge off the sheer luxury of her home for the night.

It wasn't a room, nor even a suite. It was a gorgeous villa, with pale wooden floors and white furnishings. There was her own terrace, and a huge shower and bath, but most welcoming of all was the low bed dressed in crisp linen that tempted her to climb in.

First, though, she texted Emily and let her know that she was here. But she got no response.

Hopefully her friend was asleep, Anna thought as she had a quick shower and then put on a robe. She shut the screens to block out the turbulent day and lay in silence in the blacked-out room.

But when she closed her eyes there was still Sebastián. There was also the sound of his reluctant apology and the tartness of her own brittle response.

Of course she had lied to his face. Because there was so much she wanted to discuss with him.

She lay there, fighting fury and attraction, angry at their parting and cross with herself for how much she still liked him.

'I have no handkerchief to offer.'

Why did he still make her smile?

CHAPTER SIX

ANNA SLEPT HORRIBLY and awoke to a knock on the door. She lay there, disorientated, unsure of the time and even the day.

The knock on the door sounded again, and she wished she'd put out the 'Do Not Disturb' sign—or whatever it was in Spanish. But she pulled on a robe and went to open the door. Perhaps breakfast had arrived?

But it was only evening, she realised, and Sebastián was standing there, shaved and smartly dressed. She was about to say that he was supposed to have texted, when he told her the reason for his personal call.

'It's a girl.'

'Oh, my!'

'She seems to be doing well.' Then he clarified, 'Well, that is from Alejandro, and I don't know if he's talking sense or... Can I come in?'

Given the circumstances, she opened the door for him.

He sat on the sofa and Anna took a chair. He seemed a little stunned, but still very together as he told her the little he knew. 'Emily's okay, but I think she had to take some serious drugs, so she is very tired. The baby has a machine to help her breathe.'

'She'll be terrified,' Anna said. 'It's so early. How much does she weigh?'

'I don't know.'

'Did you even ask?' Anna snapped.

'No,' he responded calmly. 'I was more focused on reassuring my brother than asking questions.'

Suitably chastised, Anna briefly closed her eyes. It was her turn to apologise.

'Sorry.'

'No problem,' he accepted with a shrug.

'Have you told your family?'

He nodded. 'Drama, drama—as always. They want to fly up. I told them to wait. Maria will just…' He paused. 'I think Alejandro and Emily may need some time…just them.'

'Yes.'

'Alejandro asked if you are okay, and I said not to worry— that I would take you for dinner.'

'I don't want to go out.'

Certainly not with him, looking like that. He was polished… almost gleaming. He wore dark trousers and suede shoes. Gone was the crumpled shirt, replaced by white linen that illuminated his dark beauty.

'I'm not even hungry.'

'Of course—you must have eaten on the plane.'

A granola bar.

'But that was hours ago,' he added, just to make his point. 'Well, I told him we would toast the baby and send a photo to cheer up Emily.'

'That's blackmail.'

'Possibly. But I'm hungry, and I actually do think the baby should be celebrated. My father is begging them to fetch a priest, so some happy messages might be nice?'

'I get it.' Anna nodded.

She headed back into her bedroom and went through her case. She selected the dress that she'd hoped to wear on a night out with Emily. It was a dark red cotton, and loose-fitting, but it would have to do. Running a comb through her hair, she saw she looked pale in the mirror, so she put on a slick of lipstick and some blusher on her cheeks.

'That's better,' he said as she came out.

'You look nice,' she suggested, rather sarcastically.

'Thank you,' he smiled.

Anna rolled her eyes. 'I've got to call my daughter and say goodnight.'

'Of course. Do you want me to wait outside?'

Anna shot him a cool look. 'It's my daughter, Sebastián, not my lover.'

It was just a quick call, and a nice goodnight, and then her mother came to the phone and updated her on how Willow had enjoyed the journey up to Scotland. And then she asked how she was.

Anna closed her eyes and chose to lie. 'I'm good. It sounds as if you're all having a brilliant time.'

She felt Sebastián's acute interest as he noticed that she'd chosen not to tell her mother anything of the day's events, but he didn't say anything when she put her phone in her bag and said she was ready to go.

'Card to get back in?' he reminded her.

'Oh, yes.'

Under normal circumstances this place would be paradise, Anna thought. Instead of eating in the hotel restaurant they walked towards the port, where there was music and beautiful people. Sebastián fitted right in, Anna thought, as she saw many heads turn when people noticed him.

'Sebastián,' the greeter said, smiling as they walked into a beautiful restaurant and were led up to the first floor, to a gorgeous table that overlooked the stunning yachts.

Chatting easily with the sommelier, who also knew him by name, Sebastián ordered champagne.

'You're well known here,' she said.

'I come here quite often.'

He might be familiar with the surroundings, but Anna had never felt more out of place in her life. She went through the menu as the champagne was poured and wished it had prices, or a few English translations...

'Pink for a girl,' Sebastián said, and as she looked up he nodded to the sky.

It was true—the sky was every shade of pink and lilac.

Why did he have to go and be so nice?

He put their two glasses on the white balcony ledge and took a picture of the blazing sky, then sent it to his brother.

Sebastián raised his glass. 'To her health!'

'To her health,' Anna replied, and they clinked glasses. 'Oh, and congratulations, Uncle Sebastián.'

'Thank you. Congratulations to you too...' He rarely paused in his English, but she heard him do it for a second. 'Aunty Anna.'

'Thank you.'

She took a breath and decided that she could at least make polite conversation with him, for the sake of Emily's new baby girl. She would have to whenever they saw each other in the future, and she decided she might as well start practising now.

'I'm glad I'm nearby. At first I didn't know if I should turn around and go home.'

'You and Emily are close?'

'Very.' Anna nodded. 'Since we were little. Our parents were friends.'

'Were?'

'Emily lost her parents.'

'That's right.'

'They died around the same time I fell out with mine, so...'

'You fell out with your parents?'

She nodded, but didn't elaborate, rather wishing he hadn't picked up on that.

'Why?'

'That's rather personal.'

'Fine.' He shrugged easily letting it go. 'Are you ready to order?'

She stared again at the menu, but still had no idea what she wanted.

'The mussels are incredible here,' he prompted kindly.

'Sounds lovely.'

They certainly looked incredible. It was a huge bowl of mussels, in a creamy white wine sauce waiting to be mopped up with crispy bread. And although their conversation was rather tense and awkward, Anna had a favour to ask.

'Can I ask you to take a photo of me? To send to my daughter?'

'It would be my pleasure.'

He took her phone, and she was so glad she'd deleted the picture of that quote!

'Smile,' he told her, and she tried. 'As if you mean it?' he suggested. 'Anna, please smile as if it's not me sitting opposite you.'

She laughed at that, and he captured the moment.

'There you go,' he said, and handed back the phone.

As Anna forwarded the message to Willow, Sebastián received a text of his own. 'Alejandro is checking that I am taking suitably good care of you.'

'You are,' Anna responded, and decided that now might be the right time to ask him something that had been on her mind— just get it out of the way in one go. 'Did you ever tell Alejandro?'

'Tell him what?'

'About us. About that night.'

'Anna!' He actually laughed at the very notion. 'I'm thirty-five. I don't keep my brother updated on my life, and I'm sure he has no interest in knowing who I slept with on his wedding night.'

'Okay…' She sighed out a soft laugh. 'I just needed to know whether Emily might know, or…'

'I would never say. But even if she did know…' He gave a casual shrug. 'It was just sex. It's hardly a crime.'

It had felt like one to her—at least afterwards it had, Anna thought as she scooped out more seriously delicious mussels from her dish.

And then it was Sebastián who had a question—or rather, an observation. 'You didn't tell your mother about the baby being born.'

'Didn't anyone ever tell you that it's rude to listen in on other people's calls?'

'No.' He shrugged again. 'And anyway, it's the only way I seem to find anything out about you—' He bit back whatever he'd been about to say next, and gave a tight smile as he referred to that awful morning.

'I didn't tell them because I don't know enough myself, and I don't want to scare Willow.'

'How old is your daughter?'

But Anna didn't answer.

She was still feeling so angry, and that wasn't like her. She tried not to let things get to her, but on this subject she was so cross that she put down her glass and looked him right in the eyes.

'How dare you think you have the right to judge me?'

Black eyes met and held hers, and she awaited his arrogant reply as she replayed in her mind his awful words that morning.

'Anna, I apologise.' He held her gaze and nodded, as if confirming his own choice of words. 'I regret what I said that morning and my reaction.'

She could feel her teeth clenching together in her tense jaw.

'I've regretted what I said for months.'

'Oh, please...' Anna responded coldly. She was about to call for the bill, but they both knew he would have to pay for dinner, and what was more, she didn't care about manners tonight, so instead she reached for her bag and stood.

'Anna,' he said calmy, 'please sit down.'

'I don't want to,' she snapped, and was suddenly confused.

Because shouldn't an apology that sounded sincere make her feel better? Instead the anger seemed to be rising inside her.

She leaned her head closer to his and in low tones expressed exactly how much he'd hurt her. 'That was my first time away from my daughter since she was born, and I didn't tell you about her because I was tearful about leaving her. In any case, it's none of your business, and I didn't think a man like you would be particularly interested in hearing about my childcare arrangements.'

'Anna, please sit down,' he said. 'Or if you want to shout let's take this conversation outside.'

'I don't want to be outside with you,' Anna said, but she did sit back down and stared angrily across at him. 'You hurt me that morning. A lot. I was already feeling bad enough about leaving her, and you have no right to judge me.'

'How old is your daughter?'

This time she answered. 'Four…almost five.' Anna took a sip of her drink and actually felt better for saying her piece—well, almost. 'As I said, you wouldn't think twice if it was a father who left his child for a weekend.'

'No, it's not that.'

She made a soft scoffing noise with pale lips that told him she was still deeply upset. And Sebastián, who rarely explained himself, knew she deserved a better explanation.

'We got too close,' he said. 'I didn't like it. I was already planning to pull back—'

'What do you mean?'

'We got too close,' he repeated, but refused to elaborate on that particular matter. 'Then I heard you say "I love you, darling", and it sounded as if you meant it. But then you said you had a daughter…'

'Did you think gold-digger Emily's friend was just like her? After a rich daddy for her child—?'

'Anna,' he broke in, his tone short, and it halted her. 'Are you going to let me explain or not? Believe me, I'd prefer not to.'

She gave a small, tense nod, which invited him to continue when he'd really rather not, but he pushed on.

'When I heard you say "I love you", I was maybe angry…a bit jealous, even…' he admitted, and then frowned, surprised to have said that.

He never revealed such things—just didn't—but her glaring eyes were waiting, which didn't make it any easier. He took a sip of his drink and for once knew he was the uncomfortable one.

'I wasn't upset that you have a daughter. I was upset with you for leaving her.'

She frowned, parted her lips to question him, but then snapped them closed, as if consciously letting him finish. He wished now he had left the whole subject alone.

'I thought we had spent enough time together that you might have spoken about her, mentioned her... Maria left when I was about ten. Alejandro was five. Carmen not even one.'

How ironic that he now wished she would interrupt, so he could draw a line under the entire thing, but she remained silent, her green eyes more curious than angry now.

'She was away a lot even before that, though. Affairs, lovers... I didn't really understand that then, but...' He had never articulated it, not even to his family, but he had spent a lot of time alone on his yacht in recent months, thinking. 'When Carmen was maybe two years old she was sick—nothing terrible, but she had a fever. The nanny was trying to calm her and the doctor came. I remember going into the lounge. My mother was on TV, doing a live interview on a talk show. Laughing, flirting, dancing. Clearly without a care or any thought as to what was happening with her children at home.'

'Out of sight, out of mind?'

Anna repeated what he had said to her that morning, but her voice was without anger now.

'Yes.' He nodded. 'I overreacted. I don't usually.'

It was possibly the understatement of his life. In the relationship department his baseline setting was freezing cold—Sebastián knew that much about himself. His passion was reserved solely for business, and not just the family one. He had major investments of his own. Certainly he would never be reliant on any one thing or person. Yet that morning he hadn't just frostily pulled back, as he always did if anyone got too close. He'd been savage.

'I should never have said what I did. But I was already smarting from the "I love you", and then...'

'I get it.'

* * *

Anna knew none of that had been easy for him to admit.

'So can you accept my apology?' he asked.

'Yes.'

And she did. It felt odd to sit there facing him, with all the anger and hurt of these past months fading away to nothing.

'Thank you,' she nodded.

'No, thank *you*,' he said.

Clearly uncomfortable with all he'd revealed, he glanced at their empty plates in relief.

'I'll get the bill.' He went to signal to the waiter, then remembered to be polite. 'Unless you want dessert?'

Anna shook her head, but although she didn't want dessert, she also did not want the night to end just yet. He made her so curious.

'Coffee would be nice though.'

He ordered coffee for Anna, and for himself his own brand of sherry. 'Spot-check,' he said.

'To make sure they keep it in stock?'

'More to make sure that it is our sherry in the bottle.'

'That's not very trusting,' she said.

'Because I'm *not* very trusting.'

It was Romero sherry, Sebastián confirmed when their drinks had been served and he had taken a sip.

'Your mother is the dancer on the bottle's label,' Anna said. 'I remember that from when Emily was doing the website.'

'She's on the label *for now*,' Sebastián said darkly.

'And your parents are back together?'

'Yes,' he nodded. 'She has wheedled her way back in since my father became ill. The wedding was their first public outing, to show off their reconciliation.'

She could better see now why he had rushed to judgement that morning.

'How is it?' Anna asked. 'Now that your mother is back?'

'We call her Maria,' he said.

'So how is it now that Maria's back?'

He gave her a brief smile, like a little reward for her persistence. 'My preference would be to have nothing to do with her. But for now, for the sake of my father, I am courteous.'

'For now?'

'I'll cut her loose when my father dies,' Sebastián said. 'I'll completely erase her from the brand.'

The cold steel in his voice sent goosebumps up her arms and served as another reminder, as if she had needed it, that this man severed ties easily.

'What about your brother and sister? Do they feel as strongly as you?'

He pondered the question for a moment. 'No. Alejandro sees both sides. Carmen loathes her and refuses to hide it. I can't blame her.' He swirled his drink and then met her eyes. 'I am concerned for Carmen.'

'Why?'

'Just am.' He shrugged, as if realising he had once again been too open, and then changed the topic. 'Enjoy the peace while it lasts,' he suggested, then drained his drink. 'The circus is coming to town.'

They wandered slowly back to their villas. The pink had gone from the sky and it was now a vivid navy expanse, with a strip of aqua where it met the horizon and stars were sparkling up high. Music was throbbing and Puerto Banús was far from sleepy, with lots of people milling about. He took her arm at one point, as a flashy car screeched down an impossibly narrow street.

Anna liked the feel of his hand on her arm and was suddenly confused.

She really had forgiven him.

The hurt she had been carrying had gone.

For months she'd looked at that incredible night through pained eyes, and yet now the sky might just as well still be pink, because she felt her rose-tinted glasses snap back on.

The time they had shared was not tainted now, although she forced herself to recall how he had hurt Emily in the past, as well his callously discarded fiancée, and how this man planned to cut off his mother without a backward glance.

'Thank you for dinner,' she said as they reached her villa.

'You're welcome,' he said.

'Text me if you hear anything from the hospital.'

'Of course… Anna?'

'Yes?'

But his mouth pressed together, perhaps changing his mind about whatever he'd been about to say, and then he shook his head, denying her the elaboration of his thoughts. Yet there was something about his silence that weakened her resolve. Something about this man that had her wanting to throw caution aside. *Again.*

The palm trees were rustling above them, and the same breeze blew her hair across her face. Anna brushed it back and met his eyes.

'I wanted to do that,' he admitted, looking at her hair.

She'd wanted him to as well. Had wanted him to smooth her hair back behind her ear and stroke his way to the kiss that had been waiting in the air. But he'd made no move.

He broke the tense silence by explaining, 'But I know I shouldn't mess up my apology.'

There was a subtle offer there, and Anna heard it. It was for her to decide if they would resume what they had started at the wedding.

But she couldn't. She just couldn't.

'Goodnight, Sebastián.'

'Sleep well.'

She let herself into the villa and stood for a moment with her back to the door, resisting the urge to change her mind, reminding herself of what Sebastián himself had said earlier.

'It was just sex.'

Only for Anna it didn't feel quite as simple as that.

There was nothing casual about her feelings.

She liked Sebastián Romero way more than could be considered wise.

CHAPTER SEVEN

ANNA WAS INCREDIBLY tempted to skip breakfast, but decided she would not hide from Sebastián and headed to the restaurant.

After selecting white shorts and a pretty cheesecloth top, she pulled on sandals and then strolled through the gorgeous grounds.

'Señorita...'

She was greeted warmly and taken to a terrace table overlooking the delicious ocean, where she gave her order for coffee. Having chosen some fruit and yoghurt from the splendid buffet, Anna was just starting to relax when the apologetic waiter came over.

'Señorita, please forgive me...but we have a group of guests and they would like privacy on the terrace.'

She glanced up and saw that two couples had arrived. While privately wondering why they couldn't sit at any one of the many vacant tables, not wanting to make a fuss, she stood up, and was about to be shown to one of the tables inside when Sebastián appeared. He looked seedy—unshaven and with bloodshot eyes. Still, even at his most ragged, he was easily the best-looking man she had ever met.

'What's going on?' he asked.

'There's a group,' Anna said. 'I think they want to close off the terrace for them.'

'Perdóneme?' he said, and frowned at the waiter who, under Sebastián's steely gaze, looked rather less authoritative as he explained in Spanish the reason for the table-change.

Sebastián answered in English. 'I don't give a damn. If they require a degree of privacy then they'll have to wait—or they can eat in their own rooms.' He looked over to her. 'Sit down, Anna.'

'It's really no problem...'

'Well, it is for me,' he said. 'I like the view.'

He took a seat, and Anna did the same.

'I really don't mind moving.'

'Well, I do.'

He ordered coffee and she watched him yawn. She guessed he hadn't returned to his villa after leaving her.

'I was just about to text Emily,' she told him. 'I didn't want to disturb her too early.'

'No need. I have just come from breakfast with Alejandro.'

Gosh, Anna thought, he certainly got things done.

'The baby is doing well for its dates and size. Though I forgot to ask what it weighed again. Emily is...' he rolled his hand '...emotional.'

'With good reason.'

'I'm not criticising,' Sebastián said. 'Just reporting.' He met her eyes and gave her a small smile. 'What else...?' He thought for a moment. 'She's asked if you will get her a few things. There's quite a list.'

He took out his phone to read from his list, and Anna took out hers so she could type the list into her Notes app. Then he suggested he just send her the list instead.

'Okay, but let's go through it so I can get her exactly what she wants.'

'Lip gloss.'

'Lip gloss?' she checked. 'Oh, do you mean lip balm?'

'I took it to be lip gloss.' He looked at her mouth, and then back to her eyes. He could flirt like a pro, with a single glance. With a single word. 'Maybe balm.'

There was no balm to be had in his gaze, so she flicked her eyes away and got back to the list.

It was quite extensive, given Emily had left Jerez with no

notice, having expected to have three more months left to prepare herself for the arrival of her baby.

'I'll drive you to the hospital once you've got the shopping,' Sebastián told her.

'I can get a taxi.'

'If you prefer,' he said. 'Carmen is arriving tomorrow.'

'What about your parents?'

'My father has a hospital appointment in Madrid later in the week. I told him things were stable enough here, and that he should keep his appointment and then come afterwards.'

'You've been busy.'

'I've barely started,' he said. 'I'll head back to Jerez soon. With Alejandro now on paternity leave, one of us has to work.'

'But I thought your yacht was…arriving?'

Or whatever the correct term was!

He nodded. 'I might tell Alejandro he can use it. They'll be good to him.'

'They?'

'My crew,' he said. 'They're like family, really.'

'Oh…' She frowned, because this really was another world to her. 'So, does it just follow you around?'

'No!' He gave a half-laugh. 'It has been out on charter, but that's just finished and they had already started preparing the yacht for me. I was going to take a break before Alejandro took time off for the new baby.'

'So you lease it out? I mean, charter it?'

'Not often—and only to friends or associates. But I have a crew who love to travel and be on the water,' Sebastián explained.

Perhaps he registered her frown.

'So do I,' he said, 'although it's more than that.'

'In what way?'

'It's something to share,' he said.

'For parties?'

'At times—though not of late.' He thought for a moment. 'It is nice for family gatherings and such. Special times. You might see it for yourself. The crew are already planning a celebration for my new niece.'

'That's nice.'

'They are far more thoughtful than I am,' he admitted. 'I have an apartment outside of Jerez, near the port. I really can't imagine having such gatherings there, nor in a hotel or function room. The yacht is different.'

'How?'

'It's home,' he said, 'with an incredible crew. They know my family. Believe me, that helps. My family is a lot to deal with...'

'I'd have loved to have a big family...' Anna sighed wistfully. 'I'd love brothers and sisters for Willow too.'

'You want more children?'

He pulled a face, looking so incredulous that it made her laugh.

'You really don't want a family?'

He shook his head. 'To my father's eternal dismay.' He rolled those black eyes. 'But I have a great life, and I don't want to complicate it.'

'What about when you're old?'

'I'll be old on my yacht,' he said, and gave her a smile. 'Don't worry. I'm too rich to be lonely.' He drained his coffee. 'I should go.'

'Should you drive back today?'

'Pardon?'

'Well, you've hardly slept.'

'Anna, we were in separate beds by midnight.' Then he added. '*Your* choice.'

'I meant...'

She flushed, because she knew she'd been caught fishing for information, and because she knew just how relieved she was that he *had* been in bed by midnight. But she didn't want him to go, Anna realised. She was inventing excuses for him not to leave.

It was just so nice to be like this with him. Even with the

annoying background of their fellow diners, one of whom was now complaining that the sun was too bright.

'No doubt she finds the water too blue,' Sebastián muttered, and then said something entirely unexpected. 'I was once engaged to a woman like that.'

He gave himself a little shake. She couldn't tell if it was because he was surprised that he'd said it, or to rid himself of the memory of this woman.

'What happened?' Anna asked, unable to help herself. 'With your fiancée?'

'Plenty.'

'It must have hurt, though?' she ventured. 'When it ended?'

'Yes.'

'Did you love her?'

'No.'

Now it was Anna who gave a slightly disparaging laugh. 'That would do it...'

'Believe me, it was never about love.' He looked over at her. 'On either side.' Perhaps he saw the slight twist of her mouth, because he added, 'Whatever you might have read.'

Anna flushed. 'I'm not usually so nosey. I just—'

'It's fine.' He gave a small shrug, as if forgiving her for her brief foray into internet stalking. 'I certainly looked *you* up after we...'

'What did you find out?'

'Nothing,' he admitted. 'I found your parents. Oh, and a photo of them, the proud grandparents, in one of your father's parish newsletters.' Now he gave her a smile. 'Your daughter was dressed as a unicorn.'

'Oh, that was so last year!' Anna laughed. 'She's into flamenco dancing now. Emily brought her back this dreadful dress—'

She halted, suddenly worried about disparaging his heritage—especially given his mother was a famous flamenco dancer.

'It's bright green with black polka dots...' she attempted,

trying to explain the fright of this dress. 'I'm sure most are gorgeous, but this one…'

Her voice trailed off as he started scrolling through his phone, but she knew she must forgive him. Because what would he know about four-year-olds who wanted to wear their flamenco dresses to the shops, to school, to church, to bed…? As well as that, he was clearly up to his eyeballs in putting out Romero fires, with the family planning to descend on Marbella at any moment.

Despite his little jab about separate beds, Sebastián was mightily relieved that they hadn't slept together last night.

She'd opened up his heart when he preferred to keep it closed.

'Do you want a lift to the hospital later?' he offered, one last time.

'If it's not too inconvenient.'

He nodded, and went to go, but then changed his mind. 'You are beyond an inconvenience, Anna Douglas.'

If she told anyone else what he'd said, or if she attempted to repeat it, it would sound like an insult or a criticism.

You probably had to be looking into his bloodshot black eyes to really interpret his meaning, Anna thought. Or you had to be inhaling the dregs of last night's cologne over the breakfast table to understand.

Because inconvenient was exactly what this attraction was.

Their attraction was so intense, so *present*, that it shocked her. She thought of his mild invitation last night and knew she could not be this playboy's occasional fling.

He would move on—that much he had told her.

One night had been a delicious oddity.

Two might break her…

'As are you,' Anna replied now, staring back at this man she would prefer not to want to quite this degree.

And with that, he got up and left.

She sat alone at the table, but without him she felt uncomfortable. And as she went to choose from the gorgeous pastry selection she knew why.

'Not so bold without your boss here.'

Anna turned. It was one of the women in the group for whom Sebastián had refused to move. She must have seen them both with their phones out and assumed that Anna worked for him. And she hadn't finished with her snide digs yet.

'And I thought the Romero brand was about elegance...'

And, no, here in Puerto Banús Anna found she *wasn't* so bold without Sebastián there.

She sat back down at her table for a few moments, trying to eat the pastry she had selected. Then she pretended to use her phone, just for something to do. But she could feel the ice of the woman's gaze upon her and soon left.

Sebastián drove her to the hospital, but declined to come inside.

'Alejandro is going to sit with the baby while you visit Emily.' He looked over at her. 'What are you going to do this afternoon?'

'I'm not sure. I'll go to the beach, maybe—see if I can go home with a tan.'

'Don't burn like a tourist. Take it slow.'

'I'm not going to get burnt.'

'Okay,' he said, in a voice that meant business. 'Now I'm going to ask the awkward question: Do you need some money?'

'No!'

'Because it is expensive here. Use the restaurant at the hotel, and room service, and when you're on the beach just charge everything to the villa.' He must have seen her eyes close. 'But you won't do that, will you?'

'I'll get some snacks at the shop to take with me.'

'Dios!' He had the audacity to laugh. 'Just—' Then he must have seen her pained face. 'Go and see your friend.'

Sebastián watched her walk off, her pale legs poking out of her ill-fitting white shorts, and he thought of her on the extremely exclusive beach, unpacking a lunch box while burning alive and being roasted by the rest of the clientele.

He did not want to get involved with Anna, but he was very aware that he'd messed up her first weekend away from her daughter.

And now circumstance was ruining Anna's first holiday without her.

Instead of relaxing, she was stuck with hospital visits.

Instead of spending time with her friend, Anna was alone.

His apology wasn't enough, Sebastián knew. He wanted to make up for that morning.

The hospital was cool—until she stepped onto the maternity ward, which was so hot Anna felt as if she might already be on the beach.

Having washed her hands, she was shown to a gorgeous room and there, looking tearful and utterly exhausted, was Emily.

'This wasn't how it was supposed to be!' Emily blurted out and promptly burst into tears.

'Oh, you poor thing!' Anna gave her a hug. 'I'm so glad I'm here...even if I can't see you very much. How is she?'

'They say she's doing well...' Emily gulped. 'But they're having to help her with her breathing. There are so many machines...'

There were indeed a lot of machines, Anna thought as they gazed through the glass at the special care unit.

Oh, gosh, she was so tiny, and yet so perfect. The hair poking out of her little knitted hat grew in blonde tufts, like Emily's, and her tiny hands were pink and reaching out, as if trying to hold on to something.

And there was Alejandro, his hand going into the porthole and taking his tiny daughter's fingers, utterly engrossed, at first unaware of his audience. Then he saw them and gave Anna a smile, pointing to the cap and gown he was wearing.

It's fine, Anna mouthed, and then put her fingers into the sign of a heart and pointed to their daughter.

'I feel dreadful that you're here alone,' Emily said when they were back in her suite.

'I'm fine. Sebastián's been great.'

'Oh, please...' Emily disparaged as she gingerly got back into bed. 'Alejandro asked him to take care of you and he's already belting back to Jerez to work. Did he give you my list?'

'He did,' Anna said, ever practical, and handed over what felt like half the contents of the *farmacia* she had been to, as well as the items of clothing Emily had asked for. 'And I made this...'

Anna passed Emily the tissue paper package and held her breath as she opened it carefully.

'Oh, Anna!'

'I'm not sure there's much call for cashmere blankets during a Spanish summer...'

She laughed, trying to make light of the gift. She had embroidered two otters, one dark and one pale, onto a mocha background, and stitched them onto a backing so both sides would be soft.

'It's perfect...' Emily was tearful again, but in a good way. 'Remember those otters at the lake?'

'Willow adores them. I'm sure our girls are going to have lots of fun watching them together.'

'I hope so.'

'I *know* so,' Anna said. 'Your daughter is beautiful. And, yes, she's early, but everyone seems very positive.'

'Yes...' Emily took a breath and gazed at the blanket. 'This is gorgeous, Anna.' She looked lovingly up at her friend and asked, 'Would it be a lot of work to add her name?'

'I can take it back home with me and do it.'

'I mean, while you're here.'

'I can't embroider a name I don't know,' Anna said, keeping her voice light while thinking of the mountain of work it would be to get it done in time. Not so much the embroidery, it was more restitching the backing without her trusty sewing machine. As well as that, the boutiques she'd seen here so far didn't really look as if they would sell the type of silk thread she required.

'Is it doable, though?'

'Of course!' Anna forced a positive tone, but it changed to one of pure delight when Emily confided the baby's name. 'That's beautiful.'

'It's top secret.'

In all, it was a lovely visit, and Anna stayed for a couple of hours, watching as glorious pink flowers and balloons were delivered, until Emily headed off for some time with her baby.

'I'll be back tomorrow,' Anna said, and hugged her friend.

'Well, hopefully I'll be better company. All I seem to do at the moment is cry.'

'Please!' Anna dismissed her concerns. 'Remember when I had Willow? I was hardly swinging from the rafters.'

'You didn't cry at the drop of a hat.'

No, she had just been silent.

She had been hurting for the tiny baby that its father didn't deign to visit. And so angry that her parents could consider her precious child a mistake.

No streams of pink flowers and *It's a girl!* balloons had arrived for her. And Anna's only visitor had been Emily.

As she took the lift to the ground floor, Anna tried to work out where she might find sewing supplies in Marbella. She did some searching on her phone, but couldn't find anything that looked promising. She knew Emily wasn't thinking clearly, but Anna didn't really want to be sewing on her holiday...

Stepping out from the cool air-conditioned hospital into the fierce midday sun felt like opening an oven door.

'Anna!'

She looked towards the source of her name being called and there he was, leaning against his car, shaved now, dressed in a dark suit and tie and wearing shades.

'I thought you were heading back to Jerez?' Anna said as she walked over.

'Maybe you are right and I am too tired to drive.' He shrugged. 'I worked online this morning instead.'

His car was like a delicious fridge as she climbed in.

'So, what are your plans?' he asked, and glanced over at her.

'I need to get a couple of things, so I might go into the old town.'

'Or we could go to the beach?'

'No, thank you.'

'You don't want to go to the beach?'

She took a breath and looked out at the gorgeous sand and sparkling waters. Of course she wanted to go to the beach. But she felt weak at the thought of an afternoon with him.

She recognised the danger of it…felt that pit-of-the-stomach recklessness she hadn't known existed until she had spent the night with him.

It would not be repeated.

But…

It was just a trip to the beach…maybe a swim.

In the middle of the day.

An afternoon in the delicious sun with him was more than she knew how to refuse.

'Yes,' Anna said, as if it were a simple decision. 'Actually, that would be lovely.'

CHAPTER EIGHT

ANNA WOULD *NOT* BURN.

She had a pump bottle of the same lotion that she used on Willow, and she slathered it on in her room, and even put it in her bag for repeat applications.

The butterflies were back as she tied on her red bikini and wrapped her pale body in the sarong, then added a straw hat. Then she headed down the path he had pointed to last night.

'*Hola!*' he said when he opened the door, wearing black swimming trunks and sunglasses, completely at ease in his own skin. 'Come through.'

'I thought we were going to the beach.'

He pointed behind him and she blinked at the sight of his bedroom and a to-die-for view of the sea.

'Wow!' she said. 'I'm going to put in a complaint about my accommodation.'

He smiled at her little joke as they walked across the cool marble floor and then through his huge bedroom and straight out onto the beach.

It was only when they arrived and she saw a couple of bronzed topless women glance over that she felt overdressed. The red and white sarong that had looked so pretty before now felt as if she'd draped herself in an English flag.

'Here,' Sebastián said, and flopped down on one of the sun loungers.

'You've given me the shaded one.'

'You *need* the shaded one,' he said. 'Or you'll burn.'

'No...' She looked up from under the brim of her hat. 'I have impenetrable sunblock on.'

She looked tense, Sebastián thought as he took off his sunglasses and placed them on the small table between them. Usually he didn't babysit anyone. He was more used to handing over his credit card and leaving his chosen date to amuse herself while he got on with work.

What was he doing here? Sebastián questioned.

He felt...*duty-bound* to stay and ensure that Anna was okay and could navigate the politics of the beach...

No, not duty-bound.

This wasn't duty.

'Dios...' he muttered as the awful group from that morning paraded past to their reserved loungers. 'This is why I prefer my yacht.'

Sebastian turned his head and gave her a lazy smile that told her he didn't mind at all being there.

'She thinks I work for you.' The words slipped out before she could stop herself.

'How do you know that?'

'Just a comment she made at breakfast, after you left.' Her lips pinched and she shook her head, not wanting to repeat it. But there was a certain patience in his silence, a space in the pause that encouraged honesty. 'She suggested the Romeros were lowering their standards of elegance by employing me.'

'She is the one who lowers things,' Sebastián said. 'Watch! She'll start complaining before she even lies down.'

Anna looked over and, sure enough, she already had the beach boys moving umbrellas and was generating unnecessary fuss on this beautiful day. Thankfully she hadn't spotted Anna, and hopefully wouldn't. Still, it did nothing to allay her tension as she lay there.

'Was your fiancée really like that?' she ventured, wondering if he'd warn her not to ask, but he didn't seem to mind.

'Not at first…' He yawned before continuing, 'But then I heard she had reprimanded one my crew.' He looked over at Anna. 'It's protocol that the *capitán* deals with such issues.'

'So, she should have gone through the captain?'

'No, she should have gone through me, and I would have spoken to Dante.'

'Your captain?'

'Yes. But in this instance there was no reason for her to complain. She was just being a bitch.'

'Don't swear.'

'Believe me, she would make a saint curse. I guess that was my first glimpse into the real her. I can usually spot her type a mile off, but Ella hid it well, I'll give her that.'

Anna forgot all about their horrible beach companion as she turned and looked at him, desperate for him to elaborate further, but he didn't.

'What really happened?' she asked.

He put his hands behind his head and said nothing.

'I don't believe you'd break things off just like that.'

'Anna, I *do* break things off just like that,' Sebastián refuted. 'Often.'

It wasn't an easy, companionable conversation. There were lots of long silences, during which they listened to the lulling, shushing waves between question and answer.

'Not if you're engaged to someone.' Anna just wouldn't buy it. 'Not when she's just lost a baby. I don't believe it.' She saw him blink, but had no idea what that blink meant. It just felt to her as if she'd hit on the truth. 'I don't believe you'd do that.'

He closed his eyes then, and for a little while Anna assumed he'd fallen asleep, but finally she heard his voice.

'I promised Ella I would never discuss it.'

'Did she agree the same?'

He gave a curt nod.

'Then why do you come off so badly in all her interviews? I don't see *her* maintaining a dignified silence.'

'Maybe not. But it's not always about setting the record

straight. Perhaps there are things that are just too...' He halted. 'I don't care what people think of me.'

But as she lay there, wishing she had a scrap of his confidence, Sebastián spoke again.

'Most of the time.'

Anna turned her head and found she was holding her breath as she met his eyes.

'I'm not going to go into details,' Sebastián said, 'but the rumours are not true.'

She nodded, and in a place deep inside she knew she was being told the truth. Her cheeks were stinging as he subtly told her that her opinion of him mattered.

'I wish I didn't care what people thought,' Anna admitted. 'Why do you?'

'I think because my parents do. I grew up being told that everything I did reflected on them. It's quite a small village where I'm from, so everyone knows everything.'

'Do you work?'

'Of course I work,' Anna said. 'I'm a receptionist at the junior school.' She looked over at him. 'It wasn't what I planned, but...' She shrugged. 'I get school holidays off, and that's going to come in very handy.'

'What *did* you plan?'

'I wanted to be an English teacher. I'm hoping to go back to college next year, once Willow is at school. There are a lot of supervised teaching days, though.'

She saw him frown.

'Do you get paid for that?'

'No, or I'd have done it already.'

'*I'll* supervise you.'

'I don't think it works like that!' Anna laughed.

She found herself pinking up, and not from the sun, and she looked at him, wondering how he could make even the most casual conversation a decadent flirtation.

'You're starting to burn,' Sebastián said, and Anna chose not to tell him that she was simply blushing.

* * *

He took her giant-sized, industrial strength sunblock from the top of her bag.

'Next time just bring a small tube.'

'Why?'

'Because you're not on a school field trip!'

He was trying to tell her gently how things were done here. He was trying to explain the world he had landed her in, which could at times be catty, but he saw her lips pinch and knew she felt criticised.

'Hold out your hand.'

She did so, and he pumped a generous dollop onto her palm. 'Left shoulder.' He watched as she rubbed it in. 'And left side of your neck.'

A beach waiter came and Sebastián ordered iced water and lime for himself. Then the waiter glanced to Anna.

'I've got mine, thanks.'

Sebastián looked at her plastic water bottle, practically coming to a boil in the sun, and changed his order.

'Two iced waters with lime, and a plate of fruit.' As the waiter walked off, he interrupted her before she could protest. 'You can save your hot water for emergencies.'

'Why are you so arrogant?'

'I'm really not.'

'Oh, you really are,' Anna said, and rolled over.

She tried to focus on her book, the same gritty biography she'd attempted to read on the plane—but it was impossible to get through a single paragraph with the presence of the demi-god by her side.

Their water came, and it was icy and delicious and served with the most gorgeous fruit platter she had ever seen.

'Have some,' he said as he bit into a slice of bright pink watermelon that had Anna's mouth watering.

But although tempted, she knew there was sand and unabsorbed sunblock on her fingers.

'No, thank you.'

She went back to her book, but still couldn't concentrate. She was just so impossibly aware of the man next to her and trying hard not to reveal it.

'Why are we fighting over fruit and water?' he asked, and she looked over.

'And sunblock,' she added curtly.

'Yes, and sunblock,' he snapped back. 'Seriously, Anna, I get that you would prefer not to be here in Puerto Banús—'

'It's not that!'

'Okay. Then I get that it's awkward for you. But please— let it go. It's a glass of water.'

'It's not the water.'

'Then what? Didn't I apologise adequately?'

She closed her eyes and let out a huff of frustration.

'Because we are still fighting and I don't get why.'

'I'm not fighting.'

'You are.'

She stared at the blurred words on the page of her book and knew he was right.

She was fighting their attraction—playing some odd whack-a-mole game with her senses.

And now Sebastián thought she was being petty by not eating the fruit that of course she wanted...

She sat up and tried to pretend that the man beside her didn't affect her, but she saw the gorgeous hair on his thighs, and knew how they felt against hers... She tried to squash down that memory.

He saw she was eating and sat up.

'Good,' he said, as if pleased their silent fight was over.

As she reached for a slice of chilled pineapple her hand hovered as she saw the opened passion fruit and the little spoons beside it, and the mixture of thinly sliced crisp green and ruby-red apples.

She watched his confident fingers move to pluck a ripe

strawberry, and it was then that she spoke, her voice breathy and bewildered. 'I'm very happy to be here.'

His olive-skinned fingers hesitated, and she watched as they took the tips of hers before he spoke. 'Good.'

She looked at their hands, lightly touching. The contact stirred the energy trapped somewhere within her, drawing it out of her, yet at the same time returning it and matching his... It was like a circuit connecting.

'*Are* we fighting?' she asked, honestly unsure.

'You are,' he said, and dropped the contact, taking up his strawberry and lying back against the headrest. 'But it is not a fight of anger. Not any more.'

She looked at him and he stared back boldly, his black eyes telling her that the next move was hers. How badly she wanted to reach over and take his hand again! How much every cell in her body wanted to let him pull her towards him, to kiss him, to stroke him!

His bed was a mere few steps away...

'I'm going in the water,' Anna said abruptly as she stood.

Perhaps in the water she could breathe and cool her heated thoughts. She would welcome the return of her common sense.

Sebastián put his hands behind his head and watched her walk towards the ocean. He saw that her shoulders were pink, and although he admired the curve of her buttocks, and the length of her thighs, it was her gorgeous back that he prized...the tension in her straight spine...

As idyllic as the beach appeared, the clientele on such exclusive resorts were not always kind—especially if they felt that they had been slighted.

He heard the woman from this morning make a comment about cheap high street bikinis and pink skin that burned, and laugh at how the English girl would suffer for lying in the sun tonight...

It was all said in Spanish, however, the mocking tone was

understood universally, and the derisive laughter from the group evident.

He saw Anna's shoulders stiffen, her stride briefly hesitate, and he held his breath.

Yes, Anna had hesitated—because being laughed at on the beach told her what she already knew: she didn't belong here.

She understood now that he *was* supervising her. Kindly, but still...

From the sunblock to the water and fruit, he was trying to help her blend in, in this rather cruel world.

She resumed walking towards the water, even though she wanted to turn and run.

'Anna!'

His voice reached her and the panic stilled.

'Wait for me.'

Anna turned and watched as he walked towards her, taking in his sheer beauty. She noted that the mocking laughter had faded into incredulous silence, because he'd grasped her hand to walk with her, and then he gave her a kiss that told all present how beautiful he found her.

It was a light kiss, an easy kiss, and even though it was delivered for the purpose of annoying her detractors, Anna revelled in it.

It made her feel beautiful.

As they walked hand in hand into the water she felt as perfect and whole as she had that night in his arms.

But the water, Anna realised, could never have shocked common sense into her. Because instead of the cold seas she was familiar with, this one was warm bliss—there wasn't even a yelp as the ocean met her stomach.

'Thank you,' she said.

'For what?'

'I don't know exactly what they said...' She looked at him. 'But you didn't have to do that, you know.'

'I wanted to,' he responded. 'Actually, I would like to do a whole lot more...'

And with that he swam off, far more expertly than her school swimming lessons would allow her to do, so instead she lay back and let the ocean support her.

The sky was the bluest she had ever seen, and the sun by far too bright to look directly at. So she squinted, and through her lashes saw the golden fire and its haze shining down on her. And then it was blocked out by the figure of Sebastián Romero. He stood there, dripping wet and looking down at her.

It was more dangerous to look directly at him than at the sun, she thought.

Yet she did.

And she floated there, recalling another time when he had looked down on her, and she knew he was remembering the same.

'Please don't...' she said.

'Don't what?'

'Don't look at me like that.'

It was odd to say it out loud. She felt uncomfortable addressing openly the warm flood of feelings his look had generated.

'As if we might...'

'Might...?' he checked, offering his hand and saving her from inelegantly trying to stand up on the sandy bottom.

He did not remove his hand.

The sand was soft, yet firm beneath her feet, the water waist-high, and his gaze drifted down her pinkening body, eventually coming to rest on the nipples that poked against her flimsy bikini.

He touched her neck where the skin was pink, and the shoulder that she must have missed with the sunblock.

'We could go back inside,' he said, and his low, throaty voice told her it was not simply to save her from burning that he made the suggestion.

Right now, standing barely dressed and facing each other, felt challenging enough to Anna.

She was unused to wanting. Naively, she'd thought that night-time was the danger zone—that walking back from dinner would be when her resolve might weaken.

When she'd said yes to the beach, it had been because surely it would be easier to keep her head at midday?

'You should stop that,' he said, as he caressed her cheek.

'Stop what?'

'Looking at me as if you want me to kiss you.'

She wanted to retort quickly, *In your dreams.* But she did not. She could feel his fingers in her hair, smoothing it back from her face as he'd wanted to last night, then sliding to the back of her head to grasp the silken strands more firmly. The sun beat down on them, and on the glistening water, and there was no place to hide.

So she stared back at him instead, and when his face came down towards hers, she closed her eyes in utter bliss at the feel of his mouth, soft and firm and capable of making her shiver on a blazing day... Her hands went to his shoulders, to the warm sun-heated skin there. She liked the noises they made as they kissed, and how hot their skin felt where it touched. Then his hand moved down to her waist, and only then did she pull back.

'I don't think...' She was trying to be honest, to thrash out a deal with the devil while there was still a chance. 'This can't go anywhere...'

'Agreed,' Sebastián said.

Clearly he did not make promises he had no intention of keeping, and she could only admire him for that.

'You don't want a relationship and...' she took a breath '... I'm in no position to have one.'

'Yes.'

'So, why would we...?'

'Because we want each other.'

She couldn't deny that truth.

'Because we can,' he said.

And his hand moved from her waist up to her ribcage, as

it had when they'd danced. He stroked her gently, but not in a calming way.

'I don't want anyone finding out,' she said.

'I'm sure we're not anyone's priority,' he said. 'We don't have to hide.'

'No!'

She was adamant. He confused every principle she held, and all her thought processes, but she was clear on this. They stood in the water, hearing the laughter and the sounds of summer around them.

'I will always be friends with Emily, and I don't want anything awkward—'

'Why would it be awkward just because we've had sex?'

And therein lay the difference between them—and Anna knew it.

Sex was sex to him. A need. A want fulfilled.

She was deliciously crazy about him and wishing it *could* just be sex…wishing that his kiss moved only her body and not her soul as well.

'Next time I'm here it will be with my daughter.' She held firm. 'I don't want there to be even a hint that you're anything more to me than my best friend's husband's brother.'

'Believe me,' he said, 'if you are here with your child I will be staying well back. I don't do relationships, and certainly not complicated ones. Stop making something simple so involved.'

He kissed her again, his mouth soothing the doubts—or was he just inflaming her desire, so that there was no room for anything other than the lust that rippled through her?

'Let's go back to the villa…'

Their foreheads were touching, their bodies barely an inch apart, but she prickled in a way that told her they very soon would be skin to skin. Anna wanted to take his hand and go to the delicious places he promised, but she attempted one last stab at reason.

'I don't want Emily to—'

'How could she know?' He attempted to reassure her. 'I go back to Jerez tomorrow.'

She felt as if the water surged beneath her as disappointment that he was leaving tomorrow hit like an invisible wave in beautiful, calm water. The shock of his words was enough to make Anna see sense.

'I can't...' She peeled herself away from him. 'I thought we had all week.'

'Anna, my brother can't work because of the baby...nor can my father because he is unwell. Carmen certainly doesn't do anything at the bodega, so someone has to be there.'

'Of course.' Logically she understood that, but her brain was pointing out that one night...or six...it didn't really matter. It was a very temporary arrangement whichever way she looked at it...

But she'd done that before, Anna realised, and she did not want the rest of her time here to be spent getting over him. Did not want to be pulled in further for only a fleeting time.

He thought she was the woman he'd met at the wedding, the persona she'd stepped into, but she was back in her own skin now.

Or halfway between the two...

'I can't,' she said, then repeated it more firmly. 'I can't be yours again just for a night. It's not enough. I want a holiday at least.'

She could justify that in her mind, Anna felt. A holiday romance, but not just sex.

It was more than that already, though. Standing in the gorgeous water, lying on the loungers, eating together... For her, at least, if not for him.

'A holiday,' she stated again.

'That's quite a demand.'

'Oh, please,' she mocked. 'Your *life's* a holiday.'

'You really think so?'

She took a breath and looked back at him. She knew how hard he worked, so she wasn't sure why she had said that.

He worked hard for his family—that much she knew too. They wouldn't be here if that wasn't the case.

'No,' she admitted. 'I don't think that. So why not take some time...?'

'It's impossible.'

'And another one-night stand with you is impossible for me.'

'I regret that.'

He didn't push. Instead he removed that beam of his attention in a way she couldn't quite define.

He still held her hand as they walked out of the water, and as she wrapped herself in her sarong there was no impatience from him. In fact, he was so polite that he even offered to prolong the day with a very late lunch.

'It's almost three,' she pointed out, smiling despite already missing the sensation of being the focus of his desire, and knowing the indefinable promise of tonight that had thrummed between them had, upon her request, been removed.

'That is lunchtime in Spain.'

'Oh, well...no, thank you. I have to go to the shops and find something for Emily. I might try Old Marbella.'

'Of course.' He nodded. 'I should do some work, anyway.' He pointed to a path. 'That takes you back to your villa.'

Only lovers got to use the bedroom route, it would seem.

Still, they parted amicably, though he didn't suggest dinner. Instead, he told her she was welcome to call Reception for a driver to take her wherever she wanted to go.

He was not, Anna guessed, going to provide extended handholding for his brother's wife's friend if he was not going to get to sleep with her again. Sebastián had found her gorgeous accommodation, had taken her to dinner the first night, had driven her to and from the hospital, had even taken her to the beach, offered to do lunch...but now there was an end to it.

'Hasta luego,' he said.

Duty done.

And she only had herself to blame.

CHAPTER NINE

ANNA WOKE TO REGRET.

It was a different kind of regret, though.

She hadn't been woken with a kiss.

Nor by her sexy lover carrying a tray bearing breakfast in bed—or however this morning might have been had she given in to another night with him...

Instead, she woke alone, in gorgeous surroundings, and wished she'd been brave enough to say yes to Sebastián.

After they'd parted yesterday she had showered and pulled on new shorts and a top and wandered around Old Marbella. She'd found an odd shop tucked away that sold silk threads for her embroidery and cotton to re-stitch the backing of the blanket.

Then she'd found a café where they'd *still* been serving lunch. She'd sat under an umbrella at a table in gorgeous Orange Square, the very heart of the old town, and had ordered what she'd thought was a steak sandwich and a beer, because that had sounded very normal.

Nothing felt normal, though, she'd thought as she'd sipped on the tall, cool glass of beer and tried to tell herself that she was proud for resisting his charms.

But Anna had known she lied.

'Your veal,' the waitress had said, putting down her plate. *'Buen provecho!'* Which Anna knew meant *Enjoy your meal*.

She would never have eaten veal at home. Not just because she couldn't afford it, but it was the principle of the thing.

And yet it would seem veal had been ordered and served, so what was she to have done?

It had been delicious!

And it was her principles that had kept her alone in her villa last night, embroidering and sewing the blanket when she could have been making reckless love.

Yes, she regretted it—especially now, when she heard a knock at the door and opened it to the stunning sight of him in a deep navy suit, but no tie, looking too sexy for words.

Clearly he was about to head for Jerez.

'Do you want to get something to eat?' he offered. 'Before I go back?'

'I'm fine,' Anna said, closing the door a little to block the view of her sewing that was laid out on the floor.

'You don't want to go to the restaurant, do you?'

'Not particularly,' Anna admitted.

'Then we can go to the marina instead.'

'Sebastián, please.' She took a breath. 'It's hard enough as it is.'

Sebastián looked at this difficult, proud woman, shutting herself away on a bright sunny day, and wondered how to make this right.

People here could be shallow sometimes, and he loathed how she'd been treated yesterday.

He thought of a way to fix things.

Of course one that might benefit him too.

'I need a favour,' he said.

'Ask away.'

'Are you going to let me in?'

'I honestly can't…'

Anna closed her eyes and knew she must sound ridiculous. 'Wait there.'

She left him at the door and hurriedly cleared the blanket she was amending away, then headed back to let him in.

'Sorry about that...'

'It's no problem.'

He came into the lounge and looked at the iced tea by the chair. He must have guessed that was where she had been sitting, so he took a seat on the sofa.

'I need a feminine perspective,' he said.

'Oh?'

'Carmen is visiting, and I am concerned about her.'

Anna saw he didn't halt himself before continuing this time.

'She has been low these past months. I know she broke up with a guy a few months ago...'

'I remember Emily saying.'

'I think it was nasty—not that she would tell me the details,' he admitted. 'It also coincided with Maria's return.'

'Ouch.' Anna felt a touch guilty, as she'd considered Carmen simply petulant and spoilt.

'I've put it down to that, as well as our father being ill, but there's something I'm missing—something she's not telling me. I wondered if you might talk to her.'

'Me?' Anna shook her head in confusion. 'Why would Carmen talk to me?'

'*I* do,' he responded simply. 'Look, Carmen is going to hit the salons and the shops when she gets here. I thought I might tell her that you are scaring the locals and need a decent wardrobe.'

'That's a horrible thing to say.'

'I say a lot of horrible things,' he said, smiling. 'I don't always mean them, though. This way, Carmen will think there's a reason for you to go with her.'

'Why are you doing this?'

'Because I want you to talk to Carmen and maybe tell me what's going on.'

'I'm not going to break her confidence—to spy and then report back to you.'

'You're not a doctor or a priest! You don't need to take her secrets to the grave,' he said. 'Just let me know if she's okay.

Because I swear there is something going on in her head, and I'm worried. Will you *try* speaking with her for me, please?'

'I'll try…'

'Okay.' He stood. 'I should go.'

'Yes.'

She saw him to the door and something close to panic quietly hit her—because she found she didn't know how to say goodbye.

It was bad enough with him here, but without him…

'Hasta luego…'

He left without a backward glance.

CHAPTER TEN

SEBASTIÁN FIXED HIS eyes on the road and tried not to notice the blue, blue Mediterranean or the glistening white yachts. And when he opened his window he quickly closed it again, because he did not want the scent of summer clouding his brain.

'Why are you doing this?' she had asked him.

Because he wanted to spoil her. Because she deserved to be spoiled.

To prevent himself thinking of Anna, he called his sister.

'I don't want to spend a day with Anna,' she sighed. 'She's boring.'

'Carmen…' He held in a tense breath. 'Just sort things out. Get the things she likes wrapped and sent to the villa without her knowing.' He gave her the address. 'Maybe go to a salon. I don't know…'

He tried to be himself, as he usually would be—curt, rude, nothing his problem. But the old him would not have given a damn that Emily's friend was feeling awkward in her clothes…

'Listen,' he said to his sister. 'I don't want Alejandro and Emily worrying about her. They have enough going on right now.'

'Okay.'

'So be nice and… I don't know…involve alcohol or something…'

He ended the call, annoyed at Carmen. He thought of Anna, feeling awkward in the boutiques and salons with his difficult sister. *He* should be the one doing this…

But she'd upped the demands, his cynical mind reminded him. A holiday!

She had looked him in the eye and asked for more.

And he had said no.

Jerez was a couple of hours away, and when he arrived there was a serious amount of work waiting, given neither he nor Alejandro had been in for the past two days.

Good—he could immerse himself in that, he thought.

Only he found himself staring out of the window as his PA filled him in on everything she'd rescheduled.

And then Alejandro's PA came in and told him of the commitments in his brother's diary…

'The next three months?' she checked. 'Or will he be back sooner?'

'I don't know,' Sebastián said honestly.

He took a breath and looked out of the window. The blue sky seemed so vivid, he thought.

Somehow he got through a meeting, then another, and another, but finally he went up to the rooftop terrace. His engagement photos had been taken there. They'd toasted the gorgeous sunset with their own sherry, of course, for the camera's sake, but he'd frowned when Ella had taken a sip.

'You're having a baby,' he'd reminded her, in his usual blunt way.

He'd stood up here, getting those photos done, feeling impatient to get back to work.

Now, when there was work to be done, he was impatient to follow that blue sky all the way back to Puerto Banús.

He could not take a holiday now—and it wasn't just the impossible timing of it.

She wanted more from him. And although Sebastián was used to that, the conflict he felt now was because he found himself wanting to give more, despite his brain telling him not to…found himself talking to her more and revealing things he never shared with anybody.

And now here he sat, watching the sun starting to dip, wanting more.

Six nights…

They were already down to five now—four if he left it until tomorrow. Then there was the family party he was planning for Saturday, so that took it down to three. He liked the safety of that low number, the expiry date written in permanent ink…

Carmen messaged, conceding:

She's actually nice. We had a great day.

He didn't respond, because usually he wouldn't care that Emily's friend had had a great day.

Yet he did.

He did care.

Then the phone went again, and it was Anna.

He let it go to voicemail, then dialled the number to listen to her message, but she hadn't left one.

'Sebastián?'

His PA came onto the terrace, no doubt wondering what time she might get home. Spanish work days were long ones, but it was nearing ten o'clock…

'Go home.' Sebastián gave her a thin smile. 'Oh, and one more thing.'

She turned around. 'Tomorrow you're going to have to re-work the schedule.'

'I already have.'

'I mean, again.'

'Oh.'

'I'm taking the rest of the week off.'

He really did have a brilliant PA. Because, to her credit, she didn't blink. He just saw her jaw tighten and then she pushed out a smile.

'Of course. I'll tell people it is a family emergency.'

'No,' Sebastián said. 'Just say that I am on vacation.'

The drive felt far shorter tonight than it had this morning—

as if the road itself was hurrying him back to be with her. He just seemed to slice his way through time and space until he stepped out of the vehicle and heard the throb of music in the air and the palm leaves rustling overhead.

He knew he had made the right decision.

'Hola,' he said as she opened the door wearing a robe, with her hair lighter than when he had left her that morning. The redness in her skin had calmed down too—or was it that she had make-up on?

'Sebastián!' Anna was startled. 'I thought you were back in Jerez.'

'Briefly,' he said. 'You look hot.'

'No, the air-conditioning is on...' She paused. 'Oh, you mean...' She swallowed at his directness. 'Thank you. We got our hair and make-up done.'

'Can I come in?'

She was about to pull open the door, but then remembered her sewing was out in the lounge.

'Actually...' She cringed again. 'Can you just...?'

'Wait?'

'Yes.'

'While you tidy up?' he smiled.

'Yes.'

Quickly she moved her sewing project into her case, and before she headed back to the door to let him in Anna allowed herself a moment to take a deep breath and exhale slowly to calm her racing heart.

She had been sitting alone in her villa, doing her sewing, verging on crying. Dressed in new clothes—a silver dress and gorgeous underwear—she'd felt like Cinderella without a ball to go to, and she had taken off the dress and hurled it at the floor.

She was in the sexiest port in the world, dressed up to the nines, and she was...sewing!

And then the sexiest man in the world had shown up at her door.

Slow down, she told her beating heart—because he was

clearly here to find out about Carmen, and actually she did have something to tell him.

'Come through,' she said, trying to breathe through her mouth and avoid the rich scent of the air whenever he was near. 'Carmen and I had a great day, and I came back to find this.' She pointed to several designer bags in her bedroom.

'A bed?'

'No!'

'I can only see the bed,' he said, and she tensed. Because he was so potent that the bags seemed to have faded and the bed was all she could see too.

'You spent far too much. You didn't need to do that.'

'So?' He shrugged and took a seat on the same chair she had been on.

'That's my seat,' Anna said.

'Come and sit here with me, then.'

He seemed lighter somehow. She didn't know this Sebastián—this lighter, less intense version of him.

She tried to get back to the reason he was here…took a seat on the sofa. 'We went shopping, and got our hair done, and—'

He closed his eyes, as if in frustration, and at her halting words took a breath and nodded for her to go on.

'She's okay,' Anna said, not wanting to break Carmen's confidence, and yet wanting to let Sebastián know it wasn't that anything dark had taken place with her ex. 'She didn't want to talk at first. I mean, she doesn't know me… But when we were getting our hair done I told her how I haven't been on a date in years…'

'To get her to talk?'

'Yes,' Anna said.

'You didn't have to exaggerate that much.'

He smiled his gorgeous, arrogant smile and Anna opened her mouth to correct him. He didn't seem to quite get it that she'd told Carmen a painful truth in an attempt to get her to open up.

It was immaterial, Anna decided, choosing not to labour the point.

'We spoke a lot. I told Carmen about some of the nastier things Willow's father said when we broke up.'

'Okay…' The smile was wiped off his face and he was serious now. 'What *did* he say to you?'

'We're talking about Carmen.' Anna put up her hand, because she was not about to get into a discussion of her ex. 'You're right—what happened with her ex was nasty, but she's okay. It's only her feelings that are hurt…'

'Okay…'

Sebastián looked both frustrated and concentrating hard. He was clearly concerned about his sister, but that didn't seem to be the whole reason he was here.

'I think she's moving on from it.'

'Thank you.' He nodded. 'I'm glad that she's spoken to someone.' He hesitated. 'To you.'

'It's not just…' Anna paused.

There was one other thing Anna wanted to share about her meeting with Carmen, because she honestly didn't know if she'd handled it right.

'It's not just about the break-up. I do think she's working through that…'

'What then?' He frowned. 'Maria?'

'Not just that either.' Anna worried at her lip for a moment. 'I don't know if I should say anything…'

'Anna, whatever your opinion of me, surely you can accept that I have my sister's best interests at heart?'

'I know you do. It's just that she said something, and I'm honestly not sure if my response was the correct one.'

'What was it about?'

'Riding,' Anna said. 'Her career.'

'Okay…'

'We went for dinner and she asked about my family. I usually don't say very much but, like I said, I was trying to get her to open up, so I told her that I'd fallen out with my parents over Willow.'

He was really concentrating, Anna could see.

'I think she's worried that your father would be disappointed if...' She saw that his frown remained. 'If she changed paths or took a break.'

He stared back at her.

'She was going to tell him that she wanted to give it up a few months ago, but he got ill and she didn't know how to.'

'She wants to stop riding?'

'I think so. I told her she was worrying needlessly. I said that it was clear to me that her father loved her, whatever she did.' She swallowed. 'I hope I said the right thing?'

'Of course.'

He nodded, but there was something in his voice that told her she might have steered Carmen wrong.

'I mean, I was just trying to—'

'It's fine,' he reassured her. 'It's good that she's spoken to you.'

She nodded, still unsure if she'd messed up. 'I tried to call you and tell you. You didn't have to drive back.'

'I didn't drive back because of Carmen,' he said.

'Then why?'

'Because...'

She was used to him ruthlessly shutting down any topic he did not wish to discuss, so she accepted that was all she was going to get. But he changed all that with the addition of two words.

'Because you're here.'

There was something missing, surely? Her brain kept trying to join the dots...

'Because you're here...'

'I took some time off,' Sebastián told her. 'I am on vacation.'

'Because of the baby?'

'No, because of what you said about wanting more than a one-night stand.' He gave her a slow smile. 'You will get your holiday...'

Looking at him really was like staring into the sun, Anna thought, because he was simply dazzling. So much so that she had to look away.

All her wishes had suddenly come true, yet she was afraid.

Anna looked at the bags scattered on the bed and heard her demand for a holiday with him in a less savoury way now.

'Do we have crossed wires?' she asked.

'Meaning?'

'I want time with you,' Anna said. 'Not…'

'I'm not hiring you, Anna.' He laughed. 'I want you to love it here,' he said. 'I want you to have the holiday you deserve.'

'Why?' she croaked.

'I like you,' he said, and only now did he falter slightly. 'I'd like a holiday with you. But as long as we're clear: no future. No falling in love. No—'

'What if…?' she cut in, but then halted, because she had a dreadful feeling it might be way too late for that.

No! She was not ruining this by getting overly emotional. Back in the real world she would see that this was not, nor ever could be, love. So she obliterated that thought from her mind.

'You were saying…?' he checked, because she knew he never missed a beat. 'What if…?'

Anna knew she had to fill the gap. Usually she would be embarrassed to bring it up, but now was grateful for the reason to blame her blush.

'What if I told you I'd gone on the Pill?'

'Oh? But, no…' He shook his head. 'We're not getting *that* close. I will take care of those details.'

He was so absolute with his boundaries that she couldn't help but ask, 'Why don't you let anyone get close to you?'

'I don't want to answer that.'

Anna was bold. Sure, she had her hang-ups, and was shy in certain things, but she dug deep and found that boldness so she could stare back at him, quietly demanding a different response.

Finally he gave one. 'I'm as incapable of love as the woman who birthed me.'

'No.'

'Anna, *yes*.' He was absolute. 'I'm not going to say the acceptable thing just because it's what you want to hear. I don't want love.' He offered another truth. 'I *do* want some time with you, though…'

'You are here until Sunday?' she checked, because if he left in the morning she would never forgive herself—let alone him.

'I have packed my bucket and spade.'

'Stop it!' She laughed, but her breathing was shallow and fast.

'I'm going to give you the holiday of your life.'

Never had she thought he'd agree to it. This was going to be a holiday—a real holiday—her first since she couldn't re-member when. A holiday with the most stunning man ever to have come into her line of vision.

'No tears at the end,' he warned. 'Because it ends on Sun-day morning. No exceptions.'

Perhaps… But Anna knew that she would possibly live off the memories for ever.

He crooked his finger and she stood and walked over to him, a little unsure if she was up to this, and still wondering if she was somehow dreaming…

He pulled her down onto his lap.

'Not just sex,' she said, as he unknotted the belt of her robe. 'Because when I said I wanted a holiday—'

'Anna,' he cut in, 'leave the details to me.'

'No,' Anna said, playing with the heavy silk of his loosened tie. 'I want a piece of that black heart.'

'You don't,' he said.

'Just a sliver,' Anna said, and kissed his very plump mouth.

She didn't know quite why, but she felt more resolute when she was with him. She kissed his scratchy cheek and then his temple…

'Let me look at you,' he said.

He pulled apart her robe and looked at her gorgeous new underwear. More than looked. He ran a finger over the lacy fabric and then moved his hand over the curve of her breast. It was the slowest perusal…unbearable in its exquisiteness.

He slid the sleeves of the robe down her arms and lifted her so that he could toss the robe to the floor. He turned her so she sat facing him, her thighs now astride his, and all he did was look. She felt as if her skin might blister and her lips might part and beg for him.

'What *are* you up to?' he asked.

'Up to?'

'What is it you have to hide when I come to the door?'

She blushed because he knew she was hiding something. 'I'm not going to tell you.'

'Tell me...' he said, running a warm finger over the lace that covered a very private place and then slipping it beneath the fabric.

'Oh...' She was lifting onto her knees at the touch of his skilled fingers. 'Don't tear them...' she said, because she liked her new knickers.

'Take them off,' he said, and removed his hand. 'And go and get it.'

'What?'

'Whatever you're using,' he said in a low whisper, his voice gruff in her ear. 'I can use it on you...'

She pulled back and stared at him. 'I genuinely don't know what you mean.'

'Don't be embarrassed,' he said. 'You don't have to hide your toys.'

'You think I'm in here with a sex toy!' She was shocked, and embarrassed for a moment, but because she was in his arms she found she had started laughing. 'You don't know me at *all*!'

'Every time I come to the door you're half-dressed and you make me wait.'

'Please don't ask me, but I promise you I am really not having the kind of fun you think.' She playfully punched his suited arm, and knew she was blushing even as she met his eyes.

And for Sebastián things suddenly changed again.

'You don't know me at all...' she had said, and yet he wanted to.

There was an innocence to her green eyes, an honesty in

her gaze that he was struggling to recognise—because usually he trusted no one.

Since the wedding he had not been able to completely erase her from his mind. Not even in his usual way.

The wild parties aboard his yacht had ended along with his engagement, but in recent months there had been no guests aboard his yacht at all. Since meeting Anna he had simply been unable to indulge in his once favourite escape.

It was just sex, he told himself as she met his gaze.

He pulled her higher up onto his lap, yet could not stop staring at her eyes, exploring them, as he might gaze into a seemingly still lake and know there was a whole world beneath that glassy surface.

It was more than sex—whatever he might tell himself.

Just for a little while he wanted to know again the pleasure of her conversation, her company—and, yes, to get to know her better. He wanted her to laugh, to smile, to have the fun she deserved, and he actually ached to be the one to give that to her.

To give her a small piece of his black heart...

A sliver...

'Get dressed,' he said.

Anna blinked, because she'd also been trapped in his gaze, feeling hot in his arms, and getting naked was the only thing on her mind.

'Dressed?'

'We're going out.'

'Sebastián!'

She was both bemused and smiling as he shifted her closer to the press of his erection and left her in no doubt that he was as turned on as she. She moved in to kiss him, but he turned so her lips met his cheek.

'I can't go out like this.'

'Oh, but you can,' he told her. 'I'm going to date you, Anna Douglas.'

CHAPTER ELEVEN

AWKWARD IN A shiny silver dress that was so not her, Anna walked with Sebastián towards the port.

'You look incredible,' he told her. 'Stop pulling at it.'

'There is nowhere else I'd wear this,' she admitted. 'I only tried it on to make Carmen laugh.'

She reached for his hand because...well, because she wanted to.

'I don't hold hands,' he said.

'When you buy six-inch heels for a woman,' Anna said, 'you have a duty to hold her hand if you don't want her to fall.'

'I'll catch you if you do.'

Anna laughed, feeling on a dizzy high as she hobbled along the jetty.

Perhaps it was because she was so dreadful in heels that he finally relented and took her hand.

If the shoe fits, the foot is forgotten...

Anna thought of the saying again, because with his hand around hers she forgot about the heels and the tight silver dress that was so inappropriate her mother would faint if she saw her in it.

'Where are we going?' she asked. 'To a bar? A club?'

'To my favourite place.'

She felt a flutter of excitement as they walked along the jetty. Anna knew nothing about yachts, but she knew beauty when she saw it. She glimpsed, too, that welcome feeling that he had told her about. For this was no luxury villa or hotel. It was his home.

'*Bienvenido a bordo, Sebastián!*' He was greeted by an immaculate man in dark trousers and a white shirt. 'Welcome aboard, *señorita*. I am Capitán Dante.' He was friendly, yet formal and respectful. 'May I ask that you remove your shoes?'

'For my decking,' Sebastián explained, and then saw her reach unsteadily to lean on the cabin wall. 'Let me help.'

'Oh...'

And then he was kneeling down and removing her shoes.

She swallowed at the touch of his hands as he undid the tiny buckles. 'Do Russian supermodels have to take their heels off?'

He let out a short burst of laughter.

Removing the silver heels, he placed them in a basket, and all she could wonder was how she might feel when she strapped them on again, because there was so much to take in.

They went up some stairs and came out on a deck so polished and soft beneath her feet that it felt like carpet. The furnishings were expensive and gorgeous—huge pale grey sofas, with tasteful splashes of colour to bring them alive—and a waiter stood at the bar, where Sebastián ordered cocktails.

'Romero's own,' he said.

It was sherry and bitter orange and something else, but she was almost too giddy to take it in as the yacht manoeuvred out of the marina.

'Have you eaten?' Sebastián asked.

'I have.'

He spoke in Spanish and soon little nibbles were being placed on a low candlelit table. She admired the glass tumblers that held tealights. They were engraved with stars to match those shining overhead. The night sky was divine, and she felt as if the stars might have been individually placed there just for her.

'Dance?' Sebastián said, once they had anchored away from the prying eyes of the marina, and he offered his hand.

The smooth deck was their dance floor, but the real luxury was being held in his arms.

'I adore your back,' he said as he held her close and ran a finger down her naked spine. 'I mean,' he said, 'you really have a beautiful back.'

They danced—and not the way they had at the wedding.

He kissed her shoulder and then grazed it with his teeth. He pulled her tighter in to him and kissed her neck. If he wasn't holding her she would be on her knees, she thought.

'The crew…'

'Shh…' he said. 'They're below.'

It felt as if they were alone in the world…alone under the stars. The slight motion of the yacht on the waves, the breeze on her skin and the heat of his mouth entranced her as he held her and kissed her neck, as if the tender skin he was focussed upon was the most vital spot on planet earth.

He took her right to the edge, and she almost folded in his arms. Then he removed his mouth, his hand, his hard body. It was disorientating to be giddy with lust and then led down some steps that were softer even than the deck.

'The floor…what is it?'

Every sensation was new.

'Leather,' he said, and guided her into the master cabin.

This was his home. That was her one coherent thought as she stepped inside. There was Spanish art on the walls, and she glimpsed an oil painting of ancient Jerez, almost out of place in such modern surroundings.

Yet not out of place, Anna thought as he slowly stripped her naked while devouring her with his mouth. It was as contradictory as this man.

Finally he kissed her all over, as he had promised that night at the wedding.

And each stroke of his tongue and velvet kiss was an apology for not ending that morning as he should have.

He undressed himself between hot, decadent kisses. She was rendered unable to assist, because each suck on her pale breasts had her bunching the crisp sheet beneath her and gasping for breath.

* * *

Sebastián was lost as he watched her breasts fall to the side a little—as real breasts did, not silicone mounds. Her stomach was flat, yet soft too. And her intimate curls were like kisses to his face as he moved down and parted her thighs.

'I want to see you,' he said as he rolled on a condom.

Anna watched as he looked, and the desire in his eyes had her clenching in anticipation and then sobbing as his mouth came down to kiss her where no mouth ever had before.

His jaw was rough, his tongue probing, and she raised herself up on her elbows briefly, to watch how absorbed he was in his task, then gave in and lay back.

She moved one hand down and gripped his hair, not sure if she was pulling him back because the contact was too intense to bear, or pressing him closer because she needed more.

He made love to her with his mouth and did not relent even when she came. He tasted her passion fully, and when she was spent, one leg draped over his shoulder, he knelt up.

'You taste incredible...'

She was panting as he looked down at her, and then he kissed her with lips that were shiny from *her*. They rolled to face each other, tumbling, still kissing, until he was on his back and she was astride him.

It felt different from when they'd been in that chair at the villa. Not just because of their lack of clothes, or the bed. It was more that they had changed since then.

Then, it had been sex.

Now, it was...

Anna didn't quite know how to describe the comparison—just that when she lowered herself down onto him there was synergy between them, both wanting more from the other.

She had never been on top before, but did not feel uncertain—just inexperienced. She closed her eyes as he filled her, because the deep penetration felt so new.

'Come here,' he demanded roughly, and pulled her head down towards him.

Her hands moved behind his shoulders and they kissed as he bucked and she responded until she found a rhythm she liked.

Awkwardly, for his shoulders and his body were big, she moved her hands to his chest. But soon there was no awkwardness in Anna, just a sense of urgency. His hands were on her breasts, thorough in their movements, and she felt the solid wall of his chest beneath her hands.

'So good...' he said, and then he said something in Spanish, and reached for a pillow to put it behind his head, so he could see her better.

Her buttocks were sliding on his thighs and his hands came up to her hips. But then he removed them.

'Help me,' Anna said, because she wanted his hands exactly where they had been...she wanted the grip and guidance of them.

'You!' he said, thrusting as she ground down.

He was denying his hands what they wanted as a form of self-torture. For now he wanted to watch her face change as she sought deeper pleasure from him. He played with her hair, pinched her nipple—anything that would help him fight not to finish until she was ready.

'Oh...'

Anna closed her eyes in deep concentration as he stroked her, every part of her body feeling spent already. Her thighs ached and she was holding back a sob of frustration—or perhaps a scream.

But then his hands slid down her damp, flushed body and took her hips firmly. She had never been so loose and so tense at the same time, because now he grasped her and moved within her at a pace she would never have found on her own.

She heard herself making humming sounds, unintelligible sounds, but they only made his grip on her hips tighter.

And then he stilled her, and Anna felt a final powerful swell within her and choked out a sound as he released himself into her.

The low shout that accompanied it was so intense that it pulled at her centre…pulled so tightly that she gave up moving, just closed her eyes and enjoyed the intimate beats of her own body's release and the fading pulse of him within her.

'I drove back for that,' he said as they lay side by side.

She gave a soft laugh. 'You can go now, then.' Anna sat up and reached for the iced water that had thoughtfully been left by the bedside. 'Oh, wait… I forgot. It's your yacht…'

It was a tease, not a threat—just light joking after something both knew had been incredible.

'Watch this,' he said. 'Lie on your back.'

Anna did so, and he lay beside her and pressed a button on a remote control.

The ceiling parted and they were bathed in stars.

'I kept it closed in case there was a drone.'

She'd fallen asleep in his arms the night of the wedding, but this time Anna was in no doubt that what they had experienced together had been beautiful—that the yacht, the stars, the pleasure had all been incredible.

What she did not know was that in that moment she'd been gifted a sliver of his heart…

CHAPTER TWELVE

'WHAT TIME IS IT?'

She woke to piercing sunlight and there was Sebastián, pulling back the drapes to reveal the dazzling ocean.

'Midday,' he said.

'Oh, my G—' She stopped, because she didn't ever blaspheme.

'Oh, my God?' he said for her, and he laughed.

'What's so funny?'

'All the things you don't do or say. We didn't go to sleep until dawn.'

'True.'

'Breakfast is ready.'

'You mean lunch?'

'No, you're on Spanish time,' he said as she climbed out of bed and picked up her once lovely but now crumpled silver dress.

He frowned. 'Why would you wear that?'

'Because it's all I have with me.' She laughed. 'Gosh, I didn't take very good care of it, did I?'

'Blame me,' Sebastián said. 'Go and shower,' he said. 'Your dress will be taken care of, and I'll find a shirt or something for you.'

She felt very untogether as she came out of the shower to…yes, a shirt. Her dress and underwear had been whisked away… And so, wearing just the shirt, carefully pulling it down over her bottom, she climbed the stairs and said good

morning to the smiling Capitán Dante, who was having coffee
with Sebastián, and stood as she ventured on deck.

'Buenos días,' he said, and Anna smiled, while wanting to
curl up and hide.

'I feel…' She knew she was cringing as she took a seat and
then halted as coffee was poured.

'Gracias,' Sebastián said, and told the server he would take
it from here. 'What's wrong?'

'They all know I stayed the night.'

'Yes.'

'And they've got my underwear!' She shot him a look. 'At
least at the hotel and villa it was a bit more anonymous.' She
broke apart a pastry. 'The sun is so bright…' She caught herself. 'I sound like that awful woman from the hotel.'

'Believe me, you don't,' he said.

They ended up on loungers, and he kept looking over to her,
as she constantly checked that she was covered.

'You could take that off and they wouldn't care.'

'I'd care,' Anna said. 'I'm sure they've seen plenty, but they
won't be seeing me.'

Even so, as they lay together quietly in the sun, she felt the
tension leave her. She lay with her eyes closed, listening to
the lap of the water and the caw of gulls, and then she heard
Sebastián talking to someone.

'Here,' he said, and she opened her eyes.

He blocked out the sun and for a second she thought her
eyes must still be closed and she was dreaming. But, no, he
handed her a small pink bag with silky rope handles.

'What's this?'

She opened it and took out a very small gold bikini. She
blinked at this Aladdin's Cave world, where thoughts and
wishes came true.

'Thank you.' She was touched that he'd noted her discomfort. 'I'll go and put it on.'

'There's no need.'

He handed her the bikini bottoms and she pulled them on

beneath the shirt, and then he handed her the top and she tied up the neck while still wearing his shirt.

He rolled his eyes as she held it over her front and he tied the back. 'Better?' he asked.

'Yes.' She looked up at him. 'I called Emily and I said I'd visit her this evening. She's moving into a suite on the NICU.'

He nodded with his eyes closed and she guessed he'd already done his due diligence with his brother.

'How's your daughter?'

'She's having fun with her grandparents.' Anna smiled, but didn't elaborate, sure he was just being polite.

But then he asked a question. 'Have you told her about the new baby?'

'Not yet.'

How odd, Anna thought, to be lying in a tiny gold bikini and having such a normal conversation. So normal that as she answered him she rolled onto her front to look at him as she spoke.

'I've told my mother, but I want to wait till I'm home to explain it to Willow. I think she'll be upset.'

'Because the baby is so small?'

'Because she isn't here to see her. I think it would just overwhelm her.'

Sebastián nodded and from behind his dark glasses stared up at the sky. There was not a single cloud in sight. He could recall lying on a beach in Corsica, with Ella beside him, a sparkling ring on her finger, and feeling no peace in his soul...

'Does her father help?'

He'd asked Anna about him before and she'd closed that down, but he wanted to be more personal now.

'No.'

'Does he see her?' he asked, and looked from the sky to her green eyes as he removed his shades.

'No.'

'Is Willow really why you fell out with your parents?'

She nodded. 'They think it was just a one-night stand.'

'Even I could tell them that it wouldn't have been.'

She blinked in surprise. 'Are you forgetting our one night?'

'Never!' He smiled and looked at her. 'I'm very good at seduction.'

'I had noticed.'

'I had to use all my skills—and they are considerable—to get you into bed... Anyway, we didn't sleep together the night we met, even though we were flirting on sight.'

'No!'

'Yes,' he refuted. 'I wanted you the first second I saw you.'

He knew he was spinning her mind, because while she thought back to the day they'd met he got back to the conversation they'd been having before.

'So, you and Willow's father weren't a one-night stand?'

'No.'

She had only ever told Emily the truth, and even then it had been a crisp version, leaving out all the feelings.

She tried to do the same now. 'He was a visiting professor when I was at university.'

'Tut-tut,' he said. 'He should have known better.'

'I *was* twenty-one.'

'He should still have known better!' he said.

And she stared back and knew then that there would be no 'crisp' versions when she was with Sebastián. His black eyes gave her permission to speak, to search herself, to be honest with herself.

'I was so naïve... I thought he was...' She frowned, because how she'd felt then was so pale in comparison to what she was experiencing now. 'I thought he was fascinating. But I was just...'

'What?'

'I'd never had a boyfriend before.'

'He was hardly a boy,' he sneered.

She knew his displeasure was not aimed at her, and she knew something else too: that he was on her side in this conversation. It was an unfamiliar feeling, after so many arguments and accusations, to know that she didn't have to speak defensively.

She didn't quite know how to tell him the full story, though.

'He was so angry when he found out I was pregnant…' She shook her head, not wanting to go on.

'How angry?'

'Just shouting…'

Anna opened her mouth to speak and then closed it, then opened it again. He watched her silently floundering and knew how hard it was for her to confide in him.

He could also guess what might be eating her up.

Maybe if he told her his truth, then she might open up? Anna had done it for Carmen—had given a piece of herself in order to learn more.

'Anna, did he use protection?'

'No.'

'So what right did he have to be angry? I've never wanted children, and I'm always careful, but even when Ella told me she was pregnant I never got angry.'

'Were you upset?'

'Maybe inwardly,' he admitted. 'But I didn't show it. I figured she was already upset enough.'

'But were *you*?'

'I'm very careful not to have unprotected sex, but when she showed me the ultrasound image I wasn't angry or shouting. Babies happen. You deal with it.'

Anna found she was holding her breath—perhaps because she was recalling Willow's father's reaction.

'I didn't love her, but I wanted to be a better parent than mine had been.' he said, as if trying to explain his thought-process. 'I didn't want to be absent, like Maria, even though I know I can be cold and selfish like her.'

'No.' Anna shook her head, adamant, for she knew he was involved with his family, there for his family.

'Yes,' he said. 'I like my career, my own space, and I would never commit myself to another person. But then I found out I was to be a father...'

'So you proposed?'

'Looking back, it was perhaps a knee-jerk reaction.' He shrugged. 'It would never have worked. And then...' He glanced over. 'I'm sure you've read what happened.'

'I want to hear what happened from you,' Anna said.

'We had an argument,' he told her. 'Here on the yacht. She was drinking—not in front of me, but Dante let me know that more champagne had been ordered.'

'I'm not with you...'

'He let me know in his very discreet way that my supplies were being topped up.'

'I'd better not crack open the bar, then.'

'Of course you can,' he said lightly, but then he looked serious. 'I dared to suggest to Ella that it might not be good for the baby. I asked to accompany her to her next doctor's appointment, and it was shortly after that when she told me she'd lost the baby.' He looked at her. 'Anna, there never was a baby.'

'But you said you saw the ultrasound picture.'

'You can buy them online, apparently.'

'She was lying all along?'

'Ella is too arrogant in her attitude towards staff to comprehend that I talk with my crew and they with me. She was in the spa, laughing with her friend about how I'd believed her. My crew don't spy. They don't judge. But...'

'They were looking out for you?'

'Yes.'

'Well!' She didn't know what to say. 'Why did you let her get away with it?'

'I told her what I thought, believe me.'

'I mean, with everyone else?'

'It's none of their business. I don't care what's said about me. *I* know the truth and so does she…'

'I'd be screaming it from the rooftops.'

'No.' He looked at her. 'It's hard to reveal what really hurts.'

He reached over and pushed her hair back from her face. He was not smoothing his way to a kiss, just trying to be gentle as he asked a question he was rather certain he already knew the answer to.

'Did you know he was married?'

'Of course not!' She was alarmed. 'How did you know…?'

'Why else would you keep his secret?'

He watched as she started to cry. He still had no handkerchief to offer, but he handed her the shirt she'd discarded instead.

'I had no idea…'

She felt stunned that he had guessed, and yet she felt as if he knew her—that he had taken care to work her out before diving in with his summing up.

'He said it would end his career, his marriage…'

'Poor professor,' he said, and then uttered a word that even in her fragile state had her pursing her lips.

'Don't say that.'

'I save it for particular types,' he said, 'and he is one.'

'Yes.' She wiped her nose on his exquisite shirt and thought of his laundry service. 'Sorry…'

'Go ahead.'

'He gave me money to have an abortion…told me to "take care of it".'

'He knows you kept the baby?'

'Yes, but he doesn't want anything to do with her.'

'Does he help financially?'

'No. I could have insisted, but I didn't want to break up his family.'

'Why can't you tell your parents the truth?'

'I'm ashamed.'

'You shouldn't be.'

'But I am,' Anna admitted, and then she told him her biggest fear. 'I don't know what to tell Willow. I just tell her our relationship didn't work out, but she's starting to ask more and more about him. How do I tell her that he has another family and wants nothing to do with her?'

She liked it that he listened carefully and thought for a long while before answering—even if she was sure there was nothing he could say that she hadn't thought of already.

'Get rid of that shame before you tell her.'

Anna looked up, because that actually sounded like a plan. 'Yes…' She blew out a breath. 'And I'll tell her in stages, I guess.'

'Yes.'

'Do you know…?' She looked out at the ocean, at the glorious day, and let herself think of the topic she'd fought so hard to avoid. 'I just wish he'd ended things nicely.'

Sebastián found that he'd tensed, because he'd been ruthless at ending things too many times. He had cut people out if they dared to get too close.

'Even if he didn't want to be part of our future, I hate that it ended in a row.' Anna gave herself a little shake and then concluded again. 'I just wish it had ended nicely.'

She took a breath of salty sea air, as if she felt better for telling him.

'I'm sorry for what happened to you,' she told him.

'We live and learn,' he said, but then he halted, because it felt for a moment as though he'd learnt the wrong lesson from his brief engagement.

He'd learnt not to trust.

CHAPTER THIRTEEN

'Hey, you.'

Sebastián smiled as Anna came up on deck, her hair rumpled and her eyes blinking from sleep. He returned reluctantly to his online conversation as she poured coffee.

Anna wore one of his T-shirts, although someone on the crew had collected her things from the villa and they now hung in his immaculate wardrobe alongside the silver dress.

'Do you want breakfast now?' he offered. 'Or I should only be another hour.'

Are you online...? she mouthed, indicating the screen.

He was so at ease with himself that he frowned, trying to understand what she was asking, but then he reminded himself this was Anna.

He stepped out of the online meeting.

'Anna, I was just asking if you wanted breakfast.'

He did not understand how the smile he had greeted her with as she'd surfaced on deck, the look in his eyes and his subsequent reaction, had told all present at the meeting—including Alejandro—that his latest temporary lover had appeared.

'I don't want anyone to know, remember?' she told him.

It was the one part of their agreement they hadn't properly thrashed out.

He still could not understand what the issue was. Her insistence on secrecy had begun to irritate him, in fact. But for Anna clearly the issue was huge.

And so he kissed her worry away, smothering her in kisses once the meeting had ended.

It was forgotten—or rather, lost—in a whirl of jet-skis, water bikes and even a slide put out by the crew that went from the yacht straight into the ocean.

'Why have you got an inflatable slide?' she asked.

'Because…' he said, and then gave her a slow, wicked smile. 'Have you never wondered about those emergency slides on a plane?'

'We're not on a plane.'

'Evacuate!' he exclaimed urgently, and stalked towards her menacingly.

'What!'

'Do not stop to collect your personal belongings…'

His deep voice was urgent, and she felt goosebumps—not so much at the imagined scenario, but because Sebastián was having fun. Real fun. And so was she. The type of fun where she screamed and laughed at the same time as he picked her up.

'Don't!' she shrilled, as he carried her to the edge.

The edge of the yacht, the edge of sheer joy, the edge of fear and ecstasy.

And she screamed as she bumped down the slide and skimmed the water for a second before crashing in.

He followed straight behind her, catching her waist and pulling her up to the surface. She did not want to know how deep the water was beneath them, or what lurked at the bottom.

She was in it.

And, oh, gosh, even as she laughed there was a new terror as she wrapped her legs around his waist and they kissed.

Because she was so deeply in…so deeply into him.

Her legs were wrapped around him…the sun was beating on her shoulders, her scalp, intensifying her feelings. His eyes were so black as she stared into them, his lashes so spiky, and now her smile was fading…

'Sebastián?'

She didn't know how to contain all that she felt...how to accept this deliciousness only for it to end...how to be his now and yet also to know that their days were numbered...how to return back to normal when they hit their expiry date...nor how to hide the passion he tapped not just in others but in her...

Tell him! Her own voice sounded in her head as she stared back at him. *Tell him how you are feeling, right this moment... right now.* Tell him that you might just be falling in...

'I think—'

He interrupted her. 'Do you want to go again?'

Sebastián was either oblivious to the turmoil in her eyes, or actively preventing her from saying words he did not want to hear.

It was the latter, Anna was sure.

Yes, the latter.

He did not want to hear any declarations outside of the bedroom. He did not want empty words that held no meaning... Nothing could come of them, so why spoil it with lies? He was stopping her from ruining a very nice thing.

'No...' She declined a second go on the slide. 'Once was enough for me.'

They swam back and she climbed up the ladder, her legs a little wobbly not so much from the thrill of the slide, but more from the words she'd been about to say to him. Unwanted words, it would seem.

'I ought to visit Emily.'

'Sure. I'll get Dante to organise the tender,' Sebastián said, but then changed his mind. 'Or we could return to port and give the crew time to do a service.'

It was protocol, apparently, to give the crew time to do their work undisturbed.

It was incredible to lie on the private deck off the main cabin as the yacht was skilfully reversed in and docked, and yet Anna's heart was still thumping as she realised how close she'd come to saying too much. To ruining their temporary arrangement...

As Sebastián went up to speak with Dante she showered and washed her hair, her tanned limbs looking unfamiliar as she washed the ocean salt from her body. Drying off, she looked at her gorgeous new clothes, but chose the familiar long skirt and cheesecloth top she had brought with her from home. She wondered if she was trying to find the old Anna…the sensible Anna who knew this could never last.

She called Willow, who seemed to have picked up a little Scottish accent!

'Three more sleeps, lassie,' Willow said.

'Yes, only three more sleeps,' Anna agreed—then inwardly panicked, because that meant only two nights left with Sebastián, because of the party on Saturday night.

How could it already be Thursday?

Their last night would likely be tomorrow…

It had gone by in a puff.

'I cannae see any photos of Emily, Mummy.'

'I'm sorry, darling.' Anna laughed at her daughter's quirky ways. 'I keep getting her to take photos of me. I'll sort that out now.'

'Can I talk to wee Emily?'

'Willow, stop!' Anna giggled. 'Emily's with Alejandro at the moment, but I'll get her to call you.'

Oh, Willow, Anna thought, sitting on the rumpled bed. She was desperate to see her daughter in person, and kept smiling long after the call had ended.

She wanted to tell Sebastián how Willow had just made her laugh, but she couldn't bear to be rewarded with only his polite, uncomprehending smile.

She came up on deck to discover that he was in another meeting. He excused himself from it and turned the microphone off when he saw her.

'I'm off,' Anna said. 'I might head back to the villa for a while.'

'Why don't you check out?'

'No…' Anna shook her head. And it wasn't because she had

the blessed blanket to finish—it was more because she needed the bolthole, a place to escape to, in moments like this, when otherwise she might say too much.

She didn't say any of that, of course... 'Emily thinks I'm staying there.'

'Sebastián?' Capitán Dante came over. 'Carmen has come to visit.' He possibly saw Anna's reaction, because he dealt with it immediately. 'The first steward is talking to her.'

Sebastián, too, must have noticed her appalled expression, but he just shrugged. 'Carmen took you out for the day.' He shrugged. 'I'll tell her it was my turn.

'No!' She was adamant. 'I don't want her finding out. I'll go into the cabin.'

She heard his irritated sigh as she scuttled off.

The cabin was in the middle of being serviced, and she felt wretched for asking the crew to leave.

Another yacht protocol broken, Anna thought as she sat on the half-made bed.

Sebastián's sigh was born of irritation—and not only because Anna insisted that they hide what they were doing.

'You can't just drop in unannounced,' he scolded his demanding sister.

'Since when?' Carmen shrugged and threw herself dramatically onto a lounger.

'I mean it, Carmen. I could have had a lover here.'

'You always have lovers here.'

Not lately, Sebastián thought. *More specifically, not since the wedding.*

He'd been too pensive to party.

Then he said all that again in his mind and realised that he was thinking in English—as if explaining his thoughts to Anna—and he thought how that one might have made her smile.

Too pensive to party...

'Why are you smiling?' Carmen snapped. 'I just told you I'm dreading Saturday.'

'It's just a celebration for the baby.'

'For you, perhaps, but I'm flying back to Jerez with them,' Carmen said and then added. 'Maybe...'

He tried to focus because, thanks to Anna, he knew what was troubling his sister. 'What do you mean *maybe*?'

'I don't know if we'll still be talking. I've got something I want to tell Papá.'

He waited, but Carmen refused to elaborate, and he guessed it wasn't *his* approval she needed in order to give up riding.

'Carmen?'

'I don't want to discuss it with you. I want to talk to Papá. But Maria's always there. I hate it that he's let her move back in. I know I'm more than old enough to leave home—but it's not as simple as just moving out. What about the horses? And who's going to be there for Papá if she decides to leave again?'

'Carmen, you don't have to be his carer.'

His heart felt as if it were on a hoist, pulled in too many different directions.

And he understood all the angles: Anna hiding in his cabin, protecting her reputation from his, Carmen wanting to break free, feeling so utterly rejected by her mother and terrified her father might do the same, and as for Alejandro...

There was a notable absence of fear in him.

Sebastián felt the snap of one of the ropes as he realised he wasn't worried about Alejandro.

His brother had a baby in Intensive Care, and yet he knew he would be okay.

What kind of flawed logic was that?

Then he sat with the answer: Alejandro loved and was loved.

And Sebastián dared not love.

Not because of his brief and meaningless engagement, but because of his mother.

'Carmen...' He spoke gravely to his sister. 'You can talk to me. I do know—'

'You don't, though,' Carmen snapped. 'She didn't leave *you* when *you* were a baby.'

No, Maria had left for the final time when he was ten, and fifty times or more prior to that.

And he *did* know. Because when Maria de Luca smiled, she was dazzling. When she told you she was your *mamá*, and would always be there for you, it raised you high.

Then she discarded you, and you fell back down to earth.

Then she left his father crying, her babies fretful and bemused—especially if she'd fired the latest nanny before she left...

He knew well the poison on the tip of all her arrows.

And it terrified him to think he was like her—cold, career-focussed, unable to commit...

'Talk to me...' he said to his sister, but Carmen shook her head.

'I have to go and check in with Anna.'

'Why?'

'Alejandro asked me to take her out again.'

'Oh?'

'I think they feel guilty about how her holiday has turned out.'

'They have just had a premature baby.'

'Yes, but she doesn't get out much.' Carmen shrugged and accepted a drink from Dante, who knew her order well. 'She's barely been out since she had Willow.'

'What?' Sebastián tried to make light of it. 'She's a hermit?'

'No!' Carmen gave a half-laugh. 'But I don't think she has the time or money for a social life.' She took a sip of her drink. 'She hasn't been on a date since she had her daughter'

'Come off it!'

'No, she told me.'

'Maybe she meant she hasn't had a serious relationship,' Sebastián countered, but then he paused with his drink on its way to his mouth, because he knew Anna better than that.

Anna had told him herself that the wedding had been her

first time away from her daughter, but he'd taken that as meaning her first trip overseas.

Had she meant her first *night* away?

Was he her first lover since Willow's father?

Surely not...

'Anyway, she's getting back out there,' Carmen said. 'Getting her confidence back...'

Sebastián said nothing.

'And I'm going to do the same... Not that I'm looking to settle down,' Carmen added.

'Is Anna?' He knew he should feign uninterest, but he couldn't not ask.

'I think she wants a family—brothers and sisters for Willow.'

It took for ever for Carmen to leave, and even when she had, he sat on deck alone for several moments.

He didn't trust himself with Anna's blossoming heart.

Nor her with his.

Was Anna dipping her toes back in the water, reclaiming her confidence, *with him*?

She had to be—he had explicitly told her it was going nowhere and that he never wanted a partner or children. Let alone someone else's.

He was watching her change, right before his eyes, like a butterfly coming out of a chrysalis, and on Sunday morning that butterfly would fly away... Back to her family, who loved her, whether she believed it or not. Back to her daughter and her future plans...

The thought hurt more than it should.

But they were an impossible match and already getting too close.

No more.

He went down to Anna in the cabin...

'She's gone,' he said, then gave her a smile and sat with her on the bed. 'I'm not usually berthed in the same port as my family. Mostly I sail away.'

'It's fine.' She looked up. 'I think it's nice that you're close to your family.'

'Carmen's about to stop by the villa and ask to take you out.'

Anna smiled at the irony. 'Is she okay?'

'Of course.'

'You look serious…'

'No.'

'I'm sorry for being pathetic,' Anna said. 'I just…'

'You don't want anyone finding out about us.'

'Not if we're not going anywhere.'

'Anna, you know we're not. You fly back on Sunday.'

'Yes, but—'

'I think,' Sebastián interrupted, 'we ought to let the crew in to service the cabin. And you need to visit Emily.'

'Sebastián—'

'Anna,' he cut in again. 'It's a holiday. It's not for ever.'

He would not let either of them forget that fact.

CHAPTER FOURTEEN

PUERTO BANÚS MIGHT be the perfect place for a holiday romance, but there was a wedge between them now and Anna couldn't quite put her finger on why.

They made love, they laughed... He gave her everything—except any further piece of that black heart.

There had been hospital visits, and trips back to the villa, but it wasn't the just the prospect of time with Sebastián that had her shaking as she trimmed the final thread of silk. It wasn't even the lure of the luxurious yacht that had her a little impatient as she carefully restitched the backing. It was the fact that their time was running out.

'I got to hold her!'

Emily was both smiling and crying when Anna took in the completed blanket.

'I actually feel like a mother now.'

'Of course you're a mother!' Anna hugged her friend.

'Alejandro is going to hold her tomorrow. It's too much for her to have us both all in one day,' Emily explained. 'How's Willow?'

'Wondering why there are so few photos of you,' Anna admitted.

'I'll put some make-up on and we can go outside and call her.'

'Thank you.'

Emily was brilliant with Willow, never letting on about the drama in her heart, and Anna loved her friend so much for that.

'She's certainly enjoying Scotland,' Emily said as they stood outside for a moment longer, enjoying the breeze and the sun. And then she looked properly at her friend. 'You look different...'

'I've been lying in the sun,' Anna said.

'No, it's more than that...'

'I got my hair done.'

'I know—Carmen told me. You just look so...' Anna watched her friend as she struggled to place what was different.

Everything was different.

She had fallen for the very man Emily had warned her about. She'd been told it would hurt, and it did.

Maybe it was good that she was leaving on Sunday, Anna thought. Time was passing fast. And now this odd wall had gone up between them and she didn't know how to push through.

She and Emily told each other so much, but Anna did not want to share this. Emily knew her well, and would know she'd be hopeless at a casual relationship.

Emily would tell her what she knew already—that Sebastián was a playboy...that he went through women like most men went through socks...

And she didn't want future visits in Spain to be uncomfortable.

So she didn't tell her friend what was going on.

More than that, Anna was trying not to admit to herself what was going on in her heart.

Certainly she could not tell Sebastián.

She didn't want it to be Friday already, and yet it was.

They met at the marina, where they sat watching expensive cars and gorgeous people descending upon the hotspot.

'Are you looking forward to tomorrow?' Anna asked as she twirled the straw in her glass.

'It'll be like herding cats...'

Anna laughed and waited for him to elaborate.

He did not.

And so they finished their drinks and wandered the streets. She peered in designer shop windows at Fabergé eggs and all things incredible...

Sebastián looked at her face, lit up by the lights of the shop windows. He knew he'd let her get too close. But he also knew she was leaving and so he was pulling away...

It was best for both of them, he'd decided.

Tomorrow his family descended. Anna would be there— but not the Anna he had come to know.

She would be the Anna who denied they even existed.

They would ignore each other, or talk politely...

The way they would have to do now, whenever she returned see her friend.

'It will be nice.' She turned and looked at him. 'To have everyone see the baby. What time are they flying in?'

'We're meeting at the hotel at four,'

'The same one Carmen's staying at?'

'No.' He gave her the address. 'From there we'll head to the hospital. I've organised a private room. After that we'll head back to the yacht for a little celebration before they fly home.'

And the next day it would be Anna who would fly home.

End it now, his head said as they walked back to his yacht.

And he knew how to: as Anna spoke with Dante, Sebastián took out his phone and fired a quick text to his sister.

'Señorita Anna!' Dante greeted her. 'Welcome aboard.'

'*Gracias*, Capitán Dante.'

Anna smiled as she practised her Spanish, but as they chatted a thought occurred: would Dante greet her by name tomorrow?

Would Emily and his entire family find out that she had been spending time on the yacht? A lot of time actually!

'Carmen's dropping by,' Sebastián said.

'When?'

'After she's visited Emily.' He pocketed his phone as if it was Carmen who had messaged him. 'At least she gave me some notice this time.'

* * *

Anna had a wish—and it was a terrible wish. She wished his family would clear off. Or that she could stop the clock…that the world would just disappear and leave them alone.

But of course life wasn't like that.

'Then I might head back to the villa.'

'I thought you might say that.'

'Sebastián, the next time I'm here it will be with my daughter.'

How? Anna begged in her mind. *How can I ever see him and act casually? How can I begin to accept that we will never have this precious time again?*

No future, he had said. No falling in love.

'I don't want anyone knowing we had a…thing.'

'A thing?' Sebastián checked.

'A fling. A sex fest. A brief romance. I don't know what to call it, but I don't want to have to explain it to them.'

'Fine,' he snapped.

'One other thing…'

'Go on,' he prompted.

'The crew…'

His eyes narrowed. 'What about them?'

'At the celebration tomorrow…' She swallowed audibly. 'Well, Emily will think…they'll all think…it's my first time on the boat…'

'Yacht,' he corrected, in a pompous, arrogant tone. 'And my crew are *always* discreet.'

'Even so…' Anna thought of how friendly they were with her now, how they called her by name. 'Could you just have a word?'

'I'm not about to explain to my crew that you wish what we have shared to remain a secret.' Sebastián shook his head. 'I can assure you that you will be greeted politely—as are all my guests.'

'Thank you.'

She stood there, feeling so uncertain because they were

fighting—not shouting or even arguing... No, Anna corrected, she was fighting herself. Fighting not to admit to herself that it was very possible, or rather very likely, she was in L-O-V-E. She didn't even want to say the word to herself, because it spelt trouble. It was impossible...

'I'd better go.'

'Adios.'

No! Was that it? Was that all he was going to say?

She wanted...

He glanced down as his phone bleeped and read the message. 'Carmen's just left the hospital, so she's ten minutes away.

Or six, the way the Romeros drove and left their cars half parked for others to deal with...or simply stepped out of a chauffeur-driven car.

She knew it wasn't really Carmen she was worried about confronting—it was her own heart. And if she stayed for even another moment she might say something she really regretted.

'I don't want them knowing because not everyone has the same attitude towards casual relationships,' Anna explained.

'I have *never* treated you casually.'

'I know that!'

'Good. So go and do what you have to do, and I shall spend time with my sister. *Adios.*'

No, no, no.

'When—?'

But she never got to finish asking when they would see each other because he interrupted.

'When what? Do you want me to text you when the coast is clear? Because that really would be crass.'

'What has changed all of a sudden?' Anna demanded.

'Nothing.'

'Something has. We used to talk—'

'Oh, please,' he broke in. 'We've been seeing each other for a matter of days. "Used to" is stretching it. You said you wanted a holiday...some fun. That was the deal.'

'The *deal*?' She gave an incredulous snort. 'Well, the deal's off—and, no, I don't want a text when the coast is clear.'

Good, he thought. *Now get out of my heart. Done.*

But not quite…

She turned and came right up to his face. 'Did I get too close?' she asked. 'Is that it?'

He said nothing.

'After all that, you can't even end it nicely.'

And with that, Anna left the yacht.

She couldn't bear the way it had all come about in the end. Despite the heat, she almost ran through the marina and towards the villa, and it felt as if the truth was chasing her the whole way. Demanding that she confront it.

Only when the door had closed behind her, as she stood in the cool, air-conditioned room, did she dare to admit it that she'd fallen head over heels with the…

'Bastard!'

She said it out loud.

Anna swore for the first time in her life.

She had been fighting the fact that she might love him since their first night together. For months it had been an easy battle. She'd just had to recall their awful first parting…or tell herself what a dreadful person he was by reading salacious gossip.

Then she'd spent days and nights being bathed in his kisses and his charm, and now he'd withdrawn it her heart felt as if was at war with itself.

Trying to hold back the truth was like trying to hold back the tide. She'd been warned. She'd been told. And she had no one to blame but herself.

She was utterly and deeply in love with Sebastián Romero.

Their row had delayed Anna's departure and Carmen arrived just a couple of moments later, but if she had seen Anna leave she said nothing to Sebastián.

'I can't stop,' she said, by way of greeting. 'Alejandro has asked me to take Anna out.'

'Again?'

'She wasn't there last time.' Carmen shrugged. 'So, what did you want?'

'To go over the arrangements for tomorrow—we're to meet at the hotel at...' He hesitated briefly. 'Five.'

'Okay.'

They chatted some more about the arrangements, but Carmen would give nothing away as to what was on her mind. If Anna hadn't spoken to him Sebastián knew he would still be none the wiser about what was troubling his sister.

Dios, he hated how things had ended with Anna. He knew full well he had pushed her away, because even if they were going nowhere Anna hadn't deserved what he had done.

He just did not know how to end things any other way.

She was right. Texting *would* be crass.

He would call her once Carmen had left.

Maybe he'd go over there...?

He should do the one thing she wished her ex had and end things nicely.

'I'd better call her,' Carmen said, picking up her phone. 'Anna! It's Carmen. Do you want to go out this evening?' She laughed. 'Get wildly drunk and dance the night away? See if there are *any* decent single men left out there?'

Sebastián couldn't help but smile at his sister.

'Okay,' Carmen said. 'I'll meet you there.'

He wasn't smiling now.

'I'm off,' Carmen said, and kissed her brother's cheek. 'Five o'clock tomorrow, yes?'

'Yes,' Sebastián said.

And a few hours later, when he checked his phone and saw his sister's latest social media update, there was Carmen...but also there was Anna, in her silver dress and heels...

There was no jealousy, just the knowledge that their row had hurt her and that she must be bleeding inside.

He knew that because he was too.

But he would not be pinning this butterfly and storing her in a display case. He wanted her to spread her wings, for she deserved more than just a sliver of him. She knew her worth and she would insist on a heart that could give.

'I got too close,' she had accused.

Too close, he quietly now agreed.

He'd come to admire her, and never more than on this night.

He raised his glass, and even smiled, because he knew how to put this a little bit right.

'Go, Anna!'

CHAPTER FIFTEEN

'WHERE'S CARMEN?' JOSÉ ASKED.

Sebastián shrugged. 'I told everyone four o'clock,' he said, even though he had told Carmen five.

He tried not to look over, but even in the periphery of his vision Anna Douglas made a stunning entrance.

She wore a lilac halter-neck dress and the flat sandals she'd arrived in. Her hair was up and she had dark glasses on.

Sebastián suppressed a smile. He knew from his sister's updates that it had been a very late night—or rather it had gone on well into the morning.

However, her eyes looked fine when she took her sunglasses off, and he watched those gorgeous green orbs sweep the gathering, feeling them linger a second on him.

He gave her a nondescript smile as she approached and left it to his brother to do the introductions 'You've met Anna, of course,' Alejandro said.

'Of course,' José said. 'At the wedding. Emily's friend. Yes?' His English was good, but not great.

'Yes.' Anna smiled. 'You must be looking forward to meeting your grandchild.'

'Very much,' Maria crooned. 'We're so excited—aren't we, darling?'

'You can only see her through the glass,' Sebastián warned. 'And only if she's well enough.'

'We don't care,' José said, squeezing Maria's hand, 'just so long as we get to see her.'

How it incensed him! Not his father—Maria. Inserting herself into the family as a doting grandmother, trying to gloss over the years of her absence.

'It is good that you have been here for Emily,' Maria said to Anna in a throaty voice. 'She needs a friend at a time like this. Poor thing…'

'Papá,' Sebastián interjected. He didn't want to hear feigned concern from his mother. 'Can we go for a walk? I want to speak with you. With us all away from the office, things are piling up.'

'Always business with you…' José grumbled.

'Can't we just keep it about family today?' Alejandro asked his brother.

'The world keeps turning,' Sebastián said. 'We can't all just take a month or three off.'

Sebastián didn't care if he came across as a cold-hearted devil. It was what they expected him to be. But he wanted to get his father on his own and work was the obvious excuse.

José, though, was rather more familiar with his eldest son's tactics, and as they stepped out into the bright son, he rolled his eyes.

'Don't worry. I know the baby is very small. I'm not going to—'

'It's not about the baby.'

'Well, I don't want to hear anything against your mother. She's excited to be here, and if you can't accept that—'

'It's not about Maria.' Sebastián signalled to a table at a café and the rope was removed so they could step in and take a seat. He ordered coffee for them both. 'Carmen is going to speak to you.'

'About?'

'Riding.'

'What about it?'

'She's unsure if it's what she wants to do with her life and—'

'Of *course* it's what she wants to do.'

'Listen—'

'No!' Jose thumped the table. 'She's world-class. It is what she loves.'

Sebastián sat and listened as his father gave every reason he had expected him to as to why Carmen shouldn't give it up.

'Finished?' he said.

'I have not finished. That girl doesn't know what she wants. This is the one thing she excels at!'

'Listen to me, Papá.' He leant forward and stared right into his father's eyes, as he had so very many times. 'She needs to know you love her—that whatever she does with her life she has your support.'

'Well, she doesn't in this,' José huffed. 'Why the hell would she give it up?'

Sebastián spooned sugar into his coffee and let him carry on. There was a certain feeling of déjà vu about this situation. Throughout Carmen's childhood and teenage years he had pre-warned or primed José, deciding it might be better for his at times fiery father to let off the inevitable steam with his eldest rather than with his sensitive and temperamental youngest.

'We should get back,' Sebastián said. 'Don't tell her I—'

'Okay, okay,' José snapped. 'I won't tell her you said any-thing.' They stopped for a moment and looked out at the yachts. 'Where's yours?'

Sebastián pointed. 'We're going there after the hospital.'

'It's been ages,' José said. 'And your mother has never been on board. It will be nice for her to see it.'

'Yes,' Sebastián said, not revealing the supreme effort be-hind that single word. He would have her walk the plank if he could, for all she had done—or rather not done. To Carmen and Alejandro too...

He glanced at his father, smiling as he looked out at the water, and for his sake kept his own emotions in check and joined in with his idle chit-chat.

'You still have Dante as the captain?'

'Of course.' Sebastián nodded. 'He'll be pleased to wel-come you.'

The cars were all ready and Carmen had arrived by the time they got back.

'You said we were meeting at five!' she accused.

'The cars are at five. You were to be here at four.'

Anna stood a little apart from everyone, and when Alejandro guided her into a car, he pointed to a different one for Sebastián.

It was a difficult day for so many reasons, yet there was so much happiness too as they all stood looking through the glass at the newest addition to their family. The incubator had been moved closer to the window, and Sebastián heard José's cry of delight at the sight of his granddaughter.

Even Maria, who lacked a single maternal bone in her body, let out a sob when she saw the tiny girl. 'Oh, *bebita*...' she crooned. 'She needs a name, Alejandro.'

'I think she might have one,' Sebastián said.

For although he was mildly enthralled with his niece, his sharp eyes had been drawn to the embroidered blanket that had been carefully hung over the incubator. The machinery on view was softened by it, and there on the delicately embroidered blanket was the date of her birth and the tiny little girl's name: *Josefa Romero Jacobs*.

'Josefa,' Sebastián said, pronouncing it *Hosefa*. 'The female for José.'

He looked quickly back to the baby as his father started to cry—a familiar sound and one he had hated all his life. But he reminded himself that today these were happy tears.

Even though to him they sounded the same as the ones from his childhood.

'Anna made it,' Emily told the little gathering. 'It's taken her months. She added the name this week.'

'You surely didn't have her sewing on her holiday?' Maria sounded appalled at the notion, and for once she almost put a smile on her eldest son's face.

He had known, of course, that Anna had a secret, but her

hiding something and returning to the villa occasionally made better sense now.

He had to fight not to turn his head and give Anna a smile... not to put his arm around her and pull her in and compliment her work. He had to stand still and not react. Because if he did, then he would break his word to her.

He would also be revealing something of himself. Because he did not do affection, or handholding, or anything of the sort. Not in public, and up until now not really in private either.

He could hear the sound of his father's tears as he looked at his tiny granddaughter. 'Josefa...' he kept saying, over and over.

Sebastián stared ahead as Emily gently told the fragile man that they had asked permission for him to hold the baby. 'Alejandro has given up his turn this afternoon.'

'Oh.' Maria sighed excitedly. 'Please let me hold her!'

'Just Papá,' Alejandro said. 'She's too little to be passed around.'

'But surely just one little cuddle...?' Maria pouted.

Now Sebastián turned around. 'Just Papá.'

Anna blinked at the tone in Sebastián's voice.

It wasn't loud, or harsh, or anything like that, but it was still the sound of a final decision.

One with which no one would argue.

She couldn't help but wonder if he was being a bit harsh on his mother. She was attention-seeking, yes, but she'd been kind about Emily—and José did seem thrilled and deeply in love with his wife.

'We'll go to the waiting room,' he said now, and put his hand on his father's shoulder. 'Congratulations, Papá...'

It was a private moment for José, so Anna went into the waiting room along with Sebastián and Carmen—who was still smarting that her mother was present at all.

'"Oh, *bebita*",' she mimicked savagely, and then translated for Anna. 'It means baby girl. I doubt she was so overcome when she saw *me*.'

'Carmen!' Sebastián said.

Anna could hear the strain in his voice, and perhaps wisely he chose not to debate the topic right now.

'Let's just try for one good night, shall we?' he suggested, and then took out his phone. 'I'll let Dante know we'll be aboard soon.'

It was only when Carmen huffed off to stare out of the window that he finally met Anna's eyes.

He gave her a half-smile—or a quarter-smile and a tiny nod—and she quickly turned her head away, because she didn't know how they were after the way things had ended between them.

'How was your night with Carmen?' he asked.

'Fun!' she said brightly.

But when she met his gaze her eyes filled with tears, because she loathed the pettiness of revenge and that was what last night had been for her.

She'd stuck to sparkling water all night, but she'd laughed and danced as if she was a glamorous and single twenty-something with no responsibilities, having the time of her life on a starry night in Puerto Banús.

She wished that she'd simply curled up and cried instead.

He gave her another smile and that made her feel even worse.

When they were finished at the hospital the cars were ready to take them to the marina, and she sat with Alejandro and Emily, who was obviously nervous at leaving her tiny baby in the hospital.

'She'll be fine,' she told her friend.

'I know,' Emily said.

'How was José when he held her?' Anna asked.

'So proud,' Emily said, and she showed her a couple of photos on her phone.

That reminded Anna of something. 'I have to take some photos of us,' she said. 'Willow keeps asking for more.'

'We'll get some on the yacht,' Emily said. 'How is she?'

'They're driving back from Scotland today. She's starting to miss me and...' A lump filled her throat but she squashed it down, and Emily squeezed her hand.

'Thanks for being here,' she said. 'And I am so sorry for asking you to do that blanket. I wasn't thinking...'

'It nearly killed me!' Anna laughed.

They began to walk along the jetty towards the yacht. Maria's flamenco shoes were clipping loudly and drawing the eyes of all around.

'Maria de Luca!' someone called out, and she smiled and waved and blew kisses with the hand that wasn't holding José's.

Emily and Alejandro were holding hands too, and Carmen was casually checking her phone. Sebastián walked ahead alone and Anna ached to walk beside him, sensing this night was incredibly hard for him.

His yacht had never looked more beautiful, Anna thought as they made their way towards it. In a sea of white, it was softly lit pink in the dusky night and she felt a little foolish for having asked Sebastián to warn the crew, because they were, of course, impeccable.

'Bienvenido a bordo, Señor Romero.'

José was welcomed back warmly, and Dante greeted all the other guests by name.

'Señorita de Luca.'

He welcomed Maria courteously, and in Spanish asked her to remove her shoes. Anna was back to being *señorita*, as she had been the first night she had been here.

'Can I ask that you...?' He gestured to her shoes and to the basket.

Carmen had already taken hers off and was heading up onto deck.

'Of course,' Anna said, and leant on the wall to remove her

shoes, trying not to recall all the tender times Sebastián had done this for her.

'Señorita de Luca?'

The *capitán* was calling Maria back. Clearly, Anna thought, she hadn't heard his request, because she was still wearing her shoes.

'Por favor?' He was politely insistent.

Anna felt her heart still as Maria shot the *capitán* a look so dark and fierce that Anna sensed a shiver on her neck before her heart suddenly beat faster.

No wonder Sebastián was so protective of his family. This was her first glimpse of Maria with her mask off—though of course she quickly snapped it back on and returned to being 'Grandmother of the Year' as she complied.

'Por supuesto,' she said, but insolently, and she did not put her shoes in the basket. Instead she left them lying in a heap on the floor.

'*Gracias*, Señorita De Luca.' Dante smiled his perfect smile.

He really was a true *capitán*!

Anna was honestly a bit shaken, but either the others hadn't noticed or they were used to it, because no comment was made.

Emily gasped when she arrived on deck. There were tiny arrangements of soft pink daisies and pink candles, and champagne corks were popping. Little Josefa's arrival was being properly celebrated.

'It's so nice to taste fresh air,' Emily said. 'Gosh, what a week…'

Anna caught Sebastián's eyes, very briefly, and she was proud of them both as they gave nothing away.

She thought of the future—years from now, perhaps. When he might be celebrating…whatever. Sebastián, old on his yacht and too rich to be lonely…

I ought to take some pictures, she thought.

She took a few of Emily and Alejandro, and of the cake when it came out. Delicate layers of pastry layered with pink jam and white chocolate ganache…

Sebastián had done all this. Or the crew, perhaps. But she had heard his meetings with Dante and the chef, and knew of the effort he'd made…

'To Josefa!' Sebastián said, and everyone clinked their glasses.

'Willow would have loved this,' Emily said. 'You'll have to take some cake back for her.'

'She'll love it!' Anna smiled.

Alejandro handed out cards for everyone, with photos of the new baby, and Anna found she had to excuse herself. She was tearful and trying not to be, missing being here already, and daunted at the prospect of leaving it all behind.

And that dreadful ending…

Anna was looking up at the stars and the rising moon, and wondering if her phone's camera was up to it, when she heard Carmen.

'I mean it!' She sounded adamant. 'I'm thinking of taking a break. Maybe travelling…'

'Come off it!' Alejandro said. 'As if anything would tear you away from the horses.'

'Why would you give up now?' Sebastián asked.

Anna held her breath, surprised by the harsh question when she'd told him how sensitive this topic was.

'An athlete is only at the top of their game for a small window of time,' he went on.

'Hey!' José interrupted his eldest son. 'If Carmen wants a break then she has earnt one. Whatever she does, we support her.'

'Papá!' Carmen let out a shriek of laughter and moved from her seat to kiss his cheek, and Anna smiled as José pulled her onto his knee.

The family were all together, and she held up her phone, wondering whether or not she should capture an image of it. Most certainly she could do it unobtrusively, and so she snapped a quick photo of the 'Elusive Five'. She knew from Emily that there were hardly any pictures of the five of them.

And then she turned back to the gorgeous night.

But all too soon it was over.

Presents were being handed out by Dante—little flamenco dolls holding Spanish sweets—and Anna just knew Willow would love one.

'Plastic Flamenco dolls!' Maria said, derisively. 'They're a bit touristy! Did you choose these, Alejandro?'

'I chose them,' Sebastián responded tartly responded. 'I'm not exactly up on baby celebrations and Alejandro has been busy.'

He caught her eyes then and Anna smiled. She knew he had somehow chosen the perfect gift to give Willow when she broke the news of the baby to her daughter.

'Well, I think it's gorgeous,' she spoke up for him. 'I'm going to give Willow mine.'

'Take two,' Sebastián said.

And that was it.

The end of their time.

Her heart was lost.

There were effusive goodbyes, with José hugging Emily and Alejandro, and Maria too. Sebastián gave his father a kiss, but as Maria moved to kiss her son he turned his cheek just enough that it missed.

Maria noticed.

Anna did too.

But for the rest it was a friendly goodbye.

'I'll see you next time, Anna.' Carmen smiled and kissed her new friend goodbye. 'Or maybe in England? We'll go raving!'

'Thank you for being here,' José said, and hugged her.

Anna turned and knew it was time to bid farewell to Sebastián. She just didn't know how to, and was pathetically grateful when her phone rang.

'Oh, excuse me. It's my daughter.'

She removed herself to take it, and chatted to Willow, who was happy but also desperate for it to be tomorrow so she could see her mum.

'One more sleep,' Anna said. 'I can't wait to see you. I've missed you so much.'

In the background she heard Sebastián speaking.

'I'll see that Anna gets back,' Sebastián said. 'You go straight to the hospital.'

'We can wait,' Alejandro said, despite his obvious eagerness to get back to his baby.

'Anna will be fine,' Sebastián insisted. 'Go and see your baby.'

'Come on,' Alejandro said to his wife. 'Sebastián says he will see that Anna gets back.'

'Tell her we'll have breakfast tomorrow.'

'For sure.'

Anna waved to her friend, and then turned her attention back to Willow, grateful to Sebastián for engineering some time for them to say goodbye privately.

The crew were clearing up, but he had a word and they melted away, and as she ended her call the cabin felt incredibly quiet.

'Peace at last,' Sebastián said.

'They are rather loud,' Anna agreed.

'I meant between us.'

'Oh…' She took a breath. 'Peace?'

'We can do better than last night, can't we?'

Yes, they could.

He poured her a fresh glass of champagne and they sat on one of the sofas. Conversation was a little awkward as they began an attempt to redefine their relationship as friends.

'Today was beautiful,' Anna said.

'It went as well as it could. Thank goodness I kept it short.'

'Your father was great with Carmen.'

'Yes.'

She didn't understand why he'd snapped at his sister when she'd told him how sensitive Carmen was about things, but she let it go, just pleased it had worked out.

'And José got to hold the baby.'

'Maria thought it should be her,' Sebastián said, rolling his eyes.

Anna frowned and felt her arms goosebump. 'She was a little jealous.'

'She disappeared for twenty-five years and yet thinks she should hold her grandchild before my father!'

'They do seem happy,' she attempted, out of politeness, but then she recalled *that* look from Maria, and knew he wasn't being harsh in his judgement.

'For now.'

He gave a low, scoffing laugh, but Anna knew it wasn't aimed at her.

'Until she changes her mind.'

'You don't think she'll leave?'

'I think she came back because we thought he only had a few weeks to live. That changed after he had his surgery. I don't know how long he's got now. I just hope it's longer than her attention span.'

'Why would she be by his side if she didn't love him?'

He didn't answer.

'Is it for the money?' Anna asked. 'Or because she wants to be sure she remains part of the brand?'

'Both, in part.' Sebastián didn't soften. 'But it's more that she wants to be his widow, and wear black, and walk behind his coffin. Be the recipient of all the attention she craves.'

'You don't think she loves him?'

'I believe she's incapable of loving anyone other than herself.'

Anna sat there and tried to take it in, stunned. Then she looked at his serious expression and wondered how bad his relationship with his mother must have been for him to draw such a conclusion.

'I saw the look she gave Dante when he asked her to remove her shoes,' she said.

'I know that look well,' he nodded.

'What was life like for you?'

Sebastián didn't answer that one. He shook his head. 'Enough about her. How's Willow?'

'Desperate for me to get home.'

'She misses you?'

'Yes.'

'Emily wants you to see her for breakfast tomorrow.'

'I heard.'

'You're in demand.'

'Yes.'

'With me too.'

'It doesn't feel like it,' Anna said, and then she looked right at him. 'Thank you, Sebastián.'

It felt imperative to say this now, before the emotion of leaving rendered her unable to say it without breaking down. She did not want to end the most perfect week of her life with tears.

'It's been wonderful.' She gave a small, wistful smile. 'All of it. Well…' She looked over. 'Apart from last night. I'm sorry I went off dancing with Carmen.'

'Anna, it was the best thing you could have done. You need to get out dancing more.'

'I wish we'd been able to talk it out.'

'We can now.' He looked at her. 'If we're both honest.'

'Something changed?'

'Yes,' he admitted.

'When Carmen came by the first time.'

'No.'

'Yes,' Anna insisted.

'Yes,' he conceded. 'She told me something about you wanting more children and to settle down, and it freaked me out.'

'I said all that to get her to open up. I said that before you came back. Before we were together.'

'It's true, though?'

'One day.' She nodded. 'Maybe. But I don't get why something I said to Carmen—'

'It changed before that, Anna.'

'No…'

'Anna.' He was both gentle and firm. 'In the water, what were you going to say?'

She shook her head. 'I don't want say it now.'

'Fair enough, but you know we were getting in too deep.'

'Only because you made it that way.'

'Do you want me to look you up when I come to England now and then? Maybe sneak away for a few days when you come to visit Emily?'

'I don't know.' She shook her head. 'Maybe.'

'No.' He shook his head. 'You want more than that for your future. So do I. And I don't want us to get closer only for you to...'

'To what?'

'Come on, Anna. You've done the tough part. Willow will soon be going to school. You're going to start the career you want. You're not going to settle for some occasional catch-up with a guy in Spain.'

He might as well have got a pen and written on the table before them in capital letters: I DON'T WANT YOUR LOVE.

And there was no point arguing with that.

'You're right.' She sniffed, and then nodded. 'I do want more than that. But not yet...'

She didn't want it to be over, but knew it was.

'We end it now,' Sebastián said. 'Nicely.'

'Yes...'

'You've got a family waiting at home who love you.' He must have seen her eyebrows rise. 'They do,' he said. 'It's time to forgive yourself for hurting them. Just be yourself.'

'I don't even know who that is,' Anna admitted, because this week had spun her around, and she felt as if her heart lived in two worlds.

'*I* do,' Sebastián said. 'And she's actually very nice. I know, because I've spent a week with her.' He gave her a smile. 'It was fun. Here...' He reached beneath the table. 'I got you a gift.'

'Please don't...'

'Why? Don't you like gifts?'

'I do but...' The dark brown box he handed her already told her it was too much. Now she was almost crying. 'I can't take this...'

'Open it.'

What she saw made her gasp.

It was a beautiful white gold Fabergé egg pendant.

'I got a long chain,' he said. 'Everyone will think it's just a necklace.'

'Nobody would think this was "just a necklace".'

It was so exquisite—the detailing, the absolute beauty of the design...

'Open it,' he said.

Anna frowned, not sure what he meant, but then she realised the egg had a catch. When she opened it, she saw that inside was a tiny yacht.

'Oh!'

She had never been one for gifts and had loathed the thought of him giving her an expensive present, but the little secret yacht was perfection. And he was right—no one even needed to see beyond the chain.

She took a breath and was honest. 'I love it. It's so beautiful...'

'Like you.'

He took it out of the box and smoothed back her hair, lifting it away from her neck. She felt the cool weight of the egg nestle between her breasts as he fastened the clasp. It was the most romantic gift—a little time capsule of their week together that she could wear, or put away and just take out sometimes...

'Thank you, Sebastián.' She leant in and kissed him lightly, feeling his warm lips on hers, and then the slide of his tongue.

She would never understand how he could kiss her in a way that felt so close to the perfect goodbye...how he could take her by the hand down to his cabin...

His suite was exquisite, the most private place on the yacht, the closest she could ever get to the centre of his world, and here he kissed her as if they weren't saying goodbye…as if he loved her.

And Anna kissed him back with deep passion…because she loved him.

He removed the straps from her shoulders and slid down her dress. 'You look…'

He took in the changes their week had made, the white breasts where her bikini had stayed firmly on. They made him smile, and as his hand dusted over her nipples and then stroked her stomach she closed her eyes to the sensation.

'Sunkissed,' was his verdict.

She was *Sebastián*-kissed, she corrected mentally. Because it wasn't just the sun that had wreaked changes in Anna. It was a week of being made love to, of moments lying together on a beach or in bed, or on a lounger, just talking,

All she had missed out on in life so far he had given her in spades. And yet, selfishly perhaps, for Anna it still wasn't enough.

He kissed her breasts as he pulled her in, and then kissed her stomach as he slid down her knickers. His breathing was heavy and her eyelashes fluttered closed as she anticipated what was to come.

One soft kiss, sweeter than any delicacy, and then he moved in for more.

Anna gave a soft moan as she fell back on plump pillows. She could smell his cologne and the sun on his shirt. She allowed herself to inhale and breathe in the pleasure as he kissed her neck and then said words in Spanish that sounded a lot like how she felt.

He took her flushed face in his hands and gave her slow, wet kisses that weakened her. He climbed on top of her and parted her legs. He couldn't know how she physically ached for him to enter her.

'Sebastián…'

He was still half dressed, but she didn't care. And he was

unsheathed, but she cared even less about that. She just had to have him inside her.

But he stopped to sheathe himself.

Always.

They'd both been burned before.

And yet there was a stab of regret—or realisation, per-haps—but then, as he kissed her hard, he dragged her back to that blurry place where details didn't matter. And he was entering her, and driving in, and she had never known such tender loving as he took every moment of their time together and condensed it into this.

Anna kissed him as she wanted to—as if it was for ever and this wasn't their final night. Their eyes locked he moved within her, but then she turned her head and looked away—because she had to.

She felt as if she were giving herself to him entirely, but even as her body rippled with pleasure she knew that he held himself back.

'Don't...' she said, but she didn't know quite what she was telling him.

She sank again, dragged back to oblivion as his tempo in-creased. His shout as he came was almost silent, breathless, but it reverberated through her, summoning her, and she felt the clench of every cell as she gave in to him. Just caved...

It was afterwards, as she lay there, the blur fading, that she knew for certain he had held back. Despite her willingness, and being on the Pill, still he'd sheathed.

Slivers of his heart was all he'd ever give.

He took care of the details, never trusting anyone else to.

He would never get that close to someone.

He didn't trust her...

Probably he never would.

CHAPTER SIXTEEN

ANNA WOKE BEFORE him and realised it was to the sound of his phone.

The buzzing faded and she found she did not know what to do. Should she simply get dressed and leave quietly, without saying goodbye?

Perhaps ending things nicely wasn't the best way after all...

Anger had felt easier to navigate than being sent off nicely with presents and best wishes...

Don't end it on a row, Anna warned herself. *Or with tears!*

Then his phone buzzed again, and his first word on waking was a swear word.

'Sebastián!' she exclaimed, and actually laughed at how incompatible they were. And then she met his lovely black eyes. 'It really is time for me to go. I'm starting to nag!'

'You can nag for a couple more hours,' he said, pulling her towards him and obliterating thought with his scratchy morning jaw—until his blessed phone buzzed again.

It was Anna who almost swore this time.

'I'd better get this.'

He rolled away from her and reached for his phone as Anna lay there, her eyes determinedly closed.

It wasn't a shout that had her opening her eyes. Instead it was a low, husky whisper that was pure anguish.

'Dios, no!' Sebastián said.

She shot to attention.

She could hear screams coming down the phone, and Sebastián saying *'Cálmate...'* clearly telling the caller to calm down.

Anna sat up, her first thought that something must have happened to the baby. She tried to stand, to reach for her clothes, to go to her friend, but then his hand came to her arm and he stroked it lightly, giving a slight shake of his head which somehow reassured her.

He'd done the same at the airport, Anna recalled. Even though they'd been barely talking, he'd seen her anguish and reassured her with his touch, with his eyes, before he'd even spoken.

And he did the same now, stroking her arm as he spoke in rapid Spanish for a couple of moments before ending the call.

What's wrong? It was the obvious question to ask. *What's happened?*

Yet they would be such pointless questions when clearly he was too stunned to answer. So instead of asking she watched as he stood there, naked, as if still taking it in. He proceeded to sit on the bed, and she watched the phone slip from his hand and fall to the floor as he put his head in his hands.

'My father...' he said.

She swallowed.

'That was Maria. They were—' He shook his head. 'I think they were making love.'

'Oh, Sebastián...'

'An ambulance and a doctor came, but no...' He shook his head. 'He's gone.'

Sometimes there were no words, so Anna knelt and put her hand on his shoulder, felt his rapid, shallow breaths.

'Carmen's hysterical,' he said, more to himself than to Anna. 'I knew he was sick, and we all knew this day was coming, but not yet...'

And then he took a shaky breath and his head went down into his hands. It felt as if the biggest, strongest tree was giving way beneath her fingers.

It was a very private moment that she was certain he would

prefer no one to see. He let out a couple of low sobs and she could see his fingers pressed into his eyes. She didn't know what to do, or how to comfort him, so she just hugged him tightly. Perhaps it was the right thing, because he brought her to his lap and it was like watching the sun go down to see the tears falling from his eyes.

'Not yet,' he said, and she clung to him. 'I thought he had more time.' He looked at her then. Right at her, as if they were in that deep water again, as if their souls were locked together. 'Will you please stay? I can't imagine the funeral...'

'Sebastián!' Her mouth gaped and Anna felt her heart split down the middle, torn completely in two. She really didn't know what to say or do.

He spoke before she could. 'You can't.' He said it for her. 'I know. I forgot for a moment that you leave today.'

'I have to get back to Willow.'

'Of course.'

He retracted his question immediately, that brief glimpse of his agony wiped away as he tipped her off his knee and went back to being the strongest tree, all signs of vulnerability erased.

'Of course you do,' he said. 'You must go—and so must I. I have so much to do.'

'I know.'

Anna sat there, hugging her knees, as he took the quickest shower and then dressed hurriedly, calling his PA as he did so, to arrange an urgent flight from Marbella to Jerez. If she didn't know better, she might think he was getting ready for work.

'I have to get to the hospital and tell Alejandro. Carmen's probably calling him now, but I asked her to wait and let me tell him face to face.'

He closed his eyes for a brief second and she saw it then— how he dealt with it all, and probably had since he was ten years old. Before that, even.

Wow.

She watched him snap back into business mode and she saw

then why they called him tough—he had to be. Because every-thing came to him, everyone looked to him, all worries landed on his shoulders. Now he was on the phone again, speaking with whom she did not know, but it sounded like a priest.

Then he paused, kissed her cheek, 'I really do have to—'

'I know.'

'Stay as long as you—'

'I can sort myself out.' She gave a shaky smile. 'Worry about yourself and your family. I'm so sorry, Sebastián.' As he threw things into a small case she hurriedly took out her phone. 'I took this photo of you all last night.'

'I haven't got time—'

'It's of the five of you,' Anna said. 'It might help, if you would like it?' she attempted.

But he was heading out through the door.

'It doesn't matter.'

Last night seemed to have taken place in a whole other world, and everything in this one was suddenly different. It was her last morning in Puerto Banús, and breakfast was served on the deck of the yacht, but she could barely manage the coffee.

It felt wrong to be on the outside.

She felt as if she should be there, with the rest of the fam-ily, but it was she herself who had demanded that they remain a secret.

Emily called an hour or so later and told Anna the news she already knew.

'How's Alejandro?' asked Anna.

'Stunned,' Emily said. 'He's flying back to Jerez now, with Sebastián.'

'Do you want me to come to the hospital?'

'Please…'

Emily was in a little suite attached to the NICU. It was a place that was used to hearing bad news—but not of an old, sick man dying.

It was still devastating…

'Do you know when the funeral is?' Anna asked.

'Sebastián is sorting it—but probably tomorrow.'

'So soon?'

'They take place much more quickly here.'

'Will you go?'

'I don't know.' Emily gave a helpless shake of her head. 'I don't know how I can be so far away from Josefa when she's so small.' She looked at her friend. 'But I know you have to go back. I understand that more than ever now.'

'I haven't seen Willow in over a week. My mother...'

'I know things are still shaky there. We'll be fine,' Emily said. 'I mean, it's not about me, is it? It's about Alejandro.'

And for Anna it was about Sebastián.

He'd asked her to stay.

To be there for the funeral.

He didn't want for ever, and yet he'd wanted her presence on the most awful day.

How could she stay, though? Her mother would never accept the excuse that she wanted to stay for her friend's father-in-law's funeral. And anyway, Willow needed her...

Nothing would keep her from her daughter. Nothing came before that love. Anna had decided that long ago.

Yet things were different now.

There wasn't a rival for her love for her daughter.

But there *was* someone else in her life whom she loved too.

And even if there could never be a future for them, Anna knew she might be able to help him a little now, just by being there.

It was surprisingly easy to call her mother...

'We're just heading to church,' said Jean. 'Willow's ever so excited that you're coming—'

'Mother,' Anna cut in, 'can you take this call away from Willow, please? I need to speak to you.'

She heard her mother talking to Willow. 'I'm just going to check if Grandpa's got his service notes.'

There was the sound of heavy breathing and she could hear

her mother climbing the stairs. And suddenly it dawned on Anna that this was what Sebastián had done when he'd asked his father to join him on a walk.

Everyone had accused him of putting work first, yet she could see now that he'd been getting his father away before Carmen joined them.

José's perfect response to his daughter had been orchestrated by Sebastián, Anna was sure of it. Because that was what he did. He had smoothed the way for his little sister, made sure her relationship with her father was protected, taken care of his family in ways they didn't even realise.

She was determined to be there for him now. Anna wasn't even nervous to speak with her mother. It was simply the right thing to do.

'Is the baby okay?' Jean asked.

'The baby's doing well,' Anna said. 'The thing is, Emily's father-in-law died this morning.'

'He's been ill for a while, hasn't he?'

'Yes, but it was still sudden and unexpected, though.'

'Okay…'

'Mum, I think I need to be here for the funeral—'

'Anna,' Jean cut in. 'I know Emily's going through a difficult time, but Willow's so looking forward—'

'This isn't about Emily.'

There was a very long silence. Her mother was waiting, and Anna was unsure how to formulate what she wanted to say, but it was more than that. It was also what she wanted—no, *needed* to happen next.

'Can I ask you to bring Willow out here to Marbella?'

'Marbella?' Her mother gave an incredulous laugh.

'I want to go the funeral and—'

'I'm sorry for their loss, but your daughter has to come first, surely?'

'She does,' Anna said, and took a breath. 'Mum, I've met someone… Alejandro's brother.' She knew that by voicing it she was opening herself up to hurt, and to her mother's scorn, but she was determined to do it anyway. 'He wants me here for the funeral and—'

'Someone you've known for a *week*?'

'We met at the wedding.'

'And was that why you flew off to Spain the first chance you got?'

'No!' She gave the Spanish *no*—the terse no...the absolute no. 'I'm not sure what's happening between us. I just know that I care about him very much, and now his father has died suddenly.' She did care very much, and there was a part of her that knew he cared too. 'We can't ever be a couple, but I can be a support to him. But I also need Willow—and she needs me.'

'I'm not just jumping on a plane with her to meet Mummy's latest—'

'That's uncalled for!' Anna snapped. 'Nothing will ever come before Willow, but she's old enough to know that her mother has a friend who's lost someone—'

'I'm sorry. No.'

'I understand,' Anna said—and perhaps she finally did. Her mother was entitled to her own opinions, but so too was Anna. She was entitled to make her own decisions and her own mistakes, and now she would make her own choices. 'I'll be home this afternoon as arranged, then, and I'll bring Willow back here myself.'

'You can't afford to do that.'

Anna couldn't afford not to. She had to listen to her heart...

It was all a little chaotic.

She booked the flights, and called Emily, and did all she could to put plans in place on her way back to England, so that by the time she walked into the vicarage she knew exactly what was happening.

'Mummy!'

Willow was the most incredible child—funny, and a bit of a show-off, wearing a tartan beret and full of smiles.

There were presents to be exchanged—Scottish rock for Anna, and the flamenco doll with sweets for Willow...

And a frosty catch-up with her parents.

When they were back in their own home, she told Willow about Josefa. And because she was only four—almost five—Willow didn't need exact details. She was simply excited to see the pictures.

'She's so cute! I want to hold her...'

'We can't hold her at the moment,' Anna said. 'Just her parents...'

And she thought of José, and how extra-precious that cuddle with his granddaughter was now.

'Willow, darling...' She took a deep breath. 'I have a friend in Spain and his father has just died. It was ever so sudden. I think I ought to go to the funeral, so I can help him.'

'You're going back?' Her daughter's eyes widened in horror. 'With *you*!'

That quickly put a smile on her face.

'Emily's going to look after you, and she's finding a nanny to help her, as I might have to stay away overnight. But we'll have a couple of days together afterwards.'

'Where are we going?'

'It's a place called Marbella.'

Willow jumped up and down at the prospect of a plane ride, and seeing Emily, going to Spain...

'Will I get to see the baby?'

'Well...' Anna took a breath. She felt as if she was balancing on a tightrope. 'It depends... But you'll definitely be with Emily. She's desperate to see you.'

'Is there a beach?'

'Yes, there's a beach.' Anna smiled.

And it was at that very beach the next morning that she and her daughter found Emily.

'Willow!'

Emily hugged her goddaughter fiercely, and didn't let on anything about the difficulties she had been through, nor ask any of the questions she had for Willow's mother. She just chatted away and introduced Dali, a highly trained nanny, who was going to help take care of Willow.

Anna insisted on paying Dali herself, even if it meant she would have to dip into her precious emergency fund. If this wasn't an emergency, she didn't know what was.

Yes, it was going to be a juggling act just to get to the funeral, but Anna did everything she could to make it easy on her daughter, answering all Dali's questions about her Willow's likes and dislikes.

Then she faced a barrage of questions from her friend, when Dali took Willow to play on the gorgeous sand—she wanted to be sure Willow was comfortable with Dali before leaving them together.

'Dali's incredible,' Emily reassured her. 'I asked the nurses at the NICU, and they recommended her. We're going to stay at the hotel next to the hospital, and Dali will take care of Willow when I need to go in…'

Anna knew she could not put off Emily's questions any longer. She really had done everything she could to help when Anna had called, even if she was uncertain what she was doing was wise.

'I thought something was going on with you and Sebastián at the wedding…' she said.

'I know…'

'Why didn't you tell me?'

'I didn't need to be warned again,' Anna admitted.

'He did everything he could to break Alejandro and me up. He got rid of me without thought, and I don't want the same thing to happen to you. It *hurt*.'

'I know… But he's hurting now,' Anna said. 'And I know we're going nowhere, but he's made me so happy. I can't tell you… This isn't about the future, or whether there's a chance for us. It's just the right thing to do.'

She gave her friend a smile.

'What happens when you come to visit me in a few months and he's seeing someone else?' asked Emily.

'I'll expect that,' Anna admitted. 'And I'm not going to let it make things awkward for the two of us, I promise. Have you told Alejandro?'

'What? That my usually sensible friend has gone completely crazy?' She gave a smile and then shook her head. 'No, I haven't told him. I was hoping to talk you out of going to the funeral.'

'Yet you found Dali?'

'I did…'

'Thank you.'

'You'd better hurry and catch your train…'

'How is Josefa?' Sebastián asked his brother.

'She is doing well.'

'She's a fighter.'

'Yes.'

'And Emily?'

'She has to stay there.'

'Of course.'

No question—Sebastián knew that.

He harboured no bitterness towards Anna for returning home. He knew, despite his first thoughts and that dreadful row, that she was a woman who was a mother first.

Unlike his.

And he admired her for it.

'I can't bear it…' Maria was weeping and waving *aromáticas* under her nose—but had managed to be in full make-up and funeral regalia.

Her day of days, Sebastián thought darkly.

But then he looked closely at his mother, and at her hands that shook as she tried to open her fan. Who was he, after all, to sit as judge and jury on love?

A dreadful mother? Yes.

An absent wife? True.

Yet José Romero's ending was the one his father would have chosen over any other, Sebastián knew.

'Here.' He handed his mother a small sherry and she nodded gratefully.

'This could be last time I'll see my photo on the bottle...' She sighed. 'You'll have every trace of me removed.'

'Let's not do this today,' Sebastián suggested firmly. 'Carmen needs—'

'Can everyone stop worrying about Carmen for a moment? *I* have just lost my husband.'

Dios, but he had to bite his tongue.

He looked at his sister, curled up in a chair, and truly wondered if she would make it through the day.

She was fragile, and she had not yet found out that the home she'd grown up in had been left to Maria. The land, the stables—all left to Maria too.

Sebastián would tell her tonight.

'I was always sniping at him...' his sister said now.

'No,' Sebastián said. 'Carmen, think of the wedding, and dancing with him. Think of that last night and how you two laughed...'

Perhaps he should text Anna and ask for that photo she had mentioned...but he dared not contact her today.

The funeral procession from home was slow as it meandered past the vines, and he watched as Carmen leant on Alejandro and sobbed.

They had always been close.

Really, he had never been close to anyone. Perhaps he was more like his mother than he would like?

Incapable of love.

He looked at Maria's black eyes and intact mascara and eyeliner. From knowing Anna, he found he actually understood his mother less.

Every night and morning Anna had called her daughter. She had spoken about her, thought about her, put her needs first...

And he wished, more than he dared admit, that she could be here today.

The hearse had stopped, so that the family could walk the last few steps to the church behind the coffin.

Sebastián checked that his sister was ready, that Maria was not fainting dramatically, and told his brother to get off the damn phone to his wife.

Then, as he watched the coffin being slid out of the hearse, he stood ramrod-straight.

He tried to do the right thing and took his mother's elbow...

She brushed it off.

Maria de Luca would make her entrance solo.

More dramatic that way, he thought bitterly.

And then, on this, the darkest of days, he saw a blonde head, and the one face he needed to see was there in the crowd.

'Anna?' he whispered, frowning.

Sebastián stepped out of the line and walked over to her.

'I thought you went home?'

'I did. I had to. But you asked... I thought it might help...'

Her lips were as white as marble, and there were black rings under her eyes—no doubt from back-to-back flights.

'If there's anything I can do...? I think they're calling for you.'

The procession into the church was about to start.

'Why did you come?' His brain was moving slowly. 'In place of Emily?'

'For *you*,' Anna said. 'I wanted to be here for you.'

That was it, he realised as he gave a slightly bewildered nod and headed back to join his siblings.

Anna was here without agenda.

She had made no demands.

She stood in the crowd outside the church, simply to be there.

For him.

'Walk with me,' he said.

He saw her swallow.

'Be with me today.'

'Okay...'

* * *

Even if they never shared another kiss, another night, another anything, it was, she knew, the right thing to have done.

One night.

One week.

No regrets.

He was not a demonstrative man in public. There was no hand-holding or anything. To all and sundry she might well be a cousin by his side, but what mattered was that she was *there*…

'*Por qué está aquí?*' his mother asked, and more from the tone than the words Anna knew Maria was asking what she was doing there.

Sebastián answered in English. 'Nothing you would understand.'

It was his one slight dig—not that his mother noticed. But she would not—*could* not understand that Anna, no matter the difficulty, had done everything she could to be here for him.

She was beside him during the service, and then afterwards, back at the bodega. She had not expected to return here so soon—and certainly not under such sad circumstances.

'I have to go and accept condolences,' Sebastián explained. 'Can we speak later?'

'Just do what you have to do,' Anna said.

On the stage there was a huge photo of José. The restaurant tables were pushed to one side and there were candles burning in the alcoves and beautiful flowers everywhere. Yet despite the stunning surroundings there was volatile edge to the mood, as if the black sherry barrels were kegs of gunpowder that at any moment might ignite.

Carmen was a mess, and Alejandro was pale and haggard—which was hardly surprising after the week he'd had. Maria looked fabulous and was graciously accepting condolences and fanning herself.

And then there was Sebastián.

He shook hands, smiled politely and said all the right things to the right people. Yet she could see the tension in his shoulders, the muscle leaping in his cheek. Even the tendons in his neck were tightly strung.

'How's it going?' she asked, when finally he escaped and came over.

'You really don't want to know.' He gave her a tight smile. 'This will go on for ever. At least as long a Spanish wedding.' He rolled his eyes. 'Just without the dancing.'

Then he looked right at her.

'Can we talk?'

'Of course.'

'Not here.' He pointed across the lavish courtyard. 'My office maybe?'

'Sure.'

She said it more casually than she was feeling, and nervously walked with him up several flights of stairs.

It was a stunning old building and his office was grand, with views over Jerez.

'You shouldn't have come.'

He said it so tersely that Anna flinched, wondering for a second if he was cross with her for turning up—for outing them, even though he'd never minded before, but then he added.

'But I'm very glad you did.'

Her eyes snapped to his, and precisely what was meant by his look Anna couldn't tell, but she saw they were blazing, angry and in agony.

She had never crossed a room so fast in her life. She moved as if to catch him—only he wasn't falling, because he met her halfway.

His kiss was fierce, rough and passionate, as if all the emotion of the past days was pouring from his lips, and she kissed him back just as hard. Blotting out everything, just offering escape.

Rough kisses crushed all incoming thought. She could feel his hands lifting her, unnecessarily, because she was already scaling him, wrapping herself around him—but not in the way she had the morning before.

This wasn't about comfort…just a final escape.

'Anna…'

Maybe the barrels below were exploding in the cellar? Or perhaps everything was falling apart in the courtyard below? But they were escaping together.

She felt her knickers tear and heard the rapid unbuckling of his belt. It was more than raw. It was necessary and urgent…

For them both.

He took her away from sorrow, as he had the very moment they'd met. He took her to a place Anna did not know.

She wanted his passion unleashed.

This was all they would ever be—she knew it even as she succumbed. It was nothing for him but sex and dark passion. She didn't care in this moment. She only cared that he had needed her and she had been there for him, and he needed her again now, but in a different way—and she needed him too.

She ground onto him as he thrust hard, but then he took over and she felt the demand of his hands, moving her hips faster. Whatever he gave, he drew out from her, because soon she was reaching a blinding climax and she felt electric in his arms.

His groan as he shot into her was almost reluctant.

She couldn't breathe properly.

Their foreheads were pressed together, and neither wanted to go back down and face reality.

'Can we stay up here?' Sebastián said, and he kissed her face.

She managed a little laugh. 'I wish!'

'When do you go back?' he asked as he lowered her down. 'Tonight?'

'A couple of days,' Anna said, straightening her dress, unable to look at him or even to speak…because he didn't need to hear how much she loved him on this day.

Or ever.

'A couple of days?' he checked.

She could hear a thousand questions in his voice.

One of her shoes had fallen off and she was slipping it back on as he sorted out his suit.

'I can stay in Jerez tonight,' Anna said, 'if you want me to. I have to be back in Marbella tomorrow.'

'Hold on…' He closed his eyes. 'You didn't just fly in for the day?'

'No.'

'What about Willow?'

'She's in Marbella.'

'What?' His voice was like the crack of a whip.

'Sebastián…' Anna kept her voice steady. 'It's fine. She's with Emily and a nanny.'

'No. No…' His eyes were like black saucers. 'Anna…?'

He knew how impossible it must have been for her to make this happen.

Knew that she'd blown up her life to be here for him.

He was thinking of her daughter, here in another country, perhaps upset and confused.

And he was trying to tell himself that funerals were not the best place to make decisions.

Nor for knee-jerk reactions.

'You need to go to her,' he said.

'Sebastián, I wouldn't have left her if I didn't know she was happy and safe.'

'No.' He shook his head. 'You need to go and be with your daughter.'

'We've just—'

She bit her lip so hard he thought she might have drawn blood. They had just had sex—the most intimate of sex—and he was telling her to get the hell out.

'Anna…' He was adamant. 'You need to go back to Willow.'

CHAPTER SEVENTEEN

THE PERILS OF SPAIN, Anna thought as sat on a sunbed in her bikini, watching Dali and Willow playing in the sea. She must stop having passionate sex the moment she had someone to look after Willow!

Dali had insisted on staying for the full twenty-four hours that Anna had paid her for. And it was perhaps just as well, because she felt dreadfully unravelled.

Sebastián did that to her, though.

Her emergency fund was practically gone, and she was undoubtedly in trouble with her parents. And Emily would be giving her *I told you so* eyes the next time she visited because, despite her brave words, Anna knew she was going to howl to her friend when she saw him with some gorgeous supermodel.

Yet even if she could go back she wouldn't change a thing.

Or would she...?

Should she have not gone yesterday?

She didn't regret it.

It was more that now she had to mourn the end of what they'd had...

'There you are.

She heard his voice and was startled, hoping he couldn't read her thoughts. She looked up and tried not to burn in a blush.

He was still in his funeral suit and unshaven. He was fully dressed, in a suit, on a beach, and she was the one melting and trying not to show it.

She wanted to leap up and fall into his embrace, or to kiss him or...

But Willow was here.

Or was she just hiding behind her daughter, and actually it was her heart that couldn't handle it?

'Willow's loving the beach,' Anna explained, watching her daughter running in the shallows. 'And Dali insisted on staying because I'd already paid her for a full twenty-four hours.'

'You paid her? I thought—'

'She's *my* daughter,' Anna said. 'And I don't expect my friends to fund—' She blushed. 'Well, if I had stayed away last night...' She tore her eyes away.

His rejection had hurt. And yet it was a pain she had invited in. No, she didn't feel used, although spending last night alone had told her she was not as brave and sure in this as she'd insisted to Emily or to her mother.

Love had got her on that plane.

Love had seen her follow him up those stairs to his office and wrap herself around him.

And he would never want it.

Sebastián spoke. 'I was thinking yesterday that I am just like my mother. Cold and—'

'You're not.'

'Sometimes I am,' he said.

'Sometimes you have to be,' Anna answered.

She was thinking of herself. Thinking how hard it was going to be in the future...visiting her friend, keeping things polite between them. Because she couldn't drag her heart through this again. She would have to learn from him and be cold too.

'Sebastián...' She took a sip of lukewarm water from her plastic bottle and wondered how to say what she had to. 'I'm going to be bringing Willow here in the future...'

'I know.'

'I don't want to confuse her.'

'Of course not—but in what way do you mean?'

'"Mummy's friend came to the beach in a black suit..."'

She watched him give a small smile and then she looked away. She stared at the beautiful blue ocean and listened to the laughter in the air, felt the breeze in the glorious, beautiful moment—and yet there was one thing missing.

'You see, I want to kiss you,' she admitted.

'I'd like that,' he said. 'But you won't do it.'

'No.'

'And I like it that you won't,' Sebastián said. 'I like it that you put Willow first. What did you tell her about coming here? That it was to see the baby?'

'No, I told her my friend had lost his father.'

Her eyes sparkled with the effort of trying to keep the love she felt for him locked in her heart, hidden from everyone. She was exhausted by constantly calling him a friend. There was no one in the world she'd have done this for—except perhaps Emily.

'What about your parents?' he asked.

'The same.' She gave a tight shrug. 'I asked them to bring her out, but no. It's fine. She's having a great time.'

'Is she still speaking Scottish?'

'Spanish now.' Anna smiled. 'How was the rest of last night?'

'Pretty grim,' he said. 'I had to tell Carmen that Maria has been left the family home. I promised her we'd fight it.'

Anna looked out at the ocean, trying not to let him see that it hurt her that he'd rather face all that alone than with her.

'Oh, and I was wrong,' he added. 'There *was* dancing. Maria kicked things off. In my father's memory, of course…'

'She really can't help herself, can she?'

'No.' He sat down on the lounger beside her. 'Anna, it was hell…'

'It sounds it.'

'No, growing up with her, I mean. She left, and then came back, then left again. I think I was eight when I swore off marriage for life.'

'I can see why…'

'So if we do this, then we have to do it right.'

She frowned.

'*I* have to do this right,' he said. 'Because the most important person in this isn't either of us.' He nodded to where Willow was playing. 'Could you see her being happy here?'

'Here?'

'Well, in Jerez. Because we need to know what we want before we tell her...'

'Tell her?'

'I love you, Anna, and it would seem we're no longer a secret.'

'Then why did you send me away?' she flared. 'You're grieving and upset. Please don't say you love me if you're going to take it back tomorrow morning.'

'I love you.'

She knew that tone, and her eyes flew to his. If anyone else had heard his terse words they might think the delivery odd, but she knew him better.

That abrupt tone was calming to her heart.

His decision was made.

'I don't think it's a complete guess that you feel the same. I don't think you'd be here otherwise—and certainly not with Willow. I had time to think last night. Look, I know I'm not ideal father material... I mean, I'm not brilliant with children...' He grimaced. 'I don't know any.'

'I happen to think you're brilliant with children,' Anna said. 'And with teenagers and troubled young women.' She looked at him. 'You told your father what I said about Carmen's riding?'

'He would have said the wrong thing otherwise. But he always steps up in the end. *Stepped.*' He closed his eyes.

'I think you've been a parent for a very long time,' Anna said. 'Since the age of ten.'

'Will you marry me, Anna?'

It was so sudden, and it came out of nowhere. And just as she caught her breath there was more.

'And, if you agree, I would like to make Willow an official cousin to Josefa and adopt her.'

He misread her frown.

'Because Alejandro and I are brothers and our children should be cousins.'

'But you've always said you don't want children...'

'I don't want children with anyone other than you.'

'You haven't even met her yet.'

'I haven't met our future children either, and nor have you. But I know we'll love them. I never want Willow to feel she is not just as important.'

He took her breath away.

'What will I do with myself if I don't have things—family—to worry about?'

He gave her a smile in the sunlight. He was nervous, Anna realised. Certain of his love for her, but as yet uncertain of what might happen next.

'We can take it slowly,' he said. 'I have to be here for a while, to make sure Carmen and Maria don't burn the family home down. And then there is the business...'

She laughed, breathless.

'You did say you wanted a big family...' he added.

'I did.'

'Mine are hard work,' he warned. 'We won't foist everyone on Willow until you think she's ready, and we'll have to sort out where we live, but—'

'Hola!'

Anna turned at the sound of her daughter's voice and smiled as she approached with Dali, who had taught her a few words of Spanish.

'Hola!' Sebastián said. 'You must be Willow.'

'Yes.' She looked up at him. 'Are you Mummy's friend whose daddy died?'

'I am.' He nodded. 'Sebastián. Pleased to meet you.'

Willow stared at him suspiciously for a moment, and Anna watched her clever girl quietly working things out.

Then, 'Are you Mummy's boyfriend?'

Anna watched Sebastián blink at the very direct question,

and before he could respond with a carefully constructed denial Anna settled for the truth.

'Yes,' Anna said, and held her breath, waiting for her daughter's response.

'Okay!' Willow said, and then turned to Dali. 'Can we have one more play in the water?'

A laughing Dali took Willow's hand and they both ran off, leaving a rather stunned couple sitting on the sun loungers.

'That went rather too well,' Anna said.

'I never thought I'd be called a boyfriend!'

'We don't have to take it slowly,' Anna turned to him, and reached over and took his hand. 'I love you so much.'

And in a complicated situation, at least one decision was easy.

'My parents will only want Willow for holidays. My family is here. *Our* family.'

'You're sure?'

'I won't tell her today, but, yes, I think so.' She looked at Willow and then back to him. 'It's the right choice.'

'You know that old Chinese saying…'

'Which one?'

She gave a vague frown—a pathetic attempt at a lie, because she still did not want to admit that it had been her screensaver for months, that she knew it off by heart and she read it every morning and again at night. A girl had some pride!

When the shoe fits, the foot is forgotten; when the belt fits, the belly is forgotten; and when the heart is right, 'for' and 'against' are forgotten. No drives, no compulsions, no needs, no attractions: Then your affairs are under control. You are a free man.

'I don't agree with Zhuangzi on everything,' Sebastián mused. 'Certainly there are needs and attractions. But with you…' he looked deeply into her eyes '…the heart is right.'

She nodded.

Her heart felt right too.

EPILOGUE

PUERTO BANÚS *LOVED* a wedding! There were cheers and whistles as the very blushing bride stepped out of the car to walk along the marina to the waiting yacht.

Anna wore a silver shot-silk dress that was high at the front and then dipped at the back.

Willow wore the awful green flamenco dress that Emily had brought back from her first trip to Spain.

And a mantilla.

As well as that she carried a fan and smiled at the cheers and waves of the people.

'I'm so excited,' Anna said—because it wasn't nervousness she felt, just utter joy as she and Emily held Willow's hands as they made their happy way to the boat.

'Welcome aboard,' said a smiling Dante. 'Everything is ready.'

'Thank you, Dante.'

'You look stunning,' he said—and not just to the bride, but to the delighted five-year-old who really was having her day of days and would soon be spending precious time with her grandparents while Anna and Sebastián enjoyed their honeymoon...

It turned out that Anna's parents really did want lots of holidays with Willow! And they'd surprised Anna by suggesting that instead of having a wedding in the village she and Sebastián should marry in Spain, with her father there to give a blessing.

'We could have Willow for a few nights while you go on your honeymoon,' her mother had said, as Sebastián had sat on their sofa drinking tea, having first asked permission for his daughter's hand from Anna's father.

Anna had never envisaged a honeymoon, and certainly not a wedding on a yacht, but now she relaxed in the cool saloon, sipping icy water beside an impatient Willow.

'How much longer?'

'Too long!' Anna laughed, because she was as impatient as her daughter, but eventually the engines slowed as the yacht reached its destination and the moment she had never thought would be hers was here.

'Good luck,' Emily said, and gave her a hug. 'I'm so happy and...' She moved her head in and whispered, 'I was so wrong about Sebastián.'

'He says the same about you!' Anna said, and they shared a laugh. Friends for ever.

She climbed the steps very carefully, not wanting to make an inelegant entrance, and as she stepped onto the deck she stopped for a moment to take it all in.

Everyone she loved was there: her parents, smiling widely when they saw little Willow, Carmen looking pale but smiling, about to head for America, Alejandro holding a still-tiny Josefa...

And there was one person whom she didn't love...

Maria wore a *lot* of black ruffles and a black lace mantilla, and she held a black fan. However, she wore suitable shoes for the yacht. Sebastián had not cut her out, but he was keeping a close watch.

Even Maria's presence couldn't unsettle Anna today, because she felt as calm as the gorgeous Mediterranean. A beautiful stillness and peace filled her as she took a breath and looked to Sebastián.

Her captain.

The captain of his family and the captain of her heart.

He wore a dark suit and a gunmetal-grey tie, and his buttonhole was lavender from her tiny garden, where she'd sat so many nights, looking at the sky and thinking of Emily's wedding night and how reckless she'd been...

But perhaps she had been wise to follow her heart?

If today proved anything it was surely that.

He smiled as she walked towards him, and then he smiled for a certain little lady who really was the belle of the ball.

'Willow,' he said, 'you're stealing the show!' He turned to his bride and said in a whisper, 'Maria is jealous of a five-year-old.' Then he looked at Anna and he gave her the smile he saved just for her. 'You look wonderful.'

'You do too,' Anna replied.

He was still not a demonstrative man in public, and he would not be reading her poetry any time soon, but his next words were for her alone, and she knew exactly what they meant. She understood that they told her of the deep well of his love for her.

'Anna...' Sebastián took her hands and she had never seen him more serious. His voice was absolutely clear. 'I love you. You have been there for me, and I promise I shall always be there for you. And for Willow.'

And even if the guests wanted more, Anna didn't need it. She knew that she had his love, that he would always be there for the people he loved.

'Always,' he emphasised, with such sincerity that it brought tears to her eyes.

'Sebastián...' She took a breath and collected herself. 'Se-bastián,' she said again, in a clearer voice. 'You made me smile the very moment I met you...'

She thought back to that day when she had walked out of the airport and smiled at the memories, and thought of all the memories still to be made.

'I will love you for the rest of my life.' She felt his hand tighten around hers and she looked right into his eyes. 'And I can't wait to share that life with you.'

Then her father forgot he wasn't officiating, and gave a long, droning speech before finally giving the blessing.

And then the celebrant read some strange Chinese quote about feet and bellies, and the bemused gathering shot sideways glances at each other.

The newly married couple knew what it meant, though.

Sebastián and Anna knew that this was *their* love.

* * * * *

HER DIAMOND DEAL WITH THE CEO

LOUISE FULLER

MILLS & BOON

CHAPTER ONE

STEADYING HERSELF ON the pale golden sand, Ondine breathed in deeply. Dipper's Beach was too narrow and steep for the tourists who flocked to the Florida coastline so, aside from the occasional crab and the seagulls that stalked the shoreline, it was almost always deserted.

But she preferred it like that.

It was the first time in nearly three weeks that she wasn't working so she could have had a lie-in this morning. Only her brain had jerked awake as it always did, one minute before her alarm went off. She could have rolled over and gone back to sleep, but she loved the early mornings when the sun was turning the sky above her beach house shell-pink. It was the one time of day she could call her own. When she wasn't working.

She squinted upwards. At work, there was never time to pause or linger. But here on the beach nobody would be trying to catch her eye or snapping their fingers. There was just the sun, the sky and an endless blue sea.

Her gaze narrowed on the shimmering water framed between the grass-edged dunes.

As a child, she was average at most things but swimming had been her 'superpower'. The one thing she'd excelled at in a family of high achievers. Every day she'd trained before school and almost every weekend she'd swum in competitions. Briefly, ludicrously, she'd even imagined herself stepping onto a podium but then she'd got injured and nowadays she swam for pleasure and for her job as a lifeguard at Whitecaps, the exclusive beachside hotel in Palm Beach favoured by the wealthy and beautiful.

Not that she got a chance to use her skills very often.

Unlike the public pool where she'd worked before, most of the Whitecaps residents preferred to lounge by the pool rather than swim in it, and the same was true of the hotel's private stretch of beach.

It was her second year at the hotel and now, as well as being a lifeguard, she worked most evenings as a waitress in the bar and restaurant. Her mouth twisted. She didn't hate either of her jobs; it just wasn't how she'd pictured her life. Two jobs. Two divorces. Living in some rented beach shack—

But the tips were phenomenal, and thanks to Vince, her useless second ex-husband, that mattered more than job satisfaction.

Thinking about the pile of brown envelopes sitting on her kitchen counter, she felt her stomach knot. Sometimes, normally after a particularly exhausting shift, she tried to work out how many glasses she would have to collect before she would be debt-free. Mostly though she was too tired to do anything but eat a bowl of pasta or, more lately, cereal and go to bed.

'Hola, Ondine. Cómo está hoy?'

Spinning round, Ondine smiled at the elderly woman with pristine grey hair who was walking towards her. Dolores was her nearest neighbour and even though she was eighty-one years old, she walked her fawn-coloured chihuahua, Hercules, along the beach twice every day.

'Are you swimming today, *chica*? But you have the day off, no?'

'*Hola*, Dolores. Hi, Herc.' She double-kissed the older woman's cheeks, then reached down to stroke the little dog's velvety ears. 'I'm not in until this evening, but I thought I'd get up and have a swim, and now I'm glad I did.' Her eyes tracked down the empty beach. 'It's so beautiful and peaceful today.'

'Not so peaceful last night.' Glancing out to the beautiful white yacht anchored close to the shoreline, Dolores clicked her tongue disapprovingly so that the dog's chin jerked upwards. 'Such noise. Music and shouting. All kinds of goings-on. Some people are so thoughtless.' She sniffed. 'Anyway, you enjoy your swim, *chica*.'

'Thanks, Dolores. See you tomorrow. Bye, Herc.' She smiled as Dolores waved the chihuahua's tiny paw.

Out at the sea, the yacht danced lightly on the waves.

Once upon a time it might have impressed her, but she worked in Palm Beach. There were as many yachts as there were palm trees.

Unzipping her hoodie, she pushed her shorts down her thighs and kicked off her flip-flops. The sand was like warm sugar and for a moment she just stood there, wiggling her toes. 'That man is richest whose pleasures are cheapest.' That was something her mum used to say but it was hard to feel rich when your kitchen counter was piled high with unpaid bills.

Her feet stilled. She should have kept a closer eye on Vince. She knew he liked to spend money but she hadn't wanted to admit to herself that she had messed up again. Married the wrong man, *again*.

Her eyes fixed on the yacht, her heart thumping heavily against her ribs as she remembered the end of her first marriage. Garrett's infidelity had been humiliating, devastating, but she could have coped, had been coping. Only then, three weeks later, before she had plucked up the courage to tell them she was getting divorced, her parents had died in a car crash.

She shivered in the warm breeze. Overnight, she had become an orphan, and her fifteen-year-old brother's guardian. She'd moved back to Florida to look after Oliver, and a month later, she'd met Vince at the hardware store. He'd made her laugh and when he'd asked her out, he'd made her laugh again. When he'd taken her out, he'd made her feel sexy.

It was a textbook rebound relationship, but that hadn't stopped her saying *yes* when Vince had proposed. A year later, the marriage had been over, confirming, as if she'd needed further proof, that she was not the marrying kind. This time her pride had taken less of a hit but she'd lost her home, and she was still paying off the credit-card bills.

The one small sliver of silver in the cloud of debt was that Oliver's college fund was tied up in some savings plan. She felt some of the tightness in her chest loosen. Unlike her, Oli knew exactly what he wanted to be and he had the brains and the determination to make it happen. Right now, he was volunteering at an outreach clinic in Costa Rica before he started medical school in September.

She frowned, her gaze snagging on the yacht.

There was someone on deck. Not someone. A man wearing a dark jacket and trousers, his white shirt loose around his throat. She watched as he crouched down and picked up a bottle, shook it and then raised his arm, crooking his elbow as if he was about to hurl it into the sea.

'Don't you dare,' she whispered.

As if he had heard her, the man looked up, and she felt a flicker of something hot and tingling like electricity snap up her spine. He couldn't see her face. She knew that because she couldn't see his, but she could see his powerful body silhouetted against the sky, sunlight clinging to his outline, gilding him in a wash of clear gold like a character in an F. Scott Fitzgerald novel.

The bottle dangled from his fingertips and then he let it fall onto the deck, straightened up and shrugged off his jacket with a conscious carelessness that made her whole body stiffen with dislike and envy.

Her mouth curled into something midway between a sneer and a scowl. It was the same gesture favoured by the hotel's trust-fund-financed clientele when they tossed tips onto the bar or used towels by their loungers.

Picturing their expensive winter tans and inherited Rolexes, she narrowed her eyes on the man as he walked across the deck. And then her pulse jerked as without warning he spun round and took a running jump over the rippling sea. There was a moment of absolute silence as he flew through the air and then he hit the water with an audible splash.

What the—?

She felt her body tense, her hand reaching up automatically for the float over her shoulder. Except it wasn't there because she wasn't at work.

Swearing softly, she moved towards the curling waves at the shoreline. She had spent the whole of spring break watching privileged young men clown around in the water. But did they have to do it when she was off duty?

Eyes fixed on the spot where he had disappeared beneath the waves, she began counting the distance in strokes as the seconds passed.

Surely he should have surfaced by now.

She was running into the sea before her brain understood the implication of that thought, barely registering the water as it splashed over her thighs, and then she was swimming, her body slicing through the surf, eyes scanning the waves, all of her training no longer theoretical but becoming in an instant so real that there was no room for panic or emotion.

What was that?

She saw a flash of gold, and then just as quickly it was gone again.

Breathing in sharply, she ducked beneath the waves, and her heart gave a huge leap forward just as the man had done moments earlier. There he was, his white shirt dazzlingly bright beneath the water, his hands reaching up.

Seconds later she reached him, her arm moved automatically around his chest and she pulled him to the surface, tilting back his head and kicking towards the shoreline. Breathing unsteadily, she dragged him onto the sand and now she saw the front of his shirt was not white but patterned.

No, not patterned. Those were bloodstains.

Over the sound of her heartbeat, she heard the voice of her instructors. *'Always start with your ABCs. Check the airways. Two breaths as soon as the victim is stable in the water or on land, then move into thirty compressions.'*

Her body was shuddering from the swim and the adrenaline but her mind was clear. Sliding two fingers under his chin, she tilted back his head, pinched his nose, put her lips to his mouth and put a breath in, waited then put a second breath in—

The man coughed, and she rolled him onto his side, and he lay there, breathing raggedly, his hand fluttering against the sand.

'It's okay, you're okay.' She squeezed his shoulder. 'You got into trouble, but you're safe now.'

Was he? She stared down at him, her heart beating like a train. The bloodstains looked shockingly vivid against the white cotton and she began unbuttoning his shirt, her hands rough with fear as she checked for injury.

'What are you doing?'

His voice was hoarse from swallowing seawater but hearing him speak cut through her panic and steadied her.

'You have blood on your shirt. I need to—'

He waved his hand dismissively. 'You don't need to worry about that. There was a fight last night, I tried to break it up—' Now he touched his mouth and she saw that there was a cut on his lip that she hadn't noticed before. 'Got punched for my efforts—'

He shivered, his arm dropping to cover his eyes and, frowning, she reached over and grabbed her hoodie and laid it over his chest. 'Should have had you there,' he mumbled. 'You must be pretty strong to pull me out of the water like that.'

'It's my job. I'm a lifeguard.'

So do your job, she told herself, tearing her gaze from his curving mouth. Taking his wrist, she felt his pulse. It was steady, she thought with relief. 'Do you have any alcohol or drugs in your system?'

'What?' He frowned. 'No, nothing—'

Remembering the bottle, she stared down at him uncertainly, but he was breathing and his pulse was firm and they could check him over at the hospital.

'Okay, well, everything is going to be fine. All you need to do is stay where you are. I'm going to go get some help—'

She didn't want to leave him alone but the chances of help turning up on the beach were slim to none. Her shoulders tensed. If only she had brought her phone, but it was sitting on the kitchen counter.

'No.' His hand clamped around her wrist, surprisingly strong. 'I don't need help. I have help. You're a lifeguard—'

'But I'm not a doctor.' She spoke calmly but firmly as she'd been taught. 'Look, I just live over there. I'm going to run back to my house and call the EMS and they'll come and check you out.'

For a moment she thought he was going to argue. It was a fairly common response. People, men particularly, were often embarrassed at being 'rescued' but medical opinion on the protocol for post-near-drownings was clear. Anyone requiring any form of resuscitation needed to be evaluated by a healthcare provider, even if they appeared alert with good breathing and a strong pulse.

'Fine. Whatever.' He let go of her arm, waving his hand in the same dismissive way as before.

Reaching for her shorts, she pulled them on and got to her feet. 'I'll be five minutes, tops. Just sit tight and try not to worry. It really is just precautionary. My name is Ondine, by the way.'

'Jack.' He shifted back against the sand, his eyes still closed. 'Jack Walcott.'

I know who you are.

She almost spoke the words out loud and her face felt suddenly hot.

Jack Walcott was the heir to the Walcott energy empire. He was also a guest at Whitecaps. In a hotel filled with beautiful, indolent people, he was the most beautiful. A baby-faced billionaire with dirty-blond hair, eyes the colour of pirate gold and a face of such absurdly perfect proportions and symmetry that it was hard not to simply stare and keep on staring.

And he knew it.

How could he not? Jack Walcott was movie-star-gorgeous with a smile that could tip the planet into meltdown.

Her mouth thinned. He was also hedonistic, self-indulgent

and arrogant. Lolling on a lounger in a pair of plain blue swim shorts designed to highlight his smooth gold skin and curving muscles, he had looked straight through her. And on the days when he'd eaten in the restaurant, he hadn't so much as glanced up from his steak when she'd brought him the mustard he'd requested. To him, she was just staff. One of the many minions paid to meet his every need.

But he would have to be in a trance or unconscious not to notice the effect he had on people. How they craned their necks to watch him walk by, elbowed their neighbours, whispered behind their hands.

Her eyes dropped irresistibly to the contoured lines of his stomach, and now she didn't just want to stare, she wanted to touch, stroke, scratch—

She felt her fingers twitch and, aware of the impropriety of her response, she clamped her hands tightly to her hips and got to her feet.

'I'll be right back, Jack,' she said quickly. His eyes stayed shut.

She ran across the sand and was halfway up the dunes when something made her look back over her shoulder to check on him. Her mouth fell open. Jack Walcott was not where she'd left him. He wasn't even lying down. He was walking along the beach, her hoodie draped across his shoulders, moving with a slow, languid grace that made her feel light-headed. Swearing under her breath, she ran back towards him.

'Hey—'

He turned, his blond hair flopping across his forehead. His shirt was almost dry now so that instead of sticking to his skin it was lifting in the breeze, revealing even more of the spectacular body beneath. She glared up into his face to stop herself from looking.

'Haven't you forgotten something?'

His eyes narrowed into the sunlight.

'Oh, yeah, my bad. Here.' The gold signet ring on his little finger glinted as he unpeeled her hoodie from around his shoulders and draped it over hers.

'That's not what I meant,' she snapped, and now finally he looked at her. Really looked at her in a way that made her feel suddenly and intensely conscious of herself, of the rise and fall of her breasts, the heavy thud of her heart, the tightness of her skin.

The gold of his eyes was steady but then something rippled beneath the flawless features, like the tremors that preceded an earthquake, almost as if he could feel her reaction, as if he was feeling it too—

Afterwards, she would wonder who made the first move. Perhaps he leaned forward or maybe she lost her footing but one moment she was glaring up at him, the next their lips were brushing and there was an emptiness in her stomach like hunger, only it was a hunger she had never felt.

His mouth was soft and warm and teasing and, dissolving with desire, she felt his hand slide round her waist and then heat was seeping through her limbs so that it was impossible not to melt against him, unthinkable not to press her body against the hard muscles of his chest.

His lips parted hers, stirring her, and she kissed him back, tasting salt and a hunger that matched her own and all the while her body was melting, her defences softening—

She breathed in sharply, and, heart hammering, she stumbled backwards. 'What the hell do you think you're doing?'

It was a good question, particularly because it meant that she didn't have to ask herself what she was doing kissing someone she had just pulled out of the sea. 'You can't just go around kissing people.'

Tilting back his head, he looked down at her. 'To be fair, you kissed me first,' he said softly.

'What I did was give you CPR. Now what are you doing?' she said breathlessly as he began backing away from her.

'I'm going back to my hotel.'

'No, you're not.' With an effort, she fought to keep her voice under control. 'You shouldn't be going anywhere, particularly on your own. That's why I told you to stay where you were.'

He shrugged. 'I got bored.'

Bored?

She could feel her nostrils flaring, and her heart was banging hard against her ribs. 'You need to see a doctor.'

'I am.' He frowned. 'Or rather I was.' He stared down at her, his beautiful mouth changing shape again, the corners curving up into a mocking smile that made her heart beat painfully fast. 'As of last night, I'm pretty sure I'm single again.'

She spoke without thinking. 'If you treat your partners with as little respect as you do your own welfare, I can't say I'm surprised.'

He stared at her in silence.

'Is that right?' The smile had vanished. 'I thought you said I needed a doctor, not a psychiatrist.' He made another of those dismissive gestures; he seemed to have an endless supply of them at his fingertips. 'Look, I'm sure you mean well, Odette, but I'm really tired, and right now I don't need a lecture, I just want to go to bed.' As if to prove his point, he yawned, extending his arms above his head, his spine curving like a cat.

'It's Ondine not Odette, and right now, you shouldn't be on your own,' she said stiffly.

His eyes were looking directly into hers. 'In bed?'

She felt her cheeks grow hot. In fact, her whole body felt as if it were on fire.

'I couldn't agree more.' The gleam in his eyes made the air leave her lungs. 'Are you offering to join me?' The mocking smile dented his cheek again. 'If so, we should probably go back to your place. It's closer.'

'I'm not offering to join you, and there is no "we",' she snapped.

He tilted his head back. 'I'm just messing with you—'

'Because this isn't a big enough mess?' She glared at him. 'You might feel fine now, but lung complications are surprisingly common after near-drownings. Chemical imbalances can develop, irregular heart rhythms can occur—'

'Okay, okay.' He held up his hands. 'I get it. But you don't need to call an ambulance. I have a car at the hotel. I can drive myself.'

Fighting an urge to roll her eyes, she shook her head. 'No, you can't.' And he probably wouldn't, she thought, remembering how he had walked off down the beach the moment she had turned her back. 'Which is why I'm going to take you myself.'

He was frowning down at her, his eyes searching her face almost as if she had suddenly started speaking gibberish. 'Why would you do that?'

'I told you. You need to see a doctor, and I don't trust you to do the right thing,'

'Impressive,' he said softly. 'It usually takes people way longer to work that out about me.'

Their eyes met and, ignoring the lurch of her pulse, she said, 'You need some shoes. We can pick some up at the house. And I'll grab my phone. Then you can call whoever you need to call to tell them you're okay. It's this way.' And without waiting, she turned and stalked away across the sand.

Five minutes later they were juddering along the road in her old in-need-of-a-clean Honda Civic. Beside her, Jack filled his chair; filled the entire car, all long muscular legs and square shoulders.

'If I didn't need to go to the hospital before, I will now,' he grumbled, wincing as she accelerated past a pizza delivery scooter. 'This feels like I'm riding a jet ski on dry land.'

'It needs new shock absorbers,' she said crisply. 'But you won't have to put up with it for long.' There were four hospitals within driving distance of her house, but she knew without asking which one to take him to. Solace Health was the private medical centre favoured by the rich and famous. There were orchids on the reception desk and, instead of disinfectant, it smelled of orange blossom and money.

'Do you mean the Solace?' He frowned. 'Isn't there another hospital?'

'Yes, but they're further away. And they're not private, which means there'll be more people there. Which means you'll have to wait,' she added, when he didn't react.

He shrugged. 'I don't mind waiting.'

She stared at him impatiently, remembering the imperious way he clicked his fingers at the poolside, but before she could respond he reached over and plucked her sunglasses from her nose and slid them in front of his eyes. She blinked as his fingers grazed her cheek. His touch was as light as the grass that brushed against her bare legs out on the dunes, only the grass never made her skin grow hot and tight.

'I'd rather wait than go to the Solace.' He frowned. 'They know me there. Know my family. I don't need any more drama.'

That she could believe, she thought, as they returned to the car an hour later.

She had told herself that it was his money and air of entitlement that made people react to him as they did, but, slouched against the reception desk in borrowed flip-flops and with half his face hidden behind her sunglasses, Jack Walcott had still created a stir. There was something about him that had made the air in the waiting room shiver with anticipation.

The doctor, a tired-looking man with greying hair, had given Jack the all-clear. But then he'd turned to Ondine and said, 'You need to keep an eye on your husband, Mrs Walcott. He needs rest but I would sit with him while he sleeps. Any difficulties in breathing, change in colour or if it's hard to wake him up, come straight back in.'

'She will—won't you, honey?' Jack had said, his eyes gleaming. 'She's a great wife. I'm a very lucky man.'

She should have corrected him but instead she'd found herself nodding. 'Yes, I can do that.'

'I'll drop you back at Whitecaps,' she said now, reversing out of the space. 'You have someone there who can keep an eye on you, don't you?'

His eyes rested on her face. 'How do you know where I'm staying?'

She swore silently but there was no way to backtrack. 'I work there,' she said finally, looking up to meet his gaze. 'I recognised you.'

He leaned back, his pupils flaring. 'I thought you seemed familiar.' His forehead creased. It gave him a puppyish air that she found immensely irritating. Or rather she found it irritating the way her body responded.

'I'm one of the lifeguards,' she said stiffly. 'You probably saw me at the pool or the beach.' Hands tightening around the wheel, she turned into the oncoming traffic. 'Or maybe in the restaurant.'

'They have lifeguards in the restaurant. Wow!' He raised

one eyebrow. 'Those soup bowls must be deeper than they look.'

He didn't need any encouragement, she knew that, and she tried to stop herself from smiling but her mouth had a mind of its own and she felt it curve upwards despite her wishes.

'I work as a waitress too. In the evenings.'

'So when do you get time off?'

It was a simple question but he made it feel complicated. Flustered, she said, 'Now. This is my day off.' And instantly regretted it as his gold eyes fixed on her face, curious and assessing.

'And you decided to spend it with me. I'm flattered.'

'Don't be,' she said quickly, pressing the air conditioning button with fingers that were suddenly shaky and incompetent. 'I'd do the same for anyone.'

That was true, she told herself firmly, only she could feel colour creeping over her cheeks and collarbone. Worse, she knew that Jack could see what she was feeling, but there was nothing she could do about that.

'If you say so,' he murmured. He shifted back against his seat, stretching out his legs. 'So why do you have two jobs? Seems very greedy. I mean, I don't even have one.'

There was an edge beneath the languid drawl she didn't understand but then she didn't want to understand Jack Walcott. Nor, more importantly, did he need to understand her.

She shrugged. 'I have a lot of outgoings.'

That was the short answer. The longer, more humiliating version was that she had let an idiot be in charge of her money. But she wasn't about to share that particular fact with Jack Walcott.

'Why not focus on one job, and get promoted?' He tipped his head back, letting the sun fall across his face. 'Or you could marry the boss,' he said, pushing her glasses back along his nose.

She glared at him. Spoken like a man who didn't need to earn a living. 'How wonderfully progressive of you. But I don't want to marry my boss.' She didn't want to marry anyone. She'd made the same mistake twice. She didn't need to do it again. 'Besides, marriage only works for men.'

'Not this man.' His fingers tapped out a rhythm against the door seal. 'I like my freedom.'

'I'm sure you do. I'm just saying that statistically marriage is good for men. They live longer. And they earn more because people think they're more dedicated, responsible, mature.'

Clearly they hadn't met her ex-husbands, she thought, flipping the indicator stalk up with unnecessary force.

'You mean, even when they're none of those things?'

Jack was looking at her. His eyes were shielded by her sunglasses but she could feel his focus.

'I suppose, yes.'

'So how does flip-flop man fit into that?'

'Who?' She glanced over at him, frowning, momentarily distracted from the traffic.

'The guy whose shoes I'm wearing.'

She had forgotten all about the flip-flops. 'Oh, those... they belong to my little brother. He lives with me.'

'Little?' He raised an eyebrow.

'I meant little in age, not size.'

Thinking about Oliver, she felt some of the tension of the morning drop from her body. He had been taller than her since he was thirteen years old. Now, at nineteen, he was six feet two, broad and handsome like their dad but with their mother's smile. He was the one good thing in her life. The one thing she hadn't messed up.

'How does your boyfriend feel about living with your kid brother?'

She felt her body still. There was one of two ways she could answer that question. Tell him the truth, which was that she was single. Or tell him that it was none of his business, but if she did that he would think she was single anyway.

'I don't have a boyfriend.' His blond hair was fluttering in the breeze and she tried to make her voice sound as casual as he looked. Oliver was the only man in her life right now, and, given her track record with men, it would be safer for it to stay that way.

'But as we're discussing partners, there is going to be someone who can sit with you while you sleep—'

'Isn't that your turn?'

'What? No—'

Caught off guard, she glanced towards him, shaking her head, but he was already reaching over to take hold of the steering wheel, jerking it left into the oncoming traffic. There was a blaring, overlapping eruption of horns.

'What is wrong with you?' She pushed his hand from the wheel. 'Do you have some sort of death wish?'

'You were going the wrong way.'

'The hotel is in that direction,' she snapped.

'Yeah, about that.' Flopping back in his seat, he screwed up his face. 'I could do with keeping this little episode off the radar so I was thinking I might come back to yours.'

CHAPTER TWO

SERIOUSLY?

Slamming her foot on the brakes, Ondine turned sharply to face him. 'Come back to mine?'

She could see her distorted reflection in the lens of her sunglasses, and irritably she reached over and snatched them from his face.

'Calm down,' he protested. 'I didn't mean it like that—'

A vivid image of what 'that' might look like with Jack popped into her head and she blinked it away. In the rear-view mirror, she could see the driver behind them mouthing something. 'Don't tell me to calm down—'

'I'm sorry.' Jack leaned forward, his golden eyes fixing on her face. 'I just don't want to go back to Whitecaps looking like this.' He gestured towards his bloodstained shirt. 'They're no different from the Solace. Someone will call my grandfather and I don't need him getting upset.'

Behind them, the driver had decided to reiterate his frustration by pressing his horn repeatedly. She watched Jack turn, a muscle pulsing in his cheek, and abruptly the hooting stopped.

'Look, I know I was a jerk earlier, and you probably want to get shot of me, but I really need somewhere to sleep for a couple of hours. On my own, just to be clear,' he added.

Ondine stared at him, her hands tightening around the steering wheel to steady herself. He was right. She did want to get shot of him. Because Jack Walcott was a dare and a temptation all wrapped up like the most beautiful present under a Christmas tree. And because she could still feel the imprint of his mouth on hers. Only where would he go if she said no?

As if sensing her weakness, he locked eyes with hers. 'Please, Ondine.'

For a few, unravelling seconds, her heart clenched. It was the first time he had used her name, and for some reason it sounded different when he said it. He made her feel different.

She gritted her teeth. He wasn't her responsibility. There was nothing in the American Lifeguard Association training programme to prepare her for having a man like Jack Walcott in her house. But there was a tension in his voice, a strain that wrenched at something inside her so that she heard herself say, 'Fine. You can come back to my house. *To sleep.* And it's just for a couple of hours.'

'Thank you,' he said softly.

She could do this, she thought as the car moved forward. It was just a couple of hours, and then Jack would leave and life would go back to how it was before.

As soon as he lay down on the bed, Jack fell asleep.

He slept, and he dreamed only it didn't feel like dreaming. It felt as though he were still awake, and he were on the yacht again, turning to run and jump, only Ondine was frowning at him in that precise, focused way of hers, her blue eyes steadying him as she took his wrist and felt for his pulse and then her hands were sliding over his shoulders, mouth fitting against his, warm and soft and—

Rolling onto his back, he blinked open his eyes.

The curtains were drawn but there was a gap the width of a tie and he could see the sun hanging high in the sky like an orange waiting to be picked and squeezed.

Feeling suddenly thirsty, he sat up, his gaze moving slowly around the room.

Aside from its tidiness, which was probably due to the absence of its usual occupant, it was a typical teenage boy's bedroom. Miami Dolphins posters were tacked to the wall. There was a desktop computer with a bunch of games piled up beside it and a life-size replica skeleton dangled from the ceiling. Left over from Halloween, he thought as the curtains lifted in the breeze.

His eyes moved to the bookshelves, skimming over the sci-fi novels and academic textbooks to lock onto a framed photo. He stared at it for a moment, feeling his body tense, and then he got to his feet and reached over to pick it up.

He scanned the faces intently. There was no doubt who they were. Mum. Dad. Oliver. And Ondine. His fingers tightened against the glass. They were on one of those log-flume rides, the kind where you meandered along a waterway, rising up a hill before dropping at speed. The photo had been taken seconds after splashdown and their eyes were wide with shock and the thrill of it.

They looked happy.

They looked like a family.

He stared down at the photo, envy cut through with a twist of bitterness filling his gut. He had a family, two really since his parents' divorce and yet he wasn't a part of either of them. And he felt the misery and the shame of it rush over his head, pulling him under—

His gaze snagged on Ondine's face and he could almost feel the grip of her hand on his shoulder. She was strong, stronger than she looked. She had confidence in her body too as if she trusted it to do what she wanted it to. And once she had agreed to let him stay, she had been as calm and pragmatic as she had been on the beach and at the hospital, he thought, remembering how she had shown him into her brother's bedroom.

'You need to sleep.' She reached past him and folded back the duvet. 'You're exhausted.'

'What are you doing?' he asked as she dragged an old rattan armchair across the room.

'I'm keeping an eye on you.' Picking up a paperback book from the bedside table, she sat down, frowning at the cover.

'You don't have to do that.'

She gave a delicate shrug. 'I told the doctor I would.'

Their eyes met, hers wide and wary; he could see her pulse hammering against the pale, thin skin of her throat and he knew that she was remembering the moment in the hospital when he told that same doctor she was his wife.

'And you always do what you say you will.'

It wasn't a question, but she acted as if it were. 'Yes. If I say I'm going to do something, I do it.'

'For better, for worse, Mrs Walcott,' he murmured as he lay down.

Her expression shifted briefly, her face contracting or retreating in a way he couldn't put a finger on, but then that smile curved her mouth and she sat back in the chair and opened the book. 'Go to sleep, Jack.'

He had no memory of his eyes closing, but he could remember Ondine sitting in the armchair, the book in her hand.

But the chair was empty now. He felt a ripple of anger scud across his skin, and a disappointment that felt disproportionate. What happened to 'if I say I'm going to do something, I do it'?

His shoulders tensed. But should he really be that surprised? Plenty of people, people who had a far stronger duty of care for him than Ondine, had made promises they couldn't or wouldn't keep.

When it came to him anyway.

Only his grandfather had ever followed through. Chiv-vying him, coaxing him, *caring*. Abruptly, he put the frame down on the shelf, and as he did so he spotted it. A piece of paper, folded in half, with his name written in block capitals.

He picked it up and opened it.

Just popped out to get some milk. Back soon. Don't wander off. O

O.

He could see Ondine's mouth forming the shape of the let-ter just as it had on the beach when he'd draped the hoodie over her shoulders and suddenly his skin was prickling again.

Was that why he had kissed her? That mouth.

He frowned, his mind liquid, the memory swelling and changing direction like a raindrop sliding down a window-pane. Or had she kissed him?

Not that it mattered.

Ondine wasn't his type. Too serious, too snitty, plus she was seriously bossy, he thought, remembering how she had more or less frogmarched him into the medical centre. Looks-wise, her hair was a fairly boring mid-brown, her cheekbones a little too pronounced, and those startlingly blue eyes seemed to be permanently narrowed in his direc-tion so that he shouldn't have found her beautiful and yet—

That mouth.

Great legs too. A pulse of heat danced across his skin as he remembered her toned calf muscles, that smooth skin.

He blinked the memory away. For him, that kiss was about the moment, not the woman. He had just nearly drowned; he'd needed to feel the warmth of breath, the firm-ness of lips, the pulse of life beating through him. And lust, desire, hunger, whatever name you gave it, was the opposite of those tenuous, liminal moments beneath the water. It was a sure thing, a talisman, as solid and real as any lifebelt.

And the reason his skin was tingling now when he thought about it was because of the salt. All he needed to do was shower and it would be as if nothing had ever happened.

The bathroom was next door. It was small—the elevator in his Manhattan apartment was larger—but the shower itself was surprisingly spacious, and there was a pile of clean towels folded on top of a wicker laundry basket.

Stripping off, he took a breath and stepped under the shower head, keeping the jet of water trained on his back.

He should have just stayed in the bar. He hadn't felt like partying and he hated boats. But everyone had wanted to go on the yacht. Plus, Carrie had stormed off by then and he hated being on his own more. If he was on his own then all those thoughts he usually had no trouble keeping at bay would come creeping out of the dark corners. Thoughts that made it impossible to sit still, because whenever you sat still they crept up and smothered you like a fog.

When he was a child everyone thought he had ADHD, and it was true that he shared some of the symptoms. But for him, it was elective. To keep moving was to keep one step ahead. He took risks too, like today. Stupid, pointless risks that flooded his body and brain with adrenaline. And if that wasn't an option then he partied because surrounding himself with people, acting as if he didn't care about what they or anyone else thought, made it easier to not think about his parents' rejection.

Except he did care what his grandfather thought.

Picking up the soap, he rubbed it over the muscles of his chest, feeling his heartbeat beneath his fingertips.

The world knew John D. Walcott IV as an oil tycoon.

The man who had turned a moderate family business into a household brand. A global company for the modern world. But to him, he was just Grandpa. Always there, always firm but fair; kind, tolerant, endlessly patient.

Until two months ago. When his patience had abruptly run out.

Even now he could picture the look of disappointment on his grandfather's familiar, lined face. And it was his fault.

Having come out of yet another meeting where his suggested investment in a renewables project had been long-grassed, he was feeling thwarted and frustrated at the Walcott Energy Corporation's snail's-pace transition to greener energy and so was careless and impatient, skim-reading a geological report rather than giving it the forensic attention it deserved before signing off on the deal.

Naturally, because not all the people employed by WEC were related to his grandfather, and therefore didn't have the luxury of letting their frustrations affect their work, the issue was spotted but by then it was too late. The paperwork was being processed and so the Canadians had to be paid off in order to terminate the deal.

To add insult to injury, when the proverbial hit the fan, he was partying in Turks and Caicos.

It was the last and very final straw for John D. Walcott IV.

He summoned his eldest grandchild to the WEC head office and told him bluntly that he needed to grow up. And that until he could demonstrate the maturity expected of an heir in waiting, the position of CEO was no longer his by birthright. As of immediate effect he was to step down from the board and clear his desk. His newly expanded free time should be spent evaluating his life, his lifestyle and his future.

Jack stared down at the water swirling into the plughole.

He had been shocked, disbelieving at first, then angry,

but above all else it had hurt, and far more than he could have imagined, to experience such cool objectivity where he had only been used to indulgent affection. After everything that had happened with his parents, he hadn't known he could still feel, still care, but he did, the more so because it was his fault, and because he hated knowing that he had let his grandfather down.

Of course his grandpa couldn't stay angry for long—

But disappointment was not the same as anger. His grandfather loved him but that didn't mean he trusted him. To become the next CEO, he was going to have to earn back that trust. Prove he could change. Make his grandfather proud.

His mouth twisted. So last night he had partied on a yacht, broken up with the woman he'd been seeing, and then jumped into the sea and nearly drowned.

Perfect. Good job, Jack!

He tipped his face up unthinkingly and water spilled into his eyes and he jerked away, his heart suddenly racing as he remembered the moment when the sea closed over his head. Breathing out unsteadily, he pressed the palms of his hands against the tiles, steadying his heartbeat, steadying himself as all the possible consequences of his actions slammed into him like a rogue wave.

Jumping off a yacht into the sea was by far the stupidest thing he'd ever done. Given that he couldn't swim, it was not just stupid but insanely dangerous.

He shivered. Except it hadn't felt dangerous at the time, just necessary. Seeing that photo of his mother with his half-brother, Penn, had made the familiar numbness start. He had felt himself disappearing and he had needed something to pull him back, something to fill the gap inside his chest. And so he'd jumped into the sea.

And the stupid thing was he had actually forgotten that

he couldn't swim. Or maybe not forgotten. It was more that it seemed implausible that was still true. That he hadn't simply learned by some kind of osmosis from all the people around him who could swim.

His stomach twisted painfully as he remembered the weight of the water, and the taste of fear in his mouth and his heartbeat filling his head—

Blanking his mind, he switched off the shower, dried himself and got dressed before making his way back to Oliver's bedroom. If only he had some actual shoes, he thought, sliding his feet back into the flip-flops, but at least his clothes were dry now, and the bloodstain on his shirt looked less vividly red.

'Good. You're awake.'

The light, husky voice knocked his train of thought off course and he turned. Ondine was standing in the doorway.

He felt his pulse change lanes and accelerate.

She had changed clothes. Now she was wearing a simple cotton dress that managed to both cover and reveal the shape of her body and even though he had told himself earlier that she wasn't his type, he had to make a conscious effort not to stare at her.

'I took a shower. You don't mind, do you?'

'Of course not. I left some towels out for you. And I thought you might want something to drink.' There was a glass of water in one hand and, judging by the steam spiralling upwards, a mug of something hot in the other.

'I didn't know what you like so I brought water and coffee. You should drink the water anyway,' she added, handing out both.

He screwed up his face. 'Didn't I drink enough earlier?'

It was the first time either of them had referred to what

happened and even though he had done so obliquely he felt the shock of it ripple through him.

'Yes, but that was salt water, so you need to rehydrate.' The careful neutrality of her voice matched the level expression on her face but there was a flicker of concern in her eyes. 'Do you have a headache? Any dizziness?'

Glancing down at the glass of water, he felt his stomach lurch, the moment when the sea had started to pull him down suddenly suffocatingly vivid inside his head.

'No, nothing. But I might start with the coffee first.'

He could no longer smell the salt on his skin but every time he breathed in, he could still taste the sea. Picking up the cup, he let the hot liquid scour his mouth and then he put the cup and the glass on the desk.

'He's studying medicine, isn't he? Your brother, I mean. How far along is he?'

She stared at him, her blue gaze level and assessing. *Unimpressed.* 'He hasn't started yet. He's on a gap year, doing medical outreach work in Costa Rica.' There was a brief silence, her obvious desire to keep her private life private vying with her curiosity. He felt a flicker of satisfaction as her curiosity won. 'How did you know he was studying medicine?'

'Elementary, my dear Mrs Walcott,' he said softly, his pulse skipping a beat as her eyes narrowed a fraction. 'The chemistry and biology textbooks, the cuddly chromosome—' leaning forward, he picked up the purple plush toy '—and of course our undernourished friend.' He gave the skeleton a gentle push. 'Where's he going?'

'Stanford.' A flush of colour seeped over her cheekbones. He could hear the pride in her voice and something pinched inside his chest. He couldn't imagine anyone sounding that way when they talked about him. Not even his grandfather.

At least not right now.

'Must be a smart kid.' Picking up his coffee, he took another sip. Ouch, he thought, wincing as the hot liquid made contact with the graze on his lip.

Her eyes arrowed in on his face. 'Do you want some antiseptic cream for that?'

He shook his head. 'I just need to be more careful.'

One fine dark eyebrow arched upwards. 'Sounds like a plan. So, what was the fight about?'

The fight? For a moment, he stared at her blankly. He had forgotten telling her that detail. Now, thinking back to it was like looking into the wrong end of a telescope. It seemed tiny and distant and unimportant.

'It was nothing—'

The evening had started well enough. They had gone to Blackjacks, and everyone had been dancing and drinking whisky sours. Everyone except him. He had wanted to, needed to, but that need had given him the willpower to stay on the soft drinks.

Only then Harry had pulled out some pills.

His shoulders tensed. He still wasn't entirely sure why, given that he had neither brought the drugs or taken them, but Harry's girlfriend, Lizzie, had got completely out of shape with him, kicking off about his 'attitude' and his 'behaviour', both of which were apparently substandard. To add insult to injury, Carrie had got involved. He couldn't remember every word but the gist of it was he was irresponsible, selfish, made poor life choices and she pitied his mother.

The tension in his shoulders spread down his spine. Even just hearing his mother mentioned had been enough to punch a hole through his chest.

That was when he'd known it was time to end things.

He felt Ondine's gaze on his face, and he tilted his head back to meet her eyes.

'Harry said something stupid about Sam's girlfriend, Maeve, and he should have just apologised but we'd all been partying pretty hard, and he was stoned, and Sam tried to hit Harry, but he punched me by mistake and the drinks went everywhere, and Maeve lost it completely and she ended up telling Harry's girlfriend Lizzie that he'd hooked up with some waitress last week—'

In other words, a fairly average night out. Only for some reason, the whole thing sounded appallingly silly and self-indulgent. He felt suddenly exhausted, as if he hadn't slept at all, and there was a weave of tension pulling his chest tight. To shake it off, he glanced over at Ondine and gave her a small, conspiratorial smile. 'Wasn't you, was it?'

She didn't laugh. Nor did she look upset or annoyed. Just stern.

'Excuse me?'

He held up his hands as he had done out on the beach. 'It was a joke.'

'A joke? You think lying to people is funny.' Two red spots of colour were burning high on her cheekbones.

Lying? He frowned. Maybe he had skimmed the truth but— 'I didn't lie.'

Her chin came up. 'I asked you at the beach and you said you hadn't taken anything. You told the doctor the same thing. Now you're telling me you'd all been "partying pretty hard".'

He felt a sting of impatience, and frustration at the injustice of her accusation. 'First off, Little Miss War-on-Drugs, who made you judge and jury? Secondly, I wasn't lying. I hadn't taken anything. Not that it's any of your business.'

'Right. That's why you jumped into the sea fully clothed, was it?'

Her eyes were the same clear blue as the ocean, and he silently replayed the moment of impact and the accompanying head rush of relief at having something real to fight for even as his thoughts flinched at the memory. It was an act of dark folly. But he had thought he was alone, and he didn't like knowing that she had seen him at his most desperate.

'You lied about that too,' she said coldly. 'You said you were messing about on deck but I saw what happened. Oh, and by the way, it is my business if I have to go fish you out of the ocean.' She shook her head. 'Let me give you a piece of advice, Jack. Next time you want to "mess about", stick to something that doesn't end with a trip to the hospital.'

He'd had enough.

'Seriously? You think I need advice from some waitress-cum-lifeguard?'

She blinked and her face stilled, and he felt her reaction as if it were his own, but his head was still spinning with shock that she knew what he'd done and that drove him to push aside any restraint or consideration.

'Maybe you need to take a good, hard look at how, where you live? Because what I think is that you should get your own life on track before you start picking holes in mine.'

She took a step backwards, and he knew he had gone too far, pushed back too hard as he always did. Even if she hadn't been inching towards the door, he could sense her withdrawing from him, and all of the certainty he'd felt as she'd waited with him at the hospital and sat by his bed began to melt away—

'Ondine, don't go.' His fists tightened, a nameless panic swamping him, pulling him under. 'Please. I don't know why I said that. I didn't mean it—'

* * *

Ondine stopped. Her legs seemed to be rooted to the floor-boards she and Oli had painted when they moved in. Her eyes were fixed on Jack's face.

He looked pale and his hair was still damp from the shower, just as it had been when she'd pulled him from the sea. And maybe that triggered some kind of reflex need to help and comfort him or maybe it was the strain in his voice, but she knew she couldn't leave him. 'I'm not going anywhere,' she said quietly.

He sat down on the bed abruptly, almost as if his legs had given way, and she realised that the shock of the morning was finally setting in.

Or more likely he had been in shock the whole time. She felt a stab of guilt. She had wanted to believe he was un-affected because that meant she could keep her distance. Now though she saw that the fleeting glimpse of his own mortality had scared him.

And her, she thought, her heart jerking into her ribs. It felt as if her breath and her heartbeat were pushing into one another inside her chest. Her skin could hardly hold it all in.

'Here, drink this. It will help.' She handed him his cof-fee, hesitated then sat down beside him. 'Is there anyone I can call?'

He looked up at her. 'Call?'

She hesitated again. 'You said you were seeing some-one. A doctor.'

'It wasn't that serious. Not for me anyway, and it's over now.' He ran a hand wearily over his face.

'Your parents, then.'

Now, he was shaking his head. 'I don't need to call any-one. I'm fine.'

He wasn't. She could see that now. It had just taken longer for him to react. She stared down at him, wondering why that was. 'Physically yes, but maybe you need to talk to someone about what happened.'

'Then I can talk to you, can't I?'

The strain was still there, and she hesitated again, then took his hand. 'Of course you can talk to me. But there are professionals—'

He was shaking his head. 'But you were there. With me.'

In the shiver of a heartbeat, she remembered her burning lungs, his heavy body. She felt his hand tighten around hers and knew that he was remembering it too.

'Only you know what happened. What it felt like. Just you and me—'

Their eyes met. Through the window she could see the sun, hear the screech of the gulls, but all of it came from another place, far away. Here it was just the two of them and this relentless pull of need between them that she could no more ignore than the tide could ignore the moon.

He was so beautiful.

Reaching up, she touched his face, her fingers following the curve of his jaw. Her pulse was raging like thunder inside her head.

'Just you and me,' she whispered and then she leaned in and kissed him.

His lips were warm and firm and their mouths fitted together just as they had before, just as if they had kissed not once but a hundred, a thousand times.

Only it was nothing like that first kiss. That had been exploratory, impulsive, organic. This was an admission of that narrow-eyed quivering creature that had been prowling around them and nipping at their heels since they'd left the hospital. It was a kiss of heat and hunger, hers and his.

She felt his hand slide around her waist, and he was pulling her onto his lap, his expression shuttered, his eyes intent on her face.

'No, not here,' she managed. 'My room.'

They moved as one, off the bed and out of the door, bodies colliding off the walls in the urgency of their haste. In the few steps it took to reach her bedroom, their mouths fused again only now, instead of her kissing him, he was kissing her, pushing her dress away from her shoulders, lifting her hair away from her neck, sucking and licking her shoulder, her throat—

His hands moved to her back, to the catch of her bra. Flicking it open, he slid it down her arms and tossed it to the floor and now his hands were cupping her breasts, his thumbs brushing against the nipples so that a moan of pleasure escaped her lips—

Finding her mouth, he kissed her deeply, urgently, his breath melting into hers, but it wasn't enough and she found the button on his waistband, jerking it open, freeing him and she heard his breath snap in his throat as her fingers wrapped around the smooth, hard length of him.

'Wait…wait!' he said hoarsely, his hand gripping her wrist. 'I don't have anything on me—'

'It's okay,' she cut him off. 'I have some.'

Was that true? It had been so long since she had needed to use contraception. Not since with Garrett before they were married. But she didn't want to think about that now. Heart thundering, she yanked open a drawer. Then another. They must be here—

Thank goodness. A rush of relief flooded her as she found the box and then she almost dropped it as his hands slid under the hem of her dress and he pulled her panties down over her thighs. And now he was turning her to face him, his fingers firm, compelling, pulling her with him onto the bed, his mouth hot against hers as she tore clumsily at the wrapper.

'Let me—'

He took the condom from her shaking hands and she watched, dry-mouthed, as he slid it onto his erection. He lifted her up so that her thighs were straddling his hips and now he slowed as he pushed inside her, taking his time, making her wait, letting her register every smooth, pulsing inch of him.

She put her hand on his arm to steady herself as he began to move against her, his hips lifting her up in a hard, intoxicating rhythm that made her head spin. Now he was touching her clitoris, working in time with his thrusts, and she sucked in a breath as his lips found the hollow below her ear.

Her fingers flexed against his warm, bare chest. She was melting, dissolving into a molten pool of need and, reaching up, she clasped his face in her hands, suddenly desperate, her mouth finding his as he rocked faster, and faster and then she cried out, back arching, breath shuddering.

Moments later, a heartbeat at most, he caught her wrists, gripping them tightly and then his lips parted and he was groaning against her mouth, body tensing as he surged inside her.

She felt his hand in her hair and, breathing hard, he fell back on the bed, taking her with him.

Head spinning, she shifted against the white heat of Jack's body. She could feel the sweat on her skin. Their sweat. But it was her face that felt as if it were on fire.

What had she done? But it was a rhetorical question. She knew what she'd done. She'd had sex with Jack Walcott. Or to put it another way, she'd made the biggest mistake of her life. Okay, maybe not the biggest, she thought, catching sight of her ring finger.

But this was definitely a mistake.

He was in the corner of her vision and she turned her head slightly until she could no longer see him. But now she could see the clothes scattered all over the floor where he had pulled them from her greedy, reckless body—

As casually as she could manage, she wriggled out of his arms.

'Where are you going?' His hand moved over her thigh, and she knew that if she let it stay there she would soon be incapable of rational thought.

'I'm just going to use the bathroom.' Sliding her legs off the bed, she stood up so quickly that she almost toppled over. 'I'll leave you to get dressed and…' She let the sentence teeter and fall into the silence between them and, snatching up her clothes, she darted out of the room.

She shut and locked the door.

Gripping the edge of the sink, she stared at her reflection. What was wrong with her? Why did she keep making the same dumb mistakes? Her fingers trembled against the cool porcelain. Since her second divorce had come through she had been single, and if not happy then focused on Oli's future and clearing the debts Vince had racked up in their names. Sex and men were off the agenda for the very simple reason that she couldn't trust herself. And it had been surprisingly easy to resist temptation.

Only then Jack had been there, his golden eyes melting into hers, his face so beautiful it made her ache, and that hard, lean body promising every kind of pleasure. Mouth dry, she stared into her reflected eyes, pressing her thighs tight. And not just promising. He had delivered.

Probably because he'd had so much practice, she thought, picturing her own shaking hands as she'd tried to unwrap the condom.

She felt her cheeks grow warm. Her lack of expertise was embarrassing to remember but at least she'd had some condoms left over, because truthfully she'd been so caught up in her hunger for him that she couldn't say for sure if she would have done something unforgivably stupid in the moment.

'Ondine—' There was a tap at the door. 'Everything all right?'

She froze. 'Yes, everything's great. I'll see you downstairs—'

Breathing out shakily, she pulled on her clothes. She should never have let him talk her into coming back to the house, not after what had happened on the beach. It had been clear then that the danger and terror of the morning had stripped away the usual reserve between strangers.

But there was no point thinking about that now. It was done. What mattered was getting Jack out of the house and back to the hotel as soon as possible and she unlocked the door and made her way downstairs. Jack was standing in the kitchen with his back to her. He was gazing down at the counter and her footsteps faltered as she saw what he was looking at.

'What are you doing with those?'

The worktop was covered in brown envelopes and she watched in horror as he picked up two and put them to one side. 'I'm playing Go Fish.'

'Do you mind?' Pushing past him, she gathered up the envelopes.

'You have a lot of unpaid bills,' he said softly.

'And you have a lot of nerve.' Her eyes narrowed on his face. 'Look, just because we had sex doesn't give you the right to go poking around in my things—'

Yanking open the drawer, she stuffed the envelopes inside, then slammed it shut. Heart thumping against her ribs, she turned to face him. He stared at her impassively.

'Putting them in there's not going to help make them go away.'

'Well, luckily for you, how I make them go away is none of your business,' she snapped.

Jack was leaning against the counter, sunlight and shadow criss-crossing his face in tigerish stripes. 'But it could be,' he said after a moment.

She glared at him. 'I think it's time for you to leave.' Snatching up her car keys, she stepped aside to let him pass, but he didn't move. Instead, he stared at her, his golden eyes hot and bright in the tiny kitchen.

'What would you say if I told you that I could make all of those bills just disappear?'

'I would say you probably need to go back to the hospital for a CAT scan,' she said stiffly.

He smiled then—a quick, devastating, get-out-of-jail-free smile that made her breath catch.

'And on any other day I'd probably agree with you, but today is different. Today is your lucky day. You see, I have a proposition, a proposal really. I need something that I think you can provide. A service.' His eyes rested on her face, then dropped to the swell of her breasts. 'And if you were to provide that service I would be willing to recompense you. Generously recompense you.'

There was another silence. Her face felt as if it were on fire. 'Are you offering to pay me for sex?'

He stared at her. 'No, actually. As much as I enjoyed myself that wasn't part of the plan, but it could be—'

'What plan?' She cut him off. The room was starting to spin.

'I want you to marry me.'

CHAPTER THREE

ONDINE STARED AT him in silence. 'Is this your idea of a joke?' she said finally.

He frowned. 'A joke? No. I couldn't be more serious.'

'Right.' She was suddenly so furious she could barely speak. 'So you want me to believe that when you woke up earlier you suddenly realised you'd fallen in love with me and that you had to marry me?'

Behind him, there was a vase of cream roses and their lush romanticism seemed to highlight the bitterness in her voice.

'Close.' His eyes flickered over her face, then past her through the window to the distant glitter of Palm Beach. 'But what I really want is for everyone else to believe that.'

What was he talking about? Her heart gave a thump. Maybe she should take him back to the hospital.

'I don't know why you're looking so worried,' he said softly. 'It was you who gave me the idea.'

'Me?' Her heart gave another lurch.

His golden eyes rested steadily on her face. 'Marriage is good for men. That's what you said. People think they're more dedicated, responsible, mature.'

'That's why you want to marry me? Because of some random comment I made—'

He was shaking his head. 'I don't want to marry anyone. But I do need a wife. Not for very long. A year or two at most, I haven't really nailed down the details—'

'And now there's no need to.' Stepping forward, she pushed her hands against his chest, ignoring the feel of his muscles, the way everything inside her pulled taut. 'Because it's time for you to go back to your hotel—'

It was as if she hadn't spoken. 'Look, I get it. It sounds crazy—'

'That's because it is crazy, Jack. You're crazy.' He wasn't moving and, glaring up at him, she snatched her hands away.

'It's not crazy. It's completely logical. Unconventional, maybe, but logical, and entirely practical for both of us,' he added, as if he were offering to do a car share to work. 'You need money and I need a wife.'

'Unconventional would be wearing a ball gown to go to the mall. And nobody *needs* a wife, Jack. Not in this century anyway. And I certainly don't need or want a husband. I've had two already.'

She had thought that would stop him in his tracks, but he just lounged back against the counter, seemingly unperturbed. 'So you're an expert.'

'Obviously not. Otherwise I'd still be married.'

'Maybe you haven't met the right man.'

Her chest was pounding with disbelief. And yet she couldn't look away. 'You can't possibly think that's you.'

He studied her now for a long, level moment. 'Actually, I do.' He tilted his head, that mouth of his pulling into a mocking curl. 'We have nothing in common and neither of us have any desire to get married but—' he held up his hand as she opened her mouth to protest '—it's for exactly those reasons that in this very specific instance I think we would be right for each other.' He took a step closer, his golden eyes holding her captive. 'Think about it. No more money worries. You could be debt-free. You wouldn't have to work two jobs.'

No debts. Only one job. The possibilities filled her, stunned her. She felt his eyes on her face. He looked calm and complacent. The complacency of one who was used to winning.

She folded her arms across her chest. 'And what do you get out of it? Why do you need a wife?'

'You don't need to worry about that.'

'Then you don't need to waste any more of my time.' She had found out the hard way that other people's agendas mattered as much as her own. Not that she was planning on taking him up on his offer.

Jack stared at her for a moment, and then he shrugged. 'My grandfather is the CEO of the family business. He's also eighty-two years old. He needs a succession plan, someone to take over when he steps down. That's me.'

'Congratulations!' She glared at him. 'But I don't see what that has to do with marrying me.'

'It doesn't. Not directly.'

Catching sight of her expression, he sighed. 'Look, I'm not going to bore you with the details but, in a nutshell, I messed up at work. So now I need to show my grandfather that I've changed, that I can change. I need to show him that I can make good life choices, that I'm mature.'

She gave a small, brittle laugh. 'And you think that proposing marriage to a total stranger nails that?'

A muscle pulsed in his jaw. 'We're not strangers.'

She felt it again, that ripple of need, and her body felt suddenly tense and loose at the same time.

'It was sex, Jack. That's all.' 'That's all' made it sound perfunctory. Mundane. It had been neither of those things. It had changed everything she thought she knew about sex. Made her catch fire, and she could still feel the flames now. His gaze hovered on her face and she knew she was blushing. 'It doesn't mean we know each other.'

'Okay, fine, we don't know each other but that isn't a problem. It's the solution. We'll be like strangers on a train.'

Her whole body felt as if it were going to implode. This was insane. Why was she even having this conversation? 'Didn't they murder each other's wives?'

His face creased with impatience. 'I just meant that together we could solve the problems we can't fix on our own.'

'I'm quite capable of fixing my own problems,' she said crisply.

He jerked open the drawer. 'So why have you got so many unpaid bills?'

Because my first husband discarded me when I couldn't get pregnant and I felt ugly and stupid and useless so I married a man on the rebound. Only he liked to have fun and I couldn't face another divorce so I shut my eyes to the fact that we were spending more than we earned.

But that was nobody's business but hers.

'They're old bills. Most of them are paid off,' she lied.

'So take the money and go on a cruise. Buy a new car. If not needing the money is the biggest problem you can come up with, then I think it's a go.'

'Our biggest problem is that nobody is ever going to believe that we're madly in love.' That wasn't true either. Everybody would believe she was in love with him, but men like Jack Walcott didn't marry waitresses or lifeguards except in the movies.

'Particularly your grandfather.'

'My grandfather's a romantic and I can be very convincing.' His eyes locked with hers and she felt heat surge through her, a heat that scorched her skin and flooded her veins. 'Look, you're overthinking this. Maybe it would be easier if you just treat it as a job.'

'I have a job.'

'You have two. Both low-paid, going nowhere.' He glanced around the small, shabby kitchen. 'I can change your life, Ondine. I can change your brother's life. Think about that. If you won't do it for yourself then do it for him.'

For a moment, she saw herself through his eyes and felt a flicker of shame. So many failures in such a short time.

And then anger bubbled up inside her. How dared he stand there and judge her when everything had been handed to him on a plate? Make that a platter, she thought, catching sight of the gold signet ring.

'My brother doesn't need your money and you know nothing about my life.'

His beautiful mouth curled. 'You have two ex-husbands, you work two jobs, and you could wallpaper your house with final demands. What more is there to know?'

'Nothing. And there's nothing more to say either,' she said coldly. 'I'll call you a cab.'

He stared at her speculatively. 'You know where to find me when you change your mind. Just be discreet—'

She yanked open the door. 'You can wait on the deck. Goodbye, Jack.'

Curling up on her side, Ondine hugged her duvet closer. It was nearly an hour since Jack had left and she had another two hours before she would have to head into work. But she was going to need every minute of those two hours to get her head straight. To get Jack and his ridiculous, patronising offer out of her head.

Her heart thudded hard as she remembered the curve of his mouth and that lift of his eyebrow. He thought he knew her but he didn't know anything about her. He didn't know what she needed.

She felt something stir inside her. Okay, maybe he did, but that didn't count. It shouldn't even have happened.

Her heart leapt against her ribs as her phone rang, and as she glanced down at the caller ID, she started to smile.

'Oli?' There was a crackling sound. 'Oli—can you hear me?'

'Yes, I can hear you.'

She could hear the excitement in his voice. 'How are you? How's it going?'

'I'm fine. And it's going really well. Yesterday I inoculated about a hundred children and today I watched a woman give birth.'

He sounded so young, so pleased with himself and she felt a rush of pride and love. 'That's amazing, Oli.'

'It really was. But we can talk about that in a minute. What's happening at home? How's Dolores and Herc? Did you get the car fixed?'

'Dolores and Herc are fine and, *no*, I haven't got around to sorting out the car yet. And everything here is the same old, same old,' she lied. 'You know...waiting tables, standing by the pool.'

Oh, and having sex with a man she'd rescued from the sea.

'I miss you—'

There was a lump in her throat. 'I miss you too. But you're enjoying it, aren't you?'

'I am.' She heard him take a breath and when he spoke again his voice was quieter, more serious. 'I didn't say anything before I left, but I was worried, O, you know, that I might come out here and realise that I'd made a mistake. Because of always being so certain. But it's everything I thought it would be, and so much—'

The crackling sound was back.

'Oli. Are you there?'

The phone clicked and she frowned as the dial tone filled her ear. This happened every single time. But he would call back—

On cue, the phone rang and she snatched it up.

'You were saying something about making a mistake,' she teased.

'Ondine?'

She almost dropped the phone. That wasn't Oliver. It was her ex-husband. 'Vince?'

'How are you?'

Her shoulders stiffened. *Poor. Stupid. Lonely. All of the above,* she thought, but instead, keeping her voice casual, she said, 'I'm good. Busy, actually.'

'Right, that's good.'

She frowned. She hadn't heard from Vince in nearly ten months. There was no need. Both of them had moved on. Which meant he was at a loose end or he wanted money.

'You know what, Vince, I'm waiting on a call so perhaps we could do this another time.' Like never.

'I wish we could, honey, but this can't wait. You see, something's come up, and we need to talk about it.' There was a silence and then Vince sighed. 'I didn't mean for it to happen. I honestly thought it would be a good investment otherwise I would never have suggested it.'

A cool shiver ran down her spine, and she felt her insides tighten. 'What are you talking about?'

'It's Oli's college fund. I'm sorry, Ondine, but it's gone. It's all gone.'

So that was that.

Breathing out unsteadily, Ondine tucked her blouse into her skirt and pushed her feet into her shoes. It had taken just over an hour for Vince to explain what had happened. Just over an hour for her brother's dreams to turn to ashes.

She couldn't just blame Vince. She might have asked him to help her invest the money but Oli was her brother. She should have looked into the fund, researched it properly, and then kept a closer eye on it, but she hadn't. Later when Vince's exuberance with money had seemed more clueless than charming, she had been relieved that the money was locked away where he couldn't get his hands on it. It had never occurred to her that the investments might tank.

There was nothing that could be done. She'd rung the college and they had been very kind but all the scholarships had been allocated. The best option, they'd said, was for him to reapply the following year, but there were no guarantees.

The lump in her throat seemed to grow a little. She needed a drink. What she didn't need was to have to go into work and face Jack. Maybe she should call in sick—

But then she thought about what she could make in tips, and right now every dime counted. Only it would never be enough. Particularly as she had other bills to pay. She thought back to how Jack had jerked open the drawer in the kitchen. No more money worries, he'd said. She could see his eyes watching her.

Feel his hot, urgent mouth against her throat.

She felt the hair on the nape of her neck rise, and then her nipples tightened.

It was indecent, the effect he had on her. And dangerous. She would be mad to spend any time in his company, much less marry him. But what other options were there? She could go to the bank. But she only had her salary. And even if she took on all the extra shifts on offer, she had less than five months to make up the difference.

Her heart felt as if it would burst through her ribs. Could she do it? Could she marry Jack Walcott?

Of course she couldn't. It was a crazy idea. He was rude and reckless—

And rich.

But also rude and reckless, plus she had failed to stay married twice before for real, so how could she possibly manage to fake it? Easy, she thought, her mouth trembling. Because Oli needed that money.

Twenty minutes later, knots forming in her belly, she was stalking through the hotel gardens to the beach bungalows. You know where to find me when you change your mind, he'd said. Arrogant bastard, she thought, but he was right. Like every other woman in the hotel, she knew exactly where Jack Walcott was staying.

Stopping in front of his door, she knocked immediately, not wanting to give herself time to change her mind. As the door opened, she felt her mouth dry. He was bare-chested, and he looked as though he had been sleeping.

'Come in.'

As she hesitated, he raised an eyebrow. 'You want to do this in the corridor.'

She didn't want to do it at all but her wishes came secondary to her need for money.

'So, how may I help?' he said softly, closing the door behind her.

'That proposal you made earlier. Is it still on the table?'

There was a short silence and, watching his lazy cat's smile tugging at his mouth, she almost turned and walked out.

'It is.'

'Then my answer is yes. I will marry you.' Taking a

breath, she steadied her nerves. 'This is how much I'll need.' She held out a piece of paper.

He looked at it, his face impassive.

'That won't be a problem.'

Silence followed, a long grainy silence that seemed to scrape against her skin. 'And I'll need some of it upfront,' she said finally. 'Shall we say half?'

The Miami-Dade courthouse was surprisingly busy for a Wednesday.

Then again, maybe it wasn't. Jack glanced at the people crossing the foyer. Maybe he was just feeling claustrophobic because today was the day.

He felt his shoulders stiffen as a door opened and a couple stepped into the hallway, hands entwined, faces lit up with happiness and relief. They might as well have had *Newlywed* stamped across their foreheads.

'Congratulations,' he murmured as they walked past. But they only had eyes for one another. Because they were in love. They believed in the power of love.

More fool them, he thought, watching them leave. He caught sight of his reflection in the mirrored lift doors. He was not, despite what people assumed, vain about his appearance. Mostly, when he looked at himself he saw the parents who had abandoned him. But it wasn't every day that a man got married.

Married.

He glanced down at the bouquet of cream roses in his hand, his heartbeat accelerating. Theoretically, he could have asked Carrie. But then it had all blown up that night on the boat and she had said that thing about his mother and after that he couldn't even look at her.

And this was better. He was calling the shots and that

meant it would be easier when he wanted to extricate himself. Which he would do at the earliest possible moment. But he still couldn't shift the feeling that he was caught in a trap. Was this really his only choice?

He could have begged his grandfather to let him come back to work. Try and prove himself worthy. Only it would be harder to quantify the change because his work ethic wasn't that far removed from his grandfather's. And he was just as, maybe more, proud of the family business as John D. Walcott IV. The difference between them was that nobody knew that because he acted as if he didn't care. It was the same with school and university. With friends and partners.

But he had learned the hard way that there was a downside to caring, and that downside was too high a price to pay.

And that was why this was his only option. Why today, just eight and a half weeks after he'd proposed to her, Ondine was going to become his wife.

Ondine Wilde: he knew her surname now, but what else did he know about her?

Truthfully, not much.

They had hardly seen one another since she had knocked on his door. Partly that was because she worked such long hours. But he also didn't want to draw attention to their 'relationship' and have it filter back to his grandfather before he was ready.

For his plan to work it needed to look as though they had married on impulse after a whirlwind romance but, as with his grandfather, that moment of recklessness would lead to a lifetime of unshakeable love and devotion.

His eyes locked with their mirror counterparts. It was going to be a tricky conversation. His grandfather might be in his ninth decade, but he was not some dithering old man.

He had a fierce, enquiring mind and much as he hoped to see Jack settle down, he would want it to be with the right woman.

Jack breathed out silently. And for the kind of wife he needed—temporary, emotionally detached, pragmatic— Ondine was the right fit.

He had a sudden, sharp memory of her frantic fingers, the press of her mouth, her body fusing with his, and his groin tensed painfully. She was the right fit in other ways too. But her mouth, her body were not part of this particular equation. Neither of them had specified that in the paperwork but they hadn't needed to. Sex meant intimacy and intimacy meant complications, and the point of this 'marriage' was to keep things simple.

His hands tightened around the bouquet. What had happened in her bedroom was a one-off. And yes, it had felt right in the moment but—

A pulse of heat ticked across his skin.

Actually, it had felt sublime. There had been a honeyed sweetness to her touch, hot and fierce, soft yet strong, so everything he wanted in a woman but had never found. But it didn't mean anything. Or rather it meant nothing more than the obvious, which was that there had been a bed, and they'd been alone and she was a woman, and he was a man. Nothing to see here, folks. Just hormones and hunger and—

He felt his pulse slow, and almost let the door slam in his face.

A woman was standing at the top of the staircase, and for a moment he didn't recognise her out of her various uniforms. And then he did.

Ondine was wearing an ivory-coloured jacket with a matching skirt that flared out above her ankles and some kind of veiled sunhat. Her glossy brown hair was loose and she wore no jewellery. But beneath the veil, her blue eyes gleamed like sapphires.

'Hi,' she said quietly.

He stared at her in silence, holding himself still. They had agreed to dress up for the ceremony, not too over the top. No morning suit or frothy meringues, but enough to make it feel romantic.

At the time, it had been just words. He didn't have a romantic bone in his body, as more than one of the women who had referred to themselves as his girlfriends had reminded him on more than one occasion. For him, romance, like falling in love, was a closed book, but then he'd had no experience of either. His grandparents were devoted to one another, but his grandmother died before he was born and all of his memories of his parents' marriage were of the two of them shouting and slamming doors. As for their remarriages—

A knot tightened in his stomach.

Even before the accident, it was clear there was no place for him in either of their reconfigured lives. Their houses, possessions, even their photographs had all been carefully separated and curated to edit out their shared past.

Nothing remained. Except him. He was the only reminder of the mess they'd made and that was why they kept him at arm's length.

'You made it,' he said, more for something to say than because he had doubted that fact.

She frowned. 'I said I'd be here.'

'You did.' He felt the knot in his stomach loosen. 'And you always do what you say you will.'

'Are those for me?' She gestured towards the flowers.

They had agreed to forgo all the wedding extras like a cake and confetti and flowers but on the way to the courthouse he'd spotted a florist and remembered the roses in Ondine's kitchen and on impulse he'd bought them.

'Yes.' He nodded. 'I know we said to keep things low-key, but I thought they'd help with the optics.' He held them out, and as she took them the movement caused her jacket to part a little. His pulse jerked. She had nothing underneath her jacket.

'You look beautiful.'

She gave him another of those 'whatever' kind of looks. 'You don't need to say that.'

'You're right, I don't. I said it because I wanted to, and because it's true.'

There was a sliver of silence like a crescent moon as her blue eyes met his through the veil and then she said with a studied carelessness, 'Do you have the rings?'

He nodded. Plain gold bands. He had been going to choose platinum but then he had remembered the flecks of gold in her irises when she had looked up at him. He could see the same flecks now.

'Shall we go in?'

As she nodded, he reached down and took her hand. He felt her tense and then her fingers tightened around his and they turned together and walked towards the marriage ceremony room.

Inside, the Florida sunshine was pouring in through the windows as if it really were a celebration of their joyful union instead of a pragmatic, mutually beneficial contract.

The officiant greeted them warmly. Jack shook hands with the courthouse-provided witnesses, and then the ceremony began. There were a couple of sentences about the promises they were making and the new life they were about to begin together. Thirty seconds later, they were on to the familiar 'do you, Jack, take Ondine to be your wife?' And then it was time to exchange rings.

Jack's teeth were suddenly on edge. Before it had been just words but now as he stepped forward to take Ondine's hand he felt his chest pull tight.

'I give you this ring as a symbol of my love and devotion as we join our lives together today.'

Now it was Ondine's turn. She repeated the vows carefully, lifting her face to his, her blue eyes wide beneath the veil, just as if she were his bride, but her hand shook a little and it suddenly occurred to him that she had said these vows for real and he felt a sharp stab of something almost like jealousy imagining her in the arms of other men, men she loved.

The officiant began speaking again. 'By the virtue of the authority vested in me by the State of Florida and the American Marriage Ministries, I now pronounce you married. Congratulations!' Taking a step backwards, he smiled at them. 'You may kiss!'

Ondine was looking up at him but instead of moving closer as he lifted the veil, she hesitated, and he felt the tension in his jaw spread down through his body.

Normally it was the women he hooked up with tying themselves up in knots about their predecessors, but he got the feeling that there was some unfinished business between Ondine and her ex-husbands, a sense that their shadows still loomed large in her life, and he found himself wanting to erase them from her memory so that, instead of the G-rated kiss he'd planned, he wrapped an arm around her waist and jerked her closer. Caught off balance, she fell against him, and he fitted his lips to hers, kissing her deliberately, thoroughly—

He felt her shock, and her breath, soft and warm against

his mouth, and then her lips parted and she was pulling him closer, her fingers tightening in his shirt and he forgot that she wasn't his for real and the mess he had made of his life and that she shouldn't move him this way, like flames licking all over his body. He didn't think, he just was, and she was fire in his hands and his mind was nothing but heat and longing and hunger—

As suddenly as he'd started the kiss, she pulled away, cheeks flushed, breasts rising and falling with each breath. She looked as stunned as he felt. But he could guarantee that she wasn't thinking about her ex-husbands, he thought with a satisfaction he didn't understand but couldn't stop himself from feeling.

'Would you like me to take some photos?'

They both turned to where the officiant and the clerk were smiling, and, reaching into his jacket, Jack pulled out his phone and handed it to the officiant. And then turning to Ondine, he smiled too. 'That's exactly what we want, isn't it, darling?'

Leaning back against the soft, suede upholstery, Ondine pressed her hand against the armrest. At the other end of the private jet, Jack was talking to one of the stewards. He looked relaxed and calm; exactly like a man should look after marrying the woman he had fallen madly in love with.

She, on the other hand, felt as if she were falling out of the plane without a parachute. There was a kaleidoscope of butterflies in her stomach, her limbs were stiff with tension, but then she had barely slept last night. Every time she dozed off, Jack would be there beside her, *inside her*, and she would jerk awake, body quivering, pulse racing because, even though she didn't want to marry him, apparently her body was in thrall to his touch, a contradiction that was making her feel even more tense.

She shifted in her seat. In the past, she had never understood the fuss people made about sex. Before her first time with Garrett, she'd wanted to have the kind of sheet-twisting, urgent sex people had in the movies, and she'd assumed that it would be like that for her. But the first time had been awkward and uncomfortable and as the months had passed and she still hadn't been pregnant, it had become charged with a kind of desperate and unspoken blame.

As for Vince... They'd met when she'd been at her lowest point, and it had been like having a golden retriever bounce into her life. He was handsome and happy, and always excited to see her and, swept along by his adoration and enthusiasm, she'd found it was easy to ignore their complete and utter lack of chemistry in bed.

And then suddenly there was Jack who was everything she had ever wanted in a lover but who lacked everything she needed in a man. Only now he was her husband.

No wonder she wasn't sleeping.

The cause of her insomnia was nodding at something the steward was saying and rubbing the back of his neck in a way that made her feel hot and irritable and on edge.

Ever since she'd agreed to marry Jack, she had been desperately ignoring the real-time consequences of that decision. Mostly it had been easy enough. Work had been full-on and she'd even taken on extra shifts. Now, though, she was on her honeymoon and there was nothing to distract her from her thoughts.

She shivered on the inside. Except Jack.

He shouldn't have kissed her like that. As if they were alone. As if it were real. And she shouldn't have kissed him back. But then again maybe it was the jolt she needed to make her wake up and smell the coffee.

She felt her stomach twist. *No, not coffee.* She was running on adrenaline as it was, she didn't need to add caffeine into the mix.

But she did need to wise up. There would be no more kissing except the closed-mouth variety. And they absolutely would not be having sex again. She would not allow one heated encounter to cloud the issue. Marrying Jack was about moving on, moving forward past this mess she'd made so that Oliver would have the future he deserved, the future her parents had planned for. Not making an even bigger, messier mess of everything.

As Jack said, this was just a job, and like all her jobs she would do it to the best of her ability. So she would play the adoring, lovestruck wife in public and keep things cordial but cool behind closed doors.

'Darling, I'm sorry that took so long.' She looked up, and her heart lurched as Jack sat down beside her. 'Did you miss me?'

Glancing at the stewards, she pasted a smile on her face. 'Of course.'

He stretched out his long legs. 'Apparently, it's forty-six degrees on Whydah. Honestly, we might as well have gone to Banff.'

They were en route to Martha's Vineyard where they would pick up a launch to his family's private island off the coast of Massachusetts.

Jack had wanted to fly to the Caribbean but then she had pointed out to him that she was supposed to have reined him in. 'I thought you wanted to show your grandfather you could change, that you were changing,' she'd said to him at one of their brief covert meetings. 'That means not having a splashy honeymoon and drinking champagne for breakfast.'

Not that the air stewards knew that, she thought a moment later, hearing the pop of a cork. 'Thank you,' she murmured as the chief steward appeared, beaming, a foaming glass in each hand.

Lifting the glass to her lips, she took a sip, and frowned. Great—now her adrenaline was making the champagne taste weird. Maybe she would just go and brush her teeth.

'I might just go and freshen up,' she murmured to Jack. 'I'll be back in a minute.'

Astonishingly there was a bedroom on board and an ensuite bathroom. If only she could stay here for ever, or at least the rest of the flight, she thought, leaning forward to rinse out her mouth.

But it wouldn't change anything. She glanced down at the plain gold band on her finger. They were married. And Jack had already spoken to his grandfather.

She had chickened out of telling Oli. But that was different. He was so far away, and alone. And besides, she was still trying to come to terms with what she had done. She let out her breath slowly, trying to steady herself. It was just a lot. Not just getting married, but this jet. The private island. *Jack.* Her pulse accelerated and she was back at the kiss at the courthouse again. There was definitely going to have to be some rules.

As she walked back into the bedroom, her stomach flipped and more annoyingly she felt her nipples tighten. Jack was stretched out on the bed, his sprawling limbs complementing the lazy-cat smile on his face.

'What is it?' she said, somewhat ungraciously she had to admit, but she felt oddly panicky at being suddenly and completely alone with him.

'What do you think it is?' His beautiful mouth curved down into a frown. 'You're my wife. We're supposed to be madly in love. So why are you skulking in the cabin like some stowaway?'

'I'm not skulking. I just needed a bit of space.'

'Since when?' Shifting against the pillow, he tipped back his head. 'You didn't seem to need any at the courthouse.'

Ignoring the treacherous warmth spreading through her limbs, she said coolly, 'You seem to be confusing your needs with mine.'

He gave a short laugh.

'So when you were pulling me closer, that was you trying to do what, exactly? Pick fluff off my jacket?' He sucked in a breath. 'Just admit it. You wanted to kiss me as much as I wanted to kiss you.'

'What if I did?' She was too shocked by his admission to be anything but honest with him. 'That doesn't make it right, and you know it. Yet you still acted on it.'

Dropping onto the bed, she kicked off her shoes. 'And that there is your problem, Jack. That lack of understanding and childish disregard for anything but what you feel in the moment is why you've ended up marrying a complete stranger to get your life back on track. Because presumably your grandfather, and everyone who has the misfortune to spend time in your company, has had enough of you.'

His face was harsh like stone. 'I cannot believe I thought we could make this charade work.'

'The feeling's mutual,' she snapped.

CHAPTER FOUR

JACK STARED DOWN at the magazine he was holding, a frown creasing his face. He liked this writer, and usually he found her accessible and informative, but she must have changed her style because he couldn't remember a word of what he'd just read.

But then he hadn't actually been reading the article, just pretending to.

His lip curled. It was bad enough having to fake things in front of Sally and the rest of the staff at Red Knots. But to be doing so on his own time, when they were alone—

He glanced over at the cause of his current inability to focus. Ondine was also reading. A book. Only, judging by the tiny vertical indentations on the smooth skin of her forehead, she was, unlike him, completely engrossed in the contents. Her mid-brown hair hung loose today, as it had most days since they'd reached the island. He liked it that way. Liked the way it shone too in the afternoon sunlight that was filtering through the window.

At that moment, she lifted her hand to tuck a stray strand of that same hair behind her ear and her cuff fell away from her wrist. Remembering what that delicate nub of bone felt like beneath his fingers, he felt his skin begin to prickle.

Oh, for—

Gritting his teeth, he swore silently as the rest of his body caught up with the scene replaying inside his head, and he felt his groin tighten. If this were a normal marriage, a normal honeymoon, he wouldn't be sitting here on this sofa pretending to read magazines, he would be in bed with his wife. Or maybe he would still be sitting here, but Ondine would not be wearing clothes and her hand would be touching him, not her hair.

But there was nothing normal about their situation.

Not that he had any idea of what 'normal' was when it came to married life. Before he'd started kindergarten, his parents' marriage was already stumbling towards the lawyer's office and a *decree nisi*. As for their remarriages. His visits were too brief, too rushed and too infrequent for him to get any insight into how their relationships worked.

Of course, his grandparents had a gold-standard marriage. But all that remained of their blissfully happy union was photos of the two of them at various stages of their lives and his grandpa's unwavering devotion to her memory.

Imagining John Walcott's reaction to finding out the truth about his grandson's marriage, Jack shifted uncomfortably in his seat.

He and Ondine had agreed to tell their families about the wedding after the ceremony, and he had called his grandfather outside the courthouse. Thinking back to that conversation now, he felt his pulse stutter. It was difficult to surprise an eighty-two-year-old man, but he had managed to surprise his grandfather.

'Married?'

'I know what you're thinking, Grandpa.' His voice had felt raw in his throat. 'And I know why you're thinking it. I've not been any kind of grandson, not the sort you deserve—'

'Jack, that's not true—'

The softness in his grandfather's voice had almost made him unravel with guilt.

'Please, just let me finish. I know I've let you down, but I do want to change, and I think I am changing, and Ondine… she's part of that change. Right from the start, it felt different with her. I feel different when I'm with her. And I know you understand that. I know you felt that with Grandma—'

His chest had tightened. His grandfather had met his future wife when she was working as a waitress. Nobody had supported the match but love had prevailed. It had felt wrong to bring up his grandmother but it had worked.

'I did. I still do,' his grandfather had said softly. 'I was so unhappy when we met. I'd inherited the business and I had all these people relying on me, only I was too proud to admit I couldn't cope. Too ashamed to admit that I hated the burden.'

Jack had frowned. He hadn't known that. 'I thought you loved the business.'

'I grew to love it. But back then, I was miserable. Then I met Candace, and it's no exaggeration to say that she saved me. She "saw" me, the real me. I found myself telling her things I'd never told anyone else. I suppose you could say I shared my soul. That's when I realised I loved her. You see, that's what love is, Jack, sharing your soul.'

'I think that's probably long enough, isn't it?'

Ondine's crisp question cut across his thoughts and he turned towards her, an anger that was both irrational and unfair skimming across the skin. Because he had wanted this cool, transactional relationship. Except now that he was living it, he didn't like it at all.

Although to say that he'd wanted this was giving him slightly too much credit. True to form, he hadn't got much further than the wedding ceremony in his head, and as a consequence he hadn't worked out how to do this part of the marriage.

Night-time was easiest. Having already told Sally that upstairs was off-limits to her housekeeping team, they slept apart, in adjacent rooms, and each morning he let himself back into what was supposedly the room they shared.

Days were harder.

They had established a routine of sorts. At some point in the morning, then again after lunch, they would retire upstairs and sit in silence at opposite ends of the bedroom. Then, after a decent amount of time had passed, he would go back downstairs, looking suitably rumpled, and say that Mrs Walcott was sleeping and anyone who happened to be there would smile and nod in silent but tacit understanding.

And on that first day it had seemed to work. But now, pretending to be exhausted from some daily honeymoon sex marathon while simultaneously enduring a period of self-imposed celibacy was pushing his buttons almost as much as these absurdly stiff and overpolite conversations.

Maybe it would have worked if they hadn't had sex. But being in such close proximity to her made him feel as if he were drowning again and the only thing he wanted to hold on to and be held by was Ondine.

'Absolutely,' he said, glancing at his watch. 'It's the penultimate day of our honeymoon so I think we could justifiably be a little worn out today.'

He had chosen his words with care, wanting to provoke a reaction, and as her chin jerked up he saw a bright flare of temper snap in her eyes like lightning across a stormy sky. But her voice was cool as she said, 'I'll be down in about an hour.'

He watched her for a moment, his breath scratching his throat.

'Take as long as you like,' he said finally, and, cutting himself off from her narrowed blue gaze, he strode across the room, wishing he could as easily excise his body's reaction to that flush of colour winging across her cheekbones.

Desire. A yearning to reach out and touch. And irritation at what she was feeling. He saw all of it. Felt all of it because he was feeling it too.

It had been like that since the flight to Martha's Vineyard. After their spat, Ondine had sat on the bed, toed off her shoe, curled up on her side and fallen asleep. Of course, having followed her in with a stupid grin on his face, he could hardly have emerged moments later looking like a puppy with his tail between his legs so he'd had to sit there, fuming, with not even his phone to keep him occupied until she'd woken up just as the plane had started its descent.

Only what was there to fight about? It wasn't as if theirs was even a real marriage.

He pictured the stubborn curve of her spine, and his mouth twisted. He shouldn't be that surprised. Everyone turned their back on him in the end. Even someone who was being paid to be his wife.

He knew why she was snippy. It was that kiss at the courthouse. But they were supposed to be crazy in love; and at some point in the not too distant future they would have to do all those things that couples in love were supposed to do, and it would need to look 'real'.

Besides, it had been their wedding day—he could hardly just have given her a peck on the cheek. And *she* had kissed *him* back.

What he really wanted to do was remind her of that fact. He clenched his hands. *Liar.* What he wanted to do was stalk back into their bedroom, snatch that book from her hands and then kiss her until she shook with need.

In reality, what he was going to do was take her to Martha's Vineyard. His jaw clenched. He hated shopping. Normally wild horses couldn't drag him near a mall. But after three endless weeks of being in forced, fruitless proximity with Ondine he would willingly wander around every upmarket boutique on the island if it meant not having to spend another hour pretending to read a magazine while trying to ignore yet another inappropriate daydream about his so-called wife.

Martha's Vineyard was every bit as charming as Ondine had expected and the total opposite of glitzy, over-the-top Palm Beach. Here, everything was quiet, low-rise, slow-paced. The one thing it shared with Palm Beach was that it was clearly a magnet for the wealthy and famous.

Just a different kind of wealth and fame, she thought, sidestepping a woman with a toddler to get a better view of a former US president, his wife and their security detail as they crossed the street and disappeared into a bookstore.

'Is that—?'

'Yes.' Beside her, Jack nodded. 'I would introduce you, but I want to keep a low profile until you've met Grandpa.'

'You know him?' She couldn't keep the surprise out of her voice, and, glancing over, she saw the pride glittering in his golden gaze.

'He's a friend of the family.' His hand, which had been holding hers loosely, tightened so that her wedding band pinched her finger. 'That's the gallery I told you about. Shall we cross over?'

It was a rhetorical question. He was already stepping off the sidewalk.

Should she have married him?

That was not a rhetorical question so much as an irrele-

vant one. They were married, but had it been the right thing
to do? Here, now, walking in the sunshine, it felt as though
it was. But only because she was pretending she was on
holiday, not on her honeymoon.

Her *fake* honeymoon.

She thought back to the strange routine that had somehow evolved without either of them saying a word. In theory those hours in the bedroom at Red Knots, when she and
Jack were supposedly making love, should be the easiest.
Nobody was watching so they didn't have to play their parts.
They should have been able to relax, but she had never felt
more tense, not even during the last gasp of her previous
two marriages.

And she knew that was absurd, only that didn't stop it
being true.

Remembering the feel of his flickering, golden eyes as
he glanced across the bedroom, a shiver moved through her
and with it a tactile memory of warm skin and his mouth
hard on hers. But obviously, the honeymoon was always
going to be the hardest part. After this, they wouldn't have
to spend nearly as much time together, so maybe she should
follow the example of the ex-president and his wife, and
enjoy this downtime.

It wasn't just politicians enjoying the lack of traffic lights
and chainstore-free vibe of Edgartown. She recognised two
actresses, one chat-show host and a comedian from one
of those late-night Saturday shows. But there were no pa-
parazzi, no passers-by filming them on their phones. Everybody just went about their business, popping in and out
of the white-painted boutiques, farm shops and cafés.

Her pulse danced forward. And yet, even dressed casually with his features disguised by a baseball cap and sunglasses, Jack, being Jack, somehow still managed to draw

admiring looks from the women walking past. It wasn't just his looks. There was something about Jack Walcott that made you look twice.

And then it was almost impossible to look away.

As if to prove her point, a pretty young woman with blonde hair and a floaty white dress who could have given Helen of Troy a run for her money glanced over, her cheeks turning a fetching shade of palest pink.

She felt a jolt of jealousy, as sharp as it was irrational. Jack was her husband, but in name only. Most of the time she wasn't even sure she liked him. They had no relationship. No shared history. Unless by history you meant one heated sexual encounter and one kiss too many.

Her skin felt suddenly too tight. She could almost excuse herself for what had happened on that first day. They had been in shock, both of them unravelling with the enormity of what could have happened. But that kiss at the courthouse had been cool-headed, unscrupulous on his part, anyway. And she was angry with him. For not knowing, or, if he did know, not caring about the effect it had had. Glancing over her shoulder, she caught the young woman staring after her enviously. But then maybe it happened so frequently, he'd stopped noticing.

If only she could do the same.

The gallery was as cool and quiet as the clientele milling in front of the paintings. She felt like a fraud. What did she know about art? Leaning in to examine what looked like a scribble of orange over a smudge of green, she noticed the price.

How much?

'Do you like it?'

She turned. Jack stood behind her, his gaze not on the

painting but on her face, his eyes narrowed as if she were a puzzle he was trying to complete.

'It's interesting,' she said cautiously.

He laughed. Several people turned around and she felt her cheeks grow warm. 'Spoken like a true art critic.'

She shrugged. 'I don't understand art.'

His mesmerising gold eyes travelled over her face. 'I disagree.' He took a step closer so that they were only inches apart and the curve of his jaw and the flawless skin over his cheekbones was more fascinating than any painting and she wanted to lean in closer. To touch. To explore. To understand him.

'You know if you like something or if you don't. If you find it compelling. Cryptic. Beautiful.' The light in his eyes sharpened, and she felt her skin grow hotter and tighter.

'If you see it. If you feel it here—' he reached out and touched her heart lightly with his fingers '—then you know all you can ever know. All you need to know. You have to trust yourself.'

Her hands twitched, then bunched into fists as if she couldn't control them. 'I don't trust easily.'

'I don't either.' He held her gaze. Maybe he was holding her breath too because her head was starting to spin and she felt suddenly fragile, adrift—

Her need for him, for it to be real, banged through her like a gong, and she felt almost queasy with panic, and, taking a step backwards, she said, 'I wish I'd come here before.' She fought to keep her voice light and careless. 'Then I wouldn't have had to marry you. I could have just bought some paints and knocked up some "art". I would have cleared my debts in no time.'

Jack stared at her in silence, his teeth on edge, his body tense.

Just for a moment there, he had forgotten all of it. The

mess he'd made at work. The water pulling him under. The spat on the plane and the tension of those hours spent barricaded in their bedroom.

Everything, everyone had been forgotten as her eyes had met his and the need in her eyes had shuddered all the way through him in a way that had made him feel undone.

Only then the shutters had come down and he felt like a fool, a stupid child again.

He needed a coffee. Actually, he needed a whisky, but a coffee would have to do. Catching hold of Ondine's elbow, he began to nudge her towards the gallery's café.

'I might just grab an espresso. Would you like something, darling?'

He felt her tense, and then her eyes widened and she tugged her arm free. 'Excuse me. I just…'

Now what? He stared after her, pulse ticcing with disbelief even as his brain followed the sway of her hips into the restroom.

'Would you like me to go and check on her?'

What?

He turned to the woman who had spoken. She was standing next to a man wearing a baby sling. The baby was facing outwards, fingers crammed into her mouth, her eyes the same startling blue as Ondine's.

The woman smiled sympathetically, then turned to the man standing beside her and said, 'I was just the same, wasn't I?' Glancing over at the coffee shop, she shuddered. 'Even just thinking about coffee used to set me off. But it's worth it.' Her face softened as the baby reached up, mouth opening to reveal two tiny white teeth. 'And it's actually a good sign.'

Jack stared at the baby. He was having to remember to breathe. 'Good sign?' he said slowly.

'My doctor always said morning sickness was a sign of a strong pregnancy.' She hesitated. 'Are you sure you don't want me to go check on her?'

'No, thank you. I'll go—'

Walking away from the couple, he felt almost drunk with shock and denial. Whatever that woman was saying was wrong. How could she be right? She knew nothing. She knew nothing about Ondine or him. She was just some random—

He stopped. Ondine was walking out of the restroom. She looked pale and shaken, but her shoulders stiffened as she saw him.

'This way,' he said curtly, grabbing her hand and towing her towards the exit.

'What is it?' He felt her fingers flex against his but he didn't loosen his grip until he had propelled her outside. He glanced up the street and, moments later, their car pulled up to the kerb.

'What is it?' Rubbing her hand, she turned to face him as the car started to move, her blue eyes narrowing on his face. 'What's so urgent that you have to pull my arm out of its socket?'

'I need to ask you something.' He swallowed. His heart was suddenly racing. 'Are you pregnant?'

She stared at him, her eyes widening with shock and confusion. 'What kind of a question is that?'

'The kind that needs answering.' His eyes locked onto hers. 'So I'm going to ask it again: is there any chance whatsoever that you could be pregnant?'

No. Absolutely not. No.

Gazing across the bathroom, Ondine felt her heart beating unevenly. That was what she had said to Jack when he had asked her if she could be pregnant, and she had believed it. She still believed it now. But the test in her hand told a different story.

Her eyes fixed on the plastic wand.

She had been here before, could picture the bathroom in the house she'd shared with Garrett, feel the swoop of disappointment as she'd stared down at the larger blank square.

They had tried for nearly two years. She had, anyway. At some point, without telling her, Garrett had given up. Suddenly conscious that her arms were shaking, she wrapped them around her waist, hugging herself tightly.

After she'd replied to his question Jack had stared at her assessingly, and then directed the driver to a side street. He had jumped out of the car, returning almost immediately without a word of explanation, and then they had been bumping in the boat across the Vineyard Sound back to Whydah Island and Red Knots.

Her throat had tightened. She had been so focused on trying not to throw up she had barely registered the huge gabled house with its shingled roof.

Not that Jack had given her any chance to do so. Holding her hand with a grip that had verged on the painful, he had more or less hauled her upstairs through the bedroom and into the bathroom. Reaching into his jacket, he had pulled out a paper bag and tossed it onto the vanity unit.

'Let me know when you're done,' he'd said, and the authority in his voice had reminded her suddenly and alarmingly that, while he might act like a playboy, he had been raised to issue orders and expect them to be followed. 'I'll be next door.'

She stared down at the two thin blue lines, and then back at the instructions leaflet. Not that she needed to read it again. When she'd been trying for a baby with Garrett she'd lost count of the number of pregnancy tests she had taken.

She knew exactly how they worked, and they all worked on the same principle.

The only difference with this one was that it was positive. *Positive.*

As in pregnant. As in having a baby.

Her fingers bit into the handle of the plastic wand. Only that wasn't possible. There must be some mistake. Only the kind of wand used by witches and wizards could conjure up the magic required for this test to be correct.

Her eyes locked onto the two lines. The first told her the test was working properly. The other told her that she was pregnant. Very slowly, she laid her hand across her stomach, her fingers flexing. But it must be faulty.

Holding her breath, she opened another box.

Then another.

And another.

Ten minutes later she was staring down at the fourth positive test when there was a knock at the door.

'Ondine—'

It was Jack. Her heart seemed to swell up and fill her throat so that breathing was suddenly almost impossible. 'Just a minute,' she said hoarsely.

'No, not another minute.' His voice was taut. 'You've been in there fifteen already.'

'All right. All right.'

From somewhere inside, she felt a snap of anger and defiance. This wasn't just happening to him. It was happening to her too.

Getting up, she unlocked the door and opened it. Jack was standing there; his handsome face was unreadable, but his eyes were bright and hard, and when they fixed on her face she felt like a deer caught in headlights.

'Well?'

It wasn't fair. She had waited for this moment for so long, hoped and prayed for it, and now it was here. But for it to happen now, with this man who didn't love her and never would, in this relationship that was a sham, a mutually convenient charade, was just too much. It was impossible to say the words out loud and instead she held out the test. He stared down at it in silence. His expression didn't change, but his breathing did.

'It's wrong,' she said quickly.

There was a tense, electric moment, and then his mouth shifted into a question mark. 'How is it wrong? There are two lines. The two lines mean you're pregnant.'

No, she thought again, swaying forward then back again. There must be some other explanation, and that would become plain. She just needed a moment to think clearly and rationally, only her head was spinning so fast that her thoughts were impossible to catch.

'I know that's what it's supposed to mean. But it's wrong. It must be faulty.' She was babbling now and he was looking at her, incredulous, stunned.

'And what about those ones?' He stalked across the bathroom to where she'd left the other tests next to the basin. 'Are these wrong too?' he said, picking them up and brandishing them at her.

'Yes. They are. They must be. I can't be pregnant.'

For a moment he didn't speak, and then, 'And yet you are,' he said slowly.

And yet she was.

Only how could it have happened? Given the odds of everything in that moment. Her history; the time of the month; the fact that Jack had worn a condom. There must be some mistake—

'You're damn right it's a mistake—'

Her chin jerked up, and, meeting Jack's angry gold gaze, she realised that she had spoken out loud. And then, registering his words, suddenly she was angry too. 'That's not what I said. I just meant that it shouldn't have happened.'

Not just shouldn't. She had thought it couldn't.

But the test in her hand said different. Her anger vanished as quickly as it had flared up and she stared down at the plastic wand dazedly, lost in the long line of failed attempts, the months of waiting, of trying not to get her hopes up. 'I don't know how it did, it's like a miracle—'

The silence that followed that remark was like a heavy, smothering blanket so that suddenly it was a struggle not just to talk but to breathe. Jack was staring at her, his powerful shoulders taut against his jacket. And then a shadow passed over his face.

'You're good,' he said softly, but there was a suggestion of contempt and menace in his voice as if he might bare his teeth at any moment.

'You really are very good.'

She stared at him in confusion. Good at what? A smile that was not a smile was curving the corners of his mouth and the fluttering queasiness she'd felt at the airport was back. Unthinkingly, she pressed her hand against her stomach and his eyes narrowed in on the movement, the not-smile vanishing from his face.

'It's impressive.'

Except he didn't sound impressed. She watched his lip curl. Or look it either.

'All of it,' he continued. 'The trembling voice. The wide-eyed shock.' He held her gaze. 'You must have had a lot of practice. Is that why you have two ex-husbands? Did you pull this sort of stunt with them too?'

Stunt.

The air snapped taut between them. Ondine blinked. A swirling misery was rising up inside her like water in a storm drain. She couldn't breathe, couldn't speak. For a moment she thought back to all the months of shame and despair and feeling a failure on so many levels. But then the hard gleam in his eyes pulled her back, and, lifting her chin, she met his gaze. 'You don't know anything about me or my ex-husbands. As for "stunts", I'm not the one jumping off boats for kicks when I'm loaded.'

'No, you get your kicks by taking someone's life and burning it to the ground. I cannot believe you thought I'd swallow this garbage.' He tossed the tests into the sink, the frustration and fury in his face rolling through her like wildfire. 'So when did you really find out? That you're pregnant, I mean.'

Her head jerked up, her gaze locking with his. 'I found out just now. The same time as you did.'

Jack leaned back against the vanity unit and again she got that suggestion of barely controlled menace. 'You expect me to believe that. I may be stupid—as I married you that's pretty much a given—but I'm not a total fool.'

Her heart gave a kick in her throat as he pushed away from the sink and took a step towards her. 'So, this is your MO, is it?'

She blinked. 'My MO?'

'Is that how you got the last two idiots to marry you?' he persisted. 'By pretending you were having their baby? Only this time you messed up. You actually got pregnant. So whose is it?' His glittering eyes tore into her. 'The baby. Who's the father?'

Shock was reverberating through her like a train hitting the buffers. Who did he think was the father?

'You are,' she said. 'You know you are.'

He straightened then: six feet three of furious, restrained male in clothes that probably cost more than her car. 'I don't know anything of the sort. I know we had sex once. I also know that I wore a condom—'

'Maybe you didn't put it on the right way.'

'The right way?' The disbelief in his voice was partnered by an expression of pure incredulity. 'I'm not some clueless teenager, Ondine. I know how to put on a condom so why don't you stop with all the games and—?'

'You think getting pregnant is a game?' She felt her stomach lurch, and she was suddenly close to tears.

His eyes gleamed dark gold beneath the recessed lights. 'No, no, no, this is not how this goes. You don't get to be affronted, Ondine. You're not the one who's being played here.'

'You haven't been played,' she snapped, focusing her panic and anger on him. 'I'm as shocked as you are.' More so, in fact.

He was shaking his head, fury and frustration imprinted in the flawless symmetry of his face. 'I don't believe you. I think you found out you were pregnant that day I came back to yours.'

'That's not true.' The intensity of his dark gold gaze made her feel light-headed. 'I didn't know I was pregnant until five minutes ago, and you are the baby's father and that's the truth.'

'No, the truth is that when I suggested you marry me, you threw me out of your house. But then, lo and behold, two hours later you turn up at the bungalow, all jittery and wide-eyed, and everything's changed and now you do want to marry me.' He laughed derisively. 'And you expect me to believe that it has nothing to do with this. That it was just some random coincidence.'

'It was,' she protested. And not just a coincidence. Finding out that Oli's fund was gone, and, worse, that she had been a passive bystander to its mismanagement, had been an enormous stomach-churning shock.

'So what happened in those two hours? Why did you change your mind?'

Her chest felt as if it were being crushed in a vice and she opened her eyes wide so that they wouldn't fill with tears. Listening to her brother talk about his day at the hospital, hearing the happiness in his voice, she had felt not just love but awe. He was such a remarkable person, and he would be a remarkable doctor. How could she have told him that he couldn't go to medical school? Not this year, maybe not ever if he couldn't get a bursary.

She might have messed up her own life, but she wasn't about to wreck his too—

Only telling Jack about the college fund would mean revealing so much more about herself and her life than she was willing to share with anyone, but particularly this man who already thought so little of her. She might not have money or power, but she still had some pride.

And, frankly, he wasn't in the mood to listen to her anyway. As far as he was concerned, she was guilty.

'You put me on the spot. And it was a lot to think about. I needed time to process it.' That was all true, but it wasn't why she had changed her mind and she knew it. Worse, Jack knew it too. She could tell by the curl of his lip.

His breath hissed through his teeth. 'Time to process it?' There was a harshness to his voice that made a shiver wash over her skin, and she could practically see the interrobang hanging in the air between them. 'You must think I was born yesterday.'

She stared at him, her breath hot and sharp in her throat.

Years ago, she had dreamed of watching that second line appear, faint at first, then strong and indisputable. She had imagined the moment of revelation and mutual joy, and now it had happened, finally, miraculously, only there was no joy, just anger and suspicion and doubt and resentment.

'Actually, oddly enough, I'm not thinking about anything but this baby.'

His perfect mouth twisted. 'Don't give me that. The only person you're thinking about is you. You got yourself knocked up, but your baby daddy doesn't want to know, does he? Did he see you for the devious, opportunistic little hustler you are? Is that why you set this whole pantomime of a marriage in motion? Or was he just not as rich as I am?'

The injustice of his words knocked the breath from her lungs, and it was almost impossible to stop herself from reacting, to restrain herself from picking up the pregnancy tests and hurling them in his beautiful, scorn-filled face.

'How dare you?' Her hands curled into fists. 'First off, this stupid marriage was your idea. And just to be clear, you might be paying me to be your wife but that's exactly why you're the last man on this planet I'd choose to impregnate me. Do you really think I'd want some arrogant, entitled trustafarian brat like you to father my child? Because I don't,' she said, answering her own question.

'And secondly, it doesn't matter whether you believe me or not, Jack. There is no "he". There is no other man in my life—'

'Do not try and tell me this baby is mine.' He was backing away from her, the dangerous, dark undertone back in his voice. 'This is on you. It's not my responsibility—'

It.

That hurt, appallingly. Not just that he didn't believe her but that he was rejecting his baby, her baby, their baby and a bud of defiance blossomed inside her as her hands moved protectively over her still-flat stomach.

'I never said it was. In fact, I don't want it to be. I don't want anything to do with you. I want out of this stupid, farcical marriage.' Not that there was much to get out of. She had signed an NDA and a prenup and Jack had given her an upfront payment, which she would return if it meant waitressing every night for the rest of her life. But neither of them had wanted to put the sordid transactional details of their arrangement in writing.

His beautiful face creased into something angular and ugly. 'You took the words right out of my mouth.'

He spun round and stalked out of the bathroom.

Ondine stared at the space where he had been standing, anger surging through her as hot and ungovernable as the hunger that had briefly flared between them and she stormed after him but he was already at the bottom of the stairs and then he disappeared from view.

Her head was spinning as if she were drunk, and then she felt wave after wave of nausea and she turned and stumbled back into the bathroom and threw up.

CHAPTER FIVE

WRENCHING OPEN THE French windows, Jack strode purpose-fully across the lawn. Or that was what someone watching him might have thought. In reality he felt like a drunk man doing a field sobriety test, and the truth was he had no idea where he was going or what he was going to do when he got there.

All he knew was that he couldn't spend another second in that bathroom with Ondine and her lies and duplicity.

And that was another reason to hate her, he thought sav-agely, glancing back at the house.

The Walcott family owned several properties. But Red Knots was different from all the rest. Since he could re-member, he'd spent part of every summer there and, for him, it was a place of simple, unthinking calm. A refuge from the uncomfortable truths of the past and the failings in the present.

It held a special place in his grandfather's heart too. John Walcott had met his wife, Candace, in Martha's Vineyard. Like Ondine, she was working as a waitress. The difference was that for John and Candace it was love at first sight. And they were still in love, holding hands and gazing into one another's eyes like loved-up teenagers in every single photo he'd ever seen of them. Right up until when his grandmother died the year before he was born.

He hadn't told Ondine that. He hadn't wanted her to get the wrong idea. To imagine that their relationship might one day blossom into something more substantial, more permanent.

But now that had happened anyway, right under his straight, patrician nose. Thanks to Ondine's duplicity, what had started out as a quid pro quo transaction was now a Gordian knot of nightmarish outcomes.

He breathed out shakily. His body was still ringing with the shock of what she had just told him. She was lying to him, of course. She must be lying. He had used a condom, *hell*, he always used a condom. It couldn't be his baby.

But what if it was?

He felt his chest tighten as Ondine's voice echoed inside his head.

'You're the last man on this planet I'd choose to impregnate me. Do you really think I'd want some arrogant, entitled trustafarian brat like you to father my child? Because I don't.'

A spasm of pressure he chose not to identify squeezed his heart.

How he lived, how he *needed* to live, was not compatible with parenthood. It wasn't even compatible with long-term relationships. That was why he'd ended up in this ridiculous sham marriage in the first place. A marriage that was supposed to be a solution to his problems, not an additional problem to solve. A marriage he had impulsively entered into knowing only half the facts.

The sound of waves broke into his thoughts and he realised that he had made his way to the jetty. Beside it, the launch bobbed jauntily on the water, her smooth fibreglass hull bumping gently against the wood in time to his heartbeat.

He shoved his hands into his pockets. He hadn't been

near the sea since that morning all those weeks ago and, looking at it, he felt his body tense. Ondine had pulled him from that same water, breathed air into his lungs. She had saved his life.

Now, though, she seemed more intent on derailing it.

His mouth thinned. It wasn't fair. He had taken precautions. So, why was this happening to him?

His shoulders tensed against the warm breeze because he knew why. He had taken too much at face value. Focused on the big picture rather than examining the details. He had looked at Ondine and seen an opportunity. A woman who needed money. And because he had money to spare he'd thought that put him in charge.

He'd thought the same about that deal with the Canadians. The one that had ended with an expensive settlement and his removal from the board. Apparently, he hadn't learned his lesson.

Gritting his teeth, he glanced up at the serene blue sky. Was that what this was? Was all of this the balancing of some vast cosmic quadratic equation of which he was just a component? It certainly felt like it. He felt insignificant, wound up, powerless.

Just like when he was a child being ferried back and forth between his parents' homes. Grudgingly welcomed then passed back with almost tangible relief as if he were a low-ranking card in Chase the Ace.

His hands balled in his pockets.

And then inevitably it had happened. In their speed to get back to their new Jack-free lives, there had been a screw-up, a misstep in communications. He had broken his arm.

Sometimes he wondered about how things might have played out afterwards. If his mother hadn't extended her holiday in St Barts. Or his father had decided to wait for her to arrive, choosing to spend a few more minutes in the company of his only son instead of leaving him in the care of the housekeeper as usual.

His throat clenched and for a moment he couldn't seem to make the deck beneath his feet stay still, and, reaching out, he gripped the railing to steady himself. Of course, neither of those things had happened and that was when his grandfather had stepped in and taken him to live in New York.

But this 'situation' with Ondine was different. Whichever way he worked through this particular equation the outcome was going to be the same.

It didn't matter if he was the father of this baby or not. He had already told his grandfather that he and Ondine were married. So, if he backed out now on his honeymoon, he was going to look more flaky, less mature, less everything he needed to be to win back John D. Walcott IV's trust and respect, and his place back on the board.

For that to happen, he needed time to prove himself worthy at work. That was why he had agreed with Ondine to stay married for at least a year. By then he would have shown his grandfather that he was capable of stepping into his shoes. Then they could gradually and quietly start to live separate lives. Or that was the plan.

If you could even call it that. He ran his hand over his face, feeling suddenly exhausted.

Everything he'd assumed would happen wasn't going to work now because in a year's time, Ondine would have given birth, and the optics of leaving your wife with a small baby were about as bad as it could get.

In other words, he was cornered. There was going to be no release from this trap he had set and sprung himself, or at least not within the timescale he'd planned. And not without tearing off a limb, metaphorically speaking. Although

Ondine probably wouldn't be averse to doing that in real life, he thought, picturing her small, furious face.

His mouth twisted. She had no right to be angry. He was the one who'd had his life turned upside down and inside out. But he wasn't a kid any more. He was in control. He made the decisions now, and he was deciding to make this sham of a marriage work.

He stopped breathing.

Although he might have said the opposite to Ondine.

Replaying the words they had flung at one another as he'd stormed out of the bathroom, he felt a flicker of unease. But she hadn't meant what she said. She wouldn't act on it, would she?

The waves slapping against the side of the launch seemed to grow louder, taking on the rhythm of his suddenly racing heart, and, swearing under his breath, he turned and began to walk swiftly back towards the house.

Red Knots looked as it always did. And, as always, gazing up at it quietened his mind. There was no way Ondine would make good on her threat. Even if she hadn't signed any paperwork, she needed money. Even more so now. But as he made his way upstairs, he felt another flicker of unease. The bedroom was empty. The bathroom too, and it was tidy. He stared for a moment at the vanity unit, remembering how he had tossed the pregnancy tests into the sink. Then he turned and checked the other bedrooms and bathrooms.

But there was no sign of her.

Downstairs, heart accelerating, he moved from room to room. In the kitchen, the housekeeper, Sally, was weighing out some flour. Aside from that, the room was empty and he was beginning to panic.

She couldn't have left the island. There was only one boat

and that was tied up at the jetty. So short of swimming back to Martha's Vineyard—

Surely she wouldn't attempt that. But then he remembered how she had pulled him through the water, and the steadiness of her grip around his chest. Only that had been close to shore. Here the currents were swift and treacherous. Slamming back outside, he made his way around the veranda, feeling sick to his stomach—

He stopped short.

Ondine was sitting on the porch swing, hugging her knees to her chest. She was wearing the same clothes as earlier but her feet were bare now. It made her look more delicate, more vulnerable, younger than before. Like a child playing dress-up. And in a way that was what she was. What this was. Except they couldn't just change out of their clothes and go back to being who they were. Not yet anyway.

'I thought you might be swimming back to the mainland.' It was harder than it should have been to keep his voice calm.

Her blue eyes met his. She looked pale and tired, but defiant. 'I agreed to be your wife. If I say I'm going to do something, I do it.'

Even as his anger simmered inside him, he felt a twitch of respect, admiration even. And relief. 'You did say that,' he agreed. 'But you also said you wanted out of this farcical marriage.'

There was a short silence.

'You said you wanted that too,' she said finally. He watched as she let go of her knees, stretching out her legs. Her feet seemed suddenly particularly bare, so bare that he was distracted by their soft curving arches and then, with crashing predictability, by a memory of how the rest of her body looked naked.

He gritted his teeth. He needed no reminder.

'I did. I do. Only I think we both know that can't happen. So, it looks like I'm stuck with you.'

He didn't bother hiding the bitterness in his voice, but as she hugged her knees closer to her chest he wished he had. Then he told himself that he didn't care. That it was her fault for trying to trick him into taking responsibility for another man's mistake.

Her chin tilted up. 'And I with you.'

She made it sound as if the idea appalled her as much as it did him and it shouldn't have stung as it did. But her words scraped against old wounds inside him. 'As if! You wanted this, all of this.'

'You're wrong,' she said flatly. 'I wanted to pay my bills. That's all. That's why I agreed to marry you. And I know you don't believe me, just like you don't believe that you're the father of this baby, but both those things are true.'

Now she got to her feet. 'I can't prove the first so I'm not going to try to.'

She was standing close enough to him that he could have counted her freckles. Close enough that he could smell the clean, floral scent of her hair. Close enough that if he wanted to, he could have reached out and pressed her body against his.

'But I can take a paternity test,' she said quietly.

His heart thumped against his ribs. If she was offering to do that she must be pretty sure he was the father. He felt an ache in his stomach, like hunger, except he had no appetite. He was the son nobody wanted. His parents had next to no input in his life. How could he possibly raise a child?

What the hell are you talking about?

He swore silently. Of course he wasn't the father. He'd get better odds on there being a white Christmas in Palm Beach. They'd had sex once. He'd worn a condom.

And condoms were only ninety-eight per cent effective.

He felt panic jump in his throat. But why? The odds of a condom failing on that one occasion were minuscule, and besides it was all too much of a coincidence her 'finding out' she was pregnant after they were married.

It was just the nearness of her throwing him into a state of confusion, making his head swim, and he hated that she could do that to him, and it was easier to hate her. Neater. Less unsettling. In fact, it was a relief.

'Do one, don't do one.' He shrugged. 'It's your call. But don't think for one moment that it's going to change anything because it won't.'

The skin over her cheeks looked taut, and her mouth was trembling a little but when she spoke her voice was steady. 'You're right, it won't.'

Staring down at her, he frowned. He'd thought she'd protest, argue, throw her offer back in his face but she was calm and her face was still and shuttered.

'Don't worry, Jack. I'll say what you want me to say. I'll hold your hand and look into your eyes and smile at you for as long as it takes to convince your grandfather that you're the man he wants you to be. The man you can never be in reality. And then we'll go our separate ways like we agreed. And as for this baby.'

She took a step backwards, just as she had that day in the bedroom when all of this had been set in motion. 'You were right about that. This baby is never going to be your responsibility so as of now that topic of conversation is off-limits.'

'That won't be a problem,' he snarled.

'I didn't imagine it wou—' She broke off, her face tensing. He frowned. 'What is it?'

'I'm going to be sick,' she said hoarsely and, eyes widening with panic, she clamped her hand to her mouth.

* * *

It was some three days now since Ondine had told Jack that he was not responsible for either her or her baby. Those words were in his head when he woke up every morning. They stayed with him as he fell asleep.

He frowned. And yet here he was, still on Whydah, watching her sleep. Shifting forward in his chair, he stared down at her, his eyes resting on her still, pale face.

But he still wasn't convinced that he should be there. In fact, most of the time he felt like an imposter.

His frown deepened. Because he was one. Their marriage might be legal, but legal was different from real. And the reality was that he was paying Ondine to be his wife; only he needed facts to fit the fiction and, ironically, the only fact that would stand up to robust scrutiny was a pregnancy that had nothing to do with him.

His hand tensed against the armrest as Ondine moaned in her sleep.

Except it did. Whether they discussed it or not, this baby was making its presence felt, twenty-four-seven, because, despite its name, the sickness didn't just happen in the morning. If anything, the nausea was worse at night. Which was why she was sleeping now, at two o'clock in the afternoon, leaving him to play the doting husband sitting by her bed.

For the optics, obviously. He could hardly abandon his wife in her hour of need. But also, because he couldn't seem to look away from the woman he had called a devious, opportunistic little hustler. All of which was still true. But in light of everything else that was happening right now, it just seemed to matter less.

The doctor had repeated what that woman had said to him at the gallery. That the sickness was typically the sign of a healthy pregnancy, and he understood the science of it. But looking over at Ondine's pale face, he still found it difficult to believe.

About as difficult as it was to believe that he was the father of this baby.

His shoulders stiffened. They hadn't talked about that particular ticking time bomb since that day out on the veranda. But then they hadn't talked much at all. Mostly because Ondine was either in the bathroom being sick or sleeping like now. If they happened to be in the same space she spoke, not to him, but in his general direction. Those occasional snatched conversations they'd had were brief and joylessly polite.

'You can go. I can manage on my own, thank you.'

She'd said that on the first day when she had unlocked the bathroom door and found him waiting for her in the bedroom. Wearing plain grey sweatpants, some kind of stretchy top and with her dark hair twisted into a kind of low, messy bun, she could have been heading off to some yoga class. Only the dark smudges beneath her ridiculously fluttery eyelashes gave any indication of the exhausting days and disrupted nights.

'You don't need to do this,' she told him after another moment as if she'd needed a breath or two to regroup before she could speak again. 'You don't have to stay. Just go and catch lobsters or whatever it is you normally do when you come here—'

'When I normally come here I'm not on my honeymoon.'

Titling back her face, her eyes met his. 'Well, I'm sorry if you're disappointed, Jack, but if you're hanging around hoping that—'

That stung. Did she really think so poorly of him? His jaw tightened. 'Seriously, don't flatter yourself. Once was enough.'

'Then you won't mind leaving,' she said coldly. 'We were only hiding out together so we could pretend we were having sex but we're obviously not doing that now.'

Her face had tensed then, just as it had out on the veranda, and she'd bolted back into the bathroom.

But she'd said exactly the same thing each time she returned to the bedroom, her mouth flattening when she saw him, and he knew he should be relieved. But for some reason her stubbornness had infuriated him, and so yesterday afternoon when she'd repeated the exact same words, he'd shaken his head and said, 'That's not going to happen.'

'Why not?' she countered immediately.

Her face had no colour at all. Even the blue of her eyes looked washed out, like faded denim, and he could hear the exhaustion in her voice. He knew that she was struggling. But she had already thrown one spectacular wrench into the works, from now on they were going to do things his way.

'Because it would look odd. What would Sally think if I just left you being sick on your own?' With Ondine being so ill, he'd had no choice but to tell the housekeeper and the rest of the staff. But he'd also made it clear the pregnancy was too early to be announced. That at least was something he could control.

She'd shrugged. 'I'm sure you'll think of some suitable explanation, Jack. You can be very convincing, remember?' Beneath the fatigue there was a jaggedness that set his teeth on edge.

'And I'm your husband, remember?'

'No, you're the man I married for money.'

That was inarguable but he still felt as though he'd been kicked by a horse. 'That still makes me your husband.'

There was a hard pause, and then she gave a small shake of her head. 'Only on paper. It isn't real.'

'But your morning sickness is.' His eyes locked with hers. 'That's why I'm staying.' During the hours of daylight anyway.

A faint tremor ran through her body. She lifted her head and stared at him mutely, her face set into taut, wary lines, and for a few half-seconds he was tempted to reach out and smooth them away with his fingers. Fortunately, before he could act on that impulse, she turned and, heart beating out of time, he watched her walk away, and he kept watching right up until she closed the bathroom door behind her.

CHAPTER SIX

AT FIRST HE thought someone was laughing. That she was laughing.

It was a quarter to midnight. He was sitting on his bed, his eyes fixed on the connecting door to Ondine's room.

It was the room his grandfather had set aside for his parents to use when they visited Red Knots. But despite having a nanny in tow, neither his mother or father had considered it relaxing to vacation with their young son, so it had been his grandfather who took him to the island, his grandfather who comforted him when he had a nightmare or a stomach ache that stopped him from sleeping.

Now he wasn't sleeping for a different reason.

There was a faint strip of light under the door but that wasn't what had caught his attention. It was the noise, faint, intermittent, jerky, fading to silence, then swelling again—

Crying, not laughing.

Shoulders tensing, he glanced away to the window. Outside everything was black on black and so quiet. Not a creature was stirring, not even a mouse. Just his conscience, he thought with a flicker of irritation as he found himself staring at the door again.

But why? Ondine wasn't his responsibility. Their marriage wasn't real. She'd said so herself.

'But your morning sickness is.' He gritted his teeth. That was what *he'd* said so that he could override her wishes.

Had she known that? He didn't know. But it appeared that he wasn't quite enough of an arrogant, entitled trustafarian brat to just sit here and let her struggle with her nausea alone.

Whether or not there was anyone there to see it.

He got to his feet. This was a mistake on so many levels—

Ondine was sitting on the bathroom floor, her face resting on her elbows, her elbows resting on the side of the bath, her back rising and falling jerkily. Her shoulder blades looked like angel's wings. Gazing down at her, he felt his ribs tightening. Now what?

'Ondine?'

At the sound of his voice, she froze, body stiffening, but she didn't look up at him. Instead, stifling a sob, she turned her head away so that he couldn't see her face, her arm curving protectively around her stomach.

'Are you okay?' He winced inside. Stupid question. She clearly wasn't. 'Can I get you anything?' Better, but not much.

She was shaking her head, not meeting his eyes. 'No, I… Could you just go?' She made a harsh little sound as if her throat were too tight. 'Please. I don't want you here.'

A muscle ticced in his jaw. Okay, job done. He had asked, and she had answered, so he had done more than most men would in his situation, but for some reason his legs didn't seem to want to move.

He gritted his teeth. 'But I can't leave you. Not like this.'

She was sick then. At first, he just stood there, feeling helpless and superfluous, but the second time it happened, he crouched down and caught hold of her hair, bunching the silky strands into a loose ball. Her neck was hot and damp but she was shivering as if she was cold, and he felt a stab of anger for the man who had let her deal with this alone.

Except she wasn't alone. He was there, he realised with a jolt.

'It's okay, you're going to be okay.' He kept talking quietly, calmly, the words forming with an ease that surprised him. It seemed unlikely that she was even listening, but then at one point she looked up at him, her face pale and tearstained.

'You don't have to do this—be here.'

The shame in her voice scraped against his skin and he had a flashback, vivid as a photograph, of coughing up seawater onto the sand and Ondine gripping his shoulder, the pulse in her hand steadying the choking panic in his chest.

'You're right, I don't. I'm choosing to be here.' Heart banging, he sat down beside her. 'And the only reason I'm here to make that choice is because of you.' She looked up at him and the soft blue of her gaze tugged at something inside him. 'Because you saved my life.'

She was only sick one more time after that. He sat on the edge of the bath while she washed her face and brushed her teeth and then followed her back into the bedroom.

'I'll be fine now.' Her voice was husky and the smudges under her eyes looked darker, but her face was no longer pinched with panic.

'Okay. But if you need anything, I'm just next door—' He cleared his throat. 'But you know that—'

She nodded, lifting her head slightly so that she was looking at a point just past his shoulder. 'I'll be fine. I just need to get some sleep. We both should.'

We.

The word pinged inside his head, tripping the automatic

alarm that was his early warning defence system against any kind of intimacy and obligation.

It was one of the many exhausting contradictions of his life. He hated being alone, but he couldn't let people get close either. To do that would mean trusting them to stick around when he messed up, and he didn't trust easily.

We was a signal to cool things down. *We* meant that he needed to take a step back. *We* conjured up a lifetime of hastily exited hotel suites, arguments and half-hearted promises that made his body brace and his weight shift to the balls of his feet like a sprinter getting ready to run.

His heart skipped a beat.

And yet he didn't feel like running now, any more than he had in the bathroom when she was being sick. On the contrary, he felt as if there were some kind of forcefield pushing the two of them together.

Of course, that was probably because, as co-conspirators in this sham marriage, he and Ondine were already a 'we' of sorts. What other reason could there be? They had no history. No trust. This baby was her future, not his. What else was there between them?

Sex.

The hair on his arms rose stiffly and he glanced over to where Ondine stood watching him in an oversized grey T-shirt he hadn't even registered before, his whole body tensing as that blunt, unprompted answer was accompanied by a crystalline memory of her lips parting as she rocked against him. Above the sound of his heart, he could hear those noises she'd made in her throat of half need, half abandonment as he'd driven into her.

Was she remembering it too?

Or was she remembering when he'd told her that once was enough?

His hands curled at his sides and he was on the verge of telling her that he hadn't meant what he'd said and that he regretted saying it, but then he came to his senses. 'I'll say goodnight, then.'

She nodded, and he was already backing away from her when she spoke.

'Goodnight. And thank you…' She hesitated as he looked over at her and he could see her pulse jerking in her throat. 'Thank you for staying with me. It was kind of you.'

She was thanking him? His chin jerked up and as his eyes met hers, he saw a confusion that matched his own as if she couldn't quite believe what she had just said.

He shrugged. 'I'm glad I could be of some help.' And strangely, he was.

For a moment, they stared at one another in silence separated by a few feet of Persian carpet and then he said quickly, 'I'll see you tomorrow.'

Except it was already tomorrow, he thought, as he finally got back into bed. Outside the darkness was fading away. Now everything looked grey. The colour of compromise.

The C-word.

His mouth twisted. Compromise was not normally part of his vocabulary. Or his life. And this marriage wasn't supposed to be any different. In his head it all seemed very black and white. His money in exchange for Ondine's collusion. Marriage as a performance.

But earlier when he had gone to find her in the bathroom, he had chosen to carry on in character even though there had been no staff around and it had been just the two of them. And while he'd been holding her hair and stroking her back, everything had loosened into something less rigid. More grey. No longer just in or out, but somewhere in between.

And he could live with that.

In fact, it had been a little naive to assume there wouldn't be some overlap, some kind of compromise. He rolled onto his side, his eyes closing. But that didn't mean he was about to get caught up in her lies.

Now that was progress.

Gazing down at her empty plate, Ondine sank back against the cushions. She had finished two whole slices of toast and, instead of nauseous, she felt light-headed, intoxicated almost. Was that possible? Could you get drunk on food?

It didn't seem likely, but the last few weeks had taught her that anything was possible, no matter how unlikely. Miracles did happen, and, frankly, she was just relieved to not be feeling sick.

For almost all her life she had taken her body for granted. Unlike, say, her ability to recall facts or make good decisions, it was the one thing she could rely on and most of her life she had done so unreservedly. And then on that day trip to Martha's Vineyard everything had changed. Each morning she woke up feeling as if she were a stranger, living in the same body but utterly changed. Since then, she had been forced to adapt on an almost hour-by-hour basis.

As of now, water and flat Gatorade were in; coffee was out. She still couldn't even think about dairy produce and watching a film where the two lead protagonists ate pizza had made her skin turn clammy. But she was definitely feeling better and, thanks to Sally, she was starting to tentatively enjoy eating again.

The housekeeper really had been incredibly kind.

And she wasn't the only one.

Pulse stumbling, Ondine glanced across the table.

She and Jack were having breakfast outside on the deck and anyone looking at them would think they were the perfect honeymooning couple. And Jack, louche in plaid pyjamas and a white T-shirt that emphasised his muscle-defined chest and arms, with his handsome face tilted up to the warm mid-morning sun, looked like the perfect husband.

He had been acting like one too.

Or maybe she didn't mean acting, because that was what he did when other people were around—like now. And that was simply a box-ticking exercise designed to corroborate their marriage.

What she was talking about was how he behaved when it was just the two of them alone.

Picking up her glass, she took a sip of water. That first night, when he'd come into the bathroom, she had wanted to crawl into a ball and hide beneath a carapace of impenetrable spines. It had been bad enough being sick but to have Jack there watching—

She had thought he would leave her to it. After all, he couldn't have made it clearer that he wasn't responsible for this baby.

Her hands moved instinctively over her stomach as she remembered her own shock and disbelief and fluttery astonishment when she'd gazed down at the positive tests. After so long trying for a baby, to discover that she was pregnant with a man who was paying her to be his wife had been too much to take in. It hadn't felt real, but then almost immediately she had started being sick and all her doubts had been confounded, forgotten. Irrelevant.

Jack's too, maybe, she thought, her gaze arrowing in on his beautiful profile. Was that why he sat with her every night? Her sole guardian in those hours when the world shrank to the walls of their ensuite bathroom? Scooping back her hair. Talking nonsense to her in that beautiful, easy drawl of his while she retched and shook and wept.

She felt her heart thud hard inside her chest. He hadn't said as much. But what other reason could there be?

'What's up?'

Looking up, she felt her pulse stumble. Jack was frowning across the table. Unlike most people when they frowned, his features didn't grow harsh. Instead, it made him appear more as if he had been cast in bronze.

Glancing away, she wondered how long would it take to get used to his beauty? A lot longer than their marriage would last, she thought with a distant sort of jolt.

'Are you feeling sick again?'

He was leaning forward now, looking concerned, and she knew he was only doing so because Sally was nearby, but she couldn't stop herself from wondering what it would be like if he weren't just playing a part but really cared about her.

She shook her head. 'No, I was just thinking that I've never seen such a perfect lawn.'

As his dark gold eyes moved past her shoulder to the rectangle of flawless green grass, she took a steadying breath. She might not be throwing up any more, but she was definitely suffering from sleep deprivation because there was no way Jack Walcott would ever see her as anything but a means to get his life back on track.

And she didn't want him to. Didn't want him.

Liar.

Her cheeks felt suddenly as if they were under a heat lamp. Okay, that might be something of an exaggeration. The truth was that whenever she let her mind wander, she could think of nothing but those feverish moments in her bedroom and how his lips had tasted and the way his hands had made her forget everything but the need pounding through her body.

But was it so surprising that memory had imprinted in her head? So much had happened that day, so many big emotions unleashed, a connection formed beneath the water, her breath moving through his body—

'You need to tell my grandfather that when you meet him.' Jack was looking at her now, his eyes glittering in the sunlight. 'The croquet lawn is his pride and joy. We could play a game if you like.'

She laughed. Because it was funny. Not that long ago she had been serving drinks to this man. Now he was her husband and he was inviting her to play croquet with him.

'Why are you laughing?'

'It's just the idea of me playing croquet. That's not who I am.'

He smiled then, a curling, devastating smile that seemed to slide over her skin like sunlight and turn the sun into just another distant, indistinguishable star and she thought, not for the first time, that it had been a lot easier in some ways when they'd had the buffer of their hate between them.

'Maybe you don't know who you are,' he said softly.

She stared at him, his words pinballing inside her head, the slow burn of his gaze making her breath catch. It was a shock to hear him say out loud what she had been thinking for so long. But the truth was Jack was right. She didn't know who she was. Had never really known even when she was growing up.

But then, it was more about what she wasn't than who she was. Her mum, her dad and Oli were all so clever, whereas she had struggled at school to be anything but average. For a short time, she had been above average at swimming, but a shoulder injury had forced her to pull out of training. A week later she'd met her first husband.

Garrett had been handsome, hard-working and impatient to begin the life he'd had mapped out. And she had been at the centre of that life. Until she couldn't get pregnant and then in the space of a few months she'd become a divorcee, an orphan and a surrogate parent to her teenage brother.

Devastated, terrified, adrift, she had stumbled into her second marriage and out the other side into her subsequent divorce. Poorer but no wiser, apparently, she thought, gazing across the table at her third husband. And even just thinking that made her cheeks hot and her skin prickle.

She had married Jack for Oli's sake, but what did that make her? A sacrifice? A fool?

And what about after it ended? Who would she be then?

Glancing up, she realised Sally was waiting to clear away the plates.

'I did think about maybe wandering down to the beach,' she said quickly, wanting, needing to change the subject and drag the path of her thoughts onto a firmer, less unsettling footing. 'I feel like I haven't left the house for weeks.'

You could see the ocean from every window, and it was pleasant sitting here in the sunshine surrounded by the artfully arranged shrubs and trees, but now she was feeling more herself, she craved the raw, untouched beauty of nature.

There was a brief blink-and-you'll-miss-it silence and then he shrugged, his smile still in place. 'Sure, why not?'

It took six, maybe seven minutes to reach the curving beach. As they walked over the top of the shallow dunes, Ondine felt like a pilgrim stepping off the *Mayflower*.

She had wanted raw and untouched, and this was it.

Pristine, powder-fine, bone-white sand, speckled at the

shoreline with pale pebbles, stretched in either direction. In the shelter of the bluff, the bleached remains of a tree lay on its side like a fallen statue. Beyond the sand, the Atlantic rippled like molten glass.

It was absurdly beautiful, spectacular, dramatic, and it seemed astonishing to her that it all belonged to just one family.

All except the sea. That didn't belong to anyone.

'It's amazing,' she said quietly.

Jack nodded, the warm breeze stirring his fringe as he toed the sand with his shoe. 'I think so.'

Shielding her eyes from the mid-morning sun, she let her gaze drift over the mesmerically shifting waves. The sea was different here...not blue like in Florida. In fact, it looked almost lavender-coloured.

'It's hard to believe that's the same ocean as back in Palm Beach. That we could have swum in that water.' As she spoke, what looked like a fishing boat chugged into view and she had a sudden, vivid flashback of Jack leaping into the air—

Beside her, she felt rather than saw him tense and she bit the inside of her mouth, wishing she could bite back her words. Was he seeing it too? Was he feeling the sudden shock of impact? The downward drag of the water, relentless, inexorable, his limbs weakening as the oxygen spilled from his lips.

'Have you gone back in? Into the sea?' She hesitated. 'Since it happened, I mean.'

There was no need to specify what 'it' was, but Jack frowned almost as if he didn't understand and then he shook his head. 'Not yet. I haven't had time.'

Hadn't he? That seemed unlikely. Unlike her, he wasn't working at the moment, and, aside from some fairly undemanding paperwork, the wedding had been a work of moments to arrange.

'You have time now. Maybe we should go for a swim after lunch.' Glancing over at the shifting water, she saw it again. His body beneath the waves, the glint of his signet ring.

'Or we could just go for a dip in the pool.' There were two. One was outside, shielded from the ocean breezes by fat laurel hedges, the other was indoors. With steps leading into the water, either would be the perfect place to regain your confidence. 'It doesn't have to be a big deal, it's just I think the longer you leave it before you get back in the water, the worse it will become. It's like falling off a horse. You need to—'

Up until that point, he'd kept silent, now though he cut across her. 'I know the theory. In fact, I've fallen off plenty of horses, so you don't need to labour the point.'

'I wasn't,' she protested. 'I just thought it might help if—'

'I don't need your help. More importantly, I don't want it, so, if you're done with your amateur sports psychology—'

His face was blank of expression but the hostility in his voice shocked her into speaking.

'I'm not an amateur. I'm a trained lifeguard and a qualified swim instructor and, as it happens, I was on the national junior swim team for two years and we worked alongside sports psychologists all the time.' She took a breath. 'Look, I know what happened was shocking and horrible but, trust me—'

'Trust you?' He stared at her in silence, a stillness forming around his beautiful golden eyes, and then she almost jumped out of her skin as he laughed, a short, biting laugh that echoed around the empty beach.

'You think I trust you? That I could ever trust you?' He

was shaking his head. 'Then you're not just devious and opportunistic, you're deluded.'

Her chest felt as if it were bound in barbed wire. She stared at him, shocked, stung by the abrupt renewal of hostilities between them. She had thought they had moved on. That something had changed and softened between them, but now she saw that she had done what she always did: read motives into actions and then turned them into a better story than the one she was living.

'I was just trying to be nice. That's all, Jack. But I don't know why I bothered because you're really not worth it.'

She was suddenly, brutally tired of him and of the two of them and the wrongness of everything and, without waiting for him to reply, she spun away and began to walk back towards the dunes.

He was unbearable. Unreasonable. Unkind. Her heart pounded in time to her footsteps across the sand, then faltered. He was also the father of this baby. Later, she would wonder if that thought made her look over her shoulder, but in the moment, all she registered was the blank-page emptiness of the beach.

Jack was gone.

She had turned and, before her brain had time to catch up with the impulse of her body, was moving across the sand and then her footsteps faltered.

He was sitting on the fallen tree, his eyes fixed on the sand, his shoulders hunched in a way that pinched at something inside her. He looked like he had that day in Oliver's bedroom when finally the shock of the day had risen like a wave and pulled him under.

And now he was drowning again.

He didn't look up as she stopped in front of him, but for some reason that made her more determined to stay. 'I know how hard it is for you to trust me because I feel the same way about you,' she said quietly. 'But I do want to help you.' If you'll let me, she wanted to add.

He flicked her a glance as if he'd heard her unspoken words. 'You wouldn't understand.'

'Try me.'

His face was taut, and she knew that whatever it was, he couldn't say it out loud. But then his stillness and silence reached inside her, pushing everything out except one tiny incontestable fact and she realised that she already knew. That, deep down, she had always known.

'You can't swim,' she said quietly.

He didn't reply but again he didn't need to. She could feel the truth in the sudden escalation of tension in the air around them.

How could that be possible? But sadly, she knew that it was not just possible but statistically unremarkable. Around half the population of the US could either not swim at all or not well enough to save themselves, although Jack was wealthier than the statistical average.

She looked over to where he sat, staring straight ahead without expression. But he didn't need her to tell him that.

'How far did you get in learning?'

Silence, then, 'Not far.'

'Does anyone know?'

His face was shuttered. 'No. It never came up.' A pause and she could feel him reaching for a plausible explanation. 'My parents split up when I was young. It was quite messy.' Another pause. 'I had two sets of nannies, and I went to a lot of different schools. I think it just got missed off the to-do list. And later on, it seemed too late to do anything about it.'

Out at sea, the fishing boat was just a tiny bobbing dot.

Watching it, she replayed the moment when she had looked out to sea and seen Jack run across the deck and leap.

The memory winded her. 'But you jumped off the yacht.'

A muscle flickered in his jaw. 'I know.' There was a note to his voice she couldn't place and as if he'd heard it too, he got to his feet. 'I didn't plan to. And I wasn't drunk or high. It was a stupid impulse thing. I was tired and I'd had enough of everyone and I wanted to get off the yacht, and I was looking at the water and it suddenly seemed ridiculous that I couldn't swim. I mean, how hard could it be?'

Now he looked winded.

As the silence stretched away from them she held herself still. He was staring down at his hands, hiding his eyes, she thought, but then she saw that they were trembling.

'Not hard. If you know what you're doing.' She kept her voice matter-of-fact. 'And it's even easier if you're not wearing clothes.' She hesitated, then took hold of his hands. 'Everyone is a beginner at some point, Jack. You'd learn in a heartbeat. You just need someone to teach you. And I can do that. If you'll let me.' She said the words out loud this time.

She watched him, waiting, on edge suddenly at how badly she wanted him to trust her. At the shoreline, the waves seemed to hover mid-air, their white caps quivering. As they toppled over, Jack shifted his gaze and when he looked back, his beauty took her breath away all over again.

'Okay.' He nodded, his mouth curving up at the corners, and in the past she would have got lost somewhere between that crooked smile and the beating of her heart, but she knew now that some of his smiles, this one, for example, were designed to distract, to divert attention away from what was going on inside that beautiful, sculptured head.

'You can teach me to swim. On one condition. You let me teach you how to play croquet.'

The lightness was back in his voice now so that it was hard to tell if he was being serious, but she decided to play along. 'Deal!'

Picturing the flawless, rectangular green lawn, she added, 'Although I'm not sure where croquet is going to fit into my life.'

His gold eyes locked with hers. 'But this is your life. Our life,' he added, after a moment.

It was just words, she told herself, but suddenly her heart was thumping inside her throat and all she could think about was his hands on her body, and the clench of her muscles around his hardness.

They were standing a breath apart, his hands still entwined with hers, and they stayed like that for what felt like a long time, not moving, not speaking, just staring at one another as the air around them shifted, and tightened, pressing against them, pushing them closer—

'We should probably be getting back,' he said, dropping her hands and taking a step backwards. 'Otherwise Sally will think something's happened and we don't want her sending out a rescue party.'

It wouldn't make any difference if she did, Ondine thought, panic beating like a gong inside her chest as they headed back to the house in silence, because the only thing she needed rescuing from was herself, and her body's senseless yearning for the man walking beside her.

CHAPTER SEVEN

'COME ON, JACK. Don't phone it in. Keep pushing, keep pushing. There you go—and rest.'

Breathing out heavily, Jack lowered the hex bar to the floor of the gym and released his grip on the hot metal. His skin was coated in sweat and it felt as if every muscle in his body was screaming abuse at him. Splaying out his fingers, he let his head fall back against the wall, his eyes narrowing on his personal trainer's impassive face.

At home, Mark was a family man, the father of twin girls and a devoted husband. In the gym he was a soft-spoken but relentless taskmaster.

As if to remind him of that fact, Mark said quietly, 'Thirty seconds left. Use the time. Stay focused.'

They worked for another ninety minutes. After strength training they did mobility drills, followed by a session with the punchbag, finishing off with a cool-down and then finally it was over.

'Good workout.' Mark smiled. 'But maybe do some yoga later. You were losing focus a little,' he added by way of explanation as Jack gave him a narrow-eyed look. 'I know you're not a big fan but building muscle and increasing endurance can only happen with the right mindset.'

They shook hands. 'See you on Wednesday.'

Jack nodded. 'Wouldn't miss it.'

'You can try,' Mark called over his shoulder. 'But you know I'll find you.'

Picking up his protein shake, Jack took a gulp. Mark was based in New York, but they had trained in London, Paris, St Barts, Tulum, Ibiza. They weren't friends. Truthfully, he knew as much about his trainer now as he did when they started working together four years ago and yet, after his grandfather, Mark was probably the most constant, most reliable person in his life.

Jack glanced around the silent gym. His heartbeat was still elevated from the training session but there was another beat behind it, not of panic, not yet, but he could feel it creeping in from the edges, just as it always did whenever he was alone and there was nothing to distract his thoughts from slipping into the dangerous territory of his past.

Not just his past, he thought, his chest tightening.

From the outside, it looked as though he were part of a series of overlapping social circles. There were friends of the family, friends of friends, people he knew from the various schools he'd attended and all of them were regular fixtures at the parties and events that punctuated his calendar. But were they his friends? Could he trust them? Did they care about him?

He stared across the gym, his breath jabbing his throat as if it were a punchbag, the panic lost in the numbness that was pushing into the gaps between his ribs.

Is there anyone I can call?

Ondine had asked him that all those weeks ago when the shock of nearly drowning had finally caught up with him. Her question had been simple enough, and it came, he knew, from a place of concern. But the answer he hadn't given, the answer he was too ashamed to give her was, no: there was no one. Not his so-called friends, none of whom had bothered to check up on him that day. Not that it was all their fault. He'd been hurt too early, too much, too often to allow friendship to happen. Speaking of which—

His muscles were burning, and his hands throbbed from hitting the punchbag but as he tried imagining his parents' reactions he felt an older ache in his chest.

He knew exactly how it would have played out. If by some miracle his mother had picked up, she would no doubt have told him to call his father. But what would be the point? His stepmother always fielded his calls and she would probably just have said what she always did, which was that his father would call back.

Fat chance.

He knew from experience that if he had waited for that to happen he would still be sitting in the hospital now.

There was only one person he could have reached out to: his grandfather.

And he'd wanted to call him so badly that day in Palm Beach. But he had called him so many times in the past. There was the DUI in LA; the party in that hotel in Cannes when the room got wrecked; the arrest in Aspen for possession of a controlled substance. All of them managed and tidied away quietly and discreetly by a man who had been a guardian, a mentor, a father as much as a grandfather. John Walcott was the one person who cared about him, and enough to dispense tough love.

And he had wanted to prove he was getting his head straight, recalibrating his life, only what had happened on the yacht hardly qualified for either. But that wasn't the only reason he hadn't dialled the number. He'd known that if he heard his grandpa's quiet, authoritative voice he would weep.

His jaw clenched. He hadn't cried since he was five years old and he fell off a chair and broke his arm. He could remember the sharp snap as his elbow hit the floor, the bright white pain that blurred his sight.

Later, at the hospital the nurses kept telling him he was brave, but he wasn't. It was just that he knew then there was no point in crying; that the power of tears to stop bad things from happening only worked in fairy tales.

None of which changed the fact that his grandfather had cared and worried about him for three decades already. For once, he hadn't wanted to add to those worries.

Besides, he was scared that if he started weeping he might never stop.

Outside the window he caught a flicker of blue the exact colour of Ondine's eyes and, glancing down at the swimming pool, he felt his heart miss a beat. That wasn't what had happened with her. Okay, he hadn't actually wept but he'd been closer to tears than he'd ever been with anyone.

He could see her fingers as they curved around his, feel their warmth and the firmness of her grip. It was the same steady grip she must have used when she'd pulled him from the sea. He had only the briefest memory of it before he'd lost consciousness but in that shifting liminal space between water and air, life and death, the touch of her hand had been reassuringly, unquestionably real.

And it had felt just as real yesterday afternoon.

When Ondine had asked whether he had been swimming since the 'accident' he had panicked and done what he always did. He'd pushed back, and, as expected, she'd stormed off. *But*—and this was a first—she had come back and he had ended up telling her the truth.

Not every sordid detail but it still felt seismic.

To her too.

He could see, *feel* her shock and confusion, but she hadn't given up on him like his parents or chosen to look the other way like his so-called friends. Instead she'd taken his hand and sat with him just as she had at the hospital and afterwards, while he'd slept in her brother's bed.

A brother she clearly adored. And yet, she was also a manipulative little hustler who had tried to convince him that he was the father of her baby.

Only how could she be both?

He felt his body tense. It was a perplexing question but now that his savage anger at being caught up in her pregnancy had subsided and he was spending more time with her, it was one he wanted and needed to answer.

Who was Ondine Walcott? At various times he had cast her as opportunistic, devious, manipulative and yet he had seen no evidence of any of those qualities. Instead she was bright and funny, intermittently furious and, on occasion, downright infuriating. But she was also patient, compassionate, a good listener. And sometimes, when she didn't know she was being watched, he could sense a shadowy fatigue that had nothing to do with the pregnancy.

Only if he had been wrong about who Ondine was, then could he be wrong about other things too? Could this baby be his? He felt a twinge of panic in his chest. Someone as damaged and incomplete as he was had no business fathering a child. He wouldn't know where to start.

But Ondine would, and maybe she could teach him.

He thought back to how she had offered to teach him to swim. *If you'll let me,* she'd added.

Would he let her? He stared down at the pool, his heart bumping against his ribs, remembering the moment out on the bluff when there had been other, more urgent things he'd wanted to let her do. Other things he'd wanted to surrender to. And not just surrender to. He had wanted to seize with both his hands—

His groin tightened, a shiver moving through him and over his skin as his body relived those heated, frantic moments in her bedroom when his mouth was hard on Ondine's and he was hard inside her, harder than he'd ever been.

He couldn't forget it; he'd wanted to. Especially after she'd told him about the baby. And he assumed he would forget as he always did, although sometimes forgetting merged with pretending it had never happened. Either way, afterwards, he'd been certain that it was just a kind of PTSD, a feverish, lost-in-the-moment compulsion to hold onto something, to someone that had been feverishly and swiftly satisfied.

A pulse of heat beat across his skin as he pictured Ondine's upturned face out on the beach.

Except he didn't feel satisfied. He felt like a person crawling out of a desert who was handed a beaker of cool water only for it to be snatched from his lips.

But if he couldn't forget, then the only other option was to avoid the teasing, treacherous rip currents of desire that seemed intent on pulling him under. His eyes fixed on the pool. Only to do that, he would need to learn how to swim.

Gazing up, Ondine watched transfixed as the coin spun up into the mid-afternoon sunshine. It seemed to hover momentarily as if defying gravity and then, still spinning, it fell back down. Jack caught it. 'Your call.'

'Tails,' she said quickly.

The corners of his mouth curved very slightly. 'Looks like you're going first, Mrs Walcott.'

Jack had invited her to play croquet after lunch and, once he'd explained the rules, including the option to 'roquet' which involved hitting your opponent's ball as far as you could, they were now standing on the immaculate green lawn. Up close, it looked even more perfect, and she had almost winced when Jack had pushed in the wickets.

Now he was handing her one of the long-handled mallets. 'You ready?'

To play croquet: yes.

To play croquet with him: less clear.

What was clear, however, was that she was having to steel herself for every interaction. She tried her hardest to ignore the effect Jack had on her, but it was getting more difficult by the day. It didn't help that he always looked so damn sexy. Today he was wearing chinos, a white button-down and a baseball cap. It was the kind of preppy look favoured by so many of the male guests at Whitecaps that when she was tired they seemed to blur into one person. But there was nothing blurry about Jack Walcott. If he had been a sketch, every angle and contour of his face would have been a clean line.

'Yes, I'm ready.'

As she nodded, he made a small bow. '*Morituri te salutant*. Those who are about to die salute you,' he said softly. 'It's what the gladiators are supposed to have said when they went into the Colosseum.'

She raised an eyebrow. 'Is that you trying to put me off my game?'

He grinned. 'I just want you to be fully prepared.'

'It's croquet, Jack, not *Battle Royale*.'

Still grinning, he backed away from her, shaking his head. 'You clearly have never seen *Heathers*. Croquet is the most brutal, unsporting game you will ever play. Don't say I didn't warn you.'

It pained her to even think it, but he wasn't exaggerating, she thought thirty minutes later as Jack whacked his ball into hers with the force of a door ram to send it spinning out of orbit to the edge of the lawn.

'Sorry.' He grinned, looking about as un-sorry as it was possible to look. 'I was going easy on you before, but I wouldn't be teaching you properly if I didn't demonstrate the correct use of the roquet,' he said, positioning his mallet and then tapping his own ball expertly through the fourth wicket. 'You see, there are two aspects to the game. The physical and the strategic. The best players are strategists.'

The same was true of life, she thought. And given that her strategy was about on a par with pinning a tail on the donkey blindfold, was it any wonder her life was such a mess? Although, strangely, given everything that was going on right now, it felt less messy than it had in a long time.

It took several fruitless, frustrating attempts but at long last she got her ball through the final wicket.

'Well done.'

She turned. Jack was standing behind her clapping slowly. He had pushed the sunglasses to the top of his head and the intensity of his gaze made her skin sting. What was he thinking when he looked at her like that? As if he couldn't look away.

Feeling exposed, she pulled a face. 'Honestly, I don't think any game has ever made me so furious or close to violence.'

He laughed then, softly, a real laugh that made his eyes gleam brighter than the sun, and she could feel the sound pulling her in.

'You're actually pretty good for a beginner. You just need to get a bit more ruthless.' His smile tugged at something loose inside her. 'Like me.'

The sun was behind him, and the light clung to him as greedily as her eyes.

'You're not ruthless.'

'Am I not?'

As his eyes found hers, her stomach knotted fiercely. She had spoken without thinking, prompted by the memory of nights when he had sat with her in the bathroom. Nobody was watching. He could have stayed in his room, but whatever his reason for not doing so, it could hardly be described as ruthless. Instead, he had been kind, and so unfazed that, after the first time, she hadn't felt self-conscious at all. And now here they were playing croquet, and he was a surprisingly good teacher. Relaxed, funny, encouraging. When the time came, he would be a good father.

Her throat tightened. But first he would have to accept that he was one.

Lifting her mallet, she let it swing gently, feeling its weight. True to her word, she hadn't raised the subject of the baby with him since that taut conversation out on the veranda, and it had been easy enough to put it to the back of her mind when she was being sick, but could it seriously stay off-limits for ever?

Then again, what had changed between them? Her morning sickness might have prompted some sort of truce, but one game of croquet didn't mean Jack was any closer to believing he was the father of their baby. Or that he even wanted to co-parent. She couldn't in all honesty say that was what she wanted either. Of course, her ideal would be to raise her child in a close, happy family. But her marriage to Jack was a long way from that ideal.

Crucially it was not based on love or permanence.

'Sometimes,' she said quickly. 'But it can't just be about ruthlessness. Surely there must be something I can do to get better because right now it feels like I'd have as much luck playing with a flamingo.'

She had kept her voice light and jokey, but Jack didn't laugh, he just stared at her speculatively, and for one horrible moment she thought he was going to ask her why she had defended him. But finally, he nodded slowly and said, 'There are some ways you can improve your swing. Offhand, I'd say you need to keep your head lower when you hit the ball and I think it would help if you loosened your grip.' He hesitated. 'I could show you. If you'll let me.'

The breath jerked in her throat.

It was the first time that he had referred, albeit obliquely, to what had happened yesterday on the beach. She still couldn't quite believe what he had told her. Not just that he couldn't swim but, knowing that, he had still leapt into the sea.

And the reason he'd given for doing so? Did she believe that? She felt the blood in her heart pull back sharply like the tide around a breakwater. Truthfully, she didn't know. Having spent time with him, she could imagine his frustration at finding himself trapped on a yacht, and he was certainly impulsive. She wouldn't be here now if he weren't. And yet she couldn't help but feel that there was more to it.

Maybe she should have pressed him, but she knew how hard it was to reveal your weaknesses to other people. Look at all the things she was keeping hidden from Jack. Only there was no reason to tell him the truth. Particularly when he was still refusing to accept the biggest truth between them.

A small shiver of sadness wound through her. Aside from a baby he wouldn't acknowledge, all that connected them was a piece of paper with some signatures on it.

Her throat was suddenly dry and tight so that it was difficult to swallow.

That was a lie. Out on the beach yesterday, they'd been

on the verge of kissing again. At some point between him telling her that all this was 'her life' and her taking his hand, something had shifted. The light dancing off the waves had changed. The breeze had softened. And that thing that they both pretended wasn't there had pulled taut, reeling them closer and closer—

Yes, but only because he had opened up to her, she told herself firmly. And because they had been on a beach again and everything had felt muddled. If she were standing that close to him now, here on this perfectly manicured lawn, it would feel completely different. Neutral.

It was then that she realised that Jack was staring at her and that she had no idea how long he had been waiting for her to reply to him.

'Go on, then. You can show me. On one condition: you join me in the pool later.' Lifting her mallet, she jabbed him lightly in the stomach. 'Oh, and try not to do the whole mansplaining thing.'

His mouth curled into one of those crooked smiles that instantly made her feel as panicky and breathless as a fish on a hook. 'Spoilsport.'

As he stepped closer, she felt her pulse change up a gear. 'Okay, what matters isn't so much how high you grip as the pressure you apply,' he said softly. 'You need to let the wood flow beneath your fingers.'

The hair on the nape of her neck rose as he moved behind her and she felt his cheek next to hers, and then his hands were overlapping hers and he was loosening her fingers, altering her grip around the smooth wooden handle. She tried to focus on what he was saying but it was difficult to concentrate when all she could think about was those same hands moving over her body, their rough urgency making her forget everything but her need for him in that moment.

'Like this,' he said, and his voice was soft and low as it vibrated against her throat. 'Then it's easier to swing. Can you feel it?'

She nodded because she couldn't speak. He was too close and his body was hot, pressed against her back so it felt as if she were melting into him, and she would have stayed like that for ever, with his arms shielding her from the world and his breath mingling with hers, but then she remembered what she had told herself seconds earlier and she slid away from him.

'I see what you mean. Thank you for showing me,' she said, suddenly stiffly polite.

'It was my pleasure. My grandfather is really the expert though.' He reached into his back pocket. 'Which reminds me. We need to take a selfie and send it to him. He'll be chuffed to bits.' He turned to where the housekeeper was putting out a jug of fresh lemonade on the table. 'Sally, could you come and take a photo for us?'

They had taken lots of photos already. At first she had found it awkward and intrusive, not to say unsettling, having to paste a smile on her face and nestle in close to Jack. Now she was more used to it, so it was easier to strike a pose, but still.

'Wait a minute. I just need to—'

Jack frowned. 'You don't need to do anything. You look beautiful.'

It was just words, but she felt a mix of panic and fascination as his golden gaze grazed her face.

'What about if you stand back-to-back?' Sally suggested. 'Lean in on your mallets. Oh, yes, that's super-cute.'

They leaned in, then turned to face one another, and Jack pulled her against him, his hand curving around her waist, his beautiful mouth curling into one of his devastating smiles. 'Thanks, Sally,' he said, taking back the phone. But as he stared down at the screen, the smile on his face stiffened.

'What is it?'

'Nothing.' He shook his head, recovering his poise. 'They just look a bit staged. Why don't we try—? No, Ondine, no—' But it was too late, she snatched the phone and was staring down at the screen.

'What are you talking about? They look great. I mean, yeah, they look like we posed for them, but that's kinda cute. It looks like we're having fun. I don't see why you don't like them.'

And then she saw why.

For a moment she couldn't breathe. She just stood there, the phone trembling in her hand in time to her pulse as she zoomed in on herself.

She was wearing a vest dress and a cropped cardigan, both from chain stores, but it wasn't her budget wardrobe that had caused Jack to recoil. It was the small but unmistakable outline of a bump pushing against the fabric.

'He doesn't know yet.' Jack's voice pulled her out of her thoughts, and she looked up at him, her throat knotting around a lump of something that was surely too solid to be tears. But why? She knew he felt this way. It was why she'd been avoiding the conversation.

Now, though, she could no longer ignore it because the camera didn't lie.

'He can't find out this way,' Jack said quietly, but firmly. 'I just need some more time—'

Her heart contracted. It was the same impulse that had stopped her from telling her parents about not getting pregnant and Garrett's betrayal. And to be fair, even though she had agreed to do so, she hadn't told Oli about marrying Jack or the pregnancy. But that was different. Her brother might be the smartest, most sensible teenager on the planet, but he was still a teenager who hadn't even had a serious girl-friend yet and it was her job to protect him, not make him anxious about what would look like a shotgun wedding.

And, given her track record with husbands, he would be anxious. Her mouth thinned—and speaking of husbands, she was done with being fair.

'What for?' She gave him a small, stiff smile. 'Just use your legendary powers of persuasion. No, actually, scrap that! I've got a better idea. You could just deny everything.' She couldn't keep the bitterness from her voice. 'You're really good at that.'

His eyes narrowed, the smiling, charming man of moments earlier vanishing before her eyes. 'I can't deny what isn't true and I'm sorry if you don't like that but—'

She suddenly felt sick, only not like before. This wasn't hormones. It was misery and anger and a horrible sense of the wrongness of what she had done, what they were doing.

'No, what I don't like is having this baby edited out before it's even born.'

He flinched, or maybe it was just the light in her eyes because now his lip was curling.

She held up her hand.

'Don't. Just don't, okay? I'm going to lie down. Alone.' And without giving him a chance to reply, she turned and stalked towards the house.

Pushing his plate away, Jack stared across the table at the empty chair where Ondine had sat at breakfast and lunch-time and would have sat this evening if she hadn't sent a message via Sally that she was tired and would be having an early night.

Maybe she was tired, but she was also avoiding him. And punishing him.

Staring down at his uneaten dessert, he had to clench his hands to stop himself from hurling the plate across the room. He had been tempted to storm up to her room and demand that she join him for dinner, but she would undoubtedly refuse and he could hardly force her to join him.

That would defeat the point anyway because what he wanted was for her to want to join him. What he wanted was for it to go back to how it was when they were playing croquet and their eyes would collide with the same force as if they were trying to roquet one another only instead of pushing them further apart, it seemed to pull them closer.

Until Sally had taken those photos, and he had reacted, *understandably*, he thought with a stab of frustration, only Ondine had got all out of shape, just as she had on the bluffs. Except this time she hadn't come back. And he missed her—

No, not that. Never that.

He pushed back his chair and got to his feet, moving swiftly out of the room and through the quiet house, panic swelling against his solar plexus.

It was her fault. *Ondine.* If she hadn't got pregnant, then all of this would have been so much more straightforward. It would have stayed transactional. But then she'd started being sick and he had tried to do the right thing, only that meant it was no longer just about the appearance of things and the money.

She had started to trust him. Worse, he'd started to trust her and he'd ended up telling her about not being able to swim and suddenly he was teaching her croquet.

His body tensed as he remembered the curve of her spine against his chest, and the sudden quickening of hunger he had felt. It had been nearly impossible to resist... His mouth thinned. And impossible to deny despite his alleged expertise in that area.

He came to an abrupt stop, his pulse jerking in his throat, somewhat surprised to find that he had made his way to the indoor pool. Gazing down, he felt a vertiginous rush of blood just as he had on the yacht. But this wasn't the sea. The water was waveless and clear. He could see the tiles on the bottom. He had strength and stamina. How hard could it be?

'Don't even think about it.'

His head snapped round, and now his pulse was beating out of time for a different reason. Ondine was hovering in the doorway, still wearing the sundress from earlier. Her face was pale and wary as if she wasn't sure of her reception, but she had said she would join him in the pool, and here she was.

'I wasn't going to jump,' he said slowly. Couldn't, not wasn't. He wanted to beat this stupid, irrational fear but he didn't know how on his own. Only he wasn't on his own, he thought as Ondine walked towards him.

'Good,' she said quietly. 'Because there are rules to follow around water.' She stopped in front of him, her blue eyes resting steadily on his face. 'And if I'm going to teach you to swim, you're going to have to follow them. And the first rule for any beginner is that you don't go into the water alone.'

'Not even the shower?' he said softly for the incomparable pleasure of watching her try and stop her mouth pulling up at the corners. But this time her mouth didn't move. Instead, her eyes locked with his and then she pulled her dress up and over her head.

Jack felt his body fill with a kind of stillness as if every pulsing, beating part had abruptly malfunctioned. And maybe it had, he thought, gazing down, dry-mouthed, at

Ondine. She was wearing what amounted to four small triangles of burnt orange-coloured fabric. To be fair, he could only see three, but he imagined— Actually he didn't want to let his imagination into this conversation.

'On this occasion, you'll be going in with me and I will be in touching distance at all times. Do you think you can remember that, Jack?'

His eyes roamed over the three triangles and he nodded, then cleared his throat. 'Yes, I can remember that.'

'Then I suggest you get changed.'

CHAPTER EIGHT

SHE WAS A good teacher. Patient. Precise. Emphatic but not overbearing. As if she spent every waking hour teaching men in their thirties how to make star shapes in the water. Maybe that was why he was not embarrassed as he'd imagined he would be whenever he'd pictured himself learning to swim.

It also helped that, as she'd predicted, he was a quick learner so that within half an hour he was pushing off from the wall of the pool and doing a fairly competent doggy-paddle.

'So who else have you taught to swim?'

They were in the shallow end now, sitting on the steps. It was the first time he could remember allowing himself to relax in water. Normally, he was too tense about someone pulling him for a joke, but he felt safe with Ondine.

'Children mostly. But plenty of adults too. You're not alone.' Their eyes met, and she gave him one of those careful smiles.

'Were you always a good swimmer? Like, when you were a kid?'

Earlier in the pool, he had congratulated himself for being so focused on her instructions. But then, only her head and shoulders were out of the water. Now though, as she nodded, he was suddenly intensely conscious of her almost nakedness, and of the excitement leaping inside him.

'I did Swim Club, but I did a lot of clubs when I was

younger.' She hesitated. 'I wasn't very academic, you see. Not like Oli. And my parents knew that I minded.' Her smile softened a little. 'They enrolled me in all these different activities so that I could find something I was really good at.'

'And that was swimming.' He dragged his gaze up and away from a droplet of water that was zigzagging between the smooth, damp skin of her cleavage.

Her mouth twitched at the corner. 'It wasn't playing the violin, that's for sure.'

'And after Swim Club?' He wanted her to keep talking, to keep watching her talk.

'I got selected for the junior swim team. The coaches were amazing. Some of the people I trained with swam in international competitions But I injured my shoulder.'

'That was bad luck.'

She shrugged. 'It happens. I'm over it now, but I would have liked to make my parents proud.'

There was a wistful note in her voice, and he frowned. 'You save lives. I'm pretty sure that would make them prouder than any medal.'

His shoulders stiffened; this was dangerous territory for him. But glancing over, he saw a tension in Ondine that matched his own.

'They would be.' She rubbed her forehead with the back of his hand. 'But they died before I finished my training.'

Died? Jack swore silently. 'I'm sorry.'

She was shaking her head. 'It's fine. You didn't know.'

But he should have done. The marriage might be fake but Ondine was a real person, and losing your parents was a huge, life-changing moment at any age, only she was so young.

'That must have been hard,' he said quietly.

'It was. That's why Oli lives with me. He had to—he was

only fourteen. And I wanted him to,' she added, her blue eyes widening as if that weren't obvious.

'I know.' He thought about how her voice softened when she talked about her brother, and the small, shabby home he'd judged and found wanting. He'd done the same to her. But the inadequacy was his, not hers: she was working two jobs to help raise her brother.

'Is that why you have no money?'

She looked down into her lap. 'No,' she said finally, and there was a flatness to her voice now that he hated, but not as much as he hated himself. 'That's down to me and my ex-husband. The second one, I mean.'

His anger was instant and so intense that for a moment he couldn't speak. 'What did he do?'

'I don't know why I said that.' She was shaking her head. 'Vince wasn't to blame. I mean, he was. He liked having fun, but I knew that right from the start. He didn't hide who he was, and it was my choice to marry him.'

'Did you love him?' His heart scraped against his ribs.

Her mouth trembled. 'No, I don't think I did, but we met just after my parents' funeral and Vince could see how miserable I was, and he's like a big, stupid dog that just wants you to be happy. But he's not a grown-up. I knew that, and I still married him.'

Jack stared at her uncertainly. He felt out of his depth. Normally, this kind of conversation was his cue to leave but he didn't want to leave Ondine. In fact, he wanted to get closer. 'You were grieving. People do all kinds of crazy stuff when they're in pain.' Look at me, he wanted to say but instead he reached out and took her hand, but she jerked it away, shaking her head.

'You don't understand. I married him because I was scared and sad, and Vince made me laugh. He made me forget. And I wanted to forget. I wanted to have fun and I wanted Oli to have fun. To have nice things. I didn't think about the future or what the money was supposed to be for. Only then the bills started to come in and it was like I woke up. Or maybe I grew up.'

He heard and hated the guilt in her voice. 'What did you do?'

'I told him to leave, and he did. We got divorced and I got the job at Whitecaps. I was managing just fine, but then after you left that day Vince rang and he told me that Oli's college fund was gone.' She swallowed. 'I rang Stanford. I thought I might be able to get a bursary but there was nothing they could do, and the bank wouldn't give me a loan— not one that would cover the fees anyway.'

And now he understood why she had come to the bungalow. 'That's why you changed your mind. Why you came to find me.'

His voice was steady but inside he was knocked sideways by the truth. That the money was for Oli because Ondine felt responsible, and she had acted on that feeling with the fierce, unthinking selflessness of a mother protecting her cub, throwing aside her clear and understandable reservations to marry a stranger for money. And he had judged her for it; been happy to judge her just as people judged him, even when it became obvious that the woman sitting beside him was incapable of living the lie he had told himself.

He felt hot with shame. His head was a swirling carousel of all the other lies he'd told himself to make his life work, truths he needed to keep hidden, questions he couldn't ask much less answer. Reaching out, he caught hold of the one solid fact.

'You wanted the money for your brother.'

She nodded. 'He's lost so much already. I couldn't take away his future as well.'

He could feel the pain in her voice inside his chest and he reached for her hand again, and this time she let him take it. 'You haven't taken anything away. You've given him a home, and love—'

'I let him down. I'm supposed to take care of him but I was stupid and careless and selfish—'

'You're not any of those things.' Jack pulled her against him. 'You're tough and brave and loyal and hard-working, and Oli is lucky to have you.'

She cried then, and he held her close until finally, she breathed out shakily and then he slid his hand under her chin, and tilted her head back so that she was looking up into his eyes. 'You don't have to worry about money, okay? You're with me now, and I can take care of you and the baby, and Oli. Whatever you need, it's yours.'

'You don't have to do that. In fact, you shouldn't do it.' Her voice was scratchy when she answered. 'Marrying me is supposed to have stopped you making impulsive decisions.'

There was silence. Her pulse was hammering against the delicate skin of her throat.

'You make me impulsive,' he said softly. He watched her shift against the tiles, a pink bloom colouring her cheeks. And then, as if to prove his point, he leaned forward and fitted his mouth to hers.

He felt her lips stiffen, and his brain froze with panic that he had got it completely wrong, that the shimmering heat between them was a mirage of his own creation, but then she captured his face in her hands and she was kissing him back, her lips soft and eager, and the taste of her was sweeter than honey.

And he just wanted a taste. Except he didn't. Now that she was in his arms, he wanted to touch her and press his body against hers and he knew that he should pull away.

Kiss her forehead. Make an excuse about boundaries but he couldn't make himself do that. Only why? Why did her kiss make him feel like this, so full of hunger, and heat and wanting her?

But then her hands slid over his chest and his mind was nothing but heat and, reaching down, he scooped her into his arms and carried her out of the pool.

Breaking the kiss, he lowered her onto the lounger. His whole body was pulsing with a need that was turning him inside out so that he could have taken her there and then, like before, but he hadn't taken time to savour that miraculous body and he forced himself to slow.

He lowered his mouth to her breast. The nipple was already stiff against the wet fabric and he sucked it into his mouth, and immediately his decision to go slow was put to the test as she arched upwards, moaning softly. Breathing unsteadily, he abandoned her breast to kiss her on the mouth again, parting her lips, tasting her again and then he licked a path down to her other breast, pushing the triangles of fabric up so that he could suck the bare, ruched tip.

Her hand was in his hair, twitching against his scalp as he licked and sucked and she was pulling down his swim shorts, freeing him into the warm air.

'Yes—' He clenched his teeth, hips jerking forward as she wrapped her hand around the already stone-hard length of his erection. And then his hand caught her hair, gripping it reflexively as she took him into her mouth and he sucked in a breath, lost. The feel of her tongue, so and sweet and irresistible.

Gazing up at Jack's face, Ondine felt her already hypersensitive nipples tighten painfully. She had really enjoyed this before but, with Jack, the desire to taste him was overwhelming, his pleasure gave her pleasure, she thought, her tongue flicking over the smooth, velvet-soft skin, feeling the blood pulsing beneath the tip—

He made a raw sound in his throat and now he shifted backwards, and she stared up at him, a pulse beating hard between her thighs. He had stood in front of her like this in her dreams. Naked. Unashamed. Beautiful. And aroused. But reality was even better than fantasy, she thought, gazing at the taut body and his hard, thick, pulsing erection. He was beautiful and aroused.

Very aroused.

She watched, mesmerised, as he slowly knelt at the end of the lounger, his dark glittering gaze trained on her face as he slid his hands under her bikini bottoms and drew them down her legs. He hesitated and then he reached up and touched her belly gently, reverentially, his fingers soft and light and magical, stroking her, stirring her, his touch melting her inside.

Now his hands moved across her thighs, sliding slowly between them, and then he lowered his mouth, trailing fire across the soft skin so she arched upwards, wanting more, wanting the ache between her thighs answered now.

Quivers of anticipation rippled across her skin and then he gently parted her legs and kissed where she was warm and slick and ready, his tongue seeking her clitoris. And the tip of his tongue… She whimpered. Oh, God, she hadn't known anything could feel so good. She was hollowed out with need, shaking inside and out, her breasts aching so that it was almost too painful to bear, and then she pressed herself closer, her head falling back against the lounger as her body splintered apart, and she was crying out, crying out his name.

She felt him shift, reach for her, his mouth seeking hers, kissing her and she was reaching for him, pressing his erection against the quivering heat between her thighs.

'Are you sure?' he said hoarsely. His eyes flicked down to her stomach. 'I can—'

'No.' She shook her head. 'I want to feel you—'

He moved forward, his golden eyes burning fiercely, and he kissed her for a long time and then he touched her between her thighs, stroking her, opening her and then he lifted her hips and he was there, hard against her, sliding in, inch by inch, stretching her—

Her pulse quickened as he shifted his weight, lifting her hips, moving inside her in a steady, intoxicating rhythm and all the time he was getting bigger and harder and she could feel herself tightening on the inside, muscles clenching, head spinning, trying to hold onto the heat of him.

His fingers tightened around her hips and then she felt him tense and she couldn't hold back the moan of pleasure as he thrust deeper, and she was grasping his hands where they held her, her body shuddering into spasms as he surged inside her.

For a moment, he stood there, hips jerking and then, breathing out raggedly, he lowered her down and she felt him pull out. Seconds later, he lay down beside her, gathering her into his arms.

Ondine buried her face against his shoulder. She could feel his heartbeat slamming into her ribs. She couldn't bring herself to open her eyes. She just wanted to stay there, breathing in the warm scent of his skin, the hard swell of his biceps keeping everything at bay. She felt his lips brush against her hair.

'It's okay, baby, it's okay.'

Was it?

In one way, the most obvious, most literal way, it was not just okay, it was amazing. Sex with Jack was a thing of wonder and beauty. It was mind-melting, dizzyingly sublime. What was less okay was that what just happened was not some feverish hook-up that could be written off as a heat-of-the-moment impulse, it was a conscious choice, for both of them.

That was if something that had been coming since the day she'd thrown him out of her house could be described as a choice.

She lifted her face. Jack was staring at her, his pupils huge and dark.

'I didn't hurt you, did I?' he said hoarsely.

Her lips felt puffy, her mouth bruised from kissing him and, breathing out shakily, she found she couldn't speak and she shook her head. It was the truth. He hadn't hurt her. But he had changed her.

Their first time together had been an explosive solar flare of hunger, a white heat of mutual need consuming them both. But this was slower, sharper, pulling everything into focus, unlocking something inside her so unashamedly sexual that she didn't know herself. Every touch, every caress, every lick seemed to shape a new understanding of who she was, who she could be, who she wanted to be.

Lying here now, with his fever-hot skin pressing into hers, everything felt so intense, so vivid. It was as if she were newly born, and seeing colour, objects, for the first time. She could hear Jack's heart beating inside her and her body felt smooth and soft, and so sensitive, and it was because of Jack. He had done this. This man who was a stranger when she married him had changed her for ever in all the ways she had assumed marriage and sex would change a person, but had never happened with either of her first two husbands.

'Are you sure?'

Suddenly close to tears, she jolted back to him, back to the shimmering golden haze of his eyes and the streaks of colour touching his hard cheekbones.

As she met his gaze, she felt a kick of panic. Was he regretting it? She stared at him, trying to take in each curve and line of his astonishing face, her heart shuddering as if he had reached inside her chest and started squeezing it in his fist.

Please, don't let him regret it—

'Yes, I'm sure. You didn't hurt me.'

He was on his side, still watching her. 'It's just so different with you. I don't…' He hesitated, his mouth twisting into a shape she didn't recognise. Not anger or confusion but something in between. 'I couldn't hold back—'

The tears that seemed to be clogging her throat pushed up and as she gazed up into his flushed, shocked face her vision blurred—

Swearing softly, he pulled her against the hard muscles of his chest, his hand soft in her hair. She held onto him, not moving, hardly breathing.

'Don't cry. I don't ever want to make you cry—'

There was an ache in his voice, and now he spoke quickly, the words spilling from his beautiful mouth. She reached up and pressed her finger to his lips.

'It's not you…it's not you…'

Not *just* you, she should have said. Jack was there at the top of the list. How could he not be? From the moment he'd jumped off that yacht, her life had not been her own. It was as if she were a kite and he were pulling the strings, making her twist and tumble in a sky as blue and endless as the sea.

But there was losing her mum and dad too and wanting but struggling to be any kind of substitute parent for Oli. And all the months of trying and failing to get pregnant ending in Garrett's betrayal, and then the stupidity of her second marriage to Vince.

And all of it had begun so quickly and in such a disconnected, haphazard way; there was never any time to think properly about what she wanted to happen, what she should do, and she had made so many mistakes, thrown away so many opportunities—

'It's just so much has happened—' So much he didn't even know about, and now it was her turn to hesitate.

He let out a long breath. 'I know.'

'And now there's you and—'

She was about to say *and the baby*, but the coward in her knew that she would have to get up and leave if he rejected their child in this most intimate of moments, and she couldn't bear to do that. 'There's this—'

She felt his heartbeat accelerate against her ribs, felt his hand tighten in her hair. 'Are you saying you regret it?'

'No. I'm not. I don't regret it, at all. Do you?' She knew she should be trying to hide the note of panic, but her voice wouldn't co-operate.

His gold eyes were the darkest she'd ever seen them.

'No.' Shaking his head, he lowered his mouth and kissed her fiercely, not just her lips but her cheeks and her forehead, the curve of her jaw and the hollow of her throat. 'I've never wanted any woman more than I want you. You make me feel things I've never felt, never wanted to feel.'

He frowned then as if he'd said too much and, reaching up, she touched his face lightly, marvelling at its smoothness and symmetry. 'I feel the same way,' she whispered.

For a moment they stared at one another and then she was leaning in and kissing him and his hands were cupping her breasts, grazing the nipples and the sensation was so sharp and intense that she squirmed against him, her body rippling to life all over again.

Ondine woke, slowly, reluctantly, blinking into the soft yellow sunlight that was spilling in through the window between the half-open curtains. At some point in the night she and Jack had left the pool house and made their way through the silent, watchful house upstairs to the bedroom, to the bed they were supposed to share, but never had.

There had been no awkward moment as they'd reached the bedroom door. She had simply opened it and led him inside and he had pushed it shut, reaching for her as he did so. And they had kept reaching for one another as the darkness around them deepened to the colour of spilt ink, again and again, until finally the sky started to lighten through all the shades of grey.

Now, though, she was alone, and even though she knew it was stupid to mind, Jack's absence seemed to have opened up some hollow in her chest.

Rolling onto her side, she reached over and pressed the flat of her hand against the mattress. She'd known he was gone the moment she woke up. Known it even before she'd opened her eyes. But maybe that was just what he did after he spent the night with a woman.

She frowned. She was making it sound like a one-night stand. But that didn't make any sense because they were married. Surely you had a one-night stand with someone you didn't know. Then again, what did she know? She'd only had three sexual partners, and she had ended up marrying all of them.

It made her feel off balance bracketing them together in that way because they were all very different. For starters, she had believed she was in love with Garrett and Vince, but the thought of love had never entered her mind with Jack.

And yet it was Jack whose touch made her shiver all the way through. Jack who made her melt on the inside. Jack who had claimed her body. And not just her body, she thought, remembering last night's tearful confession. She had never told either of her ex-husbands anything that deeply personal. Maybe that was why him being here in this bed, their bed, felt so right.

Staring blindly across the room, she saw the sun disappear behind a cloud. Or maybe she was just tired and hormonal because she had been here before.

Twice.

With Garrett, she had fallen for his certainty, trusting, expecting him to be steadfast and true. And because Vince made her laugh, she had assumed he would make her happy. Now she was doing the same thing with Jack, wanting this encounter to mean something more than bodies and skin and sweat.

She glanced down at the tangle of bedsheets.

But this was sex. Wild, sublime, incomparable sex; she doubted that any man would ever make her feel as alive and aware and as beautiful in his bed as Jack. And yet, she knew it wasn't enough. The truth was that the relationships that worked, like her parents', were more than just a chemical attraction.

Her hand moved protectively to her stomach where once there had been an indent and now there was a bump. And anyway, this relationship was about more than just her and Jack.

She thought back to what he'd said about taking care of her and Oli and the baby. He meant financially, and of course she wasn't going to pretend that Jack's money wouldn't make a difference. How could she? It was making a difference right now. And she knew he was trying to help, trying to reassure her. But it was not an acknowledgement that this baby was his any more than his concern during sex. Remembering how he'd wanted to edit all evidence of her ongoing pregnancy from the photos on his phone, she felt her throat tighten. He was still a long way from acknowledging that.

Which was why, up until now, she had pushed Jack's postpartum involvement in their baby's life to a corner of her mind she didn't visit very often.

Her fingers flexed against her abdomen.

Sometimes she wondered if she had tried hard enough to make him believe her. There were moments when she had thought about telling him about Garrett and the agonising months of disappointment and despair, as if that might prove she wasn't the manipulative little hustler he'd accused her of being. Once or twice she even felt the words form into sentences, but the pain and shame of those months were so embedded in the fascia of her body that she couldn't say them out loud.

And it had been easier before not to rock the boat.

But what about now?

'Penny for them?'

Ondine blinked. Jack was standing in the doorway. His handsome face was calm and blank, but his eyes were watching her with a lazy, predatory gleam that made her breath tangle in her throat. He was wearing loose black shorts and a black vest and his skin was flushed from working out, although how he had the energy was beyond her.

Not that she was complaining about the end results, she thought as her gaze roamed over the smooth muscles of his arms and chest.

'I was just wondering what time it is.' She shifted up the bed but as she did so the sheet fell away from her body and she felt his dark gold gaze move over her breasts with the same freedom his hands had in the hours before dawn.

So now they were both staring at each other like moonstruck idiots.

Jack recovered first.

'I'm not actually sure.' He walked across the room and stopped at the end of the bed, his fingers flexing round the top rail as if it were a barbell. 'Somewhere between brunch and lunch.'

She laughed. 'I'm guessing that means you're hungry.'

His gaze was steady and unwavering. 'It's hard not to be when I'm around you,' he said, after a moment. 'You make me hungry.' She felt her body react, skin tightening, breasts tingling, nipples suddenly incredibly sensitive. It was an echo of what he'd said to her in the pool house last night— was it really only last night?—and it was all too easy to re-member what had happened afterwards. All too tempting to turn memory into a live action replay.

'And you make me greedy,' she said quietly.

He was still watching her and she felt his gaze, felt the intensity of his concentration. 'I'm glad you've got your ap-petite back. The doctor will be too.'

She tilted her head back to meet his eyes. 'I think she was talking about food. Not sex.'

His dense, dark lashes snapped upwards at the direct-ness of her words. 'But you are. Talking about sex, I mean.'

'Yes.' Heart thudding, she pulled the sheet up to cover herself. 'We both are. Except we're not talking about it. We're tiptoeing round it—'

His gaze sharpened. 'I see. And you want us to be less coy?'

'Don't you? Or do you just want to pretend it never hap-pened?' The bitterness in her voice echoed around the bed-room.

There was a silence. His eyes narrowed. 'That's not what I said.'

It wasn't. 'I know.'

'But I could see why you might think it's what I meant.'

Their eyes met. Jack was still standing at the end of the bed, still tall and astonishingly, shockingly beautiful, but he looked serious now and yet also younger. It reminded her of when they were out on the bluff.

'You can?' she said slowly.

He nodded. 'Being married like this, it's been harder than either of us thought. And any part that's been made more challenging is almost certainly my fault. I have a lot of faults, as you've probably realised.' He gave her a small, tight smile. 'But I'm not a total idiot. Or a monster.'

'I don't think you're an idiot or a monster. I just think we should talk about what happened. Only I'm not very good at this kind of conversation.'

'And you think I am?' He hesitated, and then he walked round to where she was hunched against the pillows and sat down beside her on the bed.

'Well, you've dated more than two people so, yes, I would hope so.' She shivered, her nerves ambushed by a sudden spasm of misery imagining Jack's multiple conquests. 'It's just that last night, we said some things. And I meant what I said, and I thought you did too but then when I woke up this morning you'd gone and so I thought maybe I'd got it wrong. That it wasn't real—'

'You think I faked that?' He seemed stunned.

She frowned. 'I don't mean the mechanics. You made it sound as if you wanted me, wanted to have sex with me—'

'I did.' His voice was hoarse. 'I do. I guess I didn't want to assume— No, actually that's a lie. When I woke up this morning I wanted to make all kinds of assumptions.' His eyes fixed on her face. 'One of them was that we could just carry on without having to talk about it.' Reaching out, he uncurled her fingers and slid his hand around hers.

'But what I should have done was tell you the truth. That I wanted you since that very first day when you kicked me out of your house. And I want you now.'

Her body ached with need.

'You're not worried about it making things more complicated?'

'I think we passed complicated a long time ago,' he said softly, and, leaning forward, he fitted his mouth to hers.

For a moment they kissed, back and forth, teasing the heat from each other, then she felt him tense. 'What is it?'

'I worked out pretty hard in the gym. I definitely need to shower.' He grimaced. 'You can't want me like this.'

She did. The scent of his sweat was tugging at her senses. Then again—

Picturing Jack with water spilling over all those glorious curving muscles, she felt a shiver of anticipation dance across her skin.

'So take a shower.' Still clutching the sheet, she stood up.

'What are you doing?' His gaze had risen to meet hers and now she let the sheet drop and his eyes seemed to glow as they fixed on her naked body.

'Coming with you.' Hunger jackknifed inside her. 'I can't let you go into the water alone. Or did you forget the rules?'

She managed two steps before he caught up with her, making her shriek with laughter as he scooped her into his arms and carried her into the bathroom.

CHAPTER NINE

SHIFTING BACK IN his chair, Jack stared at his laptop and re-read the final line of text on the screen. The proposal was finished. He was just tinkering with it. What he should be doing was sending it to his grandfather, but he wasn't ready to do that yet. And yet he couldn't leave it alone either so now he was carrying his laptop around with him everywhere like a security blanket.

Not that he needed one. He felt calmer than he had in years, decades even, and happy. But then he had a lot to be happy about. His plan was working, more than working, he thought, glancing through the window.

Outside in the garden, Ondine was standing on the cro-quet lawn, practising her swing, her forehead creased with concentration, her light brown hair spilling across her shoulders. The same shoulders he'd kissed and licked earlier as she'd leaned forward, moaning softly, hands splayed against the shower wall. Remembering what had happened next, he felt his groin harden.

On waking, he had been shocked to find Ondine's soft body curled so trustingly against him. More shocking still had been how right it had felt. It was that rightness or rather his panic at seeing it in those terms that had made him slip from the bed and make his way to the gym.

He hadn't booked a session with Mark, but he had

pounded the punchbag for thirty minutes then hit the tread-mill for another fifty. But he couldn't keep away.

His eyes narrowed. Sally was on the lawn now, talking to Ondine. He watched them smile and laugh. All the staff liked her, and, having worked in hospitality, no doubt Ondine felt some kind of kinship.

But she was also a good person.

He felt a pang of guilt sharpen its point beneath his ribs. He hadn't given a thought to what she would feel like waking alone. Nor had he considered talking to her about what had started in the pool house last night.

Do you just want to pretend it never happened?

No, he hadn't wanted that. But he hadn't wanted to have a conversation that might reveal that fact because he was a coward. Because he was scared of what he might say. Because he couldn't admit to Ondine or himself that he wanted more than just one night with her. Wanting might lead to needing, and needing made you vulnerable.

But she was braver, *better* than him. When life knocked her down, she didn't just get back up, she tried to do the right thing.

Remembering how he had tried to edit out her baby bump from the photos, he felt his chest tighten. He had told her he would take care of her and the baby, but did she think he was going to pretend that had never happened too? More likely, she thought it would be beyond him. And that was entirely understandable. He could hardly manage his own life. Mismanage would be a better description, he thought, remembering the moment when he'd jumped off the yacht.

The memory cast a shadow across his thoughts. He was such a mess. Who would want him in their baby's life? His throat constricted. What if he was not just damaged, but damaging?

He pushed the question aside as he had done so many times before. This wasn't about him. It was about Ondine and making her feel safe. It was time to show her that she could trust him, that he could do the right thing, and, reaching into his pocket, he pulled out his phone.

'I thought you were on some kind of leave?'

Glancing up from his laptop, Jack stared blankly over to where Ondine lay on her side, watching him. They were lounging by the pool. Through the glass, the sun shimmered in a cloudless sky. But no blue in nature could match the beauty of Ondine's eyes.

Eyes that were now fixed steadily on his face.

Shutting his laptop, he turned to face her. 'Well, according to the WEC website, I'm currently "taking a short sabbatical to focus on personal goals". So probably everyone thinks I'm in rehab.'

He unleashed a small, curving smile, hoping to distract her, but her blue gaze stayed steady because, as he already knew, Ondine didn't get distracted easily. Lifeguard training, probably, he thought, his own gaze flickering appreciatively over her toned limbs. She was wearing another of those barely-there bikinis that theoretically should offer little to the imagination but in his case offered rather too much.

'So what are you doing on that?' she said, tapping the laptop. 'Must be pretty enthralling. I've never seen you so focused. Well, you know, aside from—' A flush of pink crept over her cheeks, and he felt his skin tighten. Yes, he knew—

'It's nothing, really. Just something I've been working on.'

'Is that all you're going to tell me?'

'No, I just didn't know if you wanted to get into the details.'

She rolled her eyes. 'I think I can manage. Or is it a secret?'

'No.' He shook his head. 'It's not a secret.' But he never

liked to show people that he cared, and he did care very much about this proposal. Then he remembered the ache in Ondine's voice when she told him about her parents, and her ex-husband, and he knew how much it must have cost her to share that with him.

Surely, he could share this.

'It's a kind of side project. A proposal to accelerate WEC's transition from fossil fuels to renewables. We're moving at a glacial pace, the whole industry is. But in five years' time, energy will look nothing like it does now. Green hydrogen. Solar. Hydropower. Geothermals. They'll be the present, not the future. Any business that doesn't get that is going to be left behind. That's why I want to push WEC to transition now.'

He saw a flicker of curiosity in her blue eyes like a wave out at sea. 'Doesn't sound much like a side project.' She glanced at the laptop. 'Could I read it? Would you mind?'

She wanted to read it. He stared at her in silence. Was she joking? But then she held out her hand. 'No, I don't mind. But don't feel like you have to.'

'I don't—'

It took her just over an hour. At one point, watching her chew her lip, he said, 'Honestly, you don't need to read the whole thing—' and she looked up, glowering at the interruption.

Now she closed the laptop. 'It's really good. I didn't have a clue about renewables before, but you made it really accessible. And exciting. So what does your grandfather think?'

He shrugged. 'It's not that he's resistant to change, it's just that, for him, WEC has always been about oil and gas.'

'Did you have a falling out? Is that why you walked out?'

Picturing that life-changing meeting with his grandfather, he felt his stomach churn with a familiar mix of regret and defiance.

'I didn't walk out. My grandfather told me to leave because I skim-read a geological report and there was a problem that we had to pay our way out of. So I never got to show him the proposal, and who knows when he'll be ready to listen to me again?'

His throat clenched as he anticipated Ondine's appraising gaze, her disappointment. 'I know what you're thinking. That it's my fault. That I messed up.'

'Everyone messes up, Jack.' She frowned. 'Even your grandfather.'

'Yeah, well, it wasn't the first time. That's why he sent me away.'

She was quiet for so long, her voice was almost a shock when finally she said, 'You make it sound like a punishment. I don't think it was. He sent you away because he thinks you're good enough to step into his shoes but he wants you to be fit for race day. And that means taking stock and being honest with yourself, about what you need to do to improve. He did what any good coach would do.'

'And what do you think?'

'Me?' Her eyes fluttered up to meet his.

He nodded. 'You're my wife. Do you think I'm good enough?' And suddenly there was nothing more important than to know her answer to that question.

'Before, no.' She hesitated, and then she smiled, a smile that filled him with wonder and hope. 'But now, I think you might just pull it off.'

She gave a squeak as he jerked her off the sun lounge and onto his lap. 'And I think you and my grandpa are going to get along very well. Maybe too well.' He paused. Her eyes were soft, open, trusting, and quickly, before he could change his mind, he said, 'I talked to him. Earlier. I told him about the baby.'

She blinked. 'Did it go okay?'

The call had been both easier and harder than he'd thought it would be, only not for the reasons he'd imagined. He'd assumed it would be hard to lie again, but it hadn't felt like a lie. Listening to the happiness in his grandfather's voice, he'd forgotten about the condom, and his suspicions about the timing of the pregnancy. All of it had retreated, and he had simply been happy and whole.

Now, though, gazing down into Ondine's face, he felt the fault lines inside him fracture. She cared about him only because she didn't know the truth. But if, make that *when*, he messed up, she would end up hating him, blaming him.

Pushing aside that thought, he cleared his throat.

'It went well. He's looking forward to meeting you at the polo. They all are.' That wasn't strictly true. He'd left messages with both his parents telling them he had news to share and that he hoped they could join him and Ondine for dinner after the tournament, but neither of them had responded. Not that he had expected them to.

'They?' She looked suddenly nervous.

'My parents. And their partners. My half-siblings.'

She grimaced. 'They certainly won't be able to miss me. I cleared tables at Whitecaps, so I know exactly what kind of women go to polo matches and I don't look like any of them.'

'That's because your beauty is real, not the result of surgery or fillers. Especially now.' He glanced down at the swell of her stomach, his pulse jerking. 'Pregnancy suits you.'

She smiled. 'You clearly have a very short memory.'

Their eyes met, both of them remembering those nights in the bathroom.

'I don't know, you were so determined. That's pretty sexy.' And she was blooming now, he thought, his gaze taking in her flushed cheeks and shining eyes.

'Did you not want children?'

He felt her whole body stiffen and the smile on her face seemed to slip sideways. 'Yes. I did. I wanted to have them with Garrett, my first husband. And we tried for so long.' Her voice stumbled. 'But nothing happened.'

Thinking back to her small, pale face when she'd handed him the positive test, it was suddenly difficult to catch his breath. She'd said it was a miracle, but by then he'd been consumed with a rage that had blocked out compassion or reason.

'Actually, it did happen for Garrett, just not with me.' She rubbed her forehead as if it hurt. Maybe it did. He could certainly feel her pain. 'He had an affair with a woman at work, and she got pregnant and then he left me.'

Glancing past her at the huge trees standing like sentinels at the edge of the gardens, Jack felt a flicker of rage. He wanted to uproot them all and smash them into firewood with his fists. What kind of man would do that?

'I think I would have been okay but then my parents were killed and it got kind of muddled up, you know, grieving for them, worrying about Oli—'

His arms tightened around her. 'I'm so sorry, Ondine.'

Now he didn't want to smash things, he wanted to sit and hold her close for ever. Protect her from the world and its random cruelties.

'It's fine. I'm fine now. I was angry before. With Garrett, and Vince, but I'm not any more.' She seemed confused, as if she had only just realised that fact. 'I don't know what changed, but I'm glad it did. They're behind me now.'

'What about after Vince?'

'There hasn't been anyone.' Her eyes were clear and blue; she was telling the truth, but if that was true—

Something was creeping up behind him like in a game of grandmother's footsteps. He felt goosebumps on his neck.

'But what about the condoms? Why would you have those if there hasn't been anyone?'

'I didn't even know I had them. They must have been from when I was with Garrett. But we stopped using them when we started trying for a baby—'

'When was that?'

'Seven years ago maybe.' Her voice was so faint now he could barely hear it. 'I was on the pill with Vince. I came off it when we broke up because I couldn't handle another relationship.'

Jack stared at her in silence, his heart hammering. He didn't know the expiry time on a condom but he was pretty sure it wasn't seven years. He felt the air quiver as if a giant, underground explosion had happened beneath their feet. But it was inside his chest.

This baby was his. His lungs were burning. He couldn't, *shouldn't* be a father. But he was. He felt a rush of panic and fear and then a joy that scared him more. He heard her swallow, knew she was watching him, and he knew that his face must be showing his shock. His understanding.

'I didn't think I could get pregnant. And I know you feel differently, but I can't regret this baby.' Looking down into her face, he felt something tear inside her. The shine had gone from her eyes. She looked small and lost. Because of him.

'It's okay. We'll work it out.' He pulled her closer, his head spinning. 'It'll be okay,' he repeated, and he kept repeating it like a mantra.

Since its inaugural match nearly fifty years ago, the annual Walcott Cup had become one of those dates in the diary that was not an official holiday but was often treated as such. For football fans, the second Sunday in February was Super Bowl Sunday. Those who preferred to mix equine talent with the chance to dress up, the first Saturday in May was reserved for John D. Walcott IV's charity polo tournament.

Normally, Jack looked forward to the tournament. He enjoyed playing and watching polo, and he was proud of what his grandfather had created. What had started out as an impromptu match between friends now raised millions of dollars for charity.

But this year, he had more important things on his mind than polo. Heart twisting, he glanced over to where Ondine sat opposite him, her eyes fixed on the view outside her window.

It was twenty-four hours since he'd worked out that he was the father of the baby in her womb. Worked out. Accepted. But not acknowledged. Not out loud anyway. So in that sense nothing had changed outwardly.

But everything had changed. All changed…changed utterly, like that Yeats poem his grandfather loved so much.

He had held her close for a long time but they hadn't talked again. Instead they had walked in silence back to the bedroom and reached for one another wordlessly.

There had been no words to express the chaos inside his head. There still weren't any.

And maybe Ondine felt the same way too.

She hadn't changed yet or done her make-up and he wished that she didn't have to. That she could just stay as she was, with her hair casually spilling over her shoulders. That they could stay on Whydah and make love and play croquet and go for a swim. Because she had kept her word. He could tread water now and move forward and back and soon he would be swimming.

Only none of it was real. At best, it was window dressing.

He was Ondine's husband in name only, and soon enough he would be named as the father on his child's birth certificate. So many signatures on so many pieces of paper.

Switching his gaze to the window, he stared across the expanse of blue to where a dark line edged with gold cut across the sky. *We'll work it out.* That was what he'd said to Ondine. But how to do that, and what 'worked out' would look like were as distant and unreachable in his mind as the horizon.

It wasn't like all those weeks ago when Ondine had told him she was pregnant. Back then he had been so focused on the statistical improbability of his being a parent that his mind had been impervious to any persuasion. Of course, the truth had been there all along. If he had paid a little more attention to what was right in front of his face, asked a few pertinent questions, he would have known that it wasn't just possible he was the father, but highly probable. But blinkered by the fear that he would be unable to undo the damage of the past or, worse, that he would recreate it, he had deliberately, determinedly done neither of those things.

Now, though, he knew he was the father. Knew it with the same, unshakeable certainty that he knew his name, almost as if he had always known, right from that moment in the gallery when she'd bolted for the restroom.

And it blew his mind that he had created a new life. Every time he thought about it, it felt like an earthquake inside him.

Because making a baby didn't mean you were qualified to raise it. Just look at his own mother and father. He felt his throat tighten so that it hurt to swallow. After the divorce they had been so eager to get rid of every reminder of one another that they had got rid of him too. They had edited him out of their lives so that now he was their son in name only.

But maybe, though, that would change today.

Thanks to the considerable gravitational pull of his grandfather's money, the Walcott Cup was the one day of the year when both his parents deigned to be in the same space as one another. Usually they were too wrapped up in their new lives to pay much attention to him. But this year would be different. For once, the spotlight would be on him, and for the right reasons. On the face of it, he had turned his life around. Finally, they would have to notice him. See the change.

His grandfather would see he was changed too. Utterly changed, and that was what he needed to focus on right now. That, after all, was what all of this was about. And this was his turf. He knew these people. He understood the rules. He knew how to leverage his looks and his charm and his status. He could make this work.

Making his way through the country club, he felt almost euphoric. He knew most of the guests by name, and those he didn't were unimportant. And he couldn't remember why he had wanted Ondine not to get dressed up.

As if she knew what he was thinking, she glanced up at him and he felt her blue gaze like a punch. She looked exquisite in a simple white dress that perfectly offset her sun-kissed limbs. Her hair was in some kind of low bun and she was wearing a fascinator in the shape of an oversized flower. And he was enthralled. Watching her smile and talk, as though this were something she did every day, only deepened his fascination.

He had thought she would be out of her depth. But Ondine was as strong a swimmer on land as she was in the water. She was making it look easy, he thought as she turned towards him again, her eyes catching fire as they met his. He felt her gaze burn through him, the lick of heat making his stomach drop so that it was the most natural thing in the world to pull her against him and kiss her hungrily.

'Everything okay?' he murmured.

She nodded. 'Everything's fine.'

His hand touched the nape of her neck, and then his eyes snagged on a woman's profile in the crowd. Tilted up to the sunlight, her eyes resting adoringly on the tall young man by her side, and suddenly he couldn't seem to make his breath reach his lungs. He stood frozen in the middle of the shifting mass of people, waiting for her to notice him, but after a moment she said something to an older man standing beside her and they all turned and moved as one towards the clubhouse.

And with every step they took, he could feel himself losing shape. As if he weren't part of the world, as if nobody could see him.

He felt a rush of panic, and then Ondine's hand found his, and that was better. He tightened his grip so that the ring on her finger pinched his skin, and some of the numbness in his chest retreated, and he felt present and connected again. But he needed to move and, looking down at Ondine, he said, 'We should go find my grandfather.'

It turned out that the Palm Beach Polo Club was actually an exclusive members-only country club. But then titles could be misleading, Ondine thought as Jack led her through the chattering groups of immaculately dressed men and long-limbed women.

Look at her: she was Mrs Jack Walcott. But her marriage was a sham, a pretence designed to reinstate her husband in his grandfather's good books.

And she had known that right from the start. Only somehow she had forgotten that their marriage wasn't real.

It wasn't only the sex. Or the baby. Or the way he had been there for her when she was throwing up and half crazy with hormones. Or even how he had comforted her, twice now. Holding her close and pushing the past back where it belonged. Because he had done that; he was the reason why she wasn't angry with Garrett and Vince any more. She just hadn't realised that yesterday.

At the centre of it all was Jack. He had changed her. Awoken her. Freed her. He had led her out of the dark, baffling woods back onto the path.

She glanced up at his handsome face.

But only so that she could meet John D. Walcott IV. He was the reason she was here. But yesterday, in the moment when Jack realised that he was the father of their baby, she had lost sight of that. She had fallen into the silence between her heartbeats.

She thought back to how he had held her close, close enough that she could feel the tension in his body as if he might break into a thousand pieces. Somehow they had made it up to the bedroom and even as he'd been pulling her close she had been sliding her hands over his beautiful, strong body, some deep-buried instinct telling her that she must hold onto him. That if she just kept holding onto him, then they could make it work as he'd said.

She wanted to believe him, but the next day, he'd got up while she was sleeping. Today he'd let her lie in, so that there had been no time to talk before they'd had to leave. And now, they were back in Florida.

Gazing down at the pristine rectangle of grass, Ondine felt a sharp pang, almost like homesickness for the croquet lawn at Red Knots. After the tranquillity of Whydah Island, the country club felt more like a nightclub. It was so noisy and there were so many people milling around her.

Actually, it was Jack they were milling around. He was at their centre too. A glittering, dazzling sun. All laughter and light. The most heavenly of bodies around which smaller, duller planets orbited. And it wasn't hard to see why. Her breath caught in her throat. He looked gorgeous in a pale blue linen suit and tan loafers.

Jack, though, seemed oblivious. 'We should go find my grandfather.' His gaze shifted to a point past her shoulder, eyes narrowing, body straining forward in that unmistakable way of someone seeing the person they were looking for in a crowd. She felt his hand tighten around hers, she tensed for the moment of reckoning when she would finally meet John D. Walcott IV, but then he turned abruptly and began towing her in the opposite direction.

'He'll probably be down by the pony lines.'

'Pony lines?'

As he turned to look at her, she felt her stomach flip. It was almost as though he didn't recognise her. But he was the one who had changed, she thought, her stomach somersaulting now as she glanced up at his high, hard cheekbones and softly curving mouth. Not outwardly. And not to anyone who didn't know him. But she was so attuned to his every move, to each and every breath he took, and there was a tautness to him as if he was holding himself in check. The relaxed, carefree man of the last few days had vanished, and with shock she realised that he was acting again.

'It's where the ponies wait. He likes to go and see them before the match. I think it reminds him of when he used to play. Although he only stopped playing a year ago.'

'But he's in his eighties!'

'And very stubborn. He only stopped because he has osteoarthritis in his shoulder. He still rides, though.'

Watching his face soften, she felt her heart slip sideways. It was one of the many things she didn't understand about Jack Walcott. That he could lie to a man he so clearly adored. Then again, up until today he'd only had to manage that contradiction over the phone. Now he was going to have to lie to his grandfather in person. They both were.

Only right now, she couldn't think about her part in those lies. This was about Jack. She had to stay focused for him. Her stomach cartwheeled. And for Oli. This was about him too, his future, and it shocked her to think that she had forgotten that momentarily. No, not forgotten, she corrected herself. It was just that at some point between signing the marriage certificate and flying down to Florida, it had stopped being Ondine and Jack conspiring for their own ends and become two people whose goals were inseparable and symbiotic.

'It'll be okay.' She squeezed his hand and, after a moment, his fingers tightened around hers. 'We can do this. Together. We can show him that you've changed.'

For a second, his eyes locked with hers, and then they narrowed past her shoulder only this time his face lit up and he started to smile. 'Grandpa.'

'Jack.'

Ondine turned, her heart thudding unevenly in her chest as John Walcott embraced his grandson, and then turned towards her, smiling. He held out both his hands. 'Ondine. It's a pleasure to meet you,' he said, kissing her on both cheeks.

If she'd wondered what Jack would look like in fifty years, now she knew. John Walcott had the same jawline and the same patrician nose. Only his eyes were different, and of course his hair was grey, but he was still a handsome man.

'You look so like Jack,' she said, without thinking.

He laughed. 'Once upon a time, maybe. I'm so pleased you are here, my dear. Welcome to our family and—' his brown eyes dropped to the slight swell of her stomach '—congratulations.'

'Thank you.'

'I couldn't be more happy for you both.'

He turned towards his grandson. 'Let's walk back up to the box, and you can tell me everything you've been up to.'

John Walcott didn't just look like Jack, he was every bit as charming, and it was clear that he doted on his grandson. And in his presence, Jack seemed to shed that strange tension of earlier.

'Now tell me, Ondine, have you ever watched a polo match before?' John Walcott said as they took their seats.

She shook her head. 'No, but, from what Jack told me, it sounds a lot like croquet on horseback but with goals instead of wickets.'

He laughed again. 'That's not a bad analogy—'

'Jack said you used to play.' Glancing over to where the sleek, muscular players and their equally sleek, muscular ponies were warming up on the pitch, that fact seemed even more astonishing.

'I did. And if it wasn't for my grandson here, fussing over me, I would probably still be playing.' Reaching out, he squeezed Jack's shoulder. 'But he's right, I'm not as young as I was. Not as young as I'd like to be. Fortunately, I have Jack to look out for me.'

He smiled and Ondine smiled back, but it seemed odd that Jack should be that person. Didn't his son look out for him?

Jack was shaking his head. 'By looking out, he means I hid his mallets.'

'And I appreciate it. That's why I'd like you to present the cup for me this year.'

'I'm not going to do that, Grandpa, it's your tournament—'

'No, it's the Walcott Cup, and you are a Walcott, and it's time I took a step back. And it could be your first public job as chair of the foundation.'

Something passed across Jack's face. 'You think I'm ready for that?'

His grandfather nodded. 'I do. And other things too, perhaps.'

Watching the two Walcott men smile at one another, Ondine didn't know how to feel. A part of her was happy. It was what Jack wanted. And she wanted it too, but if his grandfather reinstated him then where did that leave her? The answer to that question made her wish that she could just take a time-out like the players and ponies, go somewhere where she wasn't on display. Where she didn't have to smile on demand. Because she didn't feel like smiling any more.

'So when's Dad getting here?' Jack said, leaning forward, his eyes scanning the crowds of spectators who were making their way into the stands.

His grandfather's smile was suddenly a little forced. 'He won't be joining us, I'm afraid. Something came up. I'm sure he'll call you later and explain.'

There was not a flicker of reaction on Jack's perfect face, or even in his golden eyes, but he went still. Even his smile seemed to freeze. 'Why can't he come?'

'Apparently, Annie brought her boyfriend home for the weekend. She's always been so secretive. I think they felt they needed to show support.'

'Of course they did.' His words were carefully neutral, but she felt the muscles of his arm tense against her, only then his grandfather was learning forward in his chair and she saw the umpire in his black-and-white-striped shirt toss the ball into the melee of ponies and players.

CHAPTER TEN

THE POLO WAS EXCITING. But Ondine found it difficult to concentrate. The whole time she was distracted by the change in Jack's mood. Obviously he was disappointed his father had changed his plans, but was it that big a deal? Surely they could meet him on another day.

After the first match, there was an interlude when all the spectators walked onto the pitch and trod the 'divots'. Around them people were consciously not looking over in that way they did when you knew they wanted to just stop and stare, and it was a relief to return to the relative privacy of the box.

'Excuse me, Mr Walcott.' A steward wearing one of the club's branded royal-blue polo shirts stepped forward, blushing as both Jack and his grandfather nodded. 'I meant you, Mr Walcott,' she said, smiling at the older man. 'Mr Wood wondered if he could have a word.'

'Of course. Would you excuse me, Ondine? I'll be right back.'

Jack watched his grandfather make his way towards the clubhouse. 'Come on.' Grabbing her hand, he pulled her to her feet. 'Let's go.'

'Where are we going?' She was having to run almost to keep up with his purposeful strides. 'Jack, can you slow down—?'

'Sorry,' he said automatically. He turned, his face taut

and unreachable as it had been in the bathroom all those weeks ago. 'I just want to get out of here before my grandfather comes back.'

'What?' She frowned up at him in shock. 'We can't leave.'

'We can. And we are.' He started to pull her forward, but she jerked her hand free.

'We can't just leave, Jack. You're going to present the cup, remember?'

'No, I'm not. Look, I'll just tell Grandpa that you were feeling sick.' His eyes were unreadable behind his sunglasses but the tendons in his jaw were pulled tight. 'He won't mind.'

'But I do. I'm not lying to your grandfather.'

'Seriously? You want to take the moral high ground on this one?' His lip curled dismissively. 'I think it's a bit late to worry about that.'

Her stomach twisted in shock, and she clutched at the front of her dress to steady herself. The truth hurt. What hurt more was Jack throwing it in her face. But what hurt the most was the ache in his voice.

It wrenched at something inside her so that instead of turning and walking away, she stepped forward and pulled off his sunglasses. 'Yes, it is. And it's hypocritical too, and I'm going to have to find a way to live with that. But we came here today to show your grandfather that you're a different man from the one he sent away and if we leave now, then it's going to make it look as if nothing's changed.'

She saw a flicker of pain in his eyes, and a kind of angry bewilderment 'Nothing has.'

'That's not true.' Her eyes locked with his. 'I see you, Jack. I know who you are and you're not the same man I pulled out of the water. But you have to believe that. Otherwise no one else will.'

'I don't know if I can do this—' He was shaking his head; his voice sounded strained. 'I thought it would be different, I thought they'd be different—'

They? She stared at him in confusion, but there was no time to ask what he meant. His grandfather would be returning to the empty box at any moment.

'Maybe you can't. But *we* can.' She found his hand. 'Where you go, I go, so if you want to leave I'll come with you, but I think we should stay and finish this. And then we can go home.'

He was staring at her as if he was trying to read her face, see beneath the surface.

'Okay,' he said finally. 'We'll stay.'

The second match was equally thrilling but Ondine got the feeling that Jack wasn't even watching. That his eyes weren't tracking the spirited ponies as they dashed up and down the pitch, but scanning the crowd. But at least he was there, she thought, as the captain of the winning team stepped forward to receive their prize.

'Here. I want you to do it.' Ondine blinked. Jack was holding out the shining trophy. 'That's okay, isn't it, Grandpa?'

'It's better than okay, it's perfect.'

As the team celebrated their victory, John Walcott took hold of Ondine's hands and squeezed them. He was smiling but his eyes were bright with tears. 'My wife always used to present the trophy. She would be so pleased, so thank you—'

'No, thank you for inviting me today. But would it be all right if Jack took me home?' She glanced over to where he was shaking hands with the losing team. 'I just suddenly feel so tired.'

'Of course…of course.'

'I don't suppose I could email you something, could I?'

She hesitated. 'It's something Jack's been working on. I know he wants you to read it, but—'

'I'll take a look. I promise.'

After the noise and heat of the day, the plane's interior was blissfully quiet and cool.

They were in the bedroom. Ondine gazed over to where Jack sat staring out of the window. She had told his grandfather that she was tired but it was Jack who looked shattered.

He hadn't spoken in the car on the way back to the airfield but he had kept hold of her hand. Now, though, he seemed remote, and it reminded her of her fake honeymoon at Red Knots when they had sat at opposite sides of the room. Then she had been too furious to speak. Now she didn't know what to say. Except the truth.

'Your grandfather is a lovely man,' she said quietly.

He nodded. 'He liked you.'

'I liked him. I'm sorry your parents couldn't make it, but we could arrange another date.'

A muscle flickered in his jaw. 'That won't be necessary.'

Not necessary.

She stared at him, wondering if she had misheard. 'Of course, it's necessary. They're your mum and dad. I can't not meet them. Your grandfather said that your dad was going to call you so just sort something out then.'

He was shaking his head. 'He's not going to call—'

'Then call him. And then call your mum.'

'That's not going to happen.'

'Because they didn't come to the polo.' She'd forgotten this, hadn't she? This version of Jack. The handsome, spoiled brat used to getting his own way. 'You're acting like a child. Things happen—'

'Things happen?' he echoed. 'You don't know what you're

talking about. You don't know anything about what happens and you certainly don't know anything about me.'

'I know you're angry.' Blood was thudding in her ears. 'And I know you were going to leave the tournament without saying goodbye to your grandfather even though he asked you to present the trophy. I know that you wanted to use me to lie to him—'

She broke off, out of breath.

'I shouldn't have done that.' Jack's voice was faint or maybe it was just that she couldn't hear it above the pounding of her heart. 'I just needed a reason—'

There was a silence.

'You were wrong. My mother did come to the polo.' His mouth twisted. 'She was there. I saw her.'

She was there? Her eyes fluttered to his face.

'You don't believe me, do you?' he said into the silence. 'But I saw her just before we went to find my grandfather.'

Her breath scratched at her throat. 'But why didn't she come over?'

He shrugged. 'You need to ask her.'

I thought they'd be different.

Jack's words echoed inside her head. She'd wondered who he meant by 'they'. Now, though, she had a glimmer of understanding, but only Jack could confirm her suspicion. She looked at him, at his still, tense body.

'Or you could tell me.'

The seconds ticked by. 'I don't really have much of a relationship with my parents,' he said finally. 'They got divorced when I was four, and then they both remarried pretty quickly and had more children. I guess I was in the way.'

In the way.

Ondine stared at him in shock. How could he be in the way? He was their son.

As if he could read her thoughts, Jack smiled crookedly. 'I wasn't an easy child. I had a lot of tantrums, and I had night terrors too. My parents found it easier to outsource me to a nanny.'

His expression was bleak. 'Actually, I had two nannies, one for each house, only that gave my parents something else to argue about, and the nannies got caught in the cross-fire so they were always leaving. I think I averaged about five a year. But then everything changed.'

'What happened?'

For a moment, he didn't reply, and she held her breath as the silence stretched and stretched. And then he said slowly, 'I suppose if you were being charitable you'd call it a screw-up.'

He pressed his fingers into his forehead as if he were drawing out a memory. 'I was at my dad's and my mum was flying back from St Barts to pick me up, only then I found out he was taking my sisters—half-sisters—to the beach house and I had a tantrum because I wanted to go too.'

The skin was pulled taut over his cheekbones.

'Obviously that wasn't an option so, to distract me, my dad told me we could play hide-and-seek. And I went off to hide. I had this really good place in the airing cupboard, and I waited and I waited and then I heard a door slam and I knew my mum must have arrived. But I wanted my dad to find me so I stayed hidden, only I must have fallen asleep because I woke up and the house was dark.'

She felt herself tense. 'Why was it dark?'

'Because everyone had left.'

He spoke in a matter-of-fact way but she felt her face dissolve with shock. Her heart was racing. 'I don't understand,' she said slowly. Because she didn't. Before their deaths, she and Oli were at the centre of her parents' world. And Jack's family was wealthy, educated. They had childcare on tap. It made her mind boggle to think his father could leave his child home alone. Yes, in a film it would be funny, but she didn't feel like laughing. She felt sick now, sicker than she had in those first tumultuous months of her pregnancy.

'Nobody meant for it to happen. I think my dad was worried that if he came and found me I'd have another tantrum when he had to leave, so it was easier for him to just go. To be fair, Holly, the housekeeper, was there. Only she was in the garden when he drove away, and she must have thought I'd gone with him, so she locked up the house and left.'

'What about your mother?'

'She'd decided to extend her holiday so she was still in St Barts.'

Anger knifed through her. 'Without telling your dad?'

'She did tell him. She left a message. But they were always leaving messages and I guess he just didn't bother picking it up. Like I said. It was a screw-up.'

'But they must have realised and come back—'

'Nobody came back.'

His eyes were tired, empty, lost, and, sliding off the bed, she knelt in front of him and took hold of his hands. 'You must have been so scared.'

'I was a kid. I didn't really understand what had happened at first but then I realised I was locked in the house on my own and then I panicked. I got up onto a chair to try and slide one of the bolts on the back door. Only I fell off and broke my arm.'

Her lungs felt as if they might burst. Each word he spoke hurt more than the last.

'I didn't know at the time, but I triggered the alarm system and the security company saw me on the camera feed and called my grandfather and he came and took me to the hospital. I don't know what he said to my parents but after that I went to live with him.'

Jack looked down at his hands, and she saw that they were shaking. 'He's the only person who's ever looked out for me. And I lied to his face.'

Now she took his hands and held them tight. 'Not about what matters. Your grandfather wanted you to take stock of your life, and you have. And I saw how much he loves you, and he's always going to love you. He just wants you to love yourself.'

'I've hurt him. I do stupid things. Reckless things.'

'Like on the yacht,' she said quietly.

He nodded. 'I didn't lie to you. I wasn't drunk or high. And I didn't want to be there any more but I jumped because I saw this photo of my mum and Penn at some tennis match, and I got upset—'

There was a long pause. Outside the window, the sky was growing darker.

'I don't know why it happens but I start to feel numb—'

His hands tightened around hers. 'It's like I'm disappearing into this darkness and I need someone to come find me or I'll disappear for ever, and the only way I can stop it is by doing something that hurts or scares me. Because then I can focus on that and it brings me back, and I know that's not okay—'

'Oh, Jack—' Clasping his face, she kissed him gently. 'No, it's not okay.' She felt suddenly and intensely protective of him. 'But it will be.'

He buried his face into her hair. 'I'm sorry about what I said earlier. And how I was before about the baby. I know I'm the father, and I want to be there for you, for both of you. And I don't know how we can make it work or even if you want to try—'

'I do—' She bit her lip to stop herself from crying. 'I do

want that; I want you to be part of this.' She took his hand and laid it gently against her stomach.

'You do?' He seemed stunned. And it hurt that he should feel that way. That he had been hurt so often, so badly. But it was never going to happen again, she thought fiercely. She wasn't going to let it happen. And it was in that moment as she squared up to the world that it hit her.

She loved him. And just thinking it made her heart blossom like a flower.

Pressing her forehead against his, she closed her eyes, accepting the truth. Duty had sent her thundering into the water, but love was the reason she had taught him to swim. And why she had forced him to stay at the polo. She wanted what was best for him. She wanted him to be happy.

Only Jack wasn't talking about love. He was talking about making things work, and if her two previous marriages had taught her anything, it was that love had to be mutual.

She took a breath. 'We can make this work. We will make it work.'

He slid down beside her and they held each other close for a long time. At first, it wasn't about sex. It was about knowing that they had each other. But then she pressed a kiss to his mouth, and he was kissing her back. They didn't take off their clothes or get onto the bed. He pulled up her skirt and lifted her onto his lap and pushed into her.

Afterwards, she rested her head against his shoulder, feeling his shuddering heart until, finally, he loosened his arms. Tipping her off his lap, he got to his feet. 'I'm going to go speak to the pilot.' Leaning forward, he kissed her softly on the mouth. 'I need to give them enough time to change course.'

'Change course?' She frowned. 'Aren't we going back to the island?'

'Whydah wasn't for real. It was just a honeymoon.' His dark gold eyes fixed on her face. 'This is real life now.'

'So where are we going?'

'To New York.' He reached down and pulled her to her feet. Now his hands cupped her belly. 'We're going home.'

Flicking on the TV, Jack stared at the screen dazedly, watching the news ticker slide across the bottom. He felt as if he had woken from a deep sleep to find that, incredibly, the world had kept spinning and people were going on with their lives. But up here in his apartment, that all felt like a charade. And yes, the irony of that was not lost on him.

He had left Ondine in the pool to come downstairs and make breakfast. Not personally. He wasn't sure he'd ever switched on the stove before. But he was an expert at ordering breakfast. And maybe he could learn to cook. It was not something he'd considered doing before but that was the difference between the old Jack and the new. Things that had previously been off-limits felt possible, achievable. Like learning to swim. Or being a father. Ondine had made him realise that he had choices. That he wasn't condemned to staying the same.

Two days had passed since they had landed in New York. They had spent almost the entire time in bed, neither of them quite ready to leave the honeymoon behind. But then, they'd realised that they didn't have to. That it wasn't an either/or situation.

His fingers bit into the kitchen counter. Given a choice, both his parents would have opted for the other to keep him. And arriving in New York, he'd wondered why he had been so compelled to admit that to Ondine. He'd never told anyone about his childhood before. He'd felt too ashamed and scared that once they knew the real Jack Walcott they too would turn away like his parents. That they would see that he wasn't worth loving. Worth keeping.

But Ondine hadn't turned away, he thought, remembering that blaze of outrage in her eyes. She hadn't sided with his parents. She had stayed and listened and held him and then she'd told him she wanted him in her life and the baby's.

His heart beat lightly inside his chest. The baby. His baby. Their child. Ondine had been right. It was a miracle. Not just her getting pregnant against all the odds, but this new-found belief that he could be a father. A hands-on dad.

And believing that to be possible had rubbed away the last of the jagged edges. There were still bad memories, but they felt distant and softer now, as if he were looking at them through water. And he felt calmer, even when he was on his own, and that was the litmus test. Usually, he couldn't bear to be by himself, but right now, he was enjoying the quiet of the apartment. It meant he could hear the distant back and forth of the traffic; it reminded him of the sea around Whydah.

And Whydah made him think about Ondine. But that was hardly surprising. She was in his thoughts all the time.

When he could actually hold a thought.

His breath caught in his throat, his body tightening as he remembered the soft, choking noises she'd made as she'd shuddered against his mouth earlier. He wanted her all the time. Wanted her so badly it made his bones ache. But it wasn't just the sex. They had talked about her life with Oli, about her parents and her childhood. And he had told her about where he liked to buy bagels. And about walking the High Line. And the bar where they made their own spiced nuts. Nothing was off-limits. They shared everything.

Jack frowned. Something was buzzing. Not his phone. He glanced at the oven warily, and then he spotted Ondine's phone at the other end of the counter.

Glancing at the name on the screen, he felt a jolt of anticipation.

It was Oliver. For a moment, he hesitated. They hadn't been formally introduced yet, but he knew that she wanted him to like her brother and it would make her happy to come down and find the two of them getting on.

He tapped the screen. There was a slight lag, and he wondered momentarily what time it was in Costa Rica, and then Oliver's face appeared, young, grinning, relaxed, excited—

'Hi, On—' His smile froze, then faded a fraction as he saw Jack.

'Oh, I'm sorry, I thought you were—'

'Ondine.' Jack smiled. 'She's at the pool but she should be down any minute.'

He watched in amusement as Oliver slapped his forehead with the flat of his hand. 'I thought I'd catch her before she went to work.' His face stiffened. 'You're not her boss, are you?'

It took Jack longer than it should have to make sense of what Oliver was asking. But he didn't understand what he had heard. Or perhaps he had misheard it. It was the only explanation, because Oliver must know that Ondine had left Whitecaps months ago. And why hadn't he recognised him? Even without the name on screen, he would know instantly who Oli was.

'No, I'm not her boss,' he managed to say.

Even from eight thousand miles away, Oli's relief was palpable. 'Okay, I know she can't really talk at work so I'll give her a call back later. Sorry, I'm Oliver, by the way, her brother…' The silence stretched between them as Oliver politely waited for him to provide his name.

'I'm Jack.'

Oliver smiled. 'Nice to meet you, Jack.' Still smiling, he hung up.

Jack stared down at the phone in his hand, his heart pounding. He couldn't seem to move. There had been no flicker of recognition when he'd told Oli his name. But that didn't make any sense. If it did that could mean only one thing. Ondine hadn't told her brother she was married.

Only that couldn't be true. Why wouldn't she have told him? Oli was her only family. Surely she would want him to know something that significant. Surely she would have to let him know if she meant what she said on the plane about making things work.

His heart shivered inside his chest. Unless, of course, she hadn't meant it. She had simply said what was expedient in the moment to placate him. Like his father offering to play hide-and-seek.

He was still standing at the counter, frozen as if made of ice, when Ondine came into the kitchen.

Her hair was still damp from the pool and she was wearing one of his T-shirts over bare legs. The bump of her stomach pressed against the fabric. She had never looked more beautiful or natural. But looks could be deceptive.

As she slid her arms around his body his throat tightened, his body too, and it would be so easy to pull that T-shirt over her head and lift her onto the counter and lose himself in the slick heat between her thighs.

But instead he stepped backwards, his hands on hers, peeling her arms away from his waist.

'What is it?' She looked up at him, her blue eyes widening. 'Are you okay?'

She sounded worried; looked worried too, and he wanted to believe what he was hearing and seeing but—

He tapped her phone. 'Oli called.'

Her face softened as it always did when her brother was mentioned. 'That's okay. I can speak to him later.'

I can speak to him later.

Her words rolled around inside his head, like bottles on a bar-room floor. Had he ever seen her speak to Oli in real time? The answer to that question made him reach out and steady himself against the counter.

'You don't need to,' he said slowly. 'I spoke to him.'

And it was then, still watching her face, that any hopes he had that he was wrong were lost. Shattered. Relinquished.

There was silence. Now she was unnaturally still.

'He doesn't know about us. About the marriage.' He phrased it as a statement. Because he could tell from the shock on her face that he didn't need to ask the question. And then a new realisation rose like nausea in his throat. 'He doesn't know about the baby.'

'I was going to tell him.' Her voice was faint and scratchy as if the words were rough-edged. She reached out, and he flinched as she touched his arm.

'I just wanted to find the right time. When things were settled.'

He stared at her disbelieving, angry, hurting in a way that made him long for the numbness of before. 'Why bother? Why not just deny everything?'

She blinked as he threw her words back in her face.

'That's not what I was doing—'

'Oh, please—' He spun away from her into the living room, needing distance from her, from the shock and pain of her betrayal.

'It's exactly what you're doing. You know how I know that? Because I was doing it back on Whydah.'

His hands clenched and, glancing down, he stared at them dazedly as if they belonged to someone else.

'That was different. You hadn't accepted the baby was yours—'

His eyes dropped to her stomach. 'And what? You're punishing me for that?'

She took a step towards him. 'No, of course not. It's not even about you. It's about Oli. I didn't know what to say to him.' Her voice stumbled but he could see the fierce love in her eyes for her brother. 'He doesn't have anyone else but me, and he needs me. And I know he's super-smart, but you spoke to him. He's just a kid.'

'And I spoke to you. I told you things I've never told anyone. Because I trusted you—'

'You can trust me—' she began, but he was backing away from her.

'You told me that we could make this work. That we would make it work.' He was shivering now so that he had to tense his body to keep his voice from shaking. 'But you know what, Ondine? I'm really struggling to see how you could believe that when you haven't even told your brother I exist.'

Suddenly, he couldn't bear to be in the room with her any longer, to have her witness his stupidity. Without giving her a chance to reply, he turned and walked across the living room and into the hall and slammed his hand against the elevator button. The doors opened immediately, and he stepped inside, his heart pounding.

'Jack—'

He caught a glimpse of her pale, stunned face and then the doors shut and a moment later the elevator started to move. He didn't know where he was going. But it didn't matter anyway. What mattered was to keep moving. Because if he stopped, he knew the pain in his heart would swallow him whole.

CHAPTER ELEVEN

As THE DOORS closed Ondine felt as if she were back on Dipper's Beach. Only the difference was she couldn't dive after him into the elevator shaft. Instead, she hammered the button on the wall with her fist, again and again, but she knew already the lift would only come back up when Jack stepped through the doors in the entrance foyer. It was one of the perks of having the penthouse: you had your own private elevator.

But it didn't feel like a perk now. Panic clawed at her throat, strangling her.

Where was he going? Above her frantic heartbeat she could hear his voice inside her head.

'I got upset… I don't know why it happens but I start to feel numb…and the only way I can stop it is by doing something that hurts or scares me.'

And now she was scared. Pressing her hand to her mouth, she gave a sob as the lift doors opened. It was empty. He was gone because of her. She had hurt him. She hadn't meant to, but she had. Somewhere out there in Manhattan he was hurting—

Head spinning, she stared at the empty lift, panic and fear overwhelming her. She had known instantly what to do on the beach even though she'd been off duty and had no float, no phone—

Her phone.

Her heart stopped beating. Of course. She could call him.

She ran back into the apartment and snatched up her phone. Her fingers felt fat and clumsy as she pressed his name on the screen.

'Pick up, pick up…please pick up,' she whispered. She felt a jolt of relief as he answered and then she realised it was just his voicemail greeting.

'Hi, this is Jack. Leave a message and I'll get back to you.'

'It's me. I'm so sorry, Jack. I know I hurt you and I know you probably don't want to speak to me right now, but could you please call me back?'

She texted him too, and then she sat down on the sofa. She had to. Her legs felt as if they were made of blancmange. Even after her parents died, she hadn't felt this helpless. Then there had been so much to arrange, to organise, and she'd had to be strong for Oli. But here in this beautiful, silent apartment with his accusations still ringing in the air, she couldn't catch her breath, let alone think of what to do next.

The room swam. She had never meant to hurt him. She loved him, and now she realised how much because pain was the price you paid for loving someone. She knew that from losing her parents and this pain was equal to the aching loss she'd felt after the accident.

Think. *Think.* There must be something she could do. She couldn't just sit here and do nothing. But this was her first time in New York. Aside from Jack, she knew no one. Knew nothing about the city.

Except that wasn't true. They had talked a lot about his life here, she thought, her heartbeat accelerating. She knew where he bought coffee. And where he liked to walk. And he had a driver, Tom, who had picked them up from the airport.

She felt a fluttering hope, tiny but strong like a hummingbird's wings. Surely with Tom's help she would be able to find him, and then she could talk to him. She could make this right. But first she needed to get dressed. And call him again.

An hour and a half later, that hope was growing feebler by the minute. Nobody had seen Jack at any of the places she went to. And New York was so much bigger than she had imagined. A man could get lost there with hardly any effort. If he was even there.

Maybe he had left the city. She pictured the Walcott jet gleaming on the runway, her heart a leaden beat of misery. Left the country.

If only she had told Oli the truth. But when could she have told him? And what? At the beginning she had been struggling to believe that she could go through with it. That she would marry Jack for money. After the ceremony she had been angry with herself, mainly for having left herself so few options. Too angry to speak to Oli. He would have heard it in her voice. She couldn't have risked that. Couldn't have risked him coming back.

Then later she had been sick and then there was the baby and how could she have told him about the baby?

'Is there anywhere else you'd like to go, Mrs Walcott?'

Her pulse quickened. There was one place left they hadn't tried. 'Could we go back to the apartment, please, Tom?' she said quickly.

And then she offered up a prayer. *Please let him be there. Let him be safe.*

As the elevator doors opened she ran back into the apartment.

'Jack? Jack—' She called his name as she checked each

room in turn. But the apartment was as still and silent as before.

She sat down on the sofa, her phone trembling in her hand. She had called him thirty times now, left as many messages, and it was obvious he didn't want to talk to her. Remembering how he had pulled away from her, she felt as if she were drowning. Her hand reached instinctively to protect her stomach, and she forced herself to breathe. What mattered was finding Jack, making him safe. Only she couldn't do that if he wouldn't talk to her.

Her heart leapt to her throat as her phone rang shrilly. 'Jack—'

There was a beat of silence. 'Ondine, it's John Walcott. I'm back in New York, and I was just calling to invite you both to lunch on Sunday.' Another beat of silence. 'Is everything all right, my dear?'

She pressed her hand against her mouth. 'I don't think it is—'

'What's happened?' he said calmly. 'Is Jack not there?'

His simple question was what made her finally unravel.

'He left. And it's my fault. I let him down. I made him think I don't love him and I do. So much. Only he thinks I don't care—'

Jack had finally stopped shivering but he was still walking. He hadn't followed a particular route. In fact, half the time, he'd had no idea where he was. It was as if his limbs were acting of their own accord. His fingers too, he thought dully. He couldn't stop checking his phone, even though he knew that he shouldn't.

He couldn't bear to hear or read any more excuses. There had been so many over the years. So many betrayals to forgive and forget dating back to before he was too young to even understand the concept of either of those things. And it would break his heart to hear Ondine's voice repeat those same meaningless phrases, let alone have to read them in black and white.

Only why would his heart be affected? Ondine had clearly never seen their marriage as anything other than transactional.

His pulse stumbled, and, remembering the feel of her small, soft body in his arms as she told him about the misery of her first marriage, he felt his legs slow, then stop. People surged round him on the pavement, tutting and rolling their eyes, but he barely registered their irritation. He was too distracted by another memory, this time his grandfather talking about his grandmother.

'I suppose you could say I shared my soul. And that's when I realised I loved her. You see, that's what love is, Jack, sharing your soul.'

He had shared his soul with Ondine. More than that, he had opened his heart to her and the baby growing inside her. To a future he had never imagined for himself. A future with a woman he loved and their baby. A baby that would swim like a fish.

His phone vibrated, and as he glanced at the screen some of the pain in his chest softened at the edges.

It was his grandfather.

He hesitated. He didn't want to keep lying. But if he didn't answer, his grandfather would worry. Only what could he say? How was he supposed to explain the tangle of lies he had spun with Ondine? Particularly now they turned out to be true—

There was only one thing he could do. Swiping the screen up, he said quickly, 'Can I call you back, Grandpa? There's someone I need to talk to.'

'I know. Ondine called me. And you do need to talk to her.' His grandfather's voice was quiet but firm. 'But first I need to talk to you.'

Pacing back across the living room, Ondine stared at her phone, willing it to ring. It was nearly an hour since John Walcott had called, and he still hadn't rung back. She had no idea what that meant, but sitting down made her feel like a butterfly on the end of a pin. Maybe she would go back and wait outside the apartment building, see if anyone coming in had another idea of where Jack could be.

She snatched up her phone. Then if John called she could—

The elevator doors opened and she felt her legs go weak with relief as Jack walked into the entrance hall. He looked pale and tired, but he was here and he was safe.

'You came back—'

There was a silence. He seemed almost stunned to see her and she wondered if he'd thought she had left. She felt suddenly close to tears as he nodded slowly. 'I was walking around and I realised that I hadn't said everything I wanted to say.'

She could hear the struggle to keep his voice even. He felt betrayed, and maybe he wouldn't listen or believe her if he did, but she had to try and explain.

'I have too,' she said, hardly able to speak past the lump in her throat. 'I'm so sorry that I hurt you. I didn't mean to. I should have told Oli about us getting married, but I just couldn't get my head round what we were doing. And then I found out I was pregnant and I was ill and I was scared that if I told him, he'd be worried and want to come back and he's had so much to deal with. I didn't want him to have to worry about me, as well.'

Silence filled the hallway.

Jack stared at her. A muscle worked along his jaw. 'Is that it? Have you finished?'

She nodded, but he didn't speak, he just kept staring at her and then he said slowly, 'Nobody has ever looked out for me except my grandfather. I told you that on the plane, do you remember?'

He took a step forward. 'But I was wrong. You looked out for me too. Right from the start when you pulled me from the water. And then you stayed at the hospital and you watched me sleep. Even when I said awful things you didn't leave.'

'I did.' She thought back to Whydah. 'On the bluff, and after we played croquet.'

'And I deserved it both times. But you came back. Nobody's ever done that.'

'You deserve to be loved, Jack,' she whispered.

He took another step closer. 'And you went looking for me today. You made Tom take you around New York.'

'Did he tell you?'

He shook his head. 'My grandfather told me.' Leaning forward, he lifted a tendril of hair away from her face, tucking it behind her ear. 'Why did you go looking for me, O?'

She felt her heart melt. 'I couldn't not.'

Jack stared down into her eyes. 'What you said to my grandfather about loving me.' He was struggling to speak. 'Was that true? Because I love you.'

She covered her mouth with her hand, and he pulled her against him, wrapping his arms around her, holding her close against him so that she could feel his heart beating in time to hers.

'I love you,' he said again, and this time he smiled a smile that lit up his face and filled her with light and a happiness she had never known. 'You saved me, O. And I'm not talking about what happened in Palm Beach. I was drowning on dry land, and you saved me. You gave me the kiss of life. The kiss of love,' he said softly.

'You saved me too.' She felt his arms tighten around her and, looking up, she saw his golden eyes were glittering with tears. 'You make me feel special. You made me trust myself again.' She bit her lip. 'I thought I'd lost you—'

He breathed out shakily. 'You share my heart, my soul. You can't lose me. I belong to you.' His hand curved around her stomach. 'Both of you.'

Their mouths met blindly and they kissed just as they had that first day on the beach, and they were still kissing as he scooped her into his arms and carried her back into their apartment, their home.

EPILOGUE

THE GARDEN WAS starting to fill up. Guests were milling around the terrace, talking, laughing. Leaning forward to get a better view, Ondine watched as one of the animal handlers opened a brightly coloured carrier and two lop-eared rabbits hopped enthusiastically onto Red Knots' pristine lawn. 'It's getting pretty crowded down there,' she called over her shoulder.

'With people or animals?'

A flicker of heat danced over her skin as two warm hands slid round her waist, and Jack leaned in to drop a row of kisses down her throat.

'Both.'

'Who or what are we waiting for?'

His voice was casual but she knew what it cost him to ask that question. What it had cost for that question even to be possible. 'I think we're good to go,' she said softly, turning in his arms. 'Your dad is with your grandpa making friends with the ponies, and your mum is talking to Oliver.'

It was twenty months since she and Jack had stood in the Miami-Dade courthouse and exchanged vows. But the transactional relationship they had entered into that day bore no resemblance to their marriage now.

For starters, there were no more secrets. Everything was in the open. More importantly, the love they had promised one another was real. So real, she thought, looking up at him, her heart contracting so that it was suddenly difficult to breathe.

'You know we're never going to make it downstairs if you keep looking at me like that,' he said softly.

She reached out and touched his marvellous, miraculous face. 'Did I tell you how proud I am of you?'

His golden eyes were meltingly soft. 'I think you mentioned it a couple of times.'

She had. But she still liked to remind him. 'You made this happen.'

'The party!' He shook his head. 'That's all down to Martha's Farm Friends.'

'I'm not talking about the party. Well, I am. But I'm talking about why we can have a party with both our families. I'm talking about you reaching out—'

'And I could only do that because of you.' His hands firmed around the swell of her stomach. 'You're the best thing that ever happened to me, and I don't know where I would be now if I hadn't met you.'

'You'd be fine.' She touched his face lightly, letting him see her love and belief in him, and her gratitude for the life they made together. 'You're the best man I know. The best husband. The best dad, best CEO.'

His mouth curved slightly, acknowledging her words. He believed them. And there were no words for the way it made her feel to know that he did believe them. Getting to this point had been hard. He'd had to confront his past, his parents. And it was still a work in progress. But it was like swimming. You had to start with the basics and practise. Before you knew it, you were swimming triathlons for charity, she thought, her gaze snagging on the medals that were knotted casually around the bedpost. And she was proud of him for that too.

* * *

Jack looked down into Ondine's beautiful blue eyes, his heart beating in time to the distant waves. Most days he woke up and gave thanks to the ocean for bringing Ondine into his life. She had breathed, not just life into his lungs, but love into his heart. She had given him faith in himself. A beautiful daughter.

Speaking of whom…

'Do you think we should get the birthday girl up?' he said, stroking Ondine's hair. 'We wouldn't want her to miss her first party.' Their eyes met as, on cue, the baby monitor by the bed gave a squeak and then a satisfied kind of gurgle.

Esme Candace Walcott was standing up in her cot, her tousled blonde curls framing her face like a halo, a giraffe clutched in one chubby hand, the other reaching for Jack.

'Dada—'

Watching his daughter's wide blue eyes light up with delight and amazement, Jack felt his heart tumble in his chest. He gave thanks for his daughter too. If Ondine had cracked him open, Esme had pushed the crack apart and that was the thing when you opened up. You let the love in, and out. So much love.

He glanced at the row of soft toys lining one wall. Less room, though—

Tucking Esme against his shoulder, he turned to Ondine. 'You know, we should probably think about getting a bigger place when we get back to New York. Before this one arrives.' His hand reached out automatically to touch her stomach again. He couldn't stop himself. This was the part he'd missed out on before through fear and doubt. But he wasn't scared any more. And his doubts were normal, transitory, easily resolved.

'Or we could keep the apartment. Get some place up-state. With a bit of land. Kidnap some of Martha's animals.'

Ondine smiled. 'New Jack meet Old Jack.' And she loved both. Leaning into him, she wrapped her arm around his waist. 'I don't care where we live as long as we're together.'

They stood there for a moment, their bodies touching, both of them certain that wherever they lived, whatever was to come, it would all be just detail. What mattered was in their hearts and souls. There was no need for anything else.

* * * * *

COMING SOON!

We really hope you enjoyed reading this book. If you're looking for more romance be sure to head to the shops when new books are available on

Thursday 6th July

MILLS & BOON®

Coming next month

THE MAID MARRIED TO THE BILLIONAIRE
Lynne Graham

"You took me by surprise… You shocked me," she muttered unevenly, struggling to catch her breath. She was thoroughly unnerved by the sensations that had shimmied up through her taut body and then down again to a place that had ignited with a burst of warmth, mortifying her to the very bone.

Enzo released his breath on a measured hiss. "Relax. For a moment, I was tempted. But nothing is going to happen unless you want it to. I'm attracted to you. I know I shouldn't be but I'm not perfect. In fact, it seems I'm all too human. But you are completely safe with me, *piccolo mio*."

"Maybe I don't need to be safe…with you," Skye said uncertainly. "You make me feel things I didn't expect to feel. You make me curious. I know, like you said, I shouldn't be in these circumstances. But the truth is, I am and I'm attracted too."

"So…" Enzo breathed a touch raggedly. "What do you want to do about this?"

"We—we could try a kiss…just *one*," she stressed.

Continue reading
THE MAID MARRIED TO THE BILLIONAIRE
Lynne Graham

Available next month
www.millsandboon.co.uk

LET'S TALK
Romance

For exclusive extracts, competitions and special offers, find us online:

- MillsandBoon
- @MillsandBoon
- @MillsandBoonUK
- @MillsandBoonUK

Get in touch on 01413 063 232

MILLS & BOON

THE HEART OF ROMANCE

A ROMANCE FOR EVERY READER

MODERN
Prepare to be swept off your feet by sophisticated, sexy and seductive heroes, in some of the world's most glamourous and romantic locations, where power and passion collide.

HISTORICAL
Escape with historical heroes from time gone by. Whether your passion is for wicked Regency Rakes, muscled Vikings or rugged Highlanders, awaken the romance of the past.

MEDICAL
Set your pulse racing with dedicated, delectable doctors in the high-pressure world of medicine, where emotions run high and passion, comfort and love are the best medicine.

True Love
Celebrate true love with tender stories of heartfelt romance, from the rush of falling in love to the joy a new baby can bring, and a focus on the emotional heart of a relationship.

Desire
Indulge in secrets and scandal, intense drama and sizzling hot action with heroes who have it all: wealth, status, good looks…everything but the right woman.

HEROES
The excitement of a gripping thriller, with intense romance at its heart. Resourceful, true-to-life women and strong, fearless men face danger and desire - a killer combination!

To see which titles are coming soon, please visit

millsandboon.co.uk/nextmonth

MILLS & BOON
True Love
Romance from the Heart

Celebrate true love with tender stories of heartfelt romance, from the rush of falling in love to the joy a new baby can bring, and a focus on the emotional heart of a relationship.